S0-AIL-849

"Author D. Barkley Briggs braids ancient strands of Arthurian myth together with his own homespun thread into a complex tapestry of magic and meaning, bravery, and brotherhood. When the roll call of ambitious fantasy writers is called, you'll find that Briggs has earned a place in that book of names."

— JEFFREY OVERSTREET, author of *Auralia's Colors* and *Cyndere's Midnight*

"D. Barkley Briggs has penned a rousing fantasy packed full of Norse and Celtic mythology with a hearty dose of Arthurian legend. With a wide range of emotions, he moved me from the sadness of loss to the giddiness of comic relief, all the way to the excitement of heart-pounding tension. Strap on your armor, pull out your sword, and get ready for an adventure."

— M. C. PEARSON, director, Fiction in Rather Short Takes (FIRST) Blog Alliances

"Doors shall open, doors shall close. And shadows follow. Something waits for young Ewan and Hadyn Barlow in the seemingly endless tangles of the briar patch behind their new home. Fleeing grief and broken dreams, the Barlow brothers discover strange secrets and new worlds right outside their door that will change their lives forever. *The Book of Names* weaves a tale that is both thrilling and wrought with hope. D. Barkley Briggs is a new and welcome voice in fantasy fiction."

— WAYNE THOMAS BATSON, author of THE DOOR WITHIN TRILOGY

LEGENDS OF KARAC TOR: 1

THE BOOK OF NAMES

A NOVEL

D. BARKLEY BRIGGS

NAVPRESS

BE TRANSFORMED

NAVPRESS

BE TRANSFORMED

NavPress is the publishing ministry of The Navigators, an international Christian organization and leader in personal spiritual development. NavPress is committed to helping people grow spiritually and enjoy lives of meaning and hope through personal and group resources that are biblically rooted, culturally relevant, and highly practical.

**For a free catalog go to www.NavPress.com
or call 1.800.366.7788 in the United States or 1.800.839.4769 in Canada.**

© 2008 by Dean Briggs

All rights reserved. No part of this publication may be reproduced in any form without written permission from NavPress, P.O. Box 35001, Colorado Springs, CO 80935. www.navpress.com

NAVPRESS and the NAVPRESS logo are registered trademarks of NavPress. Absence of ® in connection with marks of NavPress or other parties does not indicate an absence of registration of those marks.

ISBN-10: 1-60006-227-X
ISBN-13: 978-1-60006-227-8

Cover design and illustration by Kirk DouPonce, DogEaredDesign.com
Cover photo by IstockPhoto, Shutterstock, and Dreamstime
Creative Team: Rebekah Guzman, Michael Van Schooneveld, Reagen Reed, Darla Hightower, Arvid Wallen, Kathy Guist

Some of the anecdotal illustrations in this book are true to life and are included with the permission of the persons involved. All other illustrations are composites of real situations, and any resemblance to people living or dead is coincidental.

Unless otherwise identified, all Scripture quotations in this publication are taken from the HOLY BIBLE: NEW INTERNATIONAL VERSION® (NIV®). Copyright © 1973, 1978, 1984 by International Bible Society. Used by permission of Zondervan Publishing House. All rights reserved.

Library of Congress Cataloging-in-Publication Data

Briggs, Dean, 1968-
 The book of names : a novel / D. Barkley Briggs.
   p. cm. -- (Legends of Karac Tor ; 1)
  ISBN 978-1-60006-227-8
  1. Brothers--Fiction. I. Title.
PS3552.R4556B66 2008
813'.54--dc22
                          2008003659

Printed in the United States of America

1 2 3 4 5 6 7 8 9 10 / 12 11 10 09 08

For Hanson, Evan, Gatlin, Gage.

My heroes.

What if sorrow was a doorway,

And memory, a gate?

What if we never passed through?

What worlds would go unfound?

In final days / Come final woes
Doors shall open / Doors shall close
Forgotten curse / Blight the land
Four names, one blood / Fall or stand

Lost the great one / Fallen low
Rising new / Ancient foe
Darkest path / Turn one back
Blade which breaks / Anoint, attack

Once and future / King of yore
Hidden water / Burning sword
Bone and earth / Warriors rise
Come the day / Of bloody skies

Aion's breath / Music cursed
Sings making things / Made perverse
Fate shall split / Road in twain
One shall lose / One shall gain

Secret lore / Lost now found
Eight plus one / All unbound
Beast shall come / Five must go
Doors shall open / Doors shall close

Buried deep / Hidden seen
Ancient tomb / Midst crimson green
Nine shall bow / Nine more rise
Nine horns blow / Nine stars shine

Falling flame / Burning pure
Ten thousand cries / For mercy heard
Plagues and peril / Horns of dread
End of days / Land be red

When final days / Bring final woes
Doors shall open / Doors shall close
Fate for one / For all unleashed
Come the Prince / Slay the beast

— THE RAVNA'S LAST RIDDLE

CHAPTER 1

BLACK BIRDS

The day was gray and cold, mildly damp. Perfect for magic. Strange clouds overhead teased the senses with a fragrance of storm, wind, and lightning, and the faint, clean smell of ozone. Invisible energy sparkled like morning dew on blades of grass.

Standing alone in an empty field on the back end of their new acreage, Hadyn Barlow only saw the clouds. By definition, you can't see what's invisible, and as for smelling magic? Well, let's just say, unlikely. Hadyn saw what was obvious for late November, rural Missouri: leafless trees, dead grass, winter coming on strong. Most of all he saw (and despised) the humongous briar patch in front of him, feeling anew each and every blister and callus earned hacking through its branches.

Making room for cattle next spring, or so he was told; this, even though his dad had never owned a cow in his life. He was a history teacher, for crying out loud. A college professor. Hadyn's shoulders slumped. It didn't matter. Everything was different now.

Mr. Barlow didn't let his boys curse, but low under his breath, Hadyn did, mildly, just to prove the point. Life stunk. That was the brutal truth.

All true for the most part. Yet standing alone in the field, bundled in flannel, something else prickled his skin—something hidden in the rhythm of the day, at its core—and it wasn't just the chill wind. He couldn't shake it. A sense of something. Out-of-placeness. Faced with a friendless sophomore year, Hadyn knew that feeling all too well. It attacked him every morning, right before school.

But this was something more, more than the usual nervousness and name-calling stuff. His intuition was maddeningly vague. Hadyn sniffed the air, eyeing the field. A fox scampered in the distance. Bobwhites whistled softly. This had been his routine for weeks. Go to school, come home, do chores. Today was no different. Except for the clouds.

He looked upward, struck again by the strange hues. The colors were still there; kind of creepy. They had lingered since the bus ride home. He had seen it happen with his own eyes, though he didn't think much of it at the time. Right about the time school let out and the yellow buses began winding home, the skies had opened and spilled. Low banks of clouds came tumbling from the horizon like old woolen blankets. Like that scene from *Independence Day* when the alien ships first appeared. Hues of purple, cobalt, and charcoal smeared together. Not sky blue. Not normal. Riding on the bus, face pressed against the cold window, he didn't know what to think. Only that it looked . . . *other-worldly*. Like God had put Van Gogh in charge for the day.

Strange.

Earlier, the day hadn't felt weird. If anything, he had felt relief. Two days until Friday . . . until Thanksgiving break. Only two days. He could make it. As he stood by the mailbox with his three brothers, waiting for the bus—he couldn't wait to get his own car—mild winds had stirred from the south, scampering through row after row of brittle stalks in the neighbor's cornfield across the road. He heard them in the leafless oak and elm of his own yard, hissing with a high, dry laughter. Warm winds, not cold. But about noon, the wind shifted. Again, no big deal for Missouri, always caught in the middle between the gulf winds of Mexico and Canada's bitter cold. Temperamental weather was normal in these parts.

Yet there it was. From the winding ride home through this very moment, he couldn't rid himself of that dry-mouthed, queasy feeling. It was more than a shift in wind. It was a shift in energy. Yes, the dark clouds and strange colors reminded him of the thickening air before a big, cracking Midwestern storm, but that wasn't it. This was different.

Hadyn being Hadyn, more than anything else, wanted to identify the moment. To *name* it.

Though he didn't actually speak until age three, Hadyn was born with a question mark wrinkled into his brow. Always searching, always studying something. He couldn't speak a word before then—refused to, his dad always said—yet he knew the letters of the alphabet at a precocious twelve months. When he finally did decide to talk, words gushed. Full sentences. Big vocabulary. Not surprisingly, it was clear early on that Hadyn was one of those types bent toward structure, patterns. He hated incongruities, hated not knowing how to pinpoint the strange twist in sky and mood right in the middle of an otherwise typical dreary day. If it was just nasty weather, name it! What did it feel like? *Wet fish guts?* Not quite. *A full wet diaper?* He remembered those well enough from when the twins were little, but no. *A three-day-old slice of cheese?*

Yes, that was it. Cold, damp, moldy.

Velveeta, actually, he decided, feeling a small measure of satisfaction. He fumbled for the zipper of his coat as another icy breeze prickled his skin. *Yep, another lousy Velveeta day in the life of Hadyn Barlow.*

He thought of the roaring woodstove back home. Hot cocoa. Small consolation. Until dusk, the oldest Barlow boy was stuck outside in a field with hatchet and hedge shears. Stuck in a foul mood, stuck with a knot in his throat. Just plain stuck. His task, his life, seemed endless and pointless.

"Just a little bit every day, however much you can manage after school," his father would remind him. "And don't look so grumpy. The days are shorter and shorter."

But not any warmer.

"Grr!" Hadyn grumbled aloud, snapping at the cold in his thoughts. He had chosen to "clear" the massive beast by carving tunnels in it, not just hacking mindlessly. Probably not exactly what Dad had in mind, but, well, to be honest, he didn't really care. He was the one stuck out here in the cold. He had already carved several tunnels, and reentered the biggest one now, lopping and clicking his shears at the endless mess of thorns and branches, alternating with halfhearted swings of the hatchet. The briar patch sprawled a couple hundred feet in every direction, comprised of dense, overgrown nettles, blackberry bushes, and cottonweed. Untended for generations, the underbrush was so thick and tall a person could easily get lost in it, especially toward the center, where the land formed a shallow ravine that channeled wet weather rains toward the pond on the lower field. Hadyn guessed the height at the center point would be a good twelve feet or more. Enormous.

Really, it was a ridiculous task. Dad had to know that.

"Why not just burn the thing?" Hadyn had asked him. Burn it, then brush-hog it. Throw a hand grenade in and run.

Mr. Barlow never really answered, just said he wanted him to clear it by hand. After the first day of grumbling and complaining (which proved none too popular with his father), Hadyn started carving tunnels. His plan was to craft a maze out of it, maybe create a place to escape . . . at least have some fun before his dad made him level the whole thing

Fun? He caught himself, tasting the word like a spoonful of NyQuil. *Fun is soccer with the guys back home.*

He paused for a moment to wipe his brow. Home was no longer a city, not for four months now. It was a cow pasture. Home *had* been Independence, the suburb of Kansas City whose chief claim to fame (other than being the birthplace of Harry S. Truman) was that Jesus would return there, at least according to one of numerous Mormon splinter groups. For Hadyn, it was all about skateboards and traffic and rows of houses. Noise. Friends. Now, all that—everything familiar and good—was exactly three hours and nineteen minutes straight down I-70 on the opposite end of the state. Might as well have been on the opposite side of the planet. Home now: three hundred acres in the middle of nowhere, away from all he had ever known.

The town was called Newland. The name seemed like a smack in the face.

New town. New school. New faces. New troubles to deal with. New disappointments. His dad had tried to make a big deal of the "new" thing. This would be a *new* start for their family, a *new* chapter, blah, blah, blah. A change, from sadness to hope, he said. Hadyn hated change.

He didn't want new. He wanted it how it used to be.

How it used to be was happy. Normal. Right. Fair. How it used to be meant they were a family of six, not five. Hadyn felt a familiar pang slice across his chest. He would have traded all the unknown magic in the world for five more minutes with—

Mom.

It had been a year since she died. His mental images of her remained vivid, of a beautiful woman with porcelain smooth skin, naturally blonde, witty, vivacious. All four Barlow brothers shared her wit and spirit, as well as an even mix of their parents' coloring: mom's fairness, dad's darker hair and complexion, the boys somewhere in between. Hadyn, rapidly entering his adult body, was tall for his age, muscular, lean, possessed of a some-times uncomfortably aristocratic air. Some days his eyes were smoky jade, others, iron gray. But he had Anna's cleverness.

His parents had been saving money for several years, study-ing the land all around Newland. Hadyn could not fathom why. What was so special about Podunk, America? But he knew his mom had been happy to think about life in the country. Once upon a time, that was enough. But now? Without her, what was the point? Why couldn't they have just stayed in Independence? Moving wasn't going to bring her back. Didn't Dad know that?

For the second time that afternoon, a tidal wave of loneliness nearly drowned him, left him in a goo of self-pity, the sort of sticky feeling he didn't want anyone to spoil by cheering him up. He took one more angry swing with the hatchet. Done or not, he was done for the day. Work could wait. Dad would just have to deal with it. Already, he had built a pretty impressive maze. Six unconnected tunnels so far.

Like I give a rip about these stupid tunnels, he thought as he crawled from the center toward the mouth of the largest, longest shaft. *Or this stupid land, or town, or patch of*—his knee jammed against a thorn protruding from the soil—*thorny! ridiculous!*

He clenched his jaw, flashing through dozens of choice words, using none. Honoring his dad. Pain streamed as tears down his cheek, and it wasn't just the thorn in his knee. It was life. Crawling forty more feet, he emerged to face the slowly westering sun melting down the sky. The otherworldly colors he had seen earlier were gone. Only the cold remained. And now, a bleeding, sore knee.

Behind him, he heard rustling grass and the high pitched, lilting notes of his brother's tin whistle. He wiped his eyes on his sleeve and grimaced. Ewan, like his mother, was musical. Even more like her, he was sentimental. He often carried the whistle she had brought him as a gift from Ireland. It would, no doubt, have seemed humorous to some, to see him wandering the field, playing a sprightly little tune. It only annoyed Hadyn. Thankfully, as Ewan drew closer, the song trailed away.

"Hey, Hadyn."

Hadyn grunted. "What do you want?"

Ewan shrugged, tucking the flute into his back pocket. He wore blue jeans and a blue embroidered ball cap initialed *ECB*.

"Wondered how things were going."

"Dad sent you to help, didn't he?"

Ewan frowned. "Yep. Got done with my chores sooner than planned."

"Bummer."

"Major bummer," Ewan emphasized, peering into the tunnel. "Looks like you're near the center, though. That's pretty cool."

Hadyn didn't reply. With only two years between them, the two brothers had always been the closest of friends, the fiercest competitors, the quickest of combatants. They understood each other's rhythms like no one else in the family. Whereas Hadyn was studied, wise, and cautious, Ewan was quick, fearless, and comfortable with long odds. No one could make Ewan laugh—gasping-for-air, fall-on-the-ground cackling—like Hadyn. Likewise, Ewan could frustrate Hadyn to no end or, with the sheer power of silliness, cheer him up when a sullen moment was about to strike. Not much wanting to be rescued from his mood at the moment, however, Hadyn let his silent response wrap around him like a barrier against further penetration. He didn't notice that Ewan's gaze had drifted from the briar patch to the low sky and paused there.

"What do you make of that?" he dimly heard his brother say, distracted, curious. Through the haze of his own thoughts, Hadyn followed Ewan's line of sight, his pointing finger, straight into the sunset. At first, he saw nothing. Then it was obvious. Several large black birds were swooping low on the horizon. Even at a distance, it appeared they were headed straight for the two boys, unveering over the slope of the ground, drawing swiftly nearer, a hundred yards or so away. From the sound of their raucous cry, they were like ravens, only larger, throatier, and if possible, blacker.

"Cawl-cawl," they cried.

Hadyn counted four total, wings outstretched, unflapping, like stealth bombers in formation. There was something organized and determined about their flight. It lacked animal randomness.

"Do they look strange to you?" Ewan asked, cocking his head.

Hadyn pretended to be uninterested. It didn't last. "What is that in their claws? What're they carrying?"

"Yeah, I see it. Sticks?"

"Too thick. It would be too heavy. Wouldn't it?"

"Hard to tell at this angle. Are they heading for us?" Ewan held up his hand to shield his eyes. "Man, they're fast. What are they?"

"I don't know, but they're still—"

"Look out!" Ewan dove to the side, tripping Hadyn in the process. Both boys hit the ground on a roll, turning just in time to see the birds swoop suddenly upward, arcing high into the sky, turn, then turn again. The lead bird, larger than the others, croaked loudly; the other three responded. Over and over, the same sound, like a demand: "Cawl!"

All four were pitch black, having none of the deep blue sheen of a crow's feathers, or so it seemed in the failing light. They flew as black slashes in the sky, all wing and beak, not elegant in the air, but fast. Disappearing completely against the lightless eastern expanse, they reappeared again as silhouettes skimming the western horizon. At first it seemed to Hadyn the birds would fly away, as they swept up and out in a wide arc. But the curve of their path soon came full circle. They were attempting another pass. Both boys nervously scooted further outside the angle of the birds' approach.

"What in the world?" Hadyn said, hatchet raised and ready. It was clearer now in silhouette form. Each bird carried a long, thick tube in its talons.

The brothers hunched on the ground, motionless, muscles tensed, watching as the birds continued their second approach. Hadyn held his breath. The birds didn't veer, nor aim again for the boys. Instead, they formed a precise, single-file line, a black arrow shooting toward the main tunnel of the thicket. With a final loud croak—"Cawl!"—and not a single flap of wing, all four swooped straight into the hole, one after the other. As they did, each released the object clutched in its talons. The tubes clattered together with a light, tinny sound at the mouth of the tunnel, literally at the boys' feet. The birds were already beyond sight. Their throaty noise echoed for a moment, evaporating into an obvious silence marked only by the faint breeze of wings passing over broken grass.

Hadyn and Ewan stared first at the tunnel, then at the objects. Then at each other. Then back at the tunnel. In the same instant, each of them leaped toward what the birds had left behind: four thin black metallic tubes, trimmed with milky white bands at top and bottom.

Hadyn slowly stretched out his hand and picked up a tube. He rolled it between his fingers. It was about the length of Ewan's Irish whistle, but thicker, maybe the circumference of a quarter. Not heavy at all. In the middle of each tube, finely wrought in scripted gold filigree, the letter *A* appeared.

Ewan lightly shook his tube, listening for clues to its contents. It sounded empty.

"They didn't even have us sign for delivery," he said. "What do we do with these? They look important."

"How should I know?" Hadyn said contemptuously, flicking his eyes cautiously toward the tunnel. "Where'd they even go? I mean, really. Are they just hiding back there until we leave?"

"Who cares!" Ewan said. His disgust was obvious. Hadyn was being an analyst again. "This isn't hard, Hadyn. Some big birds dive-bombed us. They dropped these cool tubes. It makes no sense. It's awesome. Totally, factor-ten cool."

Hadyn mulled it over. "Maybe they're some sort of carrier pigeon, but . . . do carrier pigeons even exist anymore?"

"Only on *Gilligan's Island*. TV Land. Listen to me, you're just guessing."

"Have you got a better idea?" Hadyn demanded.

Ewan waited, considered. Hadyn knew he hated being put on the spot like that, in the inferior position. Now it was Ewan's turn to think.

"Okay, maybe you're right. Maybe those birds really are carriers of some sort?" Ewan held up a tube. "Obviously they are. What if they need to carry these things farther still? What if they're just resting? What if they are trained to do this when they need to rest? Drop their packages, find a hole, rest, then grab their stuff and carry on?"

"So are you suggesting we flush them out? 'Cause there is no way I'm going to crawl back there. They can get out later on their own."

Ewan didn't reply. Instead he dug into his pocket, pulled out a small flashlight, and scuttled into the tunnel the birds had entered. "Wait here," he ordered.

"Hey, watch it back there!" Hadyn cautioned. Secretly, he wanted him to go, knew how to punch his brother's buttons to make it happen. "Those claws looked sharp!"

While he waited for Ewan to return, Hadyn examined the tubes further. He shook one tube, flicked it; smelled another; picked up and twirled the third and fourth tubes. His efforts yielded the same muffled sensation of something barely shifting inside. Maybe a rolled up piece of paper? If the ravens (or crows, or whatever they were) were carriers of some sort, a written message did make the most sense. But who in the world still sent paper messages . . . by bird? By raven, no less. Hello, e-mail anyone?

Presently, Ewan reappeared, breathing hard.

"They're gone," he said simply. "Must have flown out one of the other tunnels."

Hadyn creased his brow. "No way. None of the tunnels connect yet."

"They don't?" Ewan's eyes widened as it dawned on him that he hadn't seen any other tunnels. "No . . . they don't."

The two boys stared at one another in silence. Evening

enfolded them; soon, darkness. "They must have crawled through the branches," Hadyn surmised, but he hardly sounded convinced. "Are you sure you didn't see them?"

Ewan rolled his eyes. "Hello? Big, black flappy things. Yes, I'm sure." He grabbed one of the tubes, shook it again. "This band looks like ivory, but it's hard to tell in this light."

"Reminds me of one of Mom's necklaces."

Ewan grabbed the end and twisted. "Only one way to find out."

This time Hadyn didn't argue or analyze. Curiosity had gotten the best of him. The lid twisted off with surprising ease, followed by a thin hiss of sealed air. Ewan wrinkled his face. "Smells old. Yuck. Turn on your flashlight. Mine is getting weak."

He tapped the open end against the palm of his left hand. The coiled edge of a piece of thick, cream-colored parchment slipped out. Hadyn leaned in closer. Ewan gingerly teased the scroll out. It had a heavy grain of woven cotton, with rough edges trimmed in gold foil. Both boys let out a long slow breath. Neither the silver moon hanging off the tree line nor the winking stars provided light enough to clearly see. Hadyn turned on his flashlight as his brother unrolled the parchment. The paper was larger than normal, rich to the touch. Pinning both ends to the ground, both boys read at once the simple message beautifully scripted on the inside in golden ink:

You have been chosen for a life of great purpose. Adventure awaits you in the Hidden Lands.

—A

"Dude!" Ewan whistled softly. "Looks like something from King Arthur. What in the world are the Hidden Lands?"

Hadyn, who actually loved the lore of King Arthur—and Ewan knew it—was already reaching for another tube. Ewan followed his lead. Within twenty seconds, all four tubes were opened, and four identical parchments lay spread on the ground in the dark, illuminated only by flashlights. Golden ink glimmered, subtly shifting hues. Each bore the exact same message.

You have been chosen for a life of great purpose. Adventure awaits you in the Hidden Lands.

Hadyn grabbed the four sheets, quickly rolled them up, and inserted each back into its thin metal sleeve. "We need to head home before Dad gets worried," he said. "You take two, and I'll take two. Stick them under your shirt and act cool. I have no idea what these are. But for now, they're our little secret."

He puffed up for a moment, the older brother. Still out of sorts with the world.

"And none of your games, either, Ewan. I mean it. I'm not in the mood."

CHAPTER 2

ANCIENT STONE

The search for clues somehow made chores more tolerable. When Friday afternoon finally rolled around—school bell, Thanksgiving break—it was like a gift. Ewan asked his dad if he could start helping Hadyn clear the brush, and Mr. Barlow, impressed with his initiative, allowed it.

First thing Saturday morning at the briar patch, as on the previous two days, the boys took turns scanning the sky, scrambling through the tunnels, searching for clues, then backtracking and searching again. For anything: bird droppings, loose feathers, tracks, anything. No luck. The arrival of the black tubes and the curious messages held inside had piqued their interest, though they weren't really sure why, except for the wild flights of fancy a boy's mind was prone to take. They joked as if they were hacking through the Amazon or discovering a lost Mayan city. This was as close as either had ever been to a quest, Indiana Jones style. The plain fact was, birds didn't carry messages anymore, not like that.

And they certainly didn't just disappear. For whatever reason, it fell to the Barlows to solve the puzzle of where and how the birds had passed through, or out of, the maze.

About midmorning, just for fun, Ewan began referring to the whole briar patch as the Hidden Lands, just like the scroll had said. Hadyn played along, even though Avalon or Camelot was superior in his mind. While his buddies were reading *Harry Potter*, Hadyn devoured every Arthurian legend fit to print. But that was the past—for a kid Ewan's age—not a fifteen-year-old. He mentioned it anyway.

"Not bad," Ewan agreed. "Or even Narnia. But I still like Hidden Lands best."

They took turns hacking deeper into the main tunnel. It was slow going. The nettles and branches were so tangled, so thick, and so tall that even a little progress took a lot of time. Various layers of dead, matted foliage in the upper branches formed a canopy through which very little light passed. Underneath their fingers, the damp earth smelled of worms and rotten leaves, so every now and again they returned to the entrance for fresh air, casting their eyes searchingly toward the sky.

As Saturday turned from breakfast to lunch, the boys were cold, stumped, and beginning to feel disheartened. With all their clue-gathering and sky-searching, there remained zero evidence any birds had ever flown into the tunnel (except for the parchments, of course). So on the trail home for lunch, though neither of them really wanted to, they floated the idea of abandoning the secret and telling their father about the birds and message tubes. Of course, he might not take too well the news that they were wasting time searching instead of working and might move them on to other chores. Nothing could ruin a good adventure quicker than actual chores. But above all else, telling Dad meant admitting they couldn't solve the puzzle themselves—a taboo thought.

Upon arriving at the house, they peeled off their winter coats, gloves, and hats, aiming straight for the woodstove to thaw, while Mr. Barlow prepared five plates of a family favorite: PBJ with banana.

"Hi, boys," he said, wiping crumbs from the countertop. His voice sounded raspy. He looked wrung out.

"Your cold getting worse?"

Strolling to the fire, Mr. Barlow laid a strong hand on each boy's shoulder. Standing about six-foot, fairly fit, with an angular face, coffee-colored hair, and deep set eyes, their dad was no farmer, but he was masculine and strong. Not at all the bookish, retiring academic one might expect of a history professor. Each year as cool weather approached, he typically allowed himself a scruffy, short-cropped beard, and this year's model was already in place for the coming winter. Hugging their necks, he only lightly kissed their cheeks, careful not to spread germs. When he pulled away, his cough was wet and rattly.

"I'm holding my own," he said. "But I don't want to pass anything on. I think Gabe may be coming down with my bug already." He called to the twins upstairs. "Barlows . . . lunch!"

Tearing down the stairs came the twins, grabbing sandwiches, all hands and arms and energy, chewing bites and gulping milk before their rear ends were even fully seated. At length, Garret noticed Ewan. "You been working out in the field? On a Saturday?"

Ewan glanced at Hadyn and shrugged, playing it cool. "We're making progress."

Gabe wasn't impressed. "I think you're nuts. It's freezing out there. And I have a cold." He certainly didn't act sick, but Dad had expressed his concerns more than once, and Gabe had listened.

"I *want* to see what you're doing," Garret explained, rolling his eyes at Gabe. Though they were fraternal, not identical twins, they were similar in appearance. But in temperament and personality they were different as night and day. "Dad won't let me go out there, though. Why's that again, Dad?"

"It's big kid work," Mr. Barlow answered casually. "No distractions. Right guys? You are remembering to work, aren't you?"

Hadyn, mouth full, said, "You said I could make it fun."

"Double the fun with me on board!" Ewan chimed in.

"Well maybe I'll take the twins out there with me sometime to check on your progress. How's that sound? After I'm feeling a little better."

"Sure," Hadyn replied, feeling Ewan's elbow lightly nudge him. "Just tank up on vitamins first."

They ate quickly, then went back out to the briar patch. Large above them, the afternoon sky was clean and bright, the air crisp and pale and blue. Hadyn contemplated the main tunnel. Light penetrated into the shaft for twenty feet or so. Beyond, the center of the briar patch was probably another forty feet farther on.

Ewan said, "Maybe there's a nest in there somewhere."

The oldest Barlow shook his head. "If they have a nest, I imagine we've scared them away from it. I just can't believe we haven't seen a single scratch on the ground. Those were sharp claws."

"Couldn't they have just crawled through the branches?"

"Maybe. But those were big birds. Not little sparrows or even quail. Besides, we're back to tracks. That's all soft mud back in there. No grass. And yet no tracks. If they just crawled out, we'd know it."

After a moment of silence, Ewan said what both were thinking. "It's like they just flew in and disappeared."

Hadyn grabbed the hedge trimmers. "It will all disappear if Dad thinks we're moving too slow. If he shows up with a brush hog, we'll never know the truth."

So they began again, each with a flashlight this time. More crawling, more musty-smelling earth, more thorns, more cold. More clipping, snipping, hacking. Hadyn wanted to aim for the center rather than mess with connecting tunnels, and Ewan agreed. While one chopped and cut, the other would drag the severed branches outside to the discard pile. Hadyn knew his dad wouldn't approve of so much wasted, duplicate effort; definitely not the easiest or most efficient way to clean the place. But he was on a mission. For a while, at least.

"This is going nowhere," he groaned after another hour of toil. "We're well into the center. If there's anything to see, we should have seen it by now." He sighed. "I just don't get it. Are we going crazy? We saw four birds, right?"

"And have four metal tube thingies to prove it. They flew right into this tunnel. Then . . . poof!"

"Gone."

Ewan wiped a thin bead of sweat from his forehead. "Okay, what if we try to connect to that first shaft back there?" He pointed. "You know, the small one coming in from the left side. You thought it was pretty close to this tunnel, didn't you?"

Hadyn sighed. "I had that much tunneled before the birds came. Starting over means all of this," he waved his hands futilely, "has been a waste."

"Maybe not. If the other shaft is that close, maybe the branches thin out. Enough for the birds to have slipped through. Think about it—we've never even bothered looking down the other tunnels."

Hadyn was glum. "I suppose."

For lack of a better option, the two boys backtracked. Hadyn stayed in the main shaft with the trimmers, while Ewan crawled outside the briar patch with the hatchet and reentered through a smaller, narrower side shaft aimed to intersect the main shaft at about a forty-five degree angle. Ewan sounded surprisingly close, perhaps only a few feet away.

"I see your flashlight!" Ewan called. "Can you see mine?"

"I see it. But we've got some big stuff between us it looks like. Is that a tree stump?"

"I see it. Looks too tall to be a stump. Hang on."

Hadyn waited. He saw Ewan's flashlight flickering through the web of branches, heard dry cracking noises and the dull chomp of the hatchet biting into wood. After several minutes, Ewan said, "I don't think it's a tree stump. But I'm to it now. Just one more swing . . ."

Another sound, brighter, like metal on rock. It carried such force Hadyn winced at the vibration it must have caused.

"Ah . . . that's gonna leave a mark!" Ewan groaned.

"You okay?" Hadyn asked. "Sounds too big. Better just work around—"

"It's stone," Ewan said, ignoring him. His voice trailed away. "But it's . . . what in the world?" Hadyn pulled back several branches, glimpsed the outline of Ewan's head, the silhouette of the object. He heard Ewan whistle soft and low.

"Hadyn, I think you ought to come around here."

Hadyn scurried out of his tunnel and into Ewan's. He followed the line of his brother's flashlight to the object itself, or at least the part they could see. The edges revealed cut stone, not like a random chunk of rock in a field. Something else. Branches completely wrapped the surface as it curved out of reach, out of sight. Something strange stirred inside the oldest Barlow as he looked at it, something dangerous and wild, like the feeling you get on a path through forgotten woods lit only with moonlight, or on finding hidden doors in an old house, leading to secret rooms. Or words on a scroll trimmed in gold. Memory surfaced in his thoughts, a bubble rising unseen through dark water.

Great purpose.

A feeling caught in his throat. He tried but couldn't identify it.

"Let's see what this thing is," he said.

Freshly energized, they began clearing a section large enough to see the full stone, only to discover that it reached over the thicket like an arch. The process was slow, but soon the relative positions of arch and tunnels made sense. An arch has two base pillars. Ewan had discovered one. From that point, the arch curved up and over, planting its other base in an uncut portion of the briar patch just past the main tunnel's width. In other words, Hadyn had inadvertently channeled the main shaft right through the open space of the arch.

The boys worked until their lungs ached and their flashlight batteries grew weak. Hours passed. They connected the two shafts and built a mini-cave around the arch, all hidden in the belly of the briar patch. Finally, they plopped down, exhausted, to gaze upon their discovery.

In front of them, approximately five feet wide by five feet tall, stood a smooth curve of ancient stone. The stone itself was three-sided, like a wedge pointing in and down, meaning the footprint of each base was triangular. Its weathered surface was a splotchy quilt of lichen and fungi, so that neither boy could tell if the color was, indeed, black, or if the darkened surface was merely aged and dirty with decay. Thin, brittle vines wrapped round and round it, clinging to the surface so fiercely they seemed embedded. The boys scraped the vines loose, casting them aside, rubbing dried chunks of lichen and spores with their gloved fists until the growths broke off in clumps and dropped free.

Suddenly, Ewan said, "Hey, run your hands up here. Along the top curve. Do you see those?"

Hadyn shined his light, furrowed his brow. "Are those letters?" He traced the roughened surface with his fingers, felt a series of crude, oddly angled slashes and dots. "Not our alphabet. Ewan, what is this thing?"

"Maybe Indian?" Ewan replied, glancing at the back side. "Same kind of marks back here." He rolled his forefinger left to right over each carved shape. The lichen made it difficult to distinguish one from another. "I think I count nine."

"Me, too. We should get—"

Just then, three short air horn blasts echoed over the fields, cutting him short. Both boys froze in surprise. Dad called it the Von Trapp, his signal for "Come home now!" Hadyn was torn, but Ewan had already begun gathering their things. Quickly, they stumbled out of the tunnel. Stars shone overhead.

"How long have we been in there?" Ewan wondered aloud.

"Don't know. Long enough for Dad to worry. He's gonna kill you."

"Me?" Ewan cried in alarm.

Hadyn winked, then broke into a sprint over the dark fields for home.

CHAPTER 3

CURIOUS CODE

Fortunately, Dad didn't kill them.

He didn't say much of anything, actually. After dinner came free time, then bed, leaving the mysteries of the arch to torment them all night. They plotted and schemed until both were nearly hoarse, but when Sunday morning finally came, they begged their dad to let the whole family stay home.

"Take a day off," Hadyn said. "Even from church."

To their surprise, Dad agreed. Fact was, though they had been in Newland four months, they had only recently found a church everyone liked. Plus, Dad was still fighting a cold, and Gabe was starting to drag. Really, it wasn't surprising that Dad capitulated. It was probably a relief, Hadyn realized, for him to have an excuse to stay home, especially from church. Even at the one year mark, Mr. Barlow was a notably quieter man, more awkward, more tentative socially and spiritually than ever before.

Hadyn remembered, a couple of weeks after moving to

Newland, when the house was still a mess of half-emptied boxes and luggage, finding his father's laptop open, thoughts laid bare in digital ink. The words on screen were written like a confession:

> *We're here, sort of. So many boxes to unpack. I'm so proud of my boys. They're handling the move well. But how can this place ever feel like home without Anna? Now that we're finally here, I feel more stuck in No Man's Land than ever before. I'm trapped between the longings of a past I can no longer possess and a future I can no longer enjoy. From the moment Anna passed beyond my reach, all of life has become at best, second best.*

Of course, Hadyn had felt guilty for reading his father's journal, guiltier that he still remembered. Not like it was much of a secret. Dad would often take each boy in his arms and say, "I miss your mother so much," or "It shouldn't be this way." He was always apologizing, always trying to comfort, to make space for their grief and yet say hopeful things, for their sakes if not his own. And always, faraway, a wish in his eyes, an ache to see beyond earth . . . yet he was unable.

It was not a look a son is meant to see in his father's eyes. It was haunting and vacant, a black hole. Hadyn dared not enter the pull of its gravity. He didn't know how. It was hard enough for him on his own. Facing the fact that his dad hurt so much was beyond his emotional range, beyond any fifteen-year-old boy's.

Two eager voices saved him: the twins, with pleading eyes. No church meant time to play.

"Hide-and-seek, guys? C'mon! Betcha can't find us."

The older two eyed each other warily. All they really wanted to do was get out the door, but not with two nine-year-olds trailing curiously behind.

"I'm not really up for hide-and-seek right now," Ewan said, taking the initiative to steer a separate path. "Besides, I thought you guys wanted to beat that level on Mario Wii?"

"Beat it. Yesterday." Gabe smiled. Sure, he was sniffling and his eyes looked puffy, but it usually took quite a bit to knock Gabe down. "How about basketball?"

"Too cold."

"We could wrestle."

"Too much noise," Mr. Barlow answered, passing through the living room on the way to his office. "Roughhouse outside if you must." Which, of course, they were not going to do, and Dad knew it. It was the kind of impossible, inarguable logic adults were known for.

"Let's play *something*," Garret begged. "What do you guys want to do?"

Hadyn threw a curve ball. "I'll play chess. You up for a thrashing, Garret?"

Garret's eyes widened. He loved chess. Surprised, Ewan could only blink. He started to speak. Hadyn coolly intervened. "Ewan, why don't you and Gabe play something for a little while? Then maybe you and I can do something together later, while the twins do their own thing."

A slow, coy smile crept across Ewan's lips. He got it.

"C'mon Gabe," he said, scrambling upstairs.

Hadyn faced Garret gravely. "One condition," he whispered solemnly, glancing over his shoulder, as if he were telling a secret. "You can't beat me like you did last time."

Garret dashed off to find the chess board. And so the games began.

A couple of hours later, the games ended in a pillow fight upstairs, with Mr. Barlow mercifully allowing more noise than he preferred. When their dad finally called out, "All right, enough boys! Cool it down. It sounds like a herd of elephants up there!" the twins, breathless, decided to watch TV, and Hadyn and Ewan realized their golden moment had arrived. With new batteries in their flashlights, an old toothbrush, a ball of steel wool, paper, crayons, and pencils in hand, they bundled up and dashed out the back door, sprinting first through a couple hundred feet of trees before the wide fields opened in front of them.

It was a beautiful part of the country, with low ranging hills, blue streams, and many fields of corn, wheat, and soybeans. Hadyn saw the beauty through tears, hearing his mom's voice as he ran. Full of laughter. Countless times, she had tried to win his heart for the move to Newland, saying, "Out of the city, into the woods. What could be better for a bunch of boys?" or "C'mon, Hadyn, it's the home of Mark Twain. Huckleberry Finn. It'll be an adventure!" Now as he ran through those very woods, he was not sure whether he ran toward the memory or from it. He saw her face, her smile. He remembered how beautiful she was, platinum hair catching light like an angel's wings. Not long after those memories, chemotherapy started. Soon, her beautiful hair began falling out.

He ran harder, fueled by fresh anger, leaving Ewan behind. It took him roughly ten minutes to reach the briar patch, a couple minutes faster than usual. The boys' chests heaved in the chill air.

"What's gotten into you?" Ewan choked, bent over.

"Nothing. Let's just do this."

They dove into the main tunnel and scurried to their newly formed cavern. Ewan immediately began fingering every notch and crevice, as if rubbing the surface might cause the stone to change to gold.

"It's like finding treasure," he whispered. "Only better. Mom did all that stuff in Ireland, you know. All those ancient monuments. She would have loved this."

Hadyn, still hearing her echo in his head, choked something incoherent. He whipped around and shoved his brother full in the chest. "She's gone, Ewan! When are you gonna get that through your head? G-O-N-E. Gone!"

Ewan's cheeks colored with anger and embarrassment. Tears leaped to his eyes.

"You think I don't know that?" he roared, forcing Hadyn back with his feet, then lunging at his stomach. The two tumbled to the ground. In the cramped space, Ewan flailed his arms and fists wildly. "She's not gone to me! She's not! Hate life if you want, but I want to remember her!"

Caught off guard by his brother's ferocity, Hadyn was late to raise his guard. One blow landed hard on his shoulder, another in his gut. Enraged, he smacked Ewan upside the head, shoving him away. Ewan didn't try to rise or retaliate. He turned off his flashlight and lay in the dark, breathing hard.

Hadyn put his hands to his face. He couldn't believe what a fool he was.

"Ewan . . . I'm so sorry."

"Just shut up," Ewan whispered. Slowly, he rolled to a sitting position. "You think I don't know she's dead? I know it every day." He turned his flashlight on. His eyes were bloodshot and swollen. "But she'll never be gone." He raised his gaze, said one more word. "Jerk."

They sat, together, alone, on the cold ground. Time passed.

"Let's get this over with," Hadyn sighed, breathing into his cupped hands to warm his fingers. "Today's too cold to stay out for long. If we get back soon and have a more normal day at the house, it might help keep Dad from getting suspicious." Hadyn crawled to his knees. He didn't bother looking at Ewan but tried to change gears just the same. "Have you noticed? He's been watching us funny."

Ewan said nothing, but had noticed.

They took turns with the steel wool and toothbrush, gently scrubbing the top of the arch, smoothing the surface to satisfaction, careful not to mar or chip. Hadyn held a piece of lined notebook paper against the stone and Ewan colored. The tension didn't disappear, but it eased. Although his first attempt to etch with pencils didn't work so well, trial two, with crayons, did. Two sheets per side were needed to capture everything. Ewan used a different color crayon for each face, then they compared the etched paper copy to the original.

"Perfect," Hadyn declared. The marks were bold and easy to read. He felt certain they would figure out the meaning in no time. It must be some sort of language. Probably clues all over the Internet about stuff like this.

"Let's g-g-go," Ewan said, teeth chattering. "I need warmth."

Back at home, the woodstove was mercifully ablaze. Ewan cradled a warm mug of cocoa in his hands, staring soberly into the flames, silent. The fire behind the glass wildly took wing, like a caged bird thrashing about, struggling to rise in flight, to be free. As Hadyn watched his brother, he knew the feeling. Ewan had been sitting there, reading, drinking, occasionally writing in his journal, for over an hour. Hadyn knew he was still upset. He wanted to say something to make it right, but didn't know how without making it worse. Most times, as now, he just held it inside.

His job was clear. He sat with a laptop on the far couch, away from foot traffic, Googling. Gabe lay listlessly on the other couch, staring out the window through bloodshot, watery eyes. The virus had finally caught up to him. Hadyn worked studiously. Even so, it soon became apparent he had no idea how to Google for *this*. How do you describe the shape of random marks on a strange stone? Search results were nonsensical and entirely unrelated.

Suddenly, Garret plopped down beside him. Instinctively, Hadyn angled himself (and the screen) away.

"No, Garret. Not now. I'm busy."

Garret shrugged and ambled over to sit by Ewan. He folded his legs and propped his chin on his fist. Ewan sipped his steaming drink. Garret took a deep breath.

"I miss Mom," said the younger one.

Hadyn couldn't help but overhear, and, for the second time, felt like kicking himself. Really, how many times can a person screw up in one day? Quietly, almost secretly, he watched the words take their toll on Ewan, watched him close his eyes, veering through the pockmarked minefield of his own emotions. It was one thing to feel the pain yourself. It was another to force others to feel pain you don't want to feel. Hadyn knew the twins were still trying to find their grief, to give it a voice. They were only eight when she died.

Ewan looked Garret in the face, groping for words. The fire crackled, hissed.

Hadyn felt himself starting to seethe all over again. Mad at himself. At the world. At God. It was all so unfair. Ewan was right. *Jerk.*

Garret, matter-of-fact, said, "She fixed the best hot chocolate."

Ewan nudged his little brother gently, forcing a slight smile.

"Better not tell Dad. It'll hurt his feelings. Can't have that."

Garret's nose wrinkled. "He doesn't put enough chocolate in. Mom always put extra chocolate in. Plus, Dad always fixes it too hot."

Ewan put his arm around his little brother's shoulders. He had been so thrilled when they were born. Finally, *he* got to be the big brother to someone.

"I miss her," Gabe said from the couch, fighting a fever.

"I miss her, too, guys," Ewan replied.

The open space of the great room fell silent. Hadyn coughed.

"Ewan, when you get a chance. I need to show you something. Please."

"I'm busy," Ewan said.

"It's the *code.* For our . . . spy game."

"Spy game!" Garret whirled his head around. Such was life at nine years old—short attention spans. Hadyn should have known better.

"Sorry, Garret. Sorry, Gabe. It's a secret."

Gabe hadn't moved since the pillow fight and wasn't about to move now. He moaned, but didn't protest. Garret all but deflated. "Can't I just look? I never get to do this stuff with you guys!"

Ewan climbed to his feet, took his mug to the kitchen.

"Better let me check this out, Garret," he said self-righteously. "Hadyn talks without thinking of others. A *lot.*"

Touché. Hadyn glared back just the same, then dashed off, taking the stairs two at a time. Ewan followed more casually. Inside Hadyn's room, Ewan closed the door, snidely remarking, "You know we're going to have to play spy with the twins now, don't you?"

"Hey, you're the genius that put me on the spot. You knew I was working on the inscription."

"Inscription? Is that what we're calling it now? I hadn't been informed."

"Well, I'm informing you now. News flash: we aren't getting anywhere."

"You've been searching for, like, three hours. Nothing in all that time?"

"First, drop the superiority thing. I said I was sorry. And try *one* hour, maybe."

Ewan held out his hands, pretending to drop an invisible object. Hadyn rolled his eyes. "It wouldn't matter if it were days. I'm not getting anywhere."

Ewan wrinkled his brow. "Really, no hits?"

"Zip. I've Googled everything I can think of. The only logical thing is that it's Indian something-or-other. But most Indian tribes didn't even have an alphabet, and the Cherokees' looked totally different. I'm stumped."

Hadyn sat cross-legged on his bed. Four sheets of etchings were spread in front of him, taped together to form one side in brown crayon, the other in blue. Ewan stared at the rubbings for a minute, blank-faced.

"Well," Hadyn demanded. "Any ideas?"

Ewan shrugged. "Really, you're much better at this sort of thing than me. I'm clueless."

"You aren't even trying."

"Okay, try working on the papers in the tube instead of the inscription on the arch. What could *A* stand for? Maybe that will help."

Hadyn pushed the papers aside, disgusted. "*A* could stand for *anything*. Thanks a lot."

"What do you want me to say? It's gibberish! It's not an alphabet we know."

"It doesn't have to be an alphabet to have a pattern to it. Look, this mark and this mark are the same. And this one is the same as this mark on the other side. I just can't figure it out."

"Then face it, we may have to get help from Dad."

Hadyn glowered. With Ewan, it was hard to be sure whether his response was virtue or vice. He was the more flexible and adaptable of the two but also generally quicker to throw in the towel . . . on some things. Hadyn, on the other hand, walked a fine line between tenacity and stubbornness. He didn't like asking others for help, often purely for reasons of pride.

Ewan reached under Hadyn's bed and pulled out one of the slender metal tubes. He ran his finger along the scrollwork *A*.

"Do you think the birds are connected to all this?" he asked.

"You mean to the inscription?"

"I know, it doesn't really make sense."

Even so, it was a new thought. Both silently pondered.

Hadyn pulled one of the scrolls from the tube and read it silently. Vague intuitions gnawed at him. While Ewan fiddled with his tin whistle, the strands of an idea slowly knotted together in Hadyn's brain. "Listen, if we made a drawing of the marks, duplicated them by hand, we could tell Dad it was something we were working on at school. Or something like that. I don't want to lie. But that way he might not suspect anything. And we might still get help." He glanced up. "After all, we're afraid Dad's going to figure us out, but why exactly? What do we expect? Why would he automatically think we've found some ancient monument on our land, just because we showed him these marks? I mean, this is *Missouri* for crying out loud. We don't have cool stuff here."

Ewan chewed the thought like a piece of caramel, tasting it, liking it. "I get it. You mean, if the marks are written in our own handwriting, Dad wouldn't have a reason to connect it to anything else?"

"He wouldn't have a reason to think anything, really. A rubbing obviously looks like it came from something. But a drawing—"

"Is just a drawing."

Hadyn nodded. "Or a game. Or a school project. Not a strange, arched rock doohickey on the back of our land. I don't want to spend my entire Thanksgiving break stuck in translation, with no progress." He stuck out his right hand. "Deal?"

"Deal."

They shook hands.

"Okay, I've done my part. You draw. Let's hope it works."

Ewan smiled confidently. "Dad's studied stuff like this for years. He'll know what it means."

CHAPTER 4

SECRETS

Mr. Barlow frowned, puzzled. "I have no idea what it means," he answered flatly.

The two older boys stood in their father's office downstairs, located just off the den. They had presented him with a single sheet of paper, bearing Ewan's best renditions of the markings, and a flimsy story.

"It's for extra credit," Ewan said. "Hadyn couldn't figure it out. We're studying . . . Egypt . . . in class. If I get it right, it'll be cool. The whole class is clueless."

Technically, Ewan and Hadyn had reasoned, the arch *was* like an extra-credit project. Just not a *school* project. An after-school project. And Ewan had, in fact, studied Egypt at school earlier in the semester, so that part was accurate. Sort of. Lastly, his class was actually clueless about everything they were doing. Creatively worded truth. Hardly foolproof, they knew, but they wanted to keep the arch a secret at least a little while longer. The secret was part of the fun.

As his dad studied the paper once more, Hadyn glanced admiringly around his office. Familiarity had never prevented his feeling a sense of awe at his father's workspace, both in their old home and the new. Mr. Barlow's office was like some secret chamber in a faraway castle, a repository of utterly ancient things. Even in their newly furnished home, the air in this one room always smelled old, musty, like dust and oiled calf skin. Shelves were lined with old leather-bound books fastened with blackened brass clasps. Faded old maps hung on the walls, dating back hundreds of years, cataloging unrecognizable sections of land and sea with equally unrecognizable notes. Hadyn didn't have a clue what half of those were, nor the thick parchments lying in uneven bundles here and there, some tied with twine, some jumbled loose. Even the desk was old: hand-carved mahogany, with a broad, waxy top all but lost under a chaos of papers and books. The only modern item visible in the entire room was the large flat-screen monitor sitting on the left side of the desk, toward which Mr. Barlow seemed ever affixed—either pecking incessantly on the keyboard, writing his latest book, or searching, searching. Always *searching*.

For what he sought, Hadyn hadn't the foggiest—he only knew that it increasingly consumed him.

Like nearly any adult enterprise, his occupation was B-O-R-I-N-G to the kids. Reggie Barlow had taught history for fifteen-plus years at UMKC (up until last year). He was a frequently published academic, and, over the last decade, had begun dabbling more and more in archeology. Kinda cool, perhaps, but pretty straightforward stuff. What Hadyn did not realize was how controversial his dad had become. He was a notable, even revered figure in some circles, while mocked as a renegade in others. His views on "theoretical early European civilizations" were radical, to say the least. A strange intersection of archeology and legend fueled his notions, led by his digs in the British Isles, where he and Anna first met.

Anna had already spent two weeks at Newgrange, Ireland, then another three at the Hill of Tara. Mr. Barlow, digging for evidence to support his budding ideas, found her instead. At the Hill of Tara, "on the green hills of Ireland," Dad first laid his eyes upon the young and lovely Anna Leigh. Mrs. Barlow, a respected anthropologist in her own right, was no radical. Her mission was far more orthodox: to explore the local customs of primitive Celts. But, after falling in love and marrying, they published an underground rag together on "speculative archeology" that quickly developed a fierce and critical following.

Now, observing his sons, Mr. Barlow coughed to clear his throat and leaned back in his chair. The sound of supple leather and creaking springs sounded like secrets about to be found out. Suddenly, their plan seemed rather thin.

"Where did you say you found this inscription?" Mr. Barlow asked. He was not feeling well and it showed, but he seemed pleasant enough. His eyes were fixed on Ewan.

"I copied it from another sheet," Ewan said—technically true—"but don't know what it means." He tried to sound like he was answering the question, while really avoiding it. "It seems like a pattern of some sort. Are they hieroglyphs?"

"No, not at all. Your teacher, I think, would know that."

That didn't sound good. A half shade of color drained from Ewan's face. "Maybe she's trying to trick us. Maybe *that's* why there's extra credit in us figuring it out."

Mr. Barlow's red-rimmed eyes shifted between his sons. He released the paper, letting it float to his desk, grabbed a tissue, and blew his nose. "They look runic to me."

Hadyn attempted to sound casual. "Runic?"

"Think Viking. Runes were the alphabet of ancient Europe before Roman alphabets took over. There are stones with runic inscriptions all over northern Europe, left by tribes of the British Isles, by Scandinavians, by the ancient ancestors of Germany. Some of these stones with runes predate the pyramids. The people didn't have paper and pens, so they carved on rock shapes. Some small, some gigantic. Usually these were burial stones, or ceremonial stones. They were called dolmens, runestones, monoliths, menhirs. I've studied many of them. I've seen marks very similar to these, in fact."

Hadyn knew Ewan's heart was jackhammering, just like his own. Still, he couldn't believe his brother could find nothing more original to say than, "So, not Egyptian."

An unreadable smile played at the corners of Mr. Barlow's mouth. His eyes searched both their faces. "I commend you for being so committed to your school assignments. During Thanksgiving break, no less."

"Yeah, thanks."

"You know, it's interesting," Mr. Barlow continued, leaning forward to study the paper again. "There're dozens and dozens of famous sites with runic inscriptions all over Europe. But even with decades of study by many brilliant minds, the purpose of these stone monuments is still largely a mystery. Even the meaning of certain runes is unknown. A runic inscription can state one thing, but also form a riddle that means something else. For example, a runestone may tell a story, but hidden in the letters, it may also reveal a date. And that's just the tip of the iceberg, really. We know some stones performed certain, basic, highly precise calendar functions. The angle of their shadows, or a keyhole that allows a beam of sunlight through at a certain time of year, may mark the winter or summer solstice. Some of the markings record historic events. Even more puzzling, many of the monoliths seem meaningless. A bit of magic and uncertainty surrounds most of the stones. Especially," he paused for effect, slowly raising his eyes, "the runestones that have been discovered in North America."

Both boys swallowed. Neither spoke, moved, breathed.

Mr. Barlow reached behind him to the shelves lined with books, pulling out three recent editions. "The Fletcher Stone in Nova Scotia. The Spirit Pond Stones in Phippsburg, Maine. The Heavenor in Oklahoma, which may be as old as 600 AD. And the most compelling and enigmatic of all, the Kensington Runestone, discovered in 1898 in Kensington, Minnesota. Right at the head-waters of the Mississippi. All of these, in varying degrees, suggest that Scandinavian explorers traveled to North America, probably predating Columbus by at least a hundred years, possibly several hundred. Their presence may have even been more permanent than conventional wisdom allows. Settlers, not just explorers. Even if not, they left clear evidence of Viking culture behind."

"In runestones?" Ewan asked.

Mr. Barlow's tone grew thoughtful. "In one sense, there's not a lot of proof. But what we do know is hard to explain away. Triangular Scandinavian mooring holes for anchoring ships are drilled in rocks in Maine, Minnesota, Iowa, South Dakota. Viking implements—halberds, battle-axes, spears, and boat hooks—have all been identified. Several Native American words are highly suggestive of Norse origin. And there were blue-eyed Mandan Indians who knew about Christianity before the first settlers arrived. These same Indians lived in square, medieval–Norwegian style buildings. Way too coincidental to be coincidence, I think."

Ewan's eyes danced. "So, these runes. Are they letters? Does it spell something?"

"Could be letters. Could be symbols for colors. Or sounds. Or shapes. Could be anything. I must say, I'm quite intrigued. I've never seen some of these markings before. And yet . . ."

"What? Yet what?"

Mr. Barlow smiled. "I'm sure you drew the runes well, Ewan, but it would be helpful if I could study the original letters more closely. Maybe you could show me the photo your teacher used? Is it in a book?"

Ewan cleared his throat. "I'd have to look for it."

"Actually, I'd like to just talk to your teacher. This is impressive stuff. Seventh grade has come a long way—"

Mr. Barlow paused, his eyebrows gathering like storm clouds above the bridge of his nose. He studied Ewan's sheet once more. A puzzled expression, a memory, darted across his eyes. He turned, grabbed a book off the shelf and a thick pile of paper from his drawer, and hastily put on a pair of reading glasses, thumbing through the pages of the book to a fold-out sheet full of strange runes. He scanned the markings, darting back and forth between a photo of a particular stone and the meticulous, hand-drawn recreations of the runes. Then he turned to his paper, what looked like a manuscript for a new book, or maybe a doctoral thesis. Back and forth, twice more.

"I recognize these," he murmured. "I couldn't place it at first. Here, take a look at this."

He waved his sons forward excitedly, showed them the title of his manuscript: "Ancient Civilization Portals: Dimensional Travel in the Formation of Early Civilizations." Then the book. Both boys leaned over his desk for a closer view. The caption above the photo he had turned to read: "Kensington Runestone." Hadyn wiped his sweaty palms on his jeans, trying to appear calm.

Mr. Barlow pointed to three different runes in the book, all of which were circled.

Then he pointed to three different runes on Ewan's sheet. They matched.

"There are so many of these things, in America and all over the world, I created a new category for them: Ancient Civilization Portals. ACPs. I've been pressing my colleagues for answers, stirring a hornet's nest. A lot of people don't like my theories. My hunch is that they were meant for more than just calendars and markers, but the conclusions I draw are too radical for most." He pointed to the photo again. "You boys don't know it, but I've studied the Kensington Stone firsthand. I worked on one of the modern translation teams in 1998, deciphering the inscription. I assisted Dr. Nielsen in 2002, when we proved the stone's linguistics were plausible for a fourteenth-century expedition. History tells us King Magnus Erikson of Sweden authorized a voyage as far as Greenland in 1354. From there, down the Hudson Bay—it's not hard to imagine the rest, and it matches the year mentioned on the stone. Geochemical analysis helps further, suggesting pretty conclusively that the stone was buried long before the arrival of Europeans in the region. Some, however, claim the Kensington is a much more recent forgery. Part of their argument is that it contains runic forms never verified on any other runestone. These," he tapped the three circled runes, "have never been seen anywhere else. In Europe. Anywhere."

Father and sons silently absorbed the full weight of those words. Hadyn feverishly compared the runes, over and over. They were, indeed, the same. Identical, in fact.

When Mr. Barlow spoke again, his tone was soft and intimate. He looked at each boy as if telling them his own precious secret. "I've often wondered if those Scandinavians, or perhaps Viking sailors from centuries before—if they found the Hudson Bay, if they found the Mississippi—what would keep them from sailing farther south? Down the great river? Why stop at Kensington? After all, these men were unmatched explorers. Nautical geniuses. And if they did sail south, might they have left other runestones? If so, somewhere along the banks of the Mississippi is a likely choice."

He rose, moved stiffly to the east window, and gazed longingly toward the slow, unseen current of the Mississippi not far away—a mile or so—yet comfortably hidden by three more farms and many, many trees. "Boys, I will tell you a great secret. It's time you knew."

He didn't turn to measure their response. Hadyn felt his skin begin to tingle. His mouth was cotton.

"This," he continued softly, pointing to the drawing, "is *why* I bought this land. Your mother and I worked for years, searching old maps, old writings, digging around the world, reading everything we could find. Years! An old library in Norway gave us a major clue that there might be another runestone, perhaps even greater than the Kensington, somewhere in this area, specifically even on this land. Or at least a nearby farm. A thousand years ago, the Mississippi was even wider than it is now. Did you know that? We stand on its ancient shores. So when this old farm was put up for sale, we jumped at the chance."

Hadyn felt something nameless and familiar stir deep inside. Later, Ewan would tell him he had felt something too, like whispers of a song he thought he should know, but couldn't remember. For Hadyn, it was a longing, almost a sadness, rising in his throat. He pushed it aside, remembering the words on the scroll. *Chosen . . .*

Dreamlike, his father's words caused the room to fade away.

In a sudden rush, instead of Mr. Barlow's voice, Hadyn heard a raucous cry and the flapping of dark wings, saw in his mind's eye a replay of the flight of the birds from that first night, when the scrolls were given, as the sun collapsed; realized how they had formed a black arrow, pointing straight into the tunnel. To the arch. He knew in a flash, then, that Ewan was right. Things were connected. The scrolls were not the only gift left behind. The flight of the birds was part of the message.

They passed through the arch. And were gone.

Mr. Barlow turned to face them both. Hadyn saw something almost like reverence in his eyes, deep memory. And tears. He said gravely, in a drenched voice like spring fields drenched with rain: "I think we must dispense with the games. First thing tomorrow morning, I want to see the runestone you boys have found."

CHAPTER 5

DREAMSONG

That night, Ewan dreamed a strange, beautiful dream. It was dark in the dream, so dark he couldn't see the black birds, but he heard their loud wings flapping all around him. In fact, he realized, the darkness was their wings, and it shimmered. He heard their dissonant cry. It made sense to his ears, like a voice speaking.

"Call! Call!" they cried. In the color of the blackness, he felt the soft touch of mystery, like petals on a flower.

The flapping wings disappeared, and Ewan found himself standing on a green mound overlooking three white towers and a broad valley with a ribbon of blue winding toward the sea. He listened. The sound of the water tinkling over the rocks was clean and bright, as though crystal pipes were being struck. The water played like a melody in his head. It was haunting, sweet, simple—only a few notes, but seemed *so* familiar. In the dream he realized his skin had become like stone, that now he was lying in the bed of the stream, and the water on the pebbles was making music as it flowed over him. Again and again it played, ceaselessly, burning itself from deep memory into conscious thought. Soon, his skin, his teeth, his bones started vibrating. He had become the song.

Urged to movement within the dream, he stirred, humming the tune. He dressed quickly, heavy coat and boots, favorite ball cap. Stuffed a few things in his pockets. He floated, through the river, above his room, lost in the riddle of his own mind. The song must be released. Down the hall, down the stairs. On the wall, the clock read 5:13 a.m. He saw, he could read, but he moved in a dream.

Outside, the night was still dark, dark as his mind. And bitter cold. He glided along, ambivalent to the snapping of twigs underfoot. Soon he was across the field, the urgency of the tune lofting around him. It was a needful thing, this dream, whispering nine notes.

A song that *must* be sung, a tune that must be played.

Even so, when he reached the briar patch, looming large in the darkness, he hesitated. What was happening? Was he awake? Or dreaming? Why these wild compulsions? He felt foolish. Still the melody rose and fell within—a watery, lilting tide, transfixing him. He found himself staring, unable to purge the memory of silver notes strung like pearls in the air before him, straining within to be made known.

Called, the birds said.

Some things could not wait for sense to be made of them. In the dream, Ewan stood on the shores of the crystal stream again, coaxed downward into the water by melody. He resisted one last time, then fell, plunged into the depths, swimming the channel, crawling toward some unknown, dark heart.

His eyes glazed over with sleep, somewhere between the waking world and the world of dreams. Somehow he knew this; knew it, but not in a way that mattered or could be resisted. Pulling his tin whistle from his pocket, he played. Having never played the tune before, his fingers effortlessly knew the notes. He played the melody: nine sweet, beautiful notes.

Nine notes, nine times.

As he played, the runes began to glow pale blue, shining like timid December light on morning frost. Nine strange symbols pulsed, arcing up and over his eyes, carved in stone. Underneath, in the open space, the air trembled. The song felt released. In the darkness of his reverie, Ewan studied the glowing runes, curious to see what the other side looked like, if they glowed on both sides. Time slowed. He tucked his whistle in his pocket.

And crawled through.

Lights flared briefly, blinding his eyes. The darkness of the dream faded, replaced with a very real absence of light. He was awake, alert, confused. And dizzy.

Reaching out with both hands, he grasped for something firm until his senses cleared. Fumbling through his pockets, he found his flashlight, flicked it on. Beneath him was soft, moldering earth. Above him were what looked like thick, twisting roots, thrusting down into the soil, some gnarled and strong, many others rotting apart. By some strange occurrence, he was in a cramped space, a cavity of earth, surrounded by rock and mold and moss. He was on all fours, in a crawling posture. How did he get here? In his winter coat, no less. Since when did he wear his coat to bed?

Where's my room? he thought, panic rising. *Where am I?*

He clamped his hand over his mouth, turned left, right. Nothing familiar, no landmarks in sight. Softly came the remnant of a melody. Of a river, singing to him. His dream came flooding back. He had been swimming—where? crawling through the tunnel?—had played the tune, seen the runes glow. Had passed through.

That's why they disappeared! he thought, remembering four black birds, swift in flight. *They must have flown through the runestone.* The epiphany was both wonderful and terrifying.

As Ewan's eyes adjusted, he noticed a narrow hole above him, and beyond, a brighter shade of twilight. The hole he was in was warm and smothering. He wiggled free of his coat, turned off his flashlight, listening carefully for any sounds he could recognize. The loudest in his ears was his own ragged breath.

Then, a new thought. *I'm still dreaming. It's all too crazy. Waking up, playing the tune, coming here, has all been part of the dream.*

He reached out, put his hand on a rock. It was firm and cool and quite solid to the touch. He dug his fingers into it as if it might turn to dream-powder, prove ephemeral. It did not.

No. Definitely not dreaming.

He adjusted to a crouched position, carefully pulling himself up to the opening to peek out. The opening was draped with vines, obscured by a large rock to the right and underbrush to the left. Through what few cracks of space he could peer between, Ewan saw that he was in a forest of some sort—quite literally in, or at least under, a tree. He saw no signs of life, man or animal.

Until something furry and wiggly dropped on him. It landed on his neck, scampered down his shirt. Ewan, full blast awake, came *alive*.

"Ahh-ah-ooooo-ahh-aii! What in the—get—off me!—mmph—aiigh!"

If he had been an Olympic gymnast, he would have won the gold. If he had been a yodeler, he would have made the entire nation of Switzerland proud. The moment the thing slipped down his shirt, whatever it was, bug or mouse, Ewan became Elasto-Boy, contorting, shrieking, flailing his arms, whipping and cavorting about. In two seconds flat, he was out of the hole, over the rock, stripped of his shirt, and jiggling every part a body can jiggle. On the ground by his cast-off clothing, a fat, furry worm crawled away as fast as it could, probably more terrified than its unfortunate victim.

Satisfied that he was no longer under attack, Ewan slumped against a rock, breathing hard. Very slowly, he became aware of the silence surrounding him. He listened: the light rustle of leaves in the warm, buttery breeze, the skittering feet of a squirrel somewhere behind him. Blue-jeaned and shirtless, he surveyed the forest around him. The tree he had crawled from stood to his left, a large, sprawling oak with meaty roots that tangled on the surface before plunging into the earth. Funny thing, though, looking at it from ground level—

I can't see the hole.

Suddenly panicked, he dove toward the underbrush, poked his head down into the hole, felt around, shined his light, looking for anything familiar: another hole, a tunnel, runes, the arch. Just as he feared, nothing. Back on his feet, he turned a slow circle. The woods were old and stately, well-spaced, with minimal underbrush. He stood on a footpath. As best he could guess, it was early evening, though it could have just as easily been early morning.

"Think, Ewan," he told himself. He was surprised at his own

momentary calm. "Think."

It seemed pointless to call for help. The woods were empty. In his mind he tried to retrace what had happened, feeling a vague sense of body memory, dressing in his coat, wandering to the briar patch, carrying his flute. How could he have sleepwalked that whole thing? Played music, crawled through? And yet, he knew it wasn't normal sleepwalking. But then . . . what? He had obviously been transported somewhere. That would explain why it was so warm here—*here* being someplace altogether foreign. Was stuff like that even possible? Teleportation was science fiction and magic. Crazy stuff, just for fun. He donned his shirt and ball cap, grabbing his coat off the ground.

The melody from his dream lingered but had begun to fade. *If I'm still dreaming—and I know I'm dreaming—I should just do whatever I want.* It made as much sense as any other plan. But which way, left or right? What did it matter?

He turned left. When he did, she was there. He gasped.

CHAPTER 6

FAIRIES AND GNOMES

B eautiful was too kind, too tame a word, to describe the slender woman before him.

Ewan had heard of such creatures. But hearing and seeing were very different. She was like something from a picture book, those fanciful drawings of fairy-tale creatures. Luminous, silvery. Standing behind one of the trees off the path. Or floating, perhaps. She was about his height, willowy, with thin filamental wings that glittered almost beyond visibility and hair that swam in the air as if in water. The air around her appeared soft, almost liquid. She looked young, utterly captivating, staring back at him with a puzzled expression that nearly stopped his heart. He wanted to go to her, catch her like a firefly at night, just stare at her. Yes, he was thirteen, but the surge of desire he felt was not a thing of lust but of wonder.

"How?" she said. Her voice, like a plucked harp string, hummed with surprise and awareness. "How is it that you can see me?" She wasn't talking to Ewan; her question, spoken aloud, was a private musing.

"How is that you have wings?" Ewan said, marveling. "And glow?"

The fairy's eyes darted up to the sky, then left and right. "The moon is not full. There are no pools of water. No reflections. You have no silver talisman. How is it that you see?"

She seemed annoyed, intrigued. Ewan took a step toward her. She skittered back, from one tree to the next. Her dress, green and sheer, revealed nothing, floating with her. Her wings vibrated like a hummingbird's. She seemed both nervous and fascinated, no less by him than he by her.

"I'm sorry. I didn't mean to frighten you," apologized Ewan.

"I saw you come. Through one of our—what is your wordspeech?—doorgates." She blinked. "How did you find it?"

"I don't know. I played. Music."

The girl twitched and twittered her feet, like a cat with wet paws. She studied Ewan unreadably, came to a decision. "My Lady will require this news. There will be a reward."

She turned, wings blurring into motion.

"Wait!" Ewan said. His heart stirred, and he did not know why. Surely, to see her go.

The fairy paused in mid-flight, tossed her head, found Ewan's eyes. "If you were of age, you would already be lost to me. It is good you are yet young. My lady the queen awaits."

And then she was gone. Ewan realized he had been holding his breath. He let it go and looked around. Now he felt doubly lost. And very nearly heartbroken, though that made no sense at all.

He sat a moment, breathing slowly. Was she real? What was this place? He resumed his walk, heading north, or so he guessed. One thing became clear: it was evening, not morning. Light was failing. Getting stuck in an unknown forest at night was a tad creepy. Unless, of course, it meant *she* might flutter back.

He twitched his head, blinking free of her spell. The urgency of being transplanted to this land, the looming fear of night, pressed upon him. The woodland path rolled among sloping land not altogether different from their farmland, yet nothing around him was identifiable as home. A pang of longing struck his heart. Hadyn was probably still sleeping. Night fading there, approaching here. Weird.

He had to get back.

He kept up a brisk, wary pace, ranging over hills that were higher and more broad than the gentle, treeless slopes of Newland, winding up and down, left and right, rarely straight ahead. After traveling probably two or more miles, he heard a sound that stopped him in his tracks. Over the next rise, a voice.

It sounded gruff, maybe even angry. Ewan instinctively dropped to the ground. Crawling on his elbows toward the point where the path curved over the hill, he peered into the weakening light. He saw nothing, yet he heard movement. As his eyes adjusted, he noticed a figure cloaked in green that blended almost magically with the underbrush. The fabric shifted colors, matching shadows, thinning light as needed. The creature stood with its back to Ewan. It was a short, stumpy man. Short as in midget short. As in —

Dude, seriously vertically challenged.

It had a brown knapsack slung over its shoulder. It scavenged the ground with a stick. Ewan couldn't see the creature's face at all. He had to strain to hear its words.

"Bah!" the creature snorted, stomping the ground, shuffling sideways another pace or two. It pried back fallen leaves with its stick, stooping to pluck something from the ground. Its movements were neither stunted nor awkward.

"Morels, schmorels." It sniffed disdainfully, holding the object aloft. "Paltry puffballs. Bah!"

Boogie woogie boogie-boo, Ewan thought. *Whatever that means.*

As if reading his thoughts, the creature swiveled toward him, sniffing the air. Ewan ducked, waited, before slowly edging up again. The creature was back to poking and prodding the ground, but Ewan now had a full glimpse of its face. It had a snout nose set between high bulging cheekbones, a jutting forehead, and a thick, trimmed beard of bright red hair. It was every bit the little trollish monster of fairy tales, only better groomed.

Occasionally it would sample the harvested goods; more rarely, it would drop one in its knapsack. Ewan surmised them to be wild mushrooms. Perhaps berries from nearby bushes.

"Shame for Flogg!" It sneezed, inspecting one final mushroom. "Fit for pigs not priests."

With that, it gave up, trudging off along the footpath, away from Ewan. Ewan waited for the creature to get a safe lead before following. The light was fading quickly. Shadows draped the trees. The dark canopy of leaves whispered in the breeze. Moon and stars were distant, barely glimpsed promises. When Ewan finally crossed a stream of clear water, he realized he was mad with thirst. Fearing time to drink might cost him his guide, he pressed on, unsated. After rounding two more tree-thickened hills, the woods thinned abruptly. He came to stand in a wash of clear, ivory moonlight beneath a sky blazing with stars. To his left (west?) the hills flattened, hinting at a wide expanse of open fields stretching into a far, unseeable darkness. Immediately below, along the base of this hill, was a little village of uniform architecture: simple, stucco, square box dwellings. Candles flickered in the open windows, and a thick outer wall glowed with torch fire. Rising from the village came the faint sound of many voices. Singing? Chanting?

The path down the hill to the village was bereft of the cover of trees or shadows. Ewan crept along slowly — not too slow, or he would lose his guide. As he passed along the outer wall, the chanting again drew his attention. It came from somewhere farther inside one of the inner buildings. It was a somber hymn composed in a minor key. It sounded serene, austere.

EverKing, Lord of Wind,
Speed Thine arrows
To the mark.
Pluck Thy bow and loose the shaft
Ere Light succumb to Dark.
Raise the wall,
Defend us all,
Let banned and damned depart.

For a brief moment, Ewan was torn between locating the singers, who sounded like monks or something — *maybe they could help* — and continuing to follow the creature. Maybe it would be better to just stay where he was. Typical for a boy of thirteen, though, curiosity trumped caution. Just ahead, the little creature opened a heavy wooden door, ducking down a narrow atrium between buildings. When he disappeared behind another building, Ewan quickened his pace. A warm blaze of light spilled into the shadows from another door ahead and to his left. Hugging the stone wall, he caught the door just before it closed and tiptoed inside.

A metal blade was instantly pressed against his throat.

"Manling be following Flogg, now, eh?" rasped the creature. He was so short, he had to stretch his arm to reach Ewan's neck. "Thinks Flogg has no ears? Might as well three elephants a'follow me."

He grabbed Ewan by the sleeve, shoving him forward. He was surprisingly strong for his size, with an iron-fisted grip. They were in a storehouse or pantry of sorts. The walls were shelved with earthenware, boxes, and sacks of dried grains. The rafters, clogged with hanging stalks, roots, and leafy things, made the air pungent with yeast and spices. Even stronger was the smell of cheese. Ewan was shoved forward again, through another door, into a broad, rustic kitchen with a hearth fire with two large black kettles suspended over it, a heavily scarred chopping table in the center, and every size and shape of cutting instrument one could imagine hanging above.

"Flogg hunting morels to break the fast. On the morrow. Then felcher eyes." He scraped the tip of the blade against Ewan's skin, clearly warning him not to get ideas. "Look atcha . . . what kinda manling wears such strange rags ya'? From the carnivale in Portaferry maybe? Bah!"

"Please don't hurt me," Ewan said, trembling. "I'm lost. I don't know where I am. I came here for help—"

The creature spat. "Shuttin' the mouth! Whines like a lass with new dressings and no offers to dance!"

"Please . . ." Ewan whispered.

"Please, wheeze, fleas, sneeze! Sneezing and freezing. No pleases! Go you to the father, I will. Spy on Flogg no more."

In one swift motion, Flogg transferred his knife from Ewan's throat to the small of his back. "Step it, manling. To the Circles."

CHAPTER 7

THE MIRRORLING

The melody, the humming, the song Ewan had heard, increased. It pulsed along the hallways like a bass line at a rock concert. Earlier, it had sounded reverent. Now it sounded like war.

He didn't have time to notice, really. The sharp tip of metal against his lower spine kept prodding him forward. The building he found himself in was spacious but plain. The walls were made of fitted rock and mortar, well lit with ensconced torches. The roof was thatched and high. Flogg pushed and shoved Ewan down one hall and then another and then a third, before the last hallway opened into a large, round chamber with a peaked roof sweeping upward, supported by a massive cedar pole in the center. Here, the chanting crescendoed.

Something electric tingled in the room. Ewan forgot for a moment the knife stinging his back. Power radiated from the front of the room, where a clean circle of polished bronze hung from a thin wire, and where, under that bronze circle, a fierce ritual now unfolded. Nearly a dozen men wearing robes of gray stood in a circle facing inward, both arms raised, palms out as if pressing against a barrier . . . or forming one. Their chant, now wordless, thickened tones, had become a droning, sonic wall. In their midst, a vaporous creature twisted and writhed. The creature seemed the color and substance of roiling smoke, birdlike—all claws and wings and gaping, knifed maw. Something like a spine of jagged teeth ran along its massive beak, and its face was spotted with dozens of frenzied eyes darting in every direction. It was altogether otherworldly. Ewan recoiled at the sight, nicking the skin of his back on the knife. The collective energy of the robed men seemed barely able to restrain the creature. Its tortured, raging cries came from some nightmarish realm Ewan did not ever want to visit.

Ewan saw a girl now, standing in the midst of the circle, facing the beast. Her garb was more dress-like than a robe, not gray but purple, the color of squeezed summer blackberries. Unlike the men, she was young, with light brown skin and dark eyes. Her hair, black and straight, whipped about in a torrent of unseen winds, stirred as the creature writhed about. Rather than backing away, she leaned *into* the wind, her body trembling. Before her, she held something like a square of mirrored glass. Only not glass. Ewan couldn't be certain, but the mirror seemed watery, translucent. The girl's lips were moving. Ewan couldn't hear a single word, but saw her edge closer to the beast. The creature thrashed, making sounds like tearing metal, like a wild boar, cornered, run through with a spear. Still the girl edged resolutely forward. Her face tightened with strain.

The creature retaliated, swiping a claw at the girl. Ewan heard fabric tear. She nearly dropped the square, watery device. Black wings thrashed. Again, she edged closer. Gathering her strength, she raised the mirror high above her head and cried aloud.

"*Aione yl oSova!*"

At once, the encircling men grew silent, lowering their palms.

For just a moment, the entire chamber seemed to inhale its breath. The girl, the creature, paused. In that moment, the beast turned and looked right at Ewan. Something like surprise, then rage, then desperation registered in its many hollow eyes. Straining against its unseen bonds, it seemed to gather its energy for a final leap—toward him. Instinctively, Ewan shrank back. There was no need. The girl swept her mirror downward so that it passed through the vaporous form. The creature screamed a final time, a sound so raw it might melt stone or cause a man's heart to fail. Then it vanished into the glass, absorbed in an instant.

Silence.

The men bowed low as one. Though their shoulders sagged, each raised his hands, cupped his fingers, making a sign over his heart shaped like an open circle. They wordlessly dispersed then, all except four. One old man whispered intently with the girl in purple for several moments before wearily taking a seat in a wooden chair near the front of the circular chamber. He was clothed in a gray so dark as to be nearly black. Two other men, robed in lighter shades of gray, attended him. The girl with the mirror was plainly exhausted. Her chest heaved. After a few more words with the elderly man, she bowed deferentially and turned to go, bearing the mirror carefully in both hands. As she did, Ewan saw the creature, flattened, transfixed, whirling deep in the glass. Though it made no sound, it still seemed to be watching him. Ewan let slip a little panicked heave of air.

The older man lifted his eyes at the sound, noticing Ewan and

Flogg now for the first time. He registered surprise. He had a salt-and-pepper beard (mostly salt), a studied, careful face, and eyes that struck Ewan as both patient and curious.

"Master Flogg," the man said in a warm, gravelly voice. "You should have waited outside."

"Was outside," said Flogg bluntly. "Huntering sun meal. Caught other somethings."

The old man hid his mouth behind a casually placed hand. Though his eyes were disturbed, Ewan thought he seemed mostly amused. He had a fleshy, circle-shaped scar on his forehead that had whitened with age. "Master Flogg, I thought you told me morel bread and fresh berries would be the morning meal. Did you return from the forest with a different recipe in mind?"

Flogg shook his head irritably. "Too old, this manling. Already tough, the meat." He prodded Ewan in the back. "Flogg caught him sneaking. Food thief . . . spy . . . danger. One of the strange lost ones. Father will know."

The other men, whose faces were barely discernible under deep hoods, lifted their gazes ever-so-slightly toward Ewan and his captor. The older man stepped forward from his chair, leaning lightly on a long staff made of willow with a thick, knotty top.

"How many times have I told you, Flogg?" he said in a mild, scolding tone. "Cutlery is meant for the kitchen. Instruments of violence have no place in the Room of Circles."

Ewan let his eyes wander. Not only was the room itself a circle, the walls were ringed with painted patterns of endless, interlocking circles. Smaller bronze circles hung from the walls, possibly marking the cardinal points of the compass. Flogg glanced sheepishly at Ewan, then at his knife. He frowned. "Too tall the manling without blade."

"Yes, I'm sure. Of course, you do your clan proud, Master

Flogg. I will see to this boy now. Thank you."

Flogg scowled at Ewan with beady eyes. At close range, he was even more ugly than Ewan had thought possible. His skin was cracked like old leather. His eyes roamed from Ewan to the old man, back to Ewan again.

"Any ideas, and the pounding I'll givya! Ya' be singin' with your behind, it be knocked so far up ya' brain. Brg!"

He turned and stumped away. Though he stepped hard, his footsteps made almost no sound on the flagstone floor. When he had departed, Ewan exhaled, nearly collapsing. He had been tensing every muscle for so long.

The old man in front of him shaped a circle with both hands, fingers and thumb. "Peace, little brother! Goodness! Peace to you. I am Eldoran, Father of the Gray Abbey. Come . . . you look spent."

He gave Ewan a cup of water. Ewan gratefully gulped it down.

"Where am I?" he whispered, blanching. "Please tell me where I am. And what was that . . . that thing?"

"Poor lad. I can see Master Flogg has frightened you. You will have to forgive his manners. He is a master chef and a loyal friend. But we all know how grumpy gnomes can get." Eldoran studied Ewan for a moment, his clothes, his face, his ball cap. He opened his mouth. Adjusted. "It is normal to be afraid after seeing what you've seen. Watchers are evil. Spirit and air, slaves of great darkness. Do you not know of these, my boy?"

Ewan shook his head, still trembling. "How'd . . . how'd she do that? With the mirror?"

Eldoran leaned close enough for Ewan to see more clearly the circular scar on his brow, wrinkled with age. "You are not from any city or part of this kingdom, are you? Your clothing is . . . strange.

Sit and speak now. Tell me your story. Brother Melanor, bring bread and fruit for our guest. He looks hungry."

The man wearing the lightest shade of gray bowed his head, made the sign of the circle, and departed. He returned shortly with a wooden platter of simple fare: a half loaf of dried bread, grapes, and some other kind of small green fruit that was delicious. Ewan ate hungrily, mind racing. It seemed ridiculous to even attempt to tell his story. Who would believe it? But it seemed he had little choice, and nothing but time, at the moment. He told the whole tale from start to finish. Newland, Missouri. The briar patch, the tunnels, Hadyn. The birds, the scrolls. The arch. The tune and the glowing runes. When he finished, his belly was filled and his heart calmed, but a fresh ache for home nearly overwhelmed him. For the first time yet, it occurred to him that he should be very afraid.

Ding! Already there.

Eldoran didn't utter a single word while he spoke — no questions, no comments. He merely listened and watched. Upon completion, his expression turned quite serious.

"By the Nines, I have heard such things," he mused after a long silence, stroking his beard. "From long ago. Legends of old. But Call Birds haven't flown since the time of the great mirling, Tal Yssen. If even then. This is sober news, indeed."

"Call Birds?" Ewan asked. "They have a name? So you don't think I'm crazy?"

"Oh no, no!" Eldoran said gently, shaking his head. "Of all the things you have said, the Call Birds and the gifts they bore are the most strikingly true to my ears, the most impossible to deny. The arch and markings and such I am less certain of. But the Call Birds" — he shook his head, seeming to size Ewan up with new appreciation — "that part suggests you are of royal blood, to be so Called."

Ewan snorted. "Hardly."

"Call Birds are an ancient line, descendents of Runinn himself, who was present at the Mercy of Aion. It is a proverb in our land: *When you are Called, you dream. When you dream, a new world opens.* It would seem, in your case, this is literally true."

Ewan wiped his mouth. "So this isn't a dream? 'Cause I thought maybe . . ." He caught Eldoran's eyes, found no hint of humor. The other men, with no response, hid their faces under loose-fitting cowls. This was just weird. He whispered, "This is all for real? Father Eldoran of the Gray Abbey, Flogg the gnome . . . and a really *ugly* spirit bird?"

"Watcher," Eldoran said gravely. "Oh, my boy, yes. For good or ill, you are wide awake." He slapped his thigh. "Gracious, look at me! I'm ashamed of myself." He glanced at Ewan's ball cap and pointed at the letters. "Modesty has prevented you from saying your name. Young Lord Ecbee, I presume? Is that your family crest?"

Ewan pulled his cap off, saw the letters *ECB*. Embarrassed, he answered, "No, no. I'm just Ewan. Ewan Carter Barlow. E-C-B."

"Well, Ewan Carter Barlow, you have presented me a great mystery. And none too soon, for the times are troubled indeed. I must ponder further. But for now, it appears to have fallen to me to serve as first ambassador of my world to yours. Therefore, welcome, Ewan of New Land Misery. Welcome to Karac Tor!"

As he spoke these words, the door toward the kitchen burst noisily open.

"Let him go!" demanded an angry voice. A *familiar*, angry voice.

Ewan leaped to his feet. "Hadyn?"

There, wildly brandishing his Swiss Army knife like it was a sword of great doom, stood Hadyn. He wore a winter coat tied around his waist and a dangerous, wild expression.

"Let my brother go!"

He broke into a run toward the four of them.

HIGH CALLINGS

Hadyn didn't get far.

Slipping from the shadows behind the door, a gray-robed figure thrust the tip of his staff toward Hadyn's feet, sending him to the floor with a dull thud. The impact jarred the knife from his grip, sending it clattering across the flagstones. He rolled over, only to find the same staff suddenly pressed hard against his chest. When he struggled to rise, the monk bore down even harder, causing him to groan with pain.

"Relent," said the monk. "You have entered a place of peace."

Ewan shouted, "Stop it! That's my brother! That's Hadyn!"

Eldoran waved his arms. His deep voice boomed. "Sorge, release him. I am in no danger from this boy, I think."

Sorge relaxed his pressure but did not lift the staff. "If you are truly brothers, you will recognize the health of your kin. We have caused him no harm. You would be wise to treat us the same." He removed his hood and moved to one side, extending a hand of aid.

77

A thin smile played at the corners of his mouth.

"It was an ill-considered plan," he said softly. "But large of heart."

"Courageous indeed," Eldoran agreed, striding toward them with Ewan at his side.

Hadyn rubbed his sore chest and looked into the face of the monk called Sorge. He appeared to be in his forties, with a jaw like an ox and an intense, melting gaze. His skin was dark, his head completely shaven, except for a long, braided ponytail in the back. He too had a round outlined scar, about an inch wide, on his forehead. Branded. Hadyn reached for the offered hand and was pulled to his feet.

He was nearly knocked to the ground again by Ewan's fierce, grateful embrace.

"How did you get here? How in the world did you find me?" Ewan exclaimed incredulously.

"I'd like to know the same thing," Hadyn said wryly. "By the way, what world are we talking about?"

"The Royal Kingdom of Karac Tor," Eldoran replied with a flourish. "Peace upon you."

Hadyn blinked. "I don't suppose that's anywhere near St. Louis?"

"We're in a *totally* different world," Ewan whispered urgently. "I don't know how or why, or even what that means, really. All I know is that I dreamed a tune and played it at the arch. The runes glowed, and I crawled through to look at the other side. Next thing I remember, I'm here."

"Okay," Hadyn breathed. "That's a start. Because when I heard the back door open last night, I couldn't figure out what in the world you were up to. I woke up to go to the bathroom and saw a light out the window. It was you, with your flashlight, heading toward the arch. I couldn't believe it. It must have been four or five o'clock in the morning. What were you thinking?"

"I don't remember thinking," Ewan admitted. "I was kind of out of it."

Hadyn's green eyes narrowed. The gesture was one of practiced, big brother disapproval. "Anyway, I got dressed and tried to catch up to you. I heard your flute ahead of me, but when I got to the tunnel, you were gone. The runes were still glowing. I was afraid. I thought I should get Dad, but then the glow started to fade, and I didn't know if I could make it back before the glow was gone. So I crawled through too."

Ewan smiled. "Did you see her?"

Hadyn cocked his head, obviously confused.

Full of memory, Ewan addressed Eldoran. "I saw a woman. A fairy, I think—all glowy and stuff. She was slender, with large eyes and wings and silver hair that swam like in water. She acted very surprised that I could see her. She said she had to tell her queen."

"A Fey Folk?" Eldoran spluttered. "You *saw* one of them?"

"I think so." Ewan turned back to Hadyn, grinning. "Hey, did that hole under the tree freak you out? I had bugs dropping all over me."

Hadyn scrunched his face. "*What* are you talking about?"

"When you came through the arch. I landed in a nasty hole under the roots of an old tree. Before I saw the fairy . . . Fey Folk thingy . . . whatever she was."

"Not me. I was on a path on a hill. And I found this on the ground." He held up Ewan's tin whistle, adding, "Your boots leave pretty good tracks, by the way."

Ewan grabbed his flute with relief. "That's where I first saw Flogg, I bet. I had to crawl so he wouldn't see me. It must have slipped out of my pocket."

"Flogg?"

"A gnome. Mean little bugger."

"But a good cook," Eldoran said, amused by the whole exchange. He regarded Hadyn quite seriously. "Welcome, Hadyn, brother of Ewan. The tale of your coming is equally curious to me, but it seems you too have been Called."

Ewan elbowed his brother. "The birds. He's talking about the birds."

It took a moment for all the pieces to connect. "*Call,*" Hadyn exclaimed. "*That's* what they were saying."

"It is said they have the power to fly between worlds, and it seems the legends are true." Eldoran shook his head wonderingly. "I dare say a true Call has not been released in many long generations."

Hadyn pulled from his coat pocket two black metal tubes, banded with ivory, scripted on the side with a fancy capital *A*.

"If you know about the birds, I bet you'll know about these."

Eldoran took the scrolls, holding them delicately, almost reverently. Melanor pressed in to see. Sorge seemed perplexed. Father Eldoran gently removed the tube's cap and tapped the casing until the thin edge of the scroll emerged. He tugged it free, unrolling it gently, studying the grain of the parchment, the weight of the script. Then he read aloud:

"Chosen for a life of great purpose. Adventure awaits you . . ."

He eyed the boys.

"I didn't even think of them until just now," Hadyn said. "Is this good?"

Eldoran slowly raised his head. His faded blue eyes caught the oily light of a dozen torches, reflected them back like sparks in a mirror. His face was both stern and joyful.

"It is very good, little brother. Very good indeed."

"So this is the Hidden Lands?" Haydn asked. "This, right now?"

"I haven't heard that name for such a long time," Eldoran answered slowly. "But yes, little brother. You have come to the Hidden Lands, more commonly called Karac Tor."

"And where exactly *is* that?"

"Not where, perhaps, so much as what. We are a kingdom without a king. Come, both of you, and I will tell you more. We can take refreshment in my study. Elder Sorge, join us."

They moved from the large open chamber to a smaller room lit with candles—Eldoran, Sorge, Hadyn, and Ewan. Melanor and the third monk were dismissed to their chambers for meditation and rest, but not before Hadyn noticed that they too had the same round white scars on their foreheads. Sorge brought more bread and slices of sharp cheese, like cheddar, a small cup of wine for the father, and a tangy concoction of apple and lemon juice spiced with fresh mint leaf, sweetened with a touch of honey. He called it alm tea. The boys found it delicious.

"What is this stuff?" Ewan said, holding up a piece of yellow cheese. "It's amazing."

"Ah, well, how polite of you," Eldoran said, pride glinting in his eyes, though he tried to hide it. "We are simple men, but we work hard. Doolin, braghe, chaddar. We trade our cheeses around the kingdom, to help fund our work." He smiled. "Better bread with cheese than a feast without. Or so we like to think."

"He's being modest," Sorge informed them conspiratorialy. "In the south, they call that cheese you are eating *eldoran*."

Father Eldoran could not help but blush. But this was not the time for bragging. With both boys suitably refreshed, he opened his hands to them. "Allow me to share with you the history of our land."

So he began.

"As I've already said, Karac Tor is, regretably, a kingdom without a king. Yhü Hoder, the first man, ruled for five hundred years before passing the scepter to his son, who passed it to his son, and so on. A long-enduring dynasty was forged on a throne of wisdom and quiet strength. This was the Age of Crowns, followed by the even more glorious Blessed Thousand—ten centuries of unsurpassed beauty, prosperity, and advancement—the golden age of Karac Tor.

"But the Blessed Thousand ended many hundreds of years ago. The king's line was cut short, and the royal scepter passed into legend. To maintain order, the king's governors assumed power, dividing the land into their own fiefdoms. Though necessary in the short-term, it was ultimately a selfish, disastrous move."

"We exchanged one great war for dozens of smaller wars," said Sorge.

"Wars and warlords," Eldoran added. "Then, thirteen generations ago, a noble governor named Archibald rose to influence. He united the land and brought peace. He was a good man. But it was an uneasy peace."

"And much of the time, an unholy one," Sorge added.

"Caution, Elder," the father advised. His tone was soothing enough, but his eyes were stern. "The Archibalds did much for the kingdom. We are indebted to them." He turned to Hadyn and Ewan, as if apologizing. "Sorge is clear-eyed as a hawk and just as fierce. And, at least in part, he speaks the truth. The"—he groped at the air for words—"the virility, the goodness of the kingdom has languished under the Archibalds. We have our sense of history again, even our decency—"

"But we have no courage," Sorge murmured. "No heart or vision. No will to fight the rising tide."

"Tide?" Ewan asked. "What tide?"

An uneasy silence settled upon the small room. Eldoran's gaze seemed to drift through the rock walls to the green hills beyond, like a man in a cave trying to see farther into the darkness than his lamp allowed. He stirred his wine with his finger. He shook his head.

"We dare not speak it. Not yet. It is an ancient evil. And like the tide, it *is* rising."

Sorge folded his arms. "You see, little brothers, we are held in Balance. Always we waver between Order and Chaos, Virtue and Corruption. Between—"

"The Mercy of Aion and the Wrath of the Devourer," Eldoran said gravely.

"It is a perpetual cycle. The abbeys were ordained to foster balance: White, Gray, Black. The Whites serve two great tasks. They are students of the Book of Law and keepers of the Book of Names."

Ewan motioned in the air with his hands, groping. "And that's important because . . . ?" His voice trailed away. "I'm really sorry, but I'm lost."

"Is it really a book full of names?" Hadyn asked. "Like *Ewan*? Or *Anna*? What's the big deal?"

Eldoran widened his eyes. "The big deal? Names are our greatest treasure, little brother! Surely you have such a book in your world—magical and sacred?"

"The Book of Names holds the Great Plan of Aion," Sorge said, with just a touch of belligerence, as if this were a fact everyone should know.

"Tell them of Yhü," Eldoran prodded gently.

Sorge cleared his throat. "Yhü Hoder, the first man, was the friend of Aion. But he drank forbidden waters. He rebelled. Part of his judgment was to labor without rest until he had recorded the entire future of Karac Tor—every man, woman, and child who would ever be born unto the end of the age—in a book. So it was. And so it is. Every person's name who has ever lived or ever will live is written there."

"In one book?"

"Actually, no. It ended up taking thousands of scrolls to accomplish. We call all of them, collectively, the Book of Names."

Ewan was catching on. Incredulously, he said, "Let me get this straight. You mean some kid's name who will be born tomorrow is already listed somewhere in one of these scrolls . . . before he's even born?"

"Exactly."

"So when that kid grows up, he could go and read about himself? He could find out what he's going to be doing in five years? Who he's going to marry? Stuff like that?"

"Not quite," Sorge corrected. "First, though every new name is readable to all, they only become visible as each new person is born. And second, a person's deeds may be read only by that person, not another. Third, only major deeds are recorded."

"It is the greatest treasure of this kingdom," Eldoran declared with satisfaction. "And it has been entrusted to the care of the White Abbey, whose mission grew around the great library Yhü constructed to house the Book. They take the honor very seriously and are studious in the extreme as its caretakers. Rightly so, I might add. It is a stern and reverent task."

Sorge fingered a grape, ate it. "And all is for the sake of Balance. This, then, fits their portion of the Balance. The Whites are devout, unbending, and legalistic. They are the Stewards of Truth."

"Warriors, more like," the father grumbled, "being merciless on nearly all matters, for good or ill." He cleared his throat as if to clear his thoughts. "The Black Abbey to the north is quite different. They embrace the Way of Mystery—the unknowable secrets of Aion. The Blacks are curators of ritual and power, but also servants of peace. Their part of Balance relies more on awe and wonder than creeds and dictates from the Book of Law. The woman you saw in the Banishing Ring with us is Asandra, a mirling of the Black Abbey. Both her rank and her gift allow her to capture Watchers in the blessed water. That's what a mirling is supposed to do, be skilled in the mirrorling arts." He paused. "But few mirlings these days are, and none so skilled as Asandra. The practice was halted for nearly two decades, during which time many *mismyri* slipped through."

"Mismyri. Watchers," Sorge clarified.

Ewan shivered at the memory. Sorge continued.

"When a Watcher escapes, it must be recaptured, and this requires power. The problem is, over the centuries, certain Blacks, in discovering their power, have been known to lose their way and drift into blasphemy, bringing great harm to many."

Eldoran sighed. "And here we are, back to the Whites. For only the Books are true."

"Two books," Ewan said, holding up his fingers, trying to keep track. "Book of Names. Book of Law."

"For truth, yes. But power comes from the Blacks. And from the Blacks came Nemesia," Eldoran said, leaning forward. His eyes flicked a moment toward Sorge, almost with tenderness. "Nemesia was one of the Black Abbey's brightest pupils in recent memory. Not long ago, some twenty years, after achieving the rank of mirling, she strayed from the Way and refused to repent. She drifted from mystery into darkness. From ritual into sorcery. We did not discern the darkness within her as we should have. Now she ascends. And so for months now, from all over the kingdom, we have received increasing reports of children drifting about the land like wraiths. Parents are claiming their souls have been stolen. Many, many hundreds have asked for prayer."

Hadyn's curiosity was piqued. "What do you mean, stolen?"

Eldoran hesitated. "Stolen. Lost. Young people, simply wandering away. Disappearing."

"They are not disappearing," Sorge spat. "They go to the Tower of Ravens. To *her*. I would swear it."

Something about the image of his words made Ewan think of zombies. He shivered.

Sorge clenched his fists. "If I had been wiser, it would be different now. But I was a fool."

Eldoran shook his head. "It is no longer your guilt to bear, Elder Sorge. Have peace. Governor Archibald is near to her. The City of Kings overlooks the Isle of Apaté."

"Precisely. He *over* looks. He neither sees nor acts."

Eldoran unrolled one of the invitation scrolls. "Then what of these, my brother? Have faith! Apparently he has acted. He released the birds of myth and legend. And they have found these young lads. Their invitations bear his name: *A* for Archibald, the twelfth in the line of Archibalds. Even now, the governor probably has a plan. Very likely, he is wondering whether his call has been answered." Eldoran glanced admiringly at Ewan first, then Hadyn. "To think, his answer has arrived within the very walls of our own abbey! It would seem our first duty is to convey to him the glad tidings."

"Which would be . . . ?" Ewan said.

Eldoran stretched out his hands toward the Barlows like the presenter of gifts at a ceremony. "Obviously, that his Champions have arrived. You boys are the answer to our many prayers."

CHAPTER 9

HOMESICK

A lump formed in Ewan's throat. Champions? "I'm sorry, what did you say?"

Eldoran smiled. "Haven't you been listening, little brother? You have been chosen. Karac Tor's Champions are gone, too busy with their own affairs, with wine and dance and song. Many have grown old and died. Mac'Kalok is blind. Corus of Lotsley, the last truly great Champion, is lost to us. Lost among the Fey Folk."

"Worse, I fear," Sorge said quietly.

"The abbeys have prayed and Archibald has summoned repeatedly. It seems the Ever King has reached to your world for hope." His gaze drifted past the boys. "You both are so young. And yet . . ."

His voice trailed away.

"Yet what?" Hadyn snapped, shedding pretense and politeness. "*We're* your Champions, is that what you're thinking? Champions of what?"

"Of good! Champions of Aion. To you falls the privilege of righting the wrongs."

"They aren't our wrongs to right! We're here by mistake. Besides, if you're so convinced, why don't *you* fix the Balance? Why do we have to?"

Eldoran leaned back in his chair, spread his hands. "Our order is founded on peace. In the beginning, the Grays were almost entirely former warriors, men who traded weapons for vows. They were sick of war. They began growing gardens, making cheese. You grow tired of blood." He looked at Sorge, rose, and began pacing the room. "Ours is a different task, a task of prayer. We guide by finding the middle ground between reason and faith. Do the Grays really think wraiths wander about? Of course not. It's childish superstition. But the part about losing the soul . . . ah, now that part rings truer to my ears. And it shakes me to my core. If the soul of a generation is lost, the entire kingdom goes with it, slipping quietly into darkness. Already, dukes and land barons are sharpening their swords to raid each other's lands. Nemesia's shadow will engulf us all." He lowered himself to his seat again, noisily sipping his wine. "I *know* the dark is rising. Yet to see you here—new Champions, called in such rare fashion—I am shamed. The situation must be far more grave than I was willing to admit."

Ewan bit his tongue. He wore every mood on his face and rarely succeeded in hiding what he felt. Sarcasm came so easily.

I'll take 'Sorry to Disappoint You' for $200, Alex, he thought.

Hadyn touched his arm as if searching for reassurance in something familiar. He mumbled, "Ewan, I think they think we're someone we don't think we are."

"I don't even know what that means," Ewan replied. "But it sounds right."

Eldoran quietly stroked his gray beard. He held up the scrolls. "To whom do these belong?"

"I honestly don't have a clue!" Hadyn pushed back his chair, began prowling the room. "The stupid birds dropped them, that's all."

"At whose feet were they dropped?"

"It could have been *anybody's!*"

"Even so, someone was there, at that exact spot, at that exact time. Or forgive me. Were others nearby? Was there a crowd? Could the placement have been mistaken?"

Fuming, Hadyn didn't answer.

"And who picked up the scrolls? Who read the invitations? Who claimed them?"

"This is messed up," Hadyn whispered. Ewan knew the whole thing with the briar patch had been a bright spot for Hadyn, the first in months. It was a little sideline adventure—a distraction. Not a life mission. Now it was simply one more thing beyond his control.

"We don't belong here, and you know it," he continued. "We didn't know what the Hidden Lands were, or the birds. We didn't know we'd end up in another world. Is that the way this Ever King works? I might hate Newland . . . but I can't do this to my dad."

"You *answered* the Call, little brother," Sorge said solemnly.

"I'm not your brother!" Hadyn shouted so loudly even Ewan flinched. "I'm not your Champion and neither is Ewan. We're just kids. I honestly don't know what you want from us. Just show us the yellow brick road and get us out of Oz."

"The Grays have a proverb: Eventually, we are all brothers. All of us are connected. Somehow, some way."

Eldoran stroked his beard thoughtfully. "Perhaps even from

one world to the next."

Hadyn rolled his eyes. "This is *seriously* messed up."

Ewan decided to try a more diplomatic approach. After all, they couldn't force them. Could they?

"Listen, we're sorry for all the trouble your planet is in, or wherever we are. But c'mon. We shouldn't be here. It's a mistake. You can see that, can't you?"

"Providence is never mistaken," said Eldoran. "Only misunderstood."

Hadyn took a deep breath. "I'm trying to be polite. I don't want to argue anymore. Please just show us the portal, and we'll head home."

Neither monk moved.

"The runestone. Where is it?"

Sorge crossed his arms. His sleeve snagged, revealing a plain bronze band on his forearm near the elbow, which he quickly covered again, brushing his sleeve back into place. Ewan took note.

"We do not have this power," Sorge said simply. "It is of the Fey."

"Send us home now!" Hadyn demanded.

Sorge stood implacable. Even under his loose robe, his stance and grip suggested a tense, muscled frame. He squared his body to Hadyn, thick rosewood staff in hand. Ewan stepped between them. Haggard and bleary-eyed, he realized the long walk in the woods, then the stress of capture at knife-point, then all the weirdness had taken its toll. He felt himself beginning to dissolve. Behind him, edgy and protective, Hadyn said, "You can't keep us here against our will. You *can't.*"

"Stand down, little brother. You are in a place of peace, remember? It is no more our task to return you than it is your task to help us."

"Now Sorge," Eldoran chided. "Oft have the Hidden Lands been ruled by coercion and secrecy, yet never has it served to take what the heart is unwilling to give. This is not the way of Aion." He rose stiffly, placed a comforting hand on Ewan's shoulder. Ewan hid his face in his hands. He wasn't mad, like Hadyn, just scared. Even as cool as all this was, or could be, they simply weren't prepared. It was overload.

The father wrinkled his eyebrows. "You are obviously distraught. I'm sorry for that. But please believe me when I say now that you are here, I truly don't know how to send you back."

"Under the tree." Ewan raised his head hopefully. His eyes were streaked and red. "It must be there."

"Doubtful. Fey magic isn't like that."

"How do you know? We could try."

"You yourself went back and looked. You said so. Think, little brother. You both crawled through the same portal on your world, yet one came out under a tree and the other came out on a path in the woods."

The effort of hope so brief — risen, fallen — consumed the last of Ewan's strength. He turned to Hadyn, asked a fearful question, without words. His brother got the message.

"It'll be all right, Ewan. We'll figure this out."

Eldoran shrugged. "The only option, as I see it, is to send you to Stratamore. If Archibald called you, then he must know how to return you. Rest here at the abbey. Tomorrow we will make plans for your journey south."

Hadyn took a slow, calming breath. "Okay, it sounds like a start. Thank you," he added. "I'm sorry. I'm sorry we can't help. We just don't belong here."

Eldoran shuffled to the wall, rang a little service bell hanging there. Brother Melanor hurried in, hands dutifully clasped in front of him.

"Show these fine young men our guest quarters," the old man instructed. He sounded neither bitter nor angry, though perhaps a little confused.

"I'm sorry," Ewan said, looking at Sorge for some reason. "Please don't be mad at us. We're just kids."

Together, following Melanor, they passed through the halls in silence. They might as well have carried rocks in their bellies.

Behind them, unheard, Sorge continued in low tones with the Father of the Grays. "Truth be told, I did not see how those boys could be the Champions we seek," he said. "But for a moment, at least, it seemed like hope had entered our world."

"Hope never stands alone," Eldoran said in a dry, husky voice. "It is born of valor and perseverance. It rides the back of courage."

One by one, Sorge pinched the burning wicks of the lit candles. The room became progressively darker. At the moment, the darkness seemed as great as all the world.

"Then we are doomed," he said.

CHAPTER 10

ESCAPE BY NIGHT

A voice. Whispering harshly. Exasperated.

"... must I beat on a pot with a spoon? Merciful Aion! Awake, Lord Ewan! Awake!"

Ewan sat upright, eyes wide. Two faces slowly took shape, rising from the stain of night. He tried to focus. A lone candle fingered the walls with mercurial globs of shadow and light. Two murky figures loomed above him: Hadyn to the side, and Sorge leaning over his bed, shaking his head in amazement. In the darkness, Ewan could only see the man's eyes and teeth.

"Woe should the War of Swords begin while you slumber, Ewan Barlow. You sleep greatly! Rise now and make haste."

"I'll take Cheerios," Ewan mumbled sleepily, falling back onto his bed. "Some banana slices, too, thanks."

Fingers jabbed his ribs. Hadyn said, "Ewan, knock it off. Wake up. This is for real."

"What?" Ewan whined. He sat up again, rubbed his eyes.

"War of what?"

"There's no time," Hadyn snapped. "Just do it."

"Gather your things. Dress quickly. We must be away."

Wakefulness came gradually, like crawling out from under a warm, heavy blanket. Slowly, a few things became clear. First, that Hadyn was already fully dressed; furthermore, that he was garbed in native clothes, not his own—simple, loose-fitting shirt, brown trousers, sandals, cloak pinned at the neck; and third, that he appeared quite awake, even alarmed. Ewan strained his face to assemble this new information. Thankfully, Hadyn read his thoughts.

"Yes, away. To home hopefully. But there are . . . problems."

"Dangers," Sorge said plainly.

"Dangers getting us home?"

"No, to get you to Stratamore, where we will find out if it is even possible to get you home. First things first, Lord Ewan. Quickly, dress!"

Ewan rose, found Hadyn would no longer meet his gaze. He was clearly worried and trying to hide it. The younger Barlow accepted the shirt and pants Sorge gave him without question, feeling rapidly more alert. Nervousness like claustrophobia seeped into his skin.

"Leave your lettered headpiece," Sorge said.

"The hat," Hadyn whispered, replacing it in his hands with the small, thin shape of his tin whistle. "How many times do I have to find this for you?"

Ewan snatched his hat back, stuffing it into a loose back pocket. The feel of the whistle in his hands became a kind of portal to home, unpassable except for the wanting. A great, lonely distance opened inside him as they hastened along night-wrapped corridors, arriving at last in a small, torchlit antechamber which reeked of manure and old, wet straw. Beyond were the stables. Father Eldoran was there waiting, looking tired. He greeted them warmly, but his voice was grim.

"One of our brothers had a dark dream this night. In the dream, a rift opened in a gray sky, followed by thunder, as two arrows were shot from a great bow. Just then, sunlight broke through the clouds. But the sound of thunder had roused Watchers from their slumber. They pursued the arrows across the sky, intending to capture them before they found their mark."

Ewan glanced at Hadyn, uncomprehending. Eldoran continued.

"The brother who dreamed woke in a cold sweat and came to me in the middle of the night to interpret his vision. It was about the two of you, I'm certain. It troubled me enough to wake others. While you slept, we took counsel together, the Gray Elders and myself. After much deliberation and prayer, we came to one mind. Our judgment is that the dream is a clear message from Aion — a warning. Your coming to this world is not an accident, nor has it gone unnoticed by forces of evil. Last night I was too taken aback to realize the obvious: moving from one world to another does not occur without a great release of power."

Sorge spoke next. "Somehow that power has marked you, according to the dream. We don't know how. Perhaps in many ways."

"What does that mean, marked?"

Father Eldoran's answer was rough and unequivocal. "Like it or not, young men, you were Called. By accepting, you each chose that Calling, whether by will or by accident. I know this means little to you and that you have no interest in the workings of Karac Tor or the weaving of law and magic by which our world is bound. Your aim is simple — to go home. In good faith, we are utilizing every resource to aid your return. Nevertheless, when you accepted the Call, you came with power. You saw Fey Folk, with no moon. How can this be? It is because you are marked. And evil, which never sleeps, has taken notice. In short, you are now in danger."

Ewan felt a surge of fear. As if confessing, he said, "Yesterday, when that mirling did her thing with the Watcher—there was a point in the ceremony when the Watcher looked straight at me. I was at the back of the room, with Flogg. It clawed at the glass as if it was trying to get at me."

Eldoran thumped his staff on the stone floor angrily. His bushy eyebrows twitched. "Eldoran, you fool! Of *course* they are known. A Watcher saw one of them with its own eyes!" He glanced at Sorge. "Now, indeed, you must make haste. We will have even less time than I hoped."

He placed his hands on the brothers' heads, an act of benediction. "Speed and secrecy are urgent to your task, and miles matter more than sleep. You journey south under cover of night. If you are going to get home—and I make no guarantees—you must first get to the City of Kings. Archibald must know you are here."

Ewan's head spun. "We don't even know the way!"

"No, but I do," Sorge said. "I am taking you myself."

Suddenly, the door from the antechamber to the abbey swung wide, slamming against Ewan's shoulder. In stomped Flogg, mad as a hornet.

"Ready," he groused. "But no manling whines or Flogg be crackin' heads."

Eldoran glanced toward the Barlow brothers. "Flogg shall accompany you as well. Gnomes have an excellent sense of the land and . . . other skills."

Ewan started to protest. He didn't much care for the gnome. Bad first impression.

Flogg cut him short, waving a finger at Eldoran. "And no crying from Father when soupsy bowl grows cold."

"Of course," agreed the older man.

Flogg whirled to face both Barlows, wrinkling his snout. "And no complainin' for fast movings if manling feetsies start to hurt. Flogg helps get manlings home Flogg's way."

"You've got to be joking!" Ewan said. "The troll is going? Is someone going to take away all his knives first?"

"Hah!" Flogg stomped his foot. "Good! Flogg go back to kitchen. Morel stew need more salt anyway. Manlings on their own."

Eldoran waved his hand and said peaceably, "My favorite stew can wait old friend. They need you on this journey more than I need my soup—though believe me, I will miss it. And don't worry, the boy will learn better manners in time." He turned to Sorge. "Go quickly. Dawn will break soon. You should have better cover along the Old Way through the hills to Threefork. Flogg, gather your things. And please, kindly check on Asandra, if she is still in the kitchen."

"No need. I'm already here."

The mirling stepped out of the purple shadows at the far end of the hall, robed in the same color. She wore a silver chain around her neck and silver rings on every finger of her right hand. Hadyn's eyes widened to see her. Her skin was smooth, her lips full. She was exotic and beautiful—almond-shaped eyes, thick, flowing hair as black as night, like a mix of races, dark and light. Or perhaps a Native American princess.

Except this wasn't America.

"Asandra, Lords Hadyn and Ewan. Little brothers, Asandra

the mirling. She is traveling to Seabraith on official business for the Bishop Cassock and so will accompany you for the first leg of your journey."

Hadyn thrust out his hand rather awkwardly. Asandra warily regarded the gesture.

"This is how we greet on my world. We shake hands. I'm Hadyn."

"So I've been told."

Hadyn laughed nervously. "I, um . . . Eldoran just said my name, huh?" He swallowed. "That mirrorling stuff they told me about. That sounds pretty cool." Realizing how stupid he sounded, Hadyn dropped his gaze to the ground.

Ewan couldn't resist. "Nice. Smooth," he whispered in his brother's ear. "Next time, just make a circle over your heart."

"Shut up," Hadyn said.

Sorge did not address Asandra directly. His expression was both careful and blank. "Are you sure, Father? We need speed."

Eldoran missed, or overlooked, the subtlety. "Yes, I know. If only we had enough horses. But they would tire quickly in the hills, I'm afraid."

Having not missed Sorge's point, the mirling forced a polite smile, but her eyes were flint. "If you are afraid I'll slow you, don't be. I won't."

Flogg grumbled something gnomish, sounding more like a sneeze than any actual language. He dashed off, returning momentarily with a leather satchel half his size slung over his shoulder. A heavy black cudgel dangled from his belt. In the firelight, his red beard and face looked like worn leather.

"Packings and smackings. Now Flogg ready."

Eldoran turned to Sorge. "Will you carry your bow once more, Elder? The Order would permit it. You know this."

Sorge unfolded his arms from his gray robe, his fingers curving easily around four grooves worn into his quarterstaff—evidence of many miles travelled in service of the abbey. He held it easily, naturally. Too naturally, almost, like a ready threat, a trusted weapon. Polished dark with oils, it seemed an extension of his own skin.

"I took a vow. My staff will do."

The old man nodded, though Ewan thought it more a gesture of acceptance than approval. Eldoran squeezed Sorge's arm, leaned close to his ear. Ever curious, Ewan strained to hear his soft, raspy words fall like leaves to the ground.

"If trouble befalls you, have no doubt the Tower of Ravens is behind it."

Sorge's face hardened. He nodded, once, curtly. To his four companions, he said, "Jackals have been wandering far north of Redthorn, even along the southern Shimlings. It is a sign of Chaos to come. We must be alert."

He set off. The boys glanced at one another, uncertain, then followed. Flogg and Asandra brought up the rear.

Eldoran waved, blessed them. "Aion smile on your road. We shall pray the court of Archibald finds you well, then safely home."

As his voice faded, Ewan realized he would probably never see Eldoran again.

CHAPTER 11

GRAY MORNING

Together, the five travelers passed out of the abbey through the Gate of God. Sorge informed them that it was the third watch, which Hadyn, after a few more questions, estimated to be roughly two o'clock. The sky was empty of stars and moon, covered with a thick layer of clouds. Hints of turbulence could be glimpsed overhead from time to time, felt in the thickening air. South and west, lightning flashed, briefly illuminating the dark southern plains, transforming them into a vast, waving sea of rolling grasslands. Sorge watched. "Lightning is an empty promise. The Midlands beg for rain."

Ahead and to the east, like billowing sheets, the dark hills furled into utter blackness. For a time, the five climbed in silence, picking their way carefully along a goat trail up the hillside.

From the rear, Asandra hissed, speaking low. "I sense a Watcher. In the hills. He is far away. But he is searching."

Sorge flashed her a look, fell back, whispering harshly. Everyone stopped, waited. Obviously, Asandra was being chastised, probably for speaking aloud and making the boys nervous. She glared at Sorge but deferred. Sorge resumed his pace, then quickened it. They traveled without a torch or light of any kind. No moon to guide their steps. Sorge knew the way.

Ewan caught up to him. All he wanted to do was get his mind off Watchers in the dark. "What's the circle mean? On your forehead?"

The monk huffed with the effort of his pack. "Aion has no beginning. Our loyalty has no end. Thus, an endless circle."

Ewan stumbled on a rock, had to jog to catch up. "Okay. So why Gray? Why not White or Black?"

"Grays are called Waykeepers—healers, singers. Some, even, are warriors. We are part of the Balance of White and Black. We build and keep orphanages. We give aid to the hurting and stay connected to the people, to the earth, in ways the other abbeys cannot sustain, for it would dilute their task. Our task *is* those things."

"But you were a warrior once, weren't you? It sounded like that's what Eldoran—"

"I was a master bowman. Once, long ago."

Ewan heard the stiffness in his reply. It made him more curious, not less. "Is that what that bracelet on your arm means? Some sort of warrior thing?"

Sorge flicked his eyes from the trail to Ewan. Then back again. No answer. Asandra, apparently, was also curious. She had left her place at the rear and now strolled beside Ewan.

"What happened?" she asked.

Her face was as blank, as rigid, as Sorge's, and for that reason Ewan thought he heard something extra. An edge. Sorge stayed focused on the next rise of hill.

"I lost my way. Lost a friend." He wiped sweat from his brow. "I lost many things."

He pulled ahead after that. Ewan fell behind, Asandra even farther. The hills themselves grew steadily higher, rougher underfoot. More effort. Two hours slowly passed, then three. With dawn the world slowly changed clothes, exhanging the cool cloak of night for scarves of gray fog wrapped around the hills, suspended in twilight.

"Trampings and stampings. Brg! Should be cookin' and cleanin'. That's all for Flogg. But no!" It was a random complaint, and no one replied. Gnomes, it seemed, were cheerless little creatures.

The mirling, her face hidden beneath her cowl, continued to glance darkly and often to the heavens. They trekked in silence a good while, until far in the south rose a high, lonely wail. Sorge froze. The cry was faint, almost unhearable. Another echoed it. Then another. Then all three at once. Ewan shivered at the sound. They were haunting howls, lusty and anguished. Sorge glanced at Flogg.

Tensely, Asandra said, "We mustn't pause, even to rest."

They set off, dogged and wary now, moving from peak to valley, peak to valley, over the seemingly endless hills. Dawn drew near. The cover of night would soon be gone.

"Hadyn," Ewan whispered between panting breaths. "I'm scared."

Hadyn glanced back. His lips were pursed, quietly determined. "We don't have time to think that way. Just keep moving."

Which, of course, made Ewan feel even more the younger brother: small, angry, weak. But really? How could he *not* be afraid, fleeing for his life over hills he had never seen in a world totally disconnected from his own? With a gnome and a monk?

And a whatever-she-was—a mirror woman. And what was this place? Another planet? Another dimension? He dropped his head, trudging along. The hills, looming large, all seemed to be crawling with prowling beasts, at least in his imagination. He had little choice but to keep moving.

Unexpectedly, a hand touched his shoulder. He almost jumped out of his skin.

"Of course I'm scared," Hadyn admitted. "Just don't think about it. Sorge will get us there."

It wasn't much, but it was enough. Or might have been if Ewan hadn't felt Hadyn's fingers through his shirt. Trembling.

Morning broke with a mixture of relief and dread, the sun straining through low, brooding swathes of cloud. Though visibility came as a welcome companion to the five travelers—or at least to Ewan—Sorge still fretted. They had travelled hard for hours and paused now for breath on the crown of a tall hill, easily the highest yet, one which offered commanding views in all directions.

"The Watcher?" Sorge asked, leaning over, exhaling.

Asandra answered between breaths. "Not near at least, but I have felt him. Close, yet never within reach. He will try to avoid me, you know."

"Yes, but is he searching or tracking?"

From his tone, Ewan knew the latter must be the worse, though he didn't quite understand why. Neither sounded good. Asandra studied the skies.

"I don't know."

Sorge shook his head. "Not good enough. Figure it out."

Asandra eyed the monk coldly. She started to speak, instead pulled her hood down lower over her face and said nothing.

Sorge saw Ewan's fear. He pulled Ewan to his side, turned

him, pointing. Ewan followed his finger. The hills rippled away below them, miles and miles of green undulations, looking much like a crumpled green skirt flung to the floor. The ribbons of fog had thinned but still clung to the valley beds. Farther west, the hills gradually flattened, then abruptly stopped. Plains began. And right there, on the hem of the hills, tiny in proportion, so far away . . .

"The Gray Abbey," Sorge declared. "See those small lights? And the gray walls? From here, like just a few pebbles. I stood once with Corus on this very hill, on our way to see Har Halas in Brimshane. We laughed and sparred. By nightfall, we took shelter among those pebbles, at the abbey. Even then, long before my vows, it felt like home to my soul. And Eldoran, like a father to me." He sighed. "We stand now on the highest hill of the Shimlings. These are the oldest mountains in all of of Karac Tor, once high, frosty peaks. They are but little hills now—green, beautiful, and forgotten. The traders' routes all follow newer roads. We take the Old Way."

Flogg snorted. "Elder may say old. Hah! Older pathlets Flogg knowses. Under rocklings, not over."

"Thank you, Master Flogg. But no rollwols. Our friends are frightened enough at the moment."

"*Rulvôl*," Flogg corrected sternly.

"Rold Gold?" Ewan said, repeating what he heard. "That's a pretzel in my world." When all else failed, whistle in the dark. Make a joke. Distract yourself.

"What is this word you say?"

"Rold Gold. Pretzels."

Sorge frowned. They were near the dry, cracked bed of a little stream. He spat on his fingers, took a small chunk of hard clay from the ground, and began spinning it between his thumb and forefinger. He walked toward a stand of trees as he spoke.

"Rollwols are secret underground passageways," he explained. Faster than could be seen, he produced a little clay bowl in his hand. "Humans are forbidden to enter rollwols. A gnome can be cast away from his people forever for betraying one of their locations."

Though early still, the day was already hot. And quite dry. Sorge tossed his head irritably toward the sky. "Aion have mercy, how I wish it would rain! We'll take cover under those trees to break our fast, but no lingering. Here," he handed the bowl to Hadyn, "use this if you like. Flogg has water."

Soon they were munching on plums and honeybread, drinking water from the bowl. Though Sorge had tried to diffuse their fear, no one spoke.

Finally, Hadyn said, "Okay, I work better with the big picture. What's our plan, Sorge?"

Sorge nodded approvingly. "Good, yes. We aim for the foot of Avl-Argosee and the river town of Threefork. The lake is quite visible from here. Over there, on the horizon." He pointed east. The boys looked and saw a thin, vast stretch of blue. Lake Argosee, it seemed, was enormous. Sorge picked a stick off the ground, cleared a patch of dirt, and began scratching lines.

"We're here, moving southeast. In Threefork—here—is a captain friendly to the abbey. A patron, really. He's done well for himself, is mostly retired, and works only when he wants. I will send Flogg ahead to secure passage for us on his ship, south across Champion Bay to Stratamore. Simple, really—as long as nothing follows us."

Nearby, Flogg made a low warning sound.

"What?"

"Too late."

The gnome's voice sounded distant, strained. He sat with both hands pressed flat on the grass, palms down.

"Walkings and stalkings all around," he whispered.

Catlike, Sorge rolled to a coiled, crouching posture. "Hel's gates! I had a feeling." He took a breath. "What do you see?"

Flogg inhaled slowly, as if sucking up the earth's vibrations through his fingers. "Flogg feels other feet. Shadows . . . near. Manlings being watched. And wings."

Ewan scoffed. "What in the world is he talking about?"

"I sense it too," Asandra said, closing her eyes. "Something . . . not Watchers."

"Hush!" Sorge said, motioning with his hand. "Lie down. Be still."

Both boys dropped to their bellies. Flogg's white eyes, heavy-lidded in his trance, seemed oblivious. Sorge's gaze scoured the hills.

"I see nothing. Nothing! Are you sure, Flogg?"

The gnome's milky gaze slowly gained color, focus. His breath evened. "Flogg may lie," he groaned. "Rock does not."

"Swords and blood!" Sorge fumed quietly. "Where? Which way?"

A shadow in the air, far away. Asandra saw it first.

"There! Flight of Crows!"

Sorge looked, saw the darkened knot of sky, moments before clear and blue. Now thrashing with darkness. He leaped to his feet.

"Aion be merciful. No time! This way!"

Panicked, they gathered their packs, began sprinting down the hillside following the warrior monk, Sorge's ponytail whipping in the breeze behind his shaven head. Ewan's heart raced. Behind them, the raucous cries of many birds grew louder, wings beating, sounding hungry, angry. A warm wind, which had not been before, suddenly blew at their backs, bringing the birds near at frightening speed. Ewan glanced over his shoulder, stumbled on a rock, cried out. Hadyn caught his brother's arm, hauling him forward with all his might.

"Watch your eyes!" Sorge cried. "They strike the eyes!"

The birds swarmed viciously near as Hadyn pushed Ewan ahead to shield him. Ewan heard his brother hiss and scream, knew the birds were clawing him, gouging with their beaks.

"Don't look back, Ewan!" Hadyn shouted. "Run!"

He ran faster, saw at the base of the hill a tiny hut built of blue river stone, mortared with clay. Sorge, running. Flogg, surprisingly swift on such short legs. The hut. Nearby, a small pond rimmed with cattail and pampas grass. So strange, so serene. People fleeing for their lives. Birds, like demons, swarming in a dark cloud behind. Surreal.

"Inside, inside!"

He dashed in, collapsed. The birds shrieked, enraged. Hadyn dove in last of all, a raven still attached to his back, stabbing hard. Flogg slammed the door shut. The back of Hadyn's shirt was red with fresh blood, his own. Sorge leaped upon him, grabbed the bird with both hands, wrenched it free. It fought madly, croaking, biting. The monk roared, spun the weight of the bird's body in a circle, gripping its neck, snapping the spine. The flapping wings grew still.

But only inside. Outside, the wings were a storm of wind.

CHAPTER 12

THE STONE HOUSE

They all bent over, leaning against the wall, trying hard to catch their breath.

"I'm all right," Hadyn said. "Worry about me later."

Outside, the birds clattered chaotically. Their wings beat against the thatched roof. Their voices raked against the walls. They pecked on the rock. They squawked and cawed. There were dozens of them, or more.

"This is the Stone House," Sorge managed between breaths. "A waystation for pilgrims en route to the abbey." He offered a wan smile. "A shelter from rain, a place to reflect. Built many, many years ago by an Elder—a man named Crow."

No one seemed to appreciate the irony. The Stone House was really just a small room, with the one door and high up, two small, round—

"Windows," Ewan noticed, pointing.

Sorge tore off his cloak. Hadyn did the same. They stuffed

the windows full of fabric, then huddled in the corners, out of any possible lines of sight. Ewan heard his own blood ringing in his ears. He saw Flogg fingering his cudgel. He saw Sorge fretting over the west wall, the wall that faced the hill they had fled—a wall with no window, no line of sight. The monk laid his staff on the bare dirt floor and crept toward the western wall, putting his ear to the stone, then his lips. Whispering silent words, he pressed his index finger into the rock. The effect was like a hot iron sinking into soft wax. His finger slipped into the stone up to the third knuckle. Ewan let out a hushed little cry of surprise. The gesture was so simple, so effortless, it almost seemed *normal.* Still whispering, the monk twirled his finger deep in the rock, molding a channel about two inches wide. Ewan had seen a potter once spin a lump of wet clay on his wheel, then pinch it to form the cavity of a cup. Spinning so fast, the cup just seemed to appear. So did the hole. When Sorge removed his finger, Ewan saw light and grass.

The monk peered out toward the west. The birds had stopped their racket. The air was still. Ewan felt a single drop of sweat trickle down his forehead, his cheek, saw three bright red trails dripping down Hadyn's face.

"Are you okay?" he whispered.

"Hush!" Sorge commanded. "Master Flogg, I don't see anyone. What does that mean?"

"Any*who?*" Hadyn demanded. "And . . . *how in the world* are you doing that with your finger?" He surveyed the room, a wild look in his eyes. "Will somebody tell me what's going on? Why are crows hunting us?"

"They aren't crows, they're ravens," Asandra corrected. "Flight of Crows is the name of the magic."

"Whatever," Hadyn said.

He pressed his shoulder against the wall as if, by chance, he might force himself into the cracks of the mortar and disappear.

Ewan still stared at the hole. "Um, people don't just stick their fingers in solid rock where we're from."

Sorge flicked his hand in the air. "Shhh!"

He leaned closer to the hole, squinting. "Five figures," he whispered. "Approaching from the west. The ravens are with them. How can a Flight of Crows last so long?" He turned to Asandra.

"Blackest Hel," she said fiercely to herself; answer enough. "Black gates of Hel."

Sorge stared at the boys. "We could flee," he offered. "But I think it unwise."

"Fightings and smitings," Flogg snarled, patting his satchel. "Five they, five we."

"No, friend. Not a full five. These boys know nothing of battle. Nor do they want to. And we have no power over the birds. It's too dangerous."

Flogg shrugged. "*Ügthilik ngolo ligk'na bôr.*"

Both Barlows turned to Sorge for translation. Under the shadows of his hood, the monk's eyes smoldered. "He says, 'Courage, not numbers.'"

Ewan shook his head. "Oh, no. This has nothing to do with how brave we are. We don't even have anything to fight them with. What about that?"

Growling, Flogg licked the side of his cudgel. His tongue was purple. Ewan shuddered.

"Name enemy. Then fight," said the gnome.

"How do we fight birds!" Hadyn exploded. He wiped at the blood to keep it out of his eyes. "And might I point out, we are *all* hiding—all five of us. Not just Ewan and me."

Sorge observed, "First, a Watcher. Now ravens. Nemesia's will is bent on finding you. I am certain of it. We have three choices: We fight. We run. We hide. That's it. But we need to decide quickly if we are going to run."

"Fight," said Flogg.

"Hide," said Ewan, "here in the Stone House. At least we have protection."

"I agree. We close the door and lock it until they pass by," Hadyn said. "If you want to call that hiding, so be it. I call it playing it cool."

"My vote would have been to run, but"—Sorge glanced out his peephole again—"I fear it is too late for that now. And to be true, the birds are too swift. A Flight of Crows is sorcery. The birds fly swifter, with focus and greater rage, and always seem to multiply. Nemesia's doing, I'm sure. Very well. Ewan, lock the door. Everyone else up against the east wall. Stay flat and still. If Aion's eyes are on us, the door will hold."

Ewan scooted on all fours, found the latch and lock, and slid the bolt. They all pressed against the stone wall, though Flogg merely seemed irritated rather than afraid. Outside, amidst scattered, low voices, a sound drew near. Feet crunching on pebbles.

Ewan said, "Sorge, your hole!"

Sorge smeared the rock face with his fingers. The surface sealed under his touch as if made of paste. Back to the wall, he drew himself to his full height, staff in hand.

Sounds of pacing feet now ringed the Stone House. Only the four walls stood between the hunters and the hunted.

Once, then twice, the five outside circled the Stone House, unseen. Their movement was slow, deliberate. Ewan heard the light sound of flapping wings return. Claws scratching on the roof. Squawking. On the third circuit, something like fingernails began scraping the rock wall. Inside, the air thickened. Ewan grew hot, clammy. He found it hard to breathe. A strange thickness began oozing under his threshold of conscious thought, like smoke under a door, making it difficult to think. He tried to focus on a spot on the far wall. Beside him, he felt Hadyn lean hard against the stone as if to hold himself up. Matted blood was stuck in his brother's hair, dried and smeared on his face. His ragged breath, sounding like Ewan's own, made for strange comfort.

Though Sorge had counted five, a single voice now rose, directionless, drifting like a leaf in the wind, leeching through the stone, shiftless and flat.

"Who travels . . . so far?" the voice said. It was male, not old, sounding neither curious nor fearful, stringing words together like pearls on an open loop, then letting them tumble thoughtlessly to the ground, unclaimed. Other voices rose faintly in response, moaning, like wind on a barren plain. "Who journeys . . . through . . . the skies to the home . . . of despair?"

More soft strides on padded feet. More scraping. More bird noises. Strangely, no shadowed forms even attempted to peer through the high windows. They could have easily pulled the fabric loose. It was as if they truly didn't care, merely ambling and rambling. A joke meant to scare.

But they did care. A fist suddenly slammed the door so hard the wood planks rattled. Ewan jumped. Hadyn reached over, clasped his brother's wrist. Sorge reached out to his left and right, placed a steady hand on the shoulder of each boy. He put a finger to his lips to focus their thoughts. *Shhh.*

Another thump, this time harder, as if one of the people outside had taken a heavy stone from the pond and was trying to smash the door apart.

"Who crosses the hidden . . . barrier . . ."

The door rattled again, a bone-jarring sound. *Thwack!*

". . . to trouble holy men?"

Thwack! The birds went wild, dancing and squawking and flapping and pecking.

"Plans come to nothing. Yours . . . ours. Nothing. The world will . . . come to nothing. Hide and prove us true. Emerge and join us. Fight and be consumed. We are . . . the Name—"

Thwack! The door, it seemed, would surely shatter at the next blow. Ewan found himself straining to concentrate. The last word had drowned in the clatter, but Ewan thought he heard it. *The Nameless.* His head spun. The voice, so unimpressive in every other way, was oily. It stuck. It spoke words as questions, yet seemed passionless to any answer that might be given. The murky residue it left behind was paradoxical—altogether foreign on one hand, yet arriving in his brain with a sense of relief, as if invited, wanted. Ewan shook his head to clear it, saw Hadyn make a similar gesture. He wanted to scream, to force it out of his head. The voice spoke again, neither rising nor falling.

"Do not think proudly, outlanders. You have come for no great purpose. Let me show you the beginning . . . of the way of peace: nothing matters."

The other voices joined in, creating a soft, uneven chant: "Nothing. Matters. Nothing."

It seemed to crescendo. Ewan braced for the door to splinter. Wings flapped wildly. Sorge's knuckles were white on his staff. Asandra's face glistened.

"Nothing matters . . ."

Then they were gone, the sound of their feet trailing away to the south, lost amongst the whispering grass and the generous curves of dimpled land; lost in the slow circles forming on the water where the silent gulp of silver perch topped the pond for mosquitoes. Birds and voices alike. Gone.

Hadyn sank to his knees. Even in the warmish light, his face was pale. "We shouldn't have come, Ewan. We should be home right now, not here. I'm so sorry."

Actually, Ewan thought, he should be the one apologizing. He came through the runestone first. But he didn't have the words to reply. Like a song in a minor key, he felt transposed, removed from one world to this, and from this to a place of numbness.

"That kid's voice," he mumbled. "It wasn't just out *there*."

Hadyn swiveled. "What did you say?"

"It . . . was in my head. More than normal."

"I felt it too. Totally freaked me out. Who were those people?"

"No doubt, the wraiths of legend," Asandra said calmly. "Young men and women. My age. Your age. Their souls are empty. You can hear it in their voices."

Sorge moved to stand before them. "Be thankful, little brothers. I have no idea who hunted you today. But I am certain of their darkness."

"Travel now," Flogg interrupted, stepping toward the door. "Talk later."

He reached out his hand to the bolt, pulled. Pulled again. He yanked, braced his stance, and yanked again. The latch didn't budge. Flogg pounded the wood and metal shank with his fist.

Nothing.

"Rust?" the gnome said warily. The latch, obviously, was clean black iron.

Sorge inspected the bolt, along with Asandra. All three consulted in low tones.

Sorge shook his head at the gnome, who was already reaching for his bag. "No, no, friend," he sighed. "None of your fire salts.

The room is too small, and we have nothing to hide behind. The boys would likely be killed."

Ewan coughed. "We *are* in the room, you know."

Sorge turned, studied them. "Long ago, when Duke Tiernon sent his army to bring the sorcerer Zynwl to justice for his crimes, they found the keep of Zynwl fastened shut. Zynwl had built a tall tower and made it difficult to take, with no windows and only one gate at the bottom. So Tiernon called upon his great ally and dear friend, Soriah, the greatest Elder in the history of the Gray Abbey. Instead of contending with Zynwl's evil and dragging him out by force, Soriah bound the one door to the earth, as if the fortress were a tree taking root. Zynwl never escaped and eventually flung himself off the tower to his death."

"Great," Ewan said drily. "Thanks. That'll be a fun one for the kids, someday."

Asandra folded her hands behind her back, a haughty gesture, Ewan thought. Yet her words completed the riddle.

"Sometimes the way you beat an enemy is not to conquer but to confine."

"My friends," Sorge declared, touching the iron latch once more. "We are not yet done with the Stone House. The door has been wordlocked. We are sealed inside."

CHAPTER 13

BLOOD VISIONS

The small gray mouse twitched and writhed but was miserably unable to escape the delicate iron grip of the woman who held its tail. Lowering her face closer to the creature, she looked into its eyes, but they were rolled back into its head with fear. Her hair was a black fire.

"Too, too easy," the sorceress laughed. Pale pictures lingered in the steaming air around her hand, of five creatures—a monk, a gnome, a young woman with hair as dark as her own (and power she recognized), and two brothers—trapped in a small stone house of prayer, sealed inside by the strength of her will. She watched, wrapped in a cloak of silver pinned at the neck. She stood alone, surrounded by black stone and fire. Her long, silky hair, banded in silver, blew in a slight, unseen breeze. Tall and slender, she wore a plunging gown that made her beauty plain.

"Tsk, tsk," she purred. "I had not even laid my full trap."

As the evanescent image began melting into curls of misty

white, the gnome in the vision was still pounding on the door with his fist, enraged. As he faded, the circular chamber drained of power. Plumes of steam boiled atop a small pot of polished brass, engulfing both the mouse and the glistening hand of the witch. The mouse screamed at the heat. Nemesia did not. For all the fire and moisture, the air remained unusually cool—the kind of cold that makes you feel you are being watched, that runs up your spine and clings to your skin. On the woman's shoulder sat a large raven with glossy, tar-colored feathers. Unblinking, the bird stared into the roiling vapor at the small, delicious creature hanging there, squeaking, flailing, helpless. It flicked its black gaze to the table beside the pot where a dozen more little mice nervously skittered and danced, watching the boiling pot with wide, rolling eyes.

Ravens were the faraway descendents of mighty Auginn's illustrious line. Lesser birds, by far, but Nemesia took pleasure in the defiance, the symbolic act of perverting what had once been so dear to Olfadr, the Everking, in faraway Isgurd. She had made them creatures of fear. Living tokens of the invisible. Reminders that Watchers were more than legend. It helped foster suspicion in the people, to see packs of ravens flying together.

She would feed the raven soon enough, another pitiful little mouse from the cage. Feed his lust for juice and bone. Let it bite the head, pluck the fur. Of mice, there was no lack. She had dozens of cages, hundreds of mice, devoted to one simple, unswerving purpose: vision.

Vision required blood.

Well-trained by fear, the raven did not move, only croaked its hunger. This routine had happened many times before. Without the least bit of pity, the sorceress dropped the mouse into the bubbling liquid. Instantly, the creature's life mingled with the water. The steam changed from white to sickly red. Nemesia murmured strange words. Rather than dispersing, the red steam coalesced into a small cloud, suspended in midair. It swirled, gaining layers, density.

From its depths, Nemesia's visions continued. She laughed.

"Yes, foolish Gray. Wordlocked." She crossed her arms, chortling. "My word is my gift to you, though you shall never know it. Oh, yes. I know what you are thinking. How could you fall for such a simple trick? How could you not have known? Did *Nasmith* fail you?"

Nemesia reached for another mouse, tossed it into the pot. It wasn't needed. She didn't care. When she spoke again, she spoke to no one, but the chill in her voice caused the torchlight to flicker. "Such a stupid, simple plan. Does Archibald really think children from another world could become heroes in the Hidden Lands? A fool's hope. They are nothing but boys—frightened boys."

Suddenly, she moved. Expressionless, she grabbed the wire cage, turned it upside down, shook it. Every last mouse dropped into the water. Their brief screams were soon silenced. The boiling water bloomed bright red. Before Nemesia's eyes, the vision became shockingly clear. She smiled, began babbling, strange words forming like spittle on her lips. Soon, orange light glowed on her face. The beginning of a fire.

More importantly, smoke.

"Sorge, old friend . . . now I will watch you die. You *and* the precious outlanders. And with you, with them, the last hope of Aion in this world dies too."

CHAPTER 14

FEY HAVEN

The trees of Elkwood are tall and old and wild. Forest animals scamper and play. All manner of wildlife live and die in the normal rhythms of forest life.

But Elkwood is not a normal forest.

It is full of *other* things. Invisible creatures with shimmering wings. Slender beings, sprites and pixies and nymphs and brownies, human in appearance, yet entirely otherwise, in ways that made men mad with desire to possess them, if ever they were seen. Of course, this was highly rare, by design. Only in the rarest of circumstances would a spirit willingly reveal itself. Random glimpses were nearly the same: in full moons and fresh pools of rainwater, pieces of new-polished silver. Still, a few spirits had been carried away over the years. It *could* happen. These were the Fey Folk. Creatures of legend on all of the Nine fabled worlds. Luminous beings and mischief makers.

On Karac Tor, they had been progressively herded over the

centuries by the will of the Midland earls—who had long ago learned the need for such herding—into sun-dappled Elkwood. But Fey Folk didn't follow rules very well. They kept leaking out. Stealing butter and cream. Hexing cows and chickens so that their milk came out green or their egg yolks black, leaving the common people in various tizzies of fear. It had led to all sorts of superstitious practices. Copper nails over doors to snag their wings before they could enter a home. Salt thrown in wells, because salt, supposedly, would burn them. Offerings of rice and cheese.

The Fey Folk queen was a regal presence. Always, the Fey Folk had a queen, never a king. Such was the way it had always been and always would be.

In a hollowing of the woods near the center, where birds and butterflies gathered to drink from bubbling fountains, colors and shadow smeared upon each other until nothing but a fluttering, ethereal sense of wonder was left. Slanting shafts of light reached the mossy forest floor, while blossoms and feathery tufts of seedlings floated in the air, never seeming to land. At the center of Elkwood, it was nearly always spring. This was the realm of the queen.

Today, the queen was in a foul, wintry mood.

"He saw you?" she demanded of the breathless, wide-eyed spirit before her, a five-hundred-year-old pixie named Elysabel. "In plain light of sun?"

Elysabel nodded fearfully. She had known, of course, that the news might anger the queen. She had hoped for a reward. But not informing her at all would have been the most dangerous.

Queen Marielle was severely beautiful, a melting icicle in winter, filled with sunlight. Her eyes were hard and cold as diamonds. Her skin was perpetually frosted with glitter—fairy dust, mortals called it. Her hair was sage green and twirled in swirling, unseen winds.

This was Fey Haven, the court of the queen, a place of constant activity, music, and mirth. Other Fey twittered and darted about the open space, whispering to one another, chittering. Many danced and swayed, oblivious to all but the melodies of flute and drum, lingering just below what a human could ever hear. Nothing truly bothered the Fey. They were their own reality and cared for little more than song and flight and the curve of the moon in the summer sky. But the ways of men were endlessly fascinating to them, precisely because they were utterly incomprehensible. A mother's love. A warrior's sacrifice on the battlefield. The pain of death. Tears. Laughter. These were not the way of the Fey.

More to the point, the way of Fey was *secret*. The world of men and the kingdom of Fey were firmly divided, visible and invisible. Material and spirit—one of those immutable certainties upon which all reality hung. Boundaries were there for a reason and not meant to be breached casually—in daylight. Through *Fey* portals!

No, this was not good.

Elysabel tried to soften the news.

"Your mother. A long time ago. She fell in love with one of them. The great mirling."

Marielle did not blink, showed nothing resembling emotion. "Tal Yssen."

"He could see too."

The queen's wings, blurred beyond sight, made a whisper. She bobbed in the air.

"Yes."

"She showed him our secrets. He built portals. She crossed over with him. They loved and hated. But she granted him one last wish, and brought the fallen king, the great one, back with her. Across the water, with his sword. He came, as good as dead. But she sustained him even then."

"He is here still. Hidden. With his sword."

"As another has been, of late. The Champion. Only that one, *you* allowed. You wanted it."

The queen's eyes grew distant. "He was so beautiful. But I could not keep him."

Elysabel shrugged. She was not afraid anymore. The queen was lost in her own enchantment.

"It happens," she said. "The boy may be something special. But he may be nothing."

Other Fey listened, but didn't really care. Big news and small news were all the same to them. A human captive was certainly special, and rare, but a boy who saw? That was the queen's problem. Not theirs. This was the way of the Fey.

"Stay near them," Marielle commanded, refocusing. "I will reward you well or punish you greatly for this task."

No threat, no promise. Just facts.

Elysabel was surprised, but pleased. She bowed, spun away.

CHAPTER 15

WORDLOCKED

"**W**ordlocked! What in Sam Hill does that mean, wordlocked?"

Ewan had asked the question, but Hadyn wasn't paying attention to him. He was feverishly trying to recall old reruns of *MacGyver*, hoping to osmotically glean some random, brilliant escape plan. It was stupid, he knew, but it was all he had. Flogg by now had moved from fist to cudgel for his door poundings. Sorge was studying the results. Half hearing Ewan's question, he halfheartedly answered.

"Word . . . locked. They bound the metal latch to a secret word and then walked away with that word."

"Don't we have a key?"

"It doesn't need a key. It needs a word." Sorge seemed not so much puzzled as amazed. "Do they not have such simple magic in your world?"

"No!" Hadyn cried. "We open doors with keys; we don't

lock them with words. And we don't peel stone apart with our fingers!"

Sorge thoughtfully considered this information. "Then who is Sam Hill?"

Ewan's head sank to his chest. "He's the king of confusion. We're his loyal subjects. Can you get us out of here or not?"

Sorge shook his head. "Not without the word."

"Then just do your thing again!" Hadyn said, more loudly than he meant. "Stick your hand in the rock and shape another hole, big enough for us to crawl through."

"Ah, no, you overestimate me. My thing, as you say, is quite undeveloped. I came late to my vows—as a man, not a young boy. Countless Grays are far more gifted than I."

"*Slobahg*," Flogg retorted.

"Yes, I can waterbless," Sorge admitted. "But I cannot yet draw fire from wood, and I am just learning to stonemold. Such a large area of rock would be impossible for me."

"What about her?" Hadyn said, pointing to Asandra.

"The Blacks are skilled in matters of spirit and wind and mystery," Asandra said. "We are Landhealers. Such powers are not our way."

Hadyn kicked the wall, for bravado's sake, for Asandra. In frustration. No matter, it was a bad idea. He held his poise for about three seconds before succumbing to the pain, hopping around the room on one foot, whimpering. Oh, how he *wished* Dad let him curse!

"So the rock is harder than your foot," Ewan observed. "That's good information. Great, thanks."

Hadyn balled his fist, lunged. "You little turd, I'll show you rock hard."

Sorge caught Hadyn before the two came to blows. "Easy,

little brother, easy. Anger is the easiest thing of all and the least helpful. We must think. We must trust Aion."

He knelt on the ground, covering his head, and softly began to pray.

Hadyn sniffed the air. "Wait . . . what is that smell?"

It smelled faintly like someone cooking nearby. Asandra was the first to look up.

"The roof's on fire!"

"What new devilry is this?" Sorge said, rising.

Smoke had already begun clotting the air below the rafters of the thatched roof. Orange flame was blossoming through the fumes, licking at the dry sheets of grass. Everyone began to cough.

"Flogg!" Sorge shouted.

"Aye!" Flogg cried. But what could he do? The latch was a large, heavy iron assembly with no locking mechanism other than a simple sliding bolt. Feeling urgent and powerless, Hadyn stumbled to his side, his sleeve draped over his mouth and nose. The smoke was beginning to press lower into the room.

"Back! Stand!" Flogg commanded, shoving Hadyn away. With his cudgel, he struck the latch twice with a shattering force. The bolt scarred, but didn't budge. Didn't even rattle.

"Let me try," Hadyn said. He remembered burning leaves at the farm in Newland earlier in the year—how much smoke it made, how noxious it smelled. Smoke killed more people than fire, he knew. One of those useless, fire-safety factoids. It would kill them, too, if they didn't get out soon. The Stone House would become the Stone Grave. He planted his feet, raised the cudgel high above his head, and swung hard. The moment the forged iron head made contact, something like a shout blasted across the room—a cry, a single metallic word, like the declaration a hammer makes on an anvil. Hadyn spun around, holding his ears.

"What was that?" he said, panicking. "Who said that?"

"Said what?"

"Someone shouted! Right when I hit the latch. Have they come back?"

Outside, a stiff gust of wind must have whistled through the valley, for half the roof suddenly blazed. The heat became scorching; the noise overhead, a low roar. Charred pieces of wood and glowing stalks of grass began raining down, burning their skin. Ewan yelped as a piece landed on his head.

"Get low in the corners!" Sorge shouted. "Below the smoke. Cover your face. Breathe through your clothes. Hadyn, give Flogg his hammer. This is no time for games."

"I'm not *playing* games!" Hadyn said. He looked at the war club in his hands, then at the latch, confounded. Something was strange. He struck the iron bolt again—this time more lightly. The metal-on-metal sound he expected. But there was more—another sharp iron voice underneath the clang, fused into the vibration of it. He touched his ear. It was hard to concentrate. His eyes stung and watered so freely he could barely see. Too much was happening.

"You didn't hear that?" he shouted over the roar of the fire, turning to the others in amazement. "It's so clear, but it's a sound I don't understand." He swung again. "The noise is the same every time."

Ewan gasped for air. "Sorge!"

He tried to say more, but couldn't. Sorge crawled to the door.

"Hit it again and again, Hadyn. Pay close attention to the sound."

Hadyn bent near to the latch, swinging. Once, twice. He couldn't believe they didn't hear. He swung three more times, straining to hear, to form the sound in his mind.

"It sounds . . . twangy," he said, faltering.

"Tell me exactly what you hear. Quickly."

Flames dropped on Asandra. She screamed. Flogg pounced upon her, patting the flames out with his bare hands.

"The roof won't hold much longer!" she said.

Hadyn heard Ewan choking, crying. His little brother. He couldn't even see him anymore through the smoke. Furiously, he began pounding the latch.

"What . . . are . . . you . . . saying to me?" he bellowed.

"Collect yourself," Sorge urged, surprisingly calm. "Ignore the fire. Pronounce the sound. Re-create it."

Hadyn cleared his throat. "Nan? Nang . . . No . . ."

A gust of smoke left him hacking. Again, he struck. "Ninjang? That's it, but I'm not saying it right. Nuan? Rrgh! It's a nonsense word!"

He dropped the cudgel. Soon, they would all lose consciousness. Every breath was now one of poison and searing heat. It didn't matter. An overwhelming need to be with his brother, at least to touch him, one last time, seized him. He couldn't see anything, couldn't stand to open his eyes. He heard a faint voice.

"Hadyn . . ."

Hadyn fell toward the voice, desperate. Eyes pinched tight, holding his breath, he groped on the floor for Ewan's body. Found a hand. He hauled with all his might, pulling Ewan toward himself. His brother's body was limp. In the impenetrable gray, he heard Sorge say something aloud, a half-thought, a revelation; then cut himself short. Flogg and Asandra were somewhere on the floor, gasping like him. Vaguely, he sensed motion; Sorge, surging with strength, proclaimed one word. He had flung the cloth away from his face. He spoke as a command.

One nonsense word.

"*Njuang!*"

The latch rattled loosely. The bolt rotated freely under the pull of gravity. Sorge slid it open, pushed hard against the wood. The door swung wide, flooding the room with light.

Clean air.

Flogg and Asandra crawled out first, gasping. Sorge pulled on Hadyn next, who clung to Ewan's hand, dragging him along, just as a large section collapsed in a glowing heap where he had lain. All five buckled to the ground outside the open door, hacking, squeezing dry grass and rock between their fingers as though they couldn't get enough good air fast enough to make a difference. They clawed their way on elbows and knees just a few steps farther, black and grimy with soot, hair singed, skin red with heat. A few seconds later, the whole roof tumbled inward, sending a blast of smoke and cinders high into the air. Nobody moved. Hadyn lay still, near Ewan, feeling every painful, glorious expansion and contraction of his lungs. He wanted to laugh or cry. Something. He managed neither, just drank the air.

The door, having finally burned free of its hinges, toppled outward, charred and smoking. Hadyn sat up, gazing from door to grass to sky as if seeing all of it for the first time. He saw the bolt, still clinging to the door. No one spoke. No one needed to.

Ewan lay curled up in a ball, crying softly. He didn't even try to hide it. Hadyn didn't expect him to. Both their faces were dirty webs of tears. They crawled to the edge of the pond together, splashing their faces. Water never felt so good. The other three followed their lead.

They washed every part of their body they could, to scrub away the smell of smoke, to cool their skin. They were alive. But they took no more time than necessary.

Cleaned, grim, made both defiant and wary in their survival, they journeyed on.

CHAPTER 16

UNFOLDINGS

A fter about an hour of marching, of walking and nursing their wounds in silence among the barren hills — not daring to stop — Hadyn was ready for answers.

"Sorge, how did you do that?" he asked, trudging along. He was bruised, limped a little, but fit enough. "With the door?"

"I think the more appropriate question would be, how did *you* do that?" Sorge countered. *"Njuang* is of the language of the S'Qoth, the people of Quil. Idol-worshipping pagans."

"The witch," Flogg growled.

"Nemesia is also S'Qoth. Which would, of course, make the most sense."

"I am part S'Qoth," Asandra said softly from behind. Her tone held a mild challenge. "Am I part witch?"

Sorge didn't take the bait. "How *did* you discern the word, little brother? You heard it?"

"I guess so. You didn't?"

Sorge shook his head. "This is a powerful magic, to unbind what is bound."

Hadyn fought to suppress a grin. The fear had settled by now, leaving many questions, and a slow, unfolding awe. He stank of smoke, had almost died. He also felt pretty stinking cool. To top it all off, out of the corner of his eye, he saw that Asandra gazed upon him with new appreciation.

How did *I do that?* he mused.

"I didn't hear jack," said Ewan, playful with jealousy. He, too, was notably recovered. He never said thank you, and Hadyn didn't expect him to. "Not twang, nang, ninjang. Nothing." Ewan gazed into his brother's face, then broke out into a huge grin. "Dude, that was awesome. Teach me how."

"I don't know how. I just heard it."

Ewan asked Sorge, "What does njuang mean, anyway?"

"You will not like the answer," Sorge warned.

"I hardly understand the question. Try me."

"Basically, it means despair, but more as a command. Like telling someone to give up."

"Nope. Don't like it."

Typical Ewan, covering his tracks with humor—whistling in the dark. For his part, Hadyn dreaded to think what might come next. They had been magically bound to a word as a death sentence. Despair. He shivered.

"Trackerlings follow again," Flogg said during a break, fingering the earth, lost in a trance. "But gone the black croakers."

"A Flight of Crows is a burst. It cannot be maintained."

"I do not know why, but the Watcher is distant. Beyond my reach," Asandra said. "They will have a harder time finding us now."

They traveled light and fast, pausing only to catch their breath or drink, though barely either. Aiming due east, bobbing over the hills like waves on the ocean, the five drew ever closer to the Argosee. The central Shimlings were tall, just shy of low mountain height. Many were rough with crumbly shale and giant slabs of rock rather than green with grass and heather as were the hills behind them. In fact, the farther from the abbey they traveled, the more hardened and bleak the land became. Past these hills, all the land began to brown. The grass was dead. For many miles, it seemed like they made little to no progress. But thanks to Sorge's unrelenting pace, they also saw no sign of their pursuers.

Along the way, Hadyn found himself relaxing more around Asandra. She did not return the favor, gliding along in detached silence, asking nothing, adding nothing. Hadyn could not help but wonder about her. Though beautiful, she did not seem happy. He tried to strike up a conversation. He talked low, so as not to embarrass himself

"Um . . . my lady. My lady mirling,"

Too late. He felt like a fool. She answered, but her response was terse.

"Call me Asandra."

"Okay, Asandra. I was just wondering. I don't know if it's rude to ask, but how old are you?"

Her purple robe billowed in the slight breeze. "Of summers, I've seen one less than nineteen."

Hadyn tried to keep his cool. Only eighteen? Not a big enough difference to count. Not really.

"How long have you been a mirling?"

"Five years."

"Doesn't all that Watcher stuff worry your parents?"

"My only family is the Black Abbey," Asandra murmured. "I have no parents."

Common ground. They both had lost parents. But Hadyn was torn. Disclosure would leave him exposed, and he was not one to casually surrender control, mentally or emotionally. The knowledge of his pain was his own, earned with the hard stripes of life. It was part of how he remembered, how he honored his mother, by hurting for her. By carrying all that hurt deep inside, crammed and packed like a piece of paper folded over and over again, so tightly you could not make another fold, tucked away and spring-loaded into the lonely core of his being. He did not give away his secrets to strangers. Not easily.

Much to his surprise, he found himself saying aloud, "My mother died too."

Asandra spoke slowly but no less coldly, "Did I say my mother died?"

No. No, she had not. Hadyn felt his cheeks burning. Some verse in the Bible about pearls and swine rang in his ears. Asandra, he decided, was a colorless, compassionless soul. Beautiful but unfeeling. He regreted making the effort.

"I only *wish* she had died," she whispered, continuing. To Hadyn, the words were like a slap in the face. He would have given anything—*everything*—to see his mother live. Asandra never took her eyes off the hard earth. Her face was a stone. "She didn't want me. She abandoned me. At the door of the Black Abbey."

Ah . . . so everyone has a story. In spite of her prickliness, Hadyn felt a moment of empathy. He didn't know what to say. "I'm so sorry. Is that how you got to be a mirling?"

He saw one eye, half-lidded behind her cowl. A mirror full of secrets, secrets full of pain. No, he decided. She was not happy at all.

He tried, at least, to fumble forward. "I mean . . . is it a gift?

Or do they teach you?"

"Enough. Too many questions."

She fell back, leaving Hadyn, once again, feeling foolish. Mainly, though, her silence was a relief. Empathy or not, after that sweet little ice-breaker, Hadyn hardly cared if they ever spoke again. Frankly, he was more than a little disgusted with himself for finding her attractive at all.

Focus on more than the face next time, he reminded himself.

And yet.

Asandra seemed like a child who wanted more than anything to be thought an adult. Or like a little girl, acting out to gain her father's attention. Or, more simply, she was just bitter—with good cause. Hadyn had cause too.

Life could really suck sometimes.

With shock, he realized their deeper commonality. Asandra had her own little piece of pain folded up tight inside. Spring-coiled. It wasn't pretty, but she had taken the same risk he had. She had opened up. Obviously, by her demeanor, the experience was both rare and painful. After all the years, the fact of her abandonment still hurt quite deeply. So she pushed against him, against all of them, expecting more abandonment. She was a social porcupine, further confirming the story of her life. Maybe hoping, just once, that someone might push in rather than away.

Hadyn doubted he was that guy. But he felt pity just the same.

CHAPTER 17

ACCEPTANCE

At dusk, exhausted, they set up camp in a grove of oak trees, eating salted pork, raisin bread, and badly bruised carrots from the abbey.

"No smoke," Sorge said apologetically, explaining the lack of fire. "No signals."

"No problem," Hadyn muttered. "If I never smelled smoke again, it would be too soon."

Ewan passed out almost immediately after eating, under a dark cobalt sky. Soon he was snoring. Flogg and Asandra each removed themselves a little way from the others for more private rest. Sorge sat wearily awake, his quarterstaff ready on his shoulder. Hadyn lay down but did not sleep. He watched the monk tilt his face toward the silver stars, staying suspended in that posture. Soundless as the stars, his lips began to move in supplication. Yielding at last to their quiet light, the words softly turned to song, a husky mixture of night winds and shattered dreams, bare like a tree stripped clean — and all the more beautiful for it.

Across the sea, lo! the stars
Where white gulls cry for shame,
We journey as a thousand souls
In search of our true name.
The way so far, the sea so wide
our longing hearts to roam,
Should waves rise high, as seagulls cry,
Then strength drowns in the foam.
Lo! Isgurd! Silver bright!
Where brave men ne'er grow old,
My soul doth long thee in the night,
By day, I'm not so bold.
I ache that your wind holds no sway,
I yearn thy golden shores.
I fly, I fight to sail unmoored
Across the sea, and far away.
Across the sea, and far away.

The sadness of the tune trailed away to silence, gradually displaced by the alternating rhythms of Ewan's and Flogg's steady breathing.

"Wow, so lonely," Hadyn mused. "'In search of our true name.'"

Surprised to hear another voice, Sorge turned, wrapped his cloak more tightly around himself. He seemed to be chewing on his own words. "Everything, living and dead, has a name. We use the names to help us make sense of the world, to separate and identify. Rocks, birds, you, me. Common names are easy . . . and forgiving. A form of grace. I know you as Hadyn, and you know me as Sorge.

Outlander. Elder. Boy. Man. All these words start the process of knowing. They are useful. But deeper still lies our true name."

"Like a secret?"

"In a way. We all yearn to know and be known. It goes to our core. Most true names have been forgotten. Only the wise know them now, and only a few at that. To know a name is to know a thing for what it truly is, not what it appears to be. It is essence, connection, vitality—the difference between surrender and mastery. Or so I am told. You tasted some part of this mystery back at the Stone House, I think. It wasn't a true name you spoke, yet you named the binding truly. That is a rare gift."

Hadyn yawned. "Well, I need some true sleep. How can you even stay awake? We've been chased and hunted. We've run for our lives. Aren't you exhausted?"

The moon rode high. Sorge studied it, the stars, deep and layered, glittering like ice. "Our stories tell of a field of memory where an ancient battle was fought, so terrible and so full of blood the land could no longer absorb life or rain. Within a year, the ground was barren. Then one night, all the trees pulled up their own roots and moved away, lest they die."

Hadyn felt a light breeze on his face, saw the strange picture in his mind of trees hiking up their skirts and heaving up roots from the deep earth. "What does it mean?"

"No, no. You may be tired, but not just yet. Tell me what you think."

In the darkness of another world, a fifteen-year-old boy groped for words.

"I have no idea."

"Try."

"Dunno . . . trees need water, I guess."

"It means," Sorge answered, his voice hushed, "that *we do*

what we must. To live and live well, we all do what we must, when we must, even when it is hard. You have known this battle."

"I have?"

Though his face was unreadable in the darkness, Sorge's tone was gentle. "I did not know of your mother. Not until just today. I heard you speaking to Asandra. I'm very sorry, little brother. It is not right."

Hadyn lay still, felt his heart rate speed up, as if he were on display. He felt exposed. Also, comforted. A decent trade. Sorge was being sincere. He wasn't offering pity but kindness.

"Now you may sleep, Lord Hadyn. You have done what you must. I shall do what I must. I have many, many late hours practicing prayer to sustain me. We journey hard again tomorrow and the next. On the fourth day, we make Threefork."

So they did. They woke in the morning and travelled hard again. The second and third day from the abbey passed much like the first, except for no creepy people and no spooky birds. Asandra gave no Watcher warnings. Just walking, following trails, winding south and east.

On day three, trudging along, they began passing simple stone fences and herds of grazing sheep—if they could be called that. The animals were bony and thin, the fields nothing but brown stubble. Overhead, the sky was a globulous mass of unbearable heat. Creeks and streams were bone dry. They wandered past an old shepherd with long hair and a moustache, panting in the sun. He neither spoke nor looked at them, just seemed to wither in the parched air, right before their eyes.

Sorge sighed. "The land struggles to live. Blessings run thin. Curses prevail."

"And murder." Asandra's dark eyes roamed freely. "Look, there."

At the top of the hill to their left, far away, stood a grove of trees. A stone pillar.

"A place for the Wild Dance. For a Summoning. They probably sacrifice for rain and only deepen the curse."

She made the sign of the circle. They kept moving. The hills began to thin and flatten. Eastward, Avl-Argosee became plainly visible. And huge. And blue. Not like Hawaii's turquoise waters. One doesn't easily forget a color like that, or the vacation the Barlows took together before Mom died. No, the Argosee was more opaque, blue and purple, foggy with minerals and mud. Sorge, angling more south than east now, told them they were headed for the Chin, a part of the western profile of the lake that formed its last major contour before funneling into the three rivers—Luth, Hart, and Argo—and finally, Champion Bay, which, upon crossing, would bring them to Stratamore.

Their food was nearly gone, leaving enough for just one more good meal. Flogg set out to find fruits and nuts for the morning. Ewan protested that Flogg shouldn't be allowed to leave the group. Something about a larger question of safety . . . for Flogg's own good, blah, blah. Hadyn was irritated to no end.

"Ewan, knock it off," he said. "You're being an idiot."

"You're the idiot. That *thing* stuck a knife in my back, and it never said it was sorry," Ewan huffed. "Besides, he creeps me out. Am I the only one with a clue here?"

Flogg, having zero interest in Ewan's protestations, went anyway. As Sorge packed their travel gear, he chided the younger Barlow.

"You are a stranger here, Lord Ewan. Flogg is a trusted friend. Do you think I cannot see through your complaints? Tomorrow he will go ahead of us to help make arrangements in Threefork, to speed our journey. Settle it and move on, little brother. On this matter, I will pay you no mind."

That was the end of it for everyone, except maybe Ewan. The monk went on to explain how they would find the captain, restock supplies, and sail south. Foothills and spotty trees currently hid the city from view, but Sorge assured them it was no more than a half-day's journey by foot. Tomorrow, by midday, they would be at its gates.

As they drew closer to the lake, they began to see the outer tokens of a nearby city: people and homes; simple dwellings with mud walls and thatched roofs; mothers in long dresses with babies on their hips and fathers working the land. Or far in the distance, men on the water flinging huge fishing nets in the air, praying to whatever gods they chose—sea gods, fish gods, gods of net or luck (or Aion if all else failed)—for a mighty catch of bluegill and crappie to bring to market.

Sorge guided his charges through the land of these hamlets quietly. Everywhere, the people looked sour, tired, empty. No one hailed them or offered them supper. They were strangers and treated as such. A handful of folks inclined their heads to Sorge out of respect for the robe he wore, or offered him the sign of the circle. The very same folk squinted their eyes at Asandra, or averted them and cursed, or rubbed fresh mud on their doorposts and spat. Mirlings were generally feared for their strange ways, trafficking with spirits. Others thought it bad luck to rile the Darkwings, as Watchers were commonly known. Seeing their soured, resentful expressions, Hadyn felt grateful for the new clothes he had been given. They blended well with the look of others. Without them, he and Ewan would have no doubt been objects of intense scrutiny and suspicion.

Yes, it was a strange world in which he found himself enmeshed. He was now a part, unwilling or no. He had heard a name, had unbound what was bound. He had heard what not even Sorge the Gray could hear. What Flogg, whose fingers drew whispers from the land, could not hear. It was . . . rare. Or was it? Almost challenging his thoughts, he remembered the lifeless tone of the speaker at the Stone House.

You have come for no great purpose. . . . Nothing matters.

The words brought a strange, sudden rush of claustrophobia. Once again, he felt trapped at the Stone House, surrounded by fire. Trapped, really, in the struggle of Karac Tor. *Enmeshed.* Truth was, it hardly seemed like the adventure the scrolls had promised. He didn't feel up to it. Truth was, he was fearful and missed his dad and could have easily just sat down and cried, except that would have embarrassed him even more than the loneliness. The lost boy's words swarmed his brain. *Nothing . . .*

But then he remembered the feel of the cudgel in his grip, the curious whisper of the metal latch in his mind. It had spoken a word known only to him. Here, the battleground formed, between the suffocating foolishness of it all and something else. Something raw and deep and fragile, rising to oppose the fear. It snuck up on him with a secret invitation, and in that invitation a burst of intuition pounced on him, like a lion stalking its prey. The battleground grew silent. The clamor and clash of thoughts grew still.

In the span of a single breath, where before, so many things were important, now only one thing mattered; it was as if, perhaps, he had only ever known this *one thing*. He recognized the thing, weak as it was on new, shaky legs. It was a mirror image of himself. It defied the lost boy (or anyone else for that matter) to define him. Or his purpose.

He was Hadyn Barlow, and in that moment, Hadyn Barlow knew with clarity that he had been brought here for a purpose.

To fight.

CHAPTER 18

TOWER OF RAVENS

"Find them," Nemesia said coldly. Her green eyes flashed. Her face was flat with rage. "Find them. Capture them. Bring them here. I want to know how he knew the word I commanded you. I want to know what they know. I want to know what commission they bring to this world, before I destroy them."

Floating in the vapor, five youths stood on a dead, dry hill. They were all roughly the same age, but the central figure appeared to be the oldest, perhaps seventeen or eighteen. His face was slack, but a puzzle lingered in his hollow eyes. A dangerous question.

"How could they know?"

"They didn't. *He* did."

The accursed oldest one named Hadyn.

Hearing her own words, Nemesia's voice shifted slightly, became softer, more calculating. More maternal. "He's about your age, darling. How does that make you feel?"

"I feel . . ." The boy in the phantom image struggled for

words, became annoyed. "You know I never know these things. Just tell me the answer."

"Shameface, my precious bomb," Nemesia answered, sticky sweet. "I don't have any answers. No one does. There are no answers, to anything. But *if*"—and here she greatly emphasized *if* as though she were giving them a choice—"*if* I were you, I think I would feel . . . empty."

Shameface accepted this immediately, with relief. "Yes. I feel empty."

"Horribly empty, I should think! Even more than you already do. And confused, maybe? Angry? After all, why should he get to do such wonderful things and you can't? Doesn't anybody else care that you are nothing special?" She raised the volume of her voice to include the four who stood behind the leader, listening, staring with blank, fleshy eyes. Vague emotion passed over their faces.

"We are the Nameless," said one, monotone.

"Yes, nameless. All of you, my bombs, so lonely. Such a cruel task, to live this dreary life."

"I can't stand it anymore," said another. "I want to die."

"No, not die, Hurter, Hider. If you are dead, they can mourn you. They can pretend to feel bad, as if you actually mattered—as if they ever really loved you. They can bury you and forget you, with their guilt appeased."

They stared at her; five gazes of slavish simplicity. Nemesia spun her web one sticky word at a time, sowing confusion, reaping madness.

"Death is a gift to *them*, not yourselves," she explained. Her words carried both enchantment and perverse logic. "You must do something more. Something worse. You must shame them."

"How?"

"Become reckless! Become even more worthless than you already are. Become dangerous with anger. You don't need a reason to rage, my bombs! You are almost completely worthless but not yet enough to be free. You still cling to trivial hopes and dreams. Abandon these. However small, they will *never* come to pass. Forget your name, your ambitions. They are paths of iniquity—tired remnants of the empty promises of love."

"I have never . . . known love."

"Of course not, my bombs! Your fathers did not love you, and your mothers did not want you. You were not their choice. They wanted other things, better things. They gave you barely what you needed and nothing you wanted. Why? Because they did not care to be bothered. You carry this poison inside."

"I feel it. It hurts."

"Only because you still fight it! You wish to be somebody—to prove them wrong. But this can never happen. And so you hurt."

The girl nearest Shameface seemed puzzled. She spoke timidly. "But you said we had been cheated. Didn't you? That one boy—he's better than us. You said so, just now. No . . . wait. I can't remember what you said. I'm sorry, why shouldn't we fight back?"

"With what, sweet Grayday?" Nemesia intoned, clicking her nails together. "Simple, foolish girl, it's a wonder I care for you at all! None of you are good enough, smart enough, or brave enough to ever amount to anything. Listen to me, let me help you. I will speak slowly: If you feel cheated, and therefore decide to rise above your station, what have you caused yourself? You know the answer."

"Pain. Because we will always fail."

"Correct. Do you want more pain?"

"No," said Grayday firmly. "I hurt enough. More than I can bear."

"Yet you are asking for precisely that. More pain! Answer me, quickly: What does love give?"

"Love names us," Shameface said bitterly. "It gives identity." He knew the coming exchange by heart and believed the conclusions without question. Nemesia's teachings made so much sense.

"And where does identity lead?" asked the witch.

"To foolish hopes."

"Why is hope foolish?"

"Because it is the soil of dreams."

"And what do dreams cause?"

"Shame."

"Because?"

"Because the weight of dreams always collapses. Love is faithless when tested. It cannot be fulfilled. It promises what it will not surrender. It gives with one hand that it might gain with another. It demands what cannot be achieved. It remembers wrongs. Love must be earned. It is never given."

"Have you worked hard for love, my dear?"

"All my life."

"And do you have anything—any love or identity—to show for all your efforts?"

Shameface's eyes were the last embers of a dying fire, finally extinguished. He whispered, "I am empty."

"Empty and nameless. A bomb, left alone, ready to explode. Like that silly gnome carries in his satchel. And so you came to me, each of you. I am here to guide you through your pain to the comfort of numbness and rage. Perfect, my darlings. Be a slave to no man, no woman. Only yourself. Serve no one but your own desires. When you do this, when nobody matters to you, you will matter to nobody. Your nothingness will be complete. Since they

cannot own what doesn't exist, you will finally, truly, be free. This
is the gift I offer."

Her suggestion rippled through the ranks of the five shadowed
figures, who began whispering together.

"The girl keeps the Darkwings away. It makes it hard for us
to find them."

Nemesia dangled a mouse, dropped it in the water. It screamed
briefly, was silent. The witch hesitated. "I did not expect her on
this journey. But she is a broken vessel. A mistake. She means
nothing."

"The monk is strong."

"No. He is a little mouse, playing with his cheese. He is afraid
to use his strength. His guilt runs too deep."

"Then we are back to the boy—he knew your secret word.
All on his own."

Grayday broke in. "Maybe . . . we could be like *him* one
day?"

Nemesia absorbed this without reaction at first. Then her eyes
narrowed to thin slits, narrowed the flames in the black chamber
to thin points of white-hot light. Shadows scurried. Fingernails,
filed to razor points, carved grooves into the surface of the wood
table. As the vaporous image above the boiling pot began to fail,
a new thought entered the witch's mind.

Shameface begged, "Let us leave this place. We will come to
you."

"No, my bombs," she answered, sticky sweet. "I have changed
my mind. A different task, a new pleasure. I want to give you each
something very special."

"A gift?" said Grayday with surprise.

"Yes, a present for each of you. But here is what you must do.
Bring the two brothers to me. Be as devious as needed, but bring

them healthy and well, and I shall show you your own power. The power of despair."

"We are afraid."

"We are not like them. It is torment to be near them. Let us kill them quickly and return to you."

Nemesia, a hungry cat, licked her lips. "No, no, my dear Hider! That would ruin my gift. Don't you see? Since you cannot be like them, I will make *them* like you. Nameless, just like you."

Slowly, devilishly, the five teenagers smiled.

CHAPTER 19

THREEFORK

The city of Threefork was a tightly bundled knot of commerce at the southern split of the mighty Argosee, where the one great river became three. The city, which the river cut in half, was stitched back together by four great bridges. Homes were packed along tight, winding lanes around the sprawling heart of the city where the wealthy lived and worked—the eastern shore—while countless docks and the cluttered shops and peasant homes of fisherman and craftsman formed a perimeter north, west, and south.

Here seamen from Yrgavien brought fat-bellied ships laden with ore, rubies, coal, and pelts, and bargemasters came lumbering down River Conach to the Argosee bearing cedar, pine, and fir. Salty, gray-bearded captains cursed their crews with one breath, then prayed for good tailwinds the next, offering tokens at the Shrine of the Green Deep to buy favor from the sea gods for their next trek across the Bay to Vineland and back, with holds full of legendary sweet Faielyn wine. Honey mead came from Befjorg to Threefork, and from Threefork to all points of the compass; so, too, grain and produce brought by ship, cart, and donkey from traders all around the Midlands and Greenland—Slegling, Lismoych, Brimshane—and countless lesser villages besides. Even the Gray Abbey regularly sent monks pulling donkeys with carts of braghe and ghouda to Threefork. All these converged in a breathless mess of race, language, coin, bartering, trading, cursing, profit, and loss. Threefork was commerce to its bones: down every canal, inn, and shop, down every alley.

"Here," Sorge explained, "the Duke of Düshnoc came with three hundred soldiers to reclaim a large sum of money he had lost in a wager with the Earl of Seabraith. It was a fool's errand, so he was well-qualified for the task. Vastly outnumbered, even more vastly outwitted, his lone success appeared to be in greatly offending the earl, the king's most loyal ally. The earl captured the duke and had him taken to the gibbet to hang. But the duke was fortunate that day. He had come bearing the prized metal *algathon* on the spears and shields of his soldiers. He bargained with the earl: pardon in exchange for algathon. Instead of bloodshed, the two forged an alliance that lasted for two hundred years. The duke climbed down from the gibbet and left Threefork that very day with twelve champion steeds from the personal stables of the royal family as token of their covenant." Sorge squinted against the light of the sun. "In other words, in this city, the best deal is always the next deal, and the only reputation you carry is that of your last bad trade. Money talks loudly everywhere . . . but here, *everyone* is listening." He glanced behind him. "Asandra, here we take our leave of you. Will you secure passage by land or sea?"

Asandra heard well enough, but didn't answer. For the last couple of days, she had seemed to soften, however subtly. At least toward Hadyn. Now she studied the whole group, but none more than he. Her eyes, almond-shaped like Sorge's, stared at him so intently he wondered if he had food stuck in his teeth.

"I should continue with you, I think," she said slowly. "My errand to Seabraith can wait."

Sorge shook his head emphatically. "No, you must continue on. I do not agree."

"The errand is mine to decide," Asandra said, clipping her words. "I take orders from the bishop, not you."

"Well said. But these boys are *my* charges, not the bishop's. You are very skilled, Asandra, but you are young. Do not assume more wisdom than you possess. It is the path to pride."

"Pride? And where has your path taken you?" Asandra shot back. She caught herself. "Consult at the chantry if you like. We need not decide this very moment."

Sorge fumed, picking his way from the outer docks down several streets and narrow lanes, finally bringing them to the door of an attractive-looking inn in a well-appointed section of the west quarter.

"Hoods off," he advised. "No need to look like we're carrying secrets."

A voice called out from the shadows of the alley near the inn. "Sorge! Sorge, is that you, old friend? Hey, over here!"

Everyone spun. It took a moment for Hadyn's eyes to adjust to the alley's dim light, but he saw the monk's face split into a wide, troubled grin. "Cruedwyn? What are you doing here?"

The man motioned him closer. He wore a sword at his side and bright colors. He had a toothy, nervous smile.

"Wait here," Sorge commanded. He veered toward the alley, gripping his staff. Immersed in shadows, he and the man named Cruedwyn began conversing beyond hearing. Hadyn saw Sorge shake his head. Cruedwyn grasped at his sleeve, a gesture of pleading. His worried eyes glanced over to where they stood in the middle of the busy street, studying each in turn. His lips moved faster, more urgently. Again, Sorge shook his head no, then again, emphatically, *no*. The other man dropped to his knees. Sorge hesitated, touched his friend's shoulder. Turned and walked away. Toward the inn.

"Who was that?" Ewan asked.

"An old acquaintance. A swordsman and singer. He wishes to join us. I told him no."

They entered the inn. The faded sign hanging above the door read, Possum and Peacock. The innkeeper, a busy man, greeted Sorge by name, knowingly motioning toward the back room with a flick of his head. Hadyn and Ewan kept their mouths shut and their eyes straight ahead, but Asandra seemed quite at ease. The inn, though noisy, was not raucous; dim, yes, but neither cheerless nor deviant. Actually, it felt rather friendly. And by the rich aroma, Hadyn decided whatever beef stew was simmering in the kitchen, he wanted a bowl. Or two.

"Brother Sorge!" declared a lilting, cadenced voice, coming from a lean man with a shock of white hair and sagging jowls meant for a heavier man.

"You've lost weight, Gregor," Sorge said, eyeing his friend with a wry smile. "Running from pirates still?"

"Ha, t'would be an easy task. Running from me wife, more like it! Me lady wants me up on the roof, thatching for autumn rains. 'Course I come here only to think about how best to serve her every whim." He reached out to clasp Sorge's extended hand, then held it, fingering the cloth of his cuff.

"Brother no more, I'd say. The gray of an Elder? How long?"

"Nearly two years."

"Well then, I'm too late to throw a party, and not late enough to claim senility, eh? Sit, sit, my friend! 'Tis been a long time."

Sorge glanced around the room. "Where's Flogg?"

"Auginn's eyes, would ya sit first and chat awhile! Let me buy you and yer young friends here a pot of stew. Flogg'll be back soon enough. Said he had matters to attend to after finding me. Hello, boys."

He smiled pleasantly, took note of Asandra, but studied the brothers like an auctioneer assessing value. The boys nodded politely. Sorge pulled up chairs for all three. Together, they sat. The back room was small, with just six tables; only one other than Gregor's was occupied on the other side of the room.

"I need a favor," the monk said quietly.

"I know, lad. Flogg made it clear. And yes, I'll help, o'course. How soon?"

"Actually, now would be best. Haste is preferred."

He started to rise. Hadyn coughed. Sorge glanced at the brothers, both eagerly clutching wooden spoons. Slowly, he sat.

"All right then. *After* that pot of soup."

CHAPTER 20

THE ORACLE

By the time the meal was over, Flogg had rejoined their party. Ewan treated him with open contempt but withheld further challenge. Captain Gregor departed to begin preparing his ship, and the four travellers followed Sorge to the House of the Noble Way, a Gray chantry.

For the spiritual health of the land, each abbey had outposts like this — Gray chantries, White kirks, Black sanctums — scattered throughout Karac Tor, typically in major cities and larger towns. Each claimed devotees for the Way of Aion. Of course, there were plenty of pagan temples, too, boasting strange ways and stranger gods. Plenty of peasant witches and fortune-tellers in their street booths, offering to spill the bones and read your future, or sellers of charms and talismans, promising everything from love and fortune to blights upon your enemies. Plenty of normal folk, devout folk, heathens, superstitious fools, poor, rich, proud. A smorgasboard.

Today, Sorge felt a need for guidance. He felt a troubling in his spirit, he said, and he needed wisdom beyond his own. At the chantry, a gray-robed monk greeted him with the sign of the circle. They were in a quieter section of town. Wind chimes above the door tinkled lightly in voices of seashell and crystal. A gilded sign read, For Patrons and Seekers. Sorge turned to the brothers before entering.

"Would either of you like to come with me?"

"Depends on what's in there," Ewan replied.

It was a hot, muggy day. The monk's eyes glimmered in the sun.

"Surprises," he said calmly. "Truth. Revelation. Warnings. One never knows. A cat needs no eyes for milk."

"But how will *I* . . ." Ewan caught himself, cocked his head. "Huh?"

"Sometimes you just know when something is right and good. Like a cat with milk."

"Okay, nice. Never look a gift horse in the mouth. But this is kind of weird to me." He caught Hadyn's eye, silently appealing for guidance, support.

Hadyn shrugged. "If we trust him to get us home . . ."

Of course, *he* wouldn't have done it, but what did that matter? He wouldn't have crawled into the briar patch when the birds first flew in, either. Ewan was often bold and unpredictable. He loved roller coasters. Hadyn did not. Tomato, tomahto.

"Does it cost anything?" his brother asked warily.

Sorge reached into his coin purse, pushed a copper *shil* into Ewan's palm. "It is good to give, regardless."

Hadyn saw the decision being made in his brother's eyes. Ewan closed his fingers on the round coin, a shape without beginning or end. A circle. He stepped up to the door, made the sign. Together, he and Sorge entered.

"What will they tell him?" Hadyn asked Asandra.

The mirling's olive skin glistened with perspiration. "Aion's breath blows where it will."

Great, like that did any good. Could someone talk normal around here?

After nearly an hour, Sorge emerged without Ewan. He stood on the steps, staring into the faceless crowd. "At the Fourth Coming, Olfadr commanded his son, Aion, to bring gifts to men. *Lira*, *Orn*, and *Nasmith* are three of Nine."

Hadyn was exasperated. "Lira . . . and . . . *what*?"

From where she sat on a ledge of sun-baked brick, Asandra said, "Lore, Oracles, and Mysteries. Strength of Heaven. Light of Sun. Radiance of Moon."

"Oh, right," Hadyn said drily. "Why didn't you just say so?"

"Were you given insight?" Asandra probed, rising.

The monk's eyebrows gathered like storm clouds above his face. "None to tell, except for this *Orn*:

In division, completion;
In darkness, door shone;
Of water, wood dreaming;
To sunlight, from stone."

Flogg patted Sorge's arm, "Timing times. Elder will see. *Nasmith*, maybe yet."

Hadyn blinked. He was lost. Apparently, so was Ewan.

"Where's Ewan?"

A few moments later, the younger Barlow exited the chantry, as thoughtful as Sorge had been previously. His face was peaceful. "Two of the monks prayed with me. They listened. For Aion, they said—for the feel of his breath. They said I was called." He smiled. "Isn't that strange? No riddles. Just that I am called. They said my magic is meant to be heard." He looked at Sorge. "What does that mean?"

"A gift is one thing. Discovery is another." The monk turned to Asandra. "We all need light. Mirling, I do not see clearly, but I see that it *may* be best if you come. If you still wish it."

Staff in hand, he strode away, passing from smaller lanes to wider, more bustling avenues. The noise and color and movement turned the teeming central thoroughfare into a restless river of humanity. Merchants standing behind carts and under awnings loudly hawked their wares, while young children dodged in and out of traffic, playing games and screaming. Odors from bodies and countless shops assaulted them, both pleasant and foul—donkey manure and sweat on one hand, mingled with the warm, yeasty smell of freshly baked bread, flowers and apples, and a host of other aromas besides.

"Have you noticed," Hadyn whispered to Ewan, glancing around the streets. "There's old people here, and there's lots of children. But there's almost no one our age. No teenagers. They're all gone."

Ewan looked around, shuddered. "Creepy."

Near the end of the central boulevard of the city, they passed a great stone fountain at the intersection of two streets. In the center of the fountain, a statue of a bearded man, royally dressed, was slumped over as if he carried a great weight. In his hands he held a golden crown.

"Eskobar the Weak," Sorge explained. "The last king of Karac Tor."

By the smell of the air, Hadyn knew they were nearing the docks. He matched his stride to the monk's. Having chewed on the riddle for a time, he found he was more irritated than ever. "Is that all the *Orn* they've got?" he asked. "It's nonsense. It's just words."

"The stumbling dancer says the ground is uneven," Sorge replied.

"Okay, I get it. But really, how is that supposed to help us?"

"Because at some point, we *will* understand. Will God shatter stars and feed us sand?"

Hadyn rolled his eyes. "Please tell me you're running out of those."

Sorge laughed. Hadyn didn't.

"Really, how do you *know*? Is it for when we see Archibald? When we get on the boat and sail down the river? I mean, it could be nothing, right? Just a riddle."

"From Aion."

"I get that part. Aion's the good guy. But if we have no idea what it means, what does it matter?"

"*Nasmith!*" Flogg snapped.

"*Nasmith*," agreed Sorge, not breaking his stride. "It means we don't know, so we must pray. We lack wisdom, so we must ask for it as a gift."

Hadyn shook his head. "I'd ask for a good map while you're at it. We're about to get lost."

They entered the fish markets. Vendors gutting fish and rowdy pubs selling cheap beer. They passed warehouses and docks and sailors laying drunk on rotting wooden slats. They passed under the sun, to Gregor's vessel, past alleys and dark shadows. Unknowingly, they passed a man who had trailed them since the chantry, who even now watched from the shadows which vessel they boarded. They did not see him. But he saw them.

CHAPTER 21

THE WILDSTAR

They arrived to find Gregor already ready to sail. His vessel was not large, and it had a tall, single mast and clean, beautiful lines. Near the bow, in gilded silver, Hadyn read the name: *Wildstar*. The name and the vessel struck him as utterly seaworthy, though in truth, he hadn't a clue what that meant.

"I've trimmed me back to a keelboat," Gregor offered apologetically. "Don't need nothing that requires a crew n'more—just have to get on the water every now and then, y'know? Anyway, there's no room in the hold for sleeping, only stores and a bit of cargo I'm haulin'."

"I didn't think you were hauling anymore," Sorge commented.

"Oh, not really. But got me an offer too good to refuse on this here load, and just a short run. Down toward the cursed Argo"—he made a sign, as if warding off evil—"but only near, not on. Then we be on our way. I figure we take the Hart to the bay if'n it suits ya. It's clean 'n swift. Shouldn't take too long. I've got a couple more barrels coming, and some food stuff, besides. Crossing the bay will be a few days."

"So now we wait for the evening winds?" Sorge asked.

"Aye, we wait."

Sorge saw Asandra, standing alone on the starboard rail. "You are welcome on this vessel, as I have said, but I wish to be clear. You are welcome only if you do *exactly* as I say. Agreed?"

One eyebrow rose. It was a mixed gesture — part acquiescense, part defiance.

"Agreed."

Sorge started to walk away, turned back. "You disrespect me. I see it in your eyes. But I remain your elder. Take care, mirling."

Hadyn was nearby. He heard Asandra's murmured reply.

"Sorge the Gray. Friend of Corus. It is you who should take care."

He thought about asking her what that meant but, instead, chose simply to be pleased at the turn of events by which she was included on the boat rather than parting company. Yes, she was too old for him. And yes, if someone accused him of being a glutton for punishment, he couldn't have argued. Only days ago, he had been done with her. Asandra was icy, rude, antagonistic . . . beautiful, compelling. And he was a teenage boy.

But for now, he was a tired teenage boy, and there was nothing to do but wait. Asandra had already retreated back into her shell. Both Barlows seized the opportunity for some rest. They lay on the warm, oiled wooden planks of the ship's deck, watching the slow current drift ponderously south. Soon both boys were asleep.

When the ship finally unmoored from the docks, drifting into the open harbor, they stirred. The sun had long ago peaked and begun arcing lower in the sky. They stood on the edge of the deck, leaning over the railing—two Missouri boys who had never been sailing. Foreign land or not, this was fun: gulls lofting on unseen pillows of air, dangling just out of arm's reach; salty air in their noses; the clean cut of the ship through the water, awaiting her sails. They watched the old captain run his hands along the rail, surveying other boats, closing his eyes to better feel the wind on his face. It was almost something mystical, the way he seemed to feel the water, the wind. When he opened his eyes, it was to measure the harbor, waiting for the right moment to unfurl.

"C'mon boys," he said. "You're my crew, see? Grab there. Now untie that knot. And there, too. Now pull! That's right."

Soon it was done, and the boys felt almost like real sailors. The main sail hung limp for several moments before gently rippling a bit, then suddenly snapping full as a good stiff breeze blew in from the east. The boat lurched forward. Hadyn instinctively grabbed at a rope to steady his legs. At the touch, he heard. The rough woven fibers whispered in his mind, a particular blending of strands and sounds. Like a word.

He noticed but was too lost in the moment to pay attention. The pleasure on Gregor's face was evident, and Hadyn felt it too.

"There it is!" Gregor cried, heaving at the ropes. "By the gods, I love it when the wind finally grabs her!"

It was, indeed, an awesome feeling. Gregor took the helm with an easy, steady hand. The current was swift, the waters deep. The distance from the city to the branching, triplet rivers which gave it its name was short indeed. Sorge told the boys that the Hart had waters that were swift, but tame, and offered the shortest, most direct path to the bay.

"Aye," was all Gregor would say.

It only took fifteen minutes, maybe less, before the juncture of each waterway became visible ahead. To port, the Luth and

Hart were still a good ways away. But just off the bow, south and west, Hadyn saw dark, murky waters. Beyond them were the shadows of many trees.

"Redthorn," Sorge said warily. "A cursed forest. Home to jackals."

"Quick landing, 'tis all I need," Gregor said, wagging his finger. He secured the rigging, began steering hard to starboard, angling for the Argo. "This be where I drop me cargo. Then we be done with it. No worries, mates. Hardly worth the trouble for such a short trip."

Sorge eyed the countryside nervously. They were only a couple miles south of the city. The shipping lanes were clear. No other vessels could be seen up or down the channels. A few small huts dotted the land heading west, but that was about it. Gregor aimed the vessel for a small, dilapidated dock on the western shore, no doubt used by local fishermen. He put down the gangplank, handed each of the boys a thick rope, and began barking orders.

"Take these down to the dock'n lash 'em to the piers, lads. I'll follow in a moment. Go! Missy, you can go with 'em, but let them do the work, see? Sorge, my friend, you and the gnome, come and grab some of these barrels and heave 'em up the ladder to me. I'm too old for this anymore. Down there in the hold, against the far wall. Careful now, she's got a low ceiling. *Rat Trap* I should call her, not *Windstar*. That's right."

Hadyn and Ewan didn't know any good knots, but they worked their way to the dock and began tying the ropes as best they could. In the dark belly of the ship, Sorge and Flogg waited for their eyes to adjust.

"I don't see barrels anywhere—"

A creaky sound. An unoiled hinge, loud above them. The monk glanced up in time to see the hold's door slam shut. Smooth and practiced, Gregor slid a thick iron bar through heavy metal hoops on either side of the door frame, sealing the door fast. "You're the cargo now, mates," he said.

Sorge and Flogg began yelling, pounding. The sound of the staff banging against the underside of the deck drew both boys' attention.

"What's going on?" said Hadyn.

"Betrayal," Asandra said ominously.

Gregor straightened his back, took time to cooly adjust his tunic.

He laughed. "That's a smart lass ya' are, missy. As for me, I can't figure why they don't want you instead."

He unsheathed a thin rapier from his side and began slowly advancing down the gangplank, the tip pointed straight out, swishing back and forth, from boy to boy. He glanced haughtily, perhaps a little fearfully, at the mirling. "None to hear you scream lads, so go ahead. And I know for a fact a mirling's powers got nothing to do with swordfightin'. So it's just me and you here. The four of us. And some buyers with deep, deep pockets. No need for this to get ugly."

"You can't do this, Gregor!"

"Oh, but I can. It's like I told Sorge. Sometimes an offer comes along that's simply too good to refuse." He put fingers to his lips, whistled loudly. Following his line of sight, Hadyn saw five figures emerge from behind five trees scattered near the shore, fanning out, slowly converging in a half circle around the dock where the boys stood. Their march was methodical, maddeningly slow. One of them carried a small bag that jingled in his hands. The other four held long knives. They were trapped — by water, by Gregor's blade, by five hunters. Hadyn scanned the dock, the boat, the shore, trying to formulate a plan.

"Why are you doing this?" he whispered.

"Why does anyone do anything? 'Cause I wanted to. 'Cause I can."

Dimly, another voice could be heard coming from the belly of the ship. "Lord Hadyn! Lord Ewan!" It was Sorge. "How many?"

"Five on shore!" Hadyn called back. "The ones from the Stone House I think. They have knives."

"Hold your ground!"

Gregor glanced back nervously as the hold's door rattled and buckled with every blow Sorge gave it; yet it held.

Again, Sorge called out. "Gregor! Repent of this. You are a better man!"

"Gave up on being a better man, I did," Gregor shot back angrily. "Gave up on you. Gave up on Aion, most of all. I've lived long enough to see no punishment for evil, no reward for good. Besides . . . never much liked being told what to do." He paused, allowing his words to sink in, showing stained, crooked teeth. "How do you like that, Gray? Huh? What's faith worth now in invisible, legendary kings? If he be so all-powerful, why did he not warn ye you were walking into a trap? Eh? And you one of his holy servants?"

He waited for a reply. None came. Only a single, solitary, defeated thump against the hold's door.

"Aye, he didn't protect you!" Gregor shouted, his voice echoing on the water. Off in the distance, a gull cried.

And then there was silence. A slight breeze rustled the green leaves of the few trees on shore. Otherwise, the only sound was the soft whisper of the feet of five people folding the grass with each measured step, drawing closer, closer—three boys, two girls, all robed in drab brown. With drawn hoods shadowing their faces, the five advanced with both hands outstretched, as if they meant to consume their prey all at once. Standing on the gangplank,

Gregor swished his rapier in the air. The raucous thumping coming from the ship was done.

"Sorge is stuck," Ewan whispered. "What do we do?"

Gregor heard him, mocked, "Methinks what you're gonna to do is win me a prize, and then go far away. On a lovely holiday I'd wager." He called out louder to one of the five, "That better be a money bag I see in your hand there, lad. Otherwise, I'll just have to haul me cargo back on board."

Nearly to the dock, the leader of the five gazed upon Gregor dispassionately. He tossed the bag to the older man, who caught it in midair, opened it, pulled out a gold coin, and promptly bit the metal. The sailor smiled greedily, began jingling the bag, counting the number of coins.

"Outlanders," the leader said calmly, fixing his eyes on Hadyn, "do not struggle and you will not be harmed. You will come with us."

A freeway of thoughts collided in Hadyn's brain, grinding to a halt, like a traffic jam at noon. His heart pounded hot and red, but all the adrenaline in the world was pointless if he couldn't *think*. And he couldn't think, not even a little. Every muscle felt poised for action, cued and ready. Every muscle but his brain, which felt dipped in neural molasses. The sluggishness came from the five. The nearer they drew, the more powerfully their torpid, dragging will projected into his own — exactly as he had felt it at the Stone House.

Ewan made a slurred, shushing sound.

"Get *away* from us!"

He was bent over, holding his head, his ears, wobbling on his knees. He seemed pained, but his eyes were steel and grit.

"Get out of my head!" he shouted.

As long as he lived, Hadyn would never forget that moment,

standing on the dock as mild waters lapped the shore. Something about Ewan's defiance, the desperate posture of his hands clutching his face, cut through his own dullness. He knew one thing: They must not be taken. He had to do something, had to fight for himself.

For Ewan.

He formed a plan, only it wasn't a plan at all, really. It was motion. Roaring at the top of his lungs—a sound of fury and reckless abandon—he charged. He had no weapon, not even a stick. One against five. But standing still would solve nothing. If he distracted them, perhaps Ewan and Asandra might escape.

His motion was so jarring, so unexpected, the five paused, struck with uncertainty. They had formed a wall on the edge of the dock, but now the wall trembled. Hadyn was a sprinter. He was fast. He never made it. A force knocked him forward on his face, smashing him against the weathered wood of the dock.

The sound was deafening.

From deep in the hold of the ship, a blast raked across its side, shattering planks and splintering the cargo door. Flying debris smashed against the back of Gregor's head, splattering blood. He tumbled face down into the water. Ewan and Asandra were slammed to the dock. Crawling out of the smoke and tumult, Sorge heaved himself over the splintered side, collapsing into the water between the ship and the dock, snarling in pain. Behind him, Flogg seemed to have fared little better. Then came the monk's hands, grasping at piers and boards, pulling himself, wincing, to the platform. Three of the five attackers lumbered toward the dock, making weird sounds, slashing with their blades. Hadyn shook his head to clear it. Rattled, ready or not, he had to fight.

He rose unsteadily to his feet. For the second time, was saved.

He heard something, saw something. A flash of color, a musical, laughing cry, and the whisper of a blade scraping free of its scabbard. He whipped his head around, away from Sorge. There, swirling with his blade, was the man from Threefork, Cruedwyn. He moved swiftly, like a hawk diving in the sky. He cut off the three assailants before they could reach the dock, before they could even think or adapt. One of them cried out in surprise and lunged awkwardly. Cruedwyn parried, spun, thrusting his weapon deep into that one's flesh. The second swung hard, hissing like a rabid animal. Creudwyn sliced, spun again, cutting across his robe, leaving a gash of bright blood.

One of those struck folded toward the earth, never to rise again. Two more, injured, stumbled away, crying in pain. The remaining two held their ground for a brief moment. Then they, too, fled.

Cruedwyn lowered his sword, but Flogg would not yield. Hobbling past, still shouting, he heaved a bulging, leather-strapped ball in their direction. It exploded loudly above the heads of the fleeing four, knocking two more to the ground. They wailed aloud, collected themselves again, then disappeared behind the scattered trees.

Sorge turned quickly to the boys.

"Are you well?" he asked tersely. Both, obviously shaken, nodded.

Satisfied, the monk wheeled round, leaned out over the dock, ready to aid Gregor with his staff. The seaman's body, face down, floated slowly away.

"Mercy, Aion," the monk whispered, touching his closed fist to his chest. "Once, he was my friend."

The boat bubbled and frothed as it took on water from the hole blown in its hull. Slowly, it began to sink into the river. Sorge leaped aboard, gathering a few quick supplies, any food he could find, and the personal belongings all five had left on the deck. He threw them over to Flogg, one by one, then jumped back to the dock, landing hard. The vessel creaked, lurched, rolled onto its side. Within minutes, it slipped below the surface and disappeared.

Sorge's face was soot-stained, grim. He was badly bruised, with multiple cuts. Flogg, too, though he had a wild look in his eye. "There were five last time. And five this. By Auginn's eyes, we have survived their treachery each time. Cruedwyn, my thanks. Flogg sensed someone trailing us, but we assumed evil. We are in debt to your stubbornness, and I surely won't refuse your company this time, though now perhaps you see why at first I did. You join us at your own peril."

Cruedwyn, panting for breath, flashed a stunning, playful smile. "I have my own reasons to travel, if you'll accept that for now."

Sorge nodded. "It is likely too dangerous to return to Threefork. And we cannot wait for Nemesia's brood to regroup—nor will we face them in such low numbers again." He looked at Flogg, limping, felt the sticky blood on his own fingers when he wiped his face. "We need to bind our wounds and carefully plot our next move. The best we can do for now, I think, is hide. And to hide safely, we must hide dangerously, where no one would search for us."

Hadyn felt a pit in his stomach. He looked south, down the river. The sun was setting. The dark trees loomed not far away. Closer still, soon. Sorge confirmed their destination with one word.

"Redthorn."

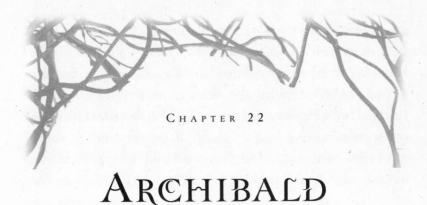

CHAPTER 22

ARCHIBALD

Vast swathes of evening light streamed through the great windows in the Hall of the King. Luminous, rose-hued beams diffused into the air, reflecting off the flagstones, catching fire on the gold filigree of the hall's six massive columns, the silver etchings trimmed into the ivory throne, the line of polished metal shields and crests hung so precisely upon the walls.

In this hall, a man shuffled aimlessly up and down the heavy blue carpet runner leading from the great double doors at one end to the ivory throne at the other, muttering, "Where are the Champions?" Though he was neither very young nor very old, he stooped as if great with age.

"*Where* are my Champions?" he bellowed again, his ragged voice echoing off the marbled walls. Then, turning in place as if searching, he murmured, "*Why* are there no Champions? Why am I alone left to rule with no aid among men?"

A dozen elite palace guards stood stone-faced at attention,

spears held tightly upright. They did not move or reply or blink. Four other men in richly embroidered robes stood at a distance with mixed expressions, either fretting or scoffing, bored or scheming. Another man, also richly arrayed, walked beside the troubled ruler. He was a slight man, full of poise and syrup; skilled in the meaningful pause, the clever phrase, the subtle gesture or expression capable of bending another mind to his point of view, however slightly; able to cloud an issue enough to seem wise, then later clarify the distortion with a simpler, more comprehensible half-truth. His name was Jonas, the Minister of Justice—a title of extravagant irony, to be sure.

"My Lord Archibald," Jonas whispered, folding his hands behind his back. On the underside of his left wrist, he bore a strange mark, like a tattoo or birthmark, shaped like a wild beast. It was nearly always buried beneath his sleeve. "You are the great governor of this dominion. Why trouble yourself with Champions and other petty matters? We have no need of relics of days gone by. This is your domain!"

Archibald was unimpressed. "My domain is crumbling to ruin."

"My liege, are the coffers empty or full?"

"Full," grumbled Archibald.

"Are barbarians from Quil threatening war at our borders?"

"Not *yet*."

"And likely never again. Is your own person healthy or ill?"

"Well."

"Have peasants gathered in an uprising or refused to pay the tax?"

Archibald shook his head irritably. "No, no, no."

"What then? Are dukes and earls plotting against you? Is Har Halas? Or Pol Shyne?"

"They are loyal to a man. Lazy, but loyal."

"Then why do you wring your hands, exaggerating woes that do not exist . . . and may *never* exist? Why agonize and compromise your health and sanity—in the prime years of your life, when you should be enjoying song and hunt and fame—grinding your teeth on unfounded fears of doom?"

Archibald grumbled low in his throat. Beneath the pasty skin of his lips, his fat teeth formed a wary, cunning smile. "Do you think I do not see through you, Jonas? With one hand you seek to flatter me and with the other play me as a fool—"

"Lord Governor, no!" Jonas pled, lowering his head.

Archibald continued, "Then do not laud the illusion of a stable kingdom while insulting my concerns as its ruler!"

Jonas withdrew two steps, wordless and submissive. They paced together in silence. Archibald nervously fingered his thin gray beard in a manner bordering on obsessive. He was a solid figure, or at least once had been. He carried a scepter but wore no crown. Archibald was not a king, and he knew it. His hands often trembled with this knowledge, and he ever felt that someone, somewhere, was measuring his royal deficit. Even now, the governor studied the chamber walls, the polished floor, with distracted, weary effort.

"The land is sickening, Jonas. Crops are yielding barely half of what they did a generation ago. Rains are flooding Vineland and forsaking the Midlands. The mountains quake in the north. My armies are thin, my Champions are scattered. The League of Assassins grows in power. And those are but trivial concerns. Across the bay but a few miles, the witch in her tower watches me. Her shadow grows, and I am powerless to stop it. Worse still, my people's children are crossing over to join her dark ways. Hundreds, perhaps thousands. My spies cannot penetrate her sorcery, but every day, we see them. The spies give reports of phantoms wandering every village, of dark ships at night, full of these youths, slipping secretly toward the Isle of Apaté. They roam as gangs, plundering at night, vanishing with more than they came with. I have stacks of letters from priests, parents, dukes, and duchesses, describing them, dreading them. Blaming me. I saw one once, when I rode the hunt. A young lass, maybe fifteen years old. Her eyes were utterly vacant, as if she had lost her soul, her very memory."

Beefy and broad-shouldered, his blue eyes could still pierce through the artifice of worry he wore as readily as a stage actor wears a mask.

He paused, ashamed. "I fear them too."

"Troublesome, to be sure," Jonas said sympathetically, stepping closer once more. "But if I may be so bold, haven't children always been difficult? I was, I know. You probably were also, great lord. In fact, tell me a time when parents haven't worried and prayed over their children. Yes? But what happens, every time? They grow up. They learn and change, and tomorrow resolves the troubles of today. Always, tomorrow."

Though he was not of royal blood, Archibald could summon a commanding presence when needed, as he did now, gazing coldly at Jonas. His blue eyes turned a pale shade of winter. "Foolish man, your tongue is made of witchcraft. These children aren't merely stubborn or troubled or even rebellious. They are *lost*. They have no connection to the land of their birth, their families, or the goodwill of the people. Good and evil are alike in their eyes, and the gods are mocked. They are our future . . . our hope for tomorrow. And if our future is lost, how will tomorrow ever dawn?"

Jonas replied with a thin, tight smile. "Heavy matters indeed.

I stand entirely corrected and will act with force. Tomorrow, I shall appoint a delegation to study these criminal activities at once."

"You appointed a delegation," Archibald said wearily, "six months ago."

"Then with my lord's leave, I shall have their report, or create a new commission!" Jonas smacked his fist in his palm. Then, smooth in its suddenness, he angled the conversation away. "But if I may be so bold, my lord, I daresay you *were* a handful as a child, weren't you? Not to overstate the point, but rowdy and raucous? Always leading the charge, eh?"

Archibald continued to pace. At first, he would not relent. But a gentle twinge of memory wet his lips. Apparently, it tasted sweet. Pride filled his voice. "Well, I don't want to boast or anything . . ."

"For shame! Truth is never a boast, my lord."

"True, true enough. The fact is, I was the finest swordsman among my six brothers. And I was the youngest! Have I ever told you of the time I found my father's sword in the livery?"

CHAPTER 23

ELDORAN

On the morning of the fourth day since his guests' departure, Eldoran rose early, as was his way, and laid a new sheet of fresh parchment on a small table in his private study. He lit two candles. The spare, waxy flames burnished the wood with a dull haze of light. Taking quill in hand and inking the tip, he began scratching the paper with his thoughts.

> *Alethes, High Priest of the White Abbey, and*
> *Cassock, Bishop of the Black Abbey*
> *From Your Humble Servant, Father Eldoran the*
> *Gray*
>
> *Troubling news continues to increase across our fair land. For more than a decade now, we have beheld, first, warning signs, then strange happenings. Most recently, truly dark events have begun to unfold.*

We have varied and wavered and argued as to their cause. But I trust your heart (as I hope you trust mine), that within our respective duties, our mission is to safeguard the ways of Aion for the health of this land. As sobering tales continue to reach our gates from every province, I have profound news to convey. Though it may be difficult to conceive, two young brothers from another world beyond the reach of ours entered the Gray Abbey three days ago. They came in response to Call Birds, which, after passing into their world, dropped royal invitations signed with a golden A. I saw these tokens myself, and for many reasons believe the veracity of their tale without question. In such troubled times, I need not tell you the importance of their coming. But I share my thoughts, knowing you will have wisdom and insights by which we can each glean a larger share of truth, to whit:

First, I am surprised that Archibald summoned the courage to send Call Birds. Such an audacious move! I know not how he came by these legendary creatures. I thought them extinct. But I fear treachery within his ranks will undo his will and betray his plans. How can we undergird him and prevent Jonas and his ilk from bringing all to ruin?

Second, my brother Alethes, I know the White Abbey is in the midst of the Days of Awe. As you review the Book of Names, I think we should look for these two young men. They are brothers named Hadyn and Ewan, surname Barlow. Since Yhü Hoder, the first man, was commissioned with divine wisdom to compose the Book as part of his doom, might not he have recorded their names and deeds and place in our history? Such travels between worlds are not entirely unknown to us, are they? Tal Yssen? The great king Artorius? I know the boys' deeds will be invisible to us, but we might still gain reassurance of their purpose if their names are recorded. Please send word immediately regarding this with the trusted brother who bears this message.

Third, my friend Cassock, I implore you to stir the seers and mirlings to greater dreams. We are blind, sickly, and wingless without them. Speaking of wings, you are so good to keep the pigeons in flight, bearing record of their dreams, but we have seen fewer and fewer for many months. Hold fast in your dark sanctuary, friend! The Black Abbey has chosen a severe solitude far in the north. But do not forget why. It is for the good of the land.

Know also that Asandra was invaluable in her time with us. By now she is well on her way to Seabraith. But her presence raised yet another issue: the number of Watchers roaming the land is becoming intolerable, and will soon outstrip the capacity of your few pupils. One recently banished at our abbey had already stirred a nearby village to madness and the slashing of their flesh. This abomination must be addressed! But how? The land is poisoned, and the great rituals of fire, land, and water have been obstructed for generations. Brothers, let us pray our fortunes are revived!

In devotion to Olfadr, EverKing, and His Imperial Prince, Aion, I sign with my own hand,

Eldoran

The father signed with a flourish, then made a second copy exactly like the first. Upon finishing the latter, he rolled both parchments into tight scrolls. He took one of the candles, tipped its flame so that hot wax dripped on the folded edge of each, waited a moment, then pressed his ring deeply into the warm, pooled substance. Rising stiffly, he opened the door, where two light gray brothers waited patiently. He caught them both in mid-yawn, gently roused them. He led them to the courtyard, where horses were saddled and ready, handed each a scroll.

"Let sleep fall away, brothers. Your task is great. Melanor, south. Velusi, north, with haste! The three abbeys must be of one mind if we are to survive the days ahead. Go!"

Iron-shod hooves clattered on the cobblestones as the men mounted and thundered away. Eldoran turned back to the abbey, heavy in his heart. Before he even reached the doors, hooves clicked on the cobblestones once more. Had one of the riders returned?

"What is it, my brother?" he said kindly, turning. "What did you forget?"

A gray robe did not greet him. It was bright yellow. The man's stallion was lathered with sweat as he reined into the courtyard, slumped against its neck, obviously exhausted. The beast heaved so hard in the chill morning air Eldoran feared its heart might explode. Both looked as if they might collapse.

"Isgurd, brother! What—"

"I am an Interpeter of the White Abbey," the man declared,

pushing himself to an upright position. His hair was short and blond, his face was dirty. "I bear urgent news from Alethes."

"Yes, yes. I know your color. What news, man? Speak."

"Alethes bids me give you grave tidings: On the first morn of the Days of Awe, according to our tradition, we entered the Hall of Ages to find our people in the Book of Names, to read the names born on that day, known in advance by the foreknowledge of Yhü Hoder. Such has been our custom for many thousand years."

"Yes, yes, and . . . ?"

The interpreter shifted his weight uncomfortably. He seemed near tears.

"Speak, brother!"

"The Book of Names, Father. The pages. They're *blank*!"

Eldoran's face soured. "What do you mean, blank?"

"They're gone! Years of names are gone. The future is gone. The record of two decades of children and life is gone. Alethes has torn his robe and cancelled the Days of Awe. Even as I bear this news, the White Abbey is fasting and mourning."

Eldoran bowed his head. His mind reeled. "The pages of the Book are . . . are . . ."

The interpreter gulped at a flagon of water, wiped his mouth. Water ran down his chin and neck and robe. It was as if he was hearing his own voice and was shocked all over again, or the voice of Fey Folk, sapping his will and strength. His final answer was void of all emotion.

". . . nameless, Father. The pages of the Book are nameless. Karac Tor is undone."

CHAPTER 24

CRUEDWYN

H is full name and title, it turned out, was Cruedwyn Creed
the Silver Tongue, Bard of the Glorious Clan Fergisfencreed.
The Fourth. Of Slegling-by-the-Sea. Wooer of Women. Master
Verseman. Tormenter of Evil. Bastion of Justice.

He had a lot of names.

Ewan only cared about one thing. "Where did you learn to
fight like that? Did you see that, Hadyn? It was like Jackie Chan
with a sword or something. Could you teach me?"

Cruedwyn basked in the praise like a flower reaching toward
the warm sun. "Teach!" he cried. "Why, young lord, I could make
a master of you in a fortnight — no, a week. Days, really, that's all
I need, skilled as I am. If I put my mind to it, I could doubtless
have you fencing like Corus himself by morning!"

As he continued speaking, a low, warbling sound rose from
somewhere alongside his voice. No one could tell exactly what
it was or where it came from, except that it seemed to surround

Creed himself—a slightly painful, irritating vibration. And it grew.

"You could teach me that fast?" Ewan said hopefully, tilting his head at the sound, as did everyone else, including Cruedwyn. For some reason, the man began hopping about nervously, as if his leather boots were on fire.

"Well, ha ha, of course it might take longer," he stammered, "you being a beginner and all. A fortnight is awfully fast. Could take years, really. Waste your whole youth. You look like a poor study if I do say so, truthfully."

"C'mon, try. Teach me."

The warbling sound began to fade. Cruedwyn listened carefully, wiggling his pinkie finger in his ear. The silence emboldened him. "Right! Done and gladly! Before I'm done with you, you'll parry like any Champion in the realm or my name's not Cruedwyn Creed!"

They all knew his name quite well by now because he said it often. In fact, he had hardly stopped talking or singing since they left the river and headed toward the safety of the trees, which, Sorge made clear, was a foolhardy thought at best—Redthorn could hardly be called safe. It was simply their only choice.

Cruedwyn wasn't finished pantomiming yet.

"I'll have you know, when Pol Shyne, the Duke of Greenland—who's practically family, being my father's brother's cousin's uncle by marriage—needed a guard for his lovely daughter Sáranyása, who did he call?"

"You?" Ewan guessed. He was quite taken with the bard, such a likable fellow.

Cruedwyn made a grand, sweeping gesture, as if to wild applause. Right in the middle of the rolling grass, he bowed low.

"Me, none other, 'tis true. Thirteen swordsmen are known

throughout the land. Duke Shyne insisted on the absolute best in Karac Tor, so he sent couriers on steed, until they found me lying naked in a bed of lilies, offering prayers for the flowers of the field, that they might be blessed with an even sweeter fragrance—"

The warbling sound began again, in earnest. This time, Cruedwyn made no attempt to hide his irritation. He glanced at his waist, seeming embarrassed, impatient.

"Oh, shut up. You know it's the truth! Okay, maybe not naked—"

A little cry escaped his lips then. A nervous sound, like laughter, like one might make if sentenced to be tied up, tickled, and pinched to death.

"I *could* teach him! That's all I said!" Cruedwyn shouted angrily. Shouted to nothing, except perhaps his . . . pants? "Is that so wrong?"

Clearly, he was uncomfortable. In pain even, with his thin, strained smile and watering eyes. Still, the sound grew. Growling, he yanked at his scabbard, talking to it as if it were a person. "Don't you dare! You besotted wedge of cursed metal! You fiend! Traitor!"

The vibration became a knife of pain for everyone. Cruedwyn spun wildly, writhing at the waist. He jerked on the haft with his gloved hand, wisked the blade free. Against the dark, mossy earth, the metal glowed as if heated in a smithy's fire. Where it touched a bed of fallen leaves, it sizzled. The air smelled burnt.

"It was all in fun!" the bard cried. "Mere jest! Aargh! Why am I cursed with your wretched ways! I've never shown you anything but kindness!"

As if in answer, a leaf touching the blade caught fire. Then, silence.

All this took place like a one-act play before the eyes of a rather stunned group of curious onlookers. As one, they all burst into laughter, even Flogg. Everyone except Cruedwyn, whose feelings appeared more than a little hurt.

"Easy, friend," Sorge said at length, patting him on the back. "We'll get you another sword. You are far too great a swordsman to go without one."

"Oh, it'll cool down," the bard said irritably. "Maybe in minutes. Maybe by tonight. The hothead! But I can't bring myself to part with it—traded my own beloved harp for this sword, and what's a bard without a harp? Only to find it was cursed by Loki himself. Can you believe it?"

Flogg made a warding sign against that name. Loki. The Prince of Mischief. A Fey Folk.

They continued south, shadowing the Argo, drawing ever nearer to the northern rim of Redthorn. The woods loomed larger and larger on the edge of the land. Hadyn's knees felt weak to look at them, though he couldn't fathom why. From here at least, dark or no, they just looked like trees. Asandra didn't help.

"It is said even Watchers do not go there," she said.

"A true saying," Sorge observed. "Though I cannot imagine why evil would not be drawn to evil."

"Tell me about Watchers," Hadyn said suddenly, trying to divert himself. With each step, a foul and sullen mood increasingly fell upon the whole group. Watchers hardly seemed the right topic to lighten it. But hey, it was a start. Even Cruedwyn had grown glum. His sword, safely returned to its scabbard, still caused a slight limp as he walked. "So, what are they?"

"Fallen spirits," Sorge answered. "Slaves of the Devourer. When evil reigns, they fly with the Horned Lord, Haurgne, on his wild hunts."

"Long ago," Asandra said softly, "before memory, they were

the eyes of Olfadr, at the making of the world. But Haurgne, the Devourer, ensnared them. Now they are his. Dark, birdlike spirits."

"When a mirling captures them, as Asandra did in a mirror of blessed water, they are bound by the code which binds all the earth together. And in this Law, all waters lead to Hel, which is their prison. That day, Asandra took the frame of water to the river near the abbey, with the Watcher still trapped inside. She laid it in the flowing waters and cracked the glass. This released the Watcher into the river, on which it traveled, bound in liquid, down to the rushing current of the Goldfoam. From Goldfoam, eventually—as all waters must—it passes into Undrwol. There the water shall be purged of its evil. In this way, Watchers are removed from the earth."

"I thought you said they were banished to Hel?"

"Helheim, the kingdom of ice and terror far in the north. In the mountains of Bitterland. It is the the entrance to Undrwol. The living do not enter there."

"Nor should the living enter *there*." Cruedwyn pointed straight ahead. They had arrived. Redthorn sprawled before them, dark and somber. Sorge scouted the area before the last light failed. There was a good campsite outside the forest amongst a few straggling trees, where the land gradually sloped down the embankment toward the Argo. Pleasantly, on the way down, a large bit of soft, flat earth was hemmed in by enormous boulders. There was a makeshift fire pit and old ashes. The place had been used before.

"Good lines of sight," Sorge said, peering below to the water's edge. East was the river. "To the west and north we are hidden by the rocks. We can defend this place if needed."

"Pray not, brother monk. Remember, I am regrettably

swordless." Creed slapped his sheath, not so much to emphasize the point, it seemed, as to insult his weapon. "Even when the blade cools, and wearing gloves, the haft can be unbearable. Sometimes the blade gets so hot it actually deforms. It melts. Or something. I wish it would just rot and fall to pieces. But it always comes back, curse it." He shook his head ruefully. "Strange magic, the Fey."

Ewan said, "What's strange is how you were following us. I mean, I'm glad for once. But I don't know that I should be." He glanced toward Flogg. "I'm not much on that sort of thing."

Cruedwyn turned away with flair. "Take no thought of it, my young friend! A Creed seeks adventure wherever it may be found. Luck and happenstance led me to you. That's all." From his waist, the already warm sword began moaning in protest. The bard snapped. "All right, fine! I'm being hunted. Sort of. It's nobody, really. Just a man named Quillian. I needed help getting out of the Midlands, and quickly. So I thought I might wave you down from the shore for another try. Like a poor, pitiful beggar. There, are you happy?"

Hadyn couldn't tell if Cruedwyn had lashed out at Ewan or the sword. But he wasn't offended on Ewan's behalf. The bard's blond, moppy hair, receding chin, and fast, toothy grin already reminded the oldest Barlow of a puppy, which Hadyn wisely decided was not a good comparison to make at the moment. Nor was it an easy thought to avoid, for whenever Cruedwyn moved, his mail undershirt, tucked safely under a blue vest, tinkled. Like a dog collar. Hadyn had to bite his lip.

"Did you say Quillian?" Sorge swooped into the conversation. "Of the League?"

"You've heard of him, then?"

The monk's eyes narrowed. "You should have told me, Creed. You know it."

"Pish-posh! Let's not dwell on the past, shall we? He thinks he won my sword in a game of Bones, and he didn't. That's that. A simple misunderstanding. Now let's do something useful and plan for tomorrow, eh? You do have a plan, right—besides Redthorn? It's a fool's errand to enter those cursed woods, but we can't camp here forever, either, because apparently I'm not the only one with enemies." He eyed the brothers, mostly with respect. "Boys, let me give you some advice. An enemy is nothing to be ashamed of. Fact is, if you don't have at least one enemy in your life, you're probably doing something wrong."

Deep within Redthorn rose a lone, wolfish howl. Its barren cry, ragged with hunger, triggered a chorus of other howls all over the forest. The voices emanated outward, surrounding the band of six as they made camp, clinging like dew to their tingling skin. Ewan unconsciously edged closer to Hadyn.

Flogg stumped away. "Flogg going to trees for listening. Then come and tell again."

"It's a bit dangerous, but I'm going to risk a fire," Sorge said. "I suspect those four that escaped are too wounded to travel very fast, nor will they want to challenge us again without more aid. Hot food might lift our spirits, and the fire will keep the jackals at bay. We all need our strength. For the woods, tomorrow."

Cruedwyn gasped. "You're going to do it then? Sorge, we would need an army! Before it was over, we'd all be mad. Or dead."

Hadyn didn't like the sound of that, but what he noticed, strangely, was Asandra. She studied Sorge's face, arching one eyebrow almost imperceptibly. Waiting.

"I'll take your counsel over rabbits and onions, happily, Creed. But not one more word on an empty stomach. Build me a fire. Asandra, tend to wounds. I'll be back soon."

He stalked into the night. Asandra's gaze lingered on him with a curious expression, like she was hearing a familiar song, or wishing for a visit from an old friend who will never be seen again.

When she felt Hadyn's eyes resting upon her, her countenence fell.

"Leave me alone," she said.

CHAPTER 25

NIGHT AT REDTHORN

Later, with a cool breeze whispering from the north, the fire crackling warmly, and three rabbits hung on a spit, Sorge called for attention.

"Hadyn, Ewan, listen to me now. You are strangers to our ways, but you have learned some, mostly of the Grays. It is time to learn of the Blacks, they who listen to soil and water, trees and rocks. In Aion's name, wherever evil is committed, they purge. It is a spiritual act, for the construct of their order is predominantly spiritual. Grays are physical. Whites are mental. Among the Blacks, mirlings are second in rank." He turned to Asandra. "I know these woods weigh heavily on you. Do not withhold your grief. Tell us the tale of the darkening of Redthorn."

Asandra lifted her heavy purple cowl so that Hadyn could see her eyes again, brown and warm. He was suprised to see that she did not resent the request. As the embers swirled, dancing in the updraft like fireflies, her face shone.

"Redthorn was once the most beautiful of forests. It is also called *Salieré*, which means Red Rock, though no one can remember why. Here, Aion and Yhü would go hunting together. Aion would ride his great steed and laugh and tell tales of Isgurd. But sometime long ago, lost in mist and sorrow—some say even before the Age of Crowns—a great evil occurred in these woods. An evil so great even the trees themselves were forever defiled. The Argo was darkened, as were oak, ash, and elm. One of the five Great Trees, the Ash of Uisnwch, once put down roots here. It would have died had not Soriah the Gray carried from it a seed, long ago, replanted now in the court of the White Abbey. He saw in a dream and obeyed."

Her voice took on a certain cadence, broken only a little by Flogg's return from surveying the forest perimeter. As the gnome stepped into the circle of firelight, Hadyn shifted his hearing away from Asandra, who quietly continued her tale anyway.

"Quiet bugger," Hadyn said admiringly. "I didn't even hear him coming."

Ewan curled his lips. "Sneaky, I'd say. Why'd he have to go to the woods again? And why does it seem we are attacked after he leaves for a while?"

"Get over it, Ewan. Sorge would know better."

"It happened in Threefork. He went ahead of us—for what? Then Gregor betrayed us. And think about it. If he can listen through the land with his fingers, all weird and stuff, who's to say he can't send signals through the land? Same thing, but reversed, telling them where we are? Maybe that's what happened at the Stone House, with the ravens."

Prodded by the memory, Hadyn poked at the scabs on his

head left from bird peckings. "You're stretching like rubber. He's almost died protecting us each of those times."

He heard how loud he sounded. Or rather, how strangely quiet the camp had grown. Night birds, crickets, the hissing fire. Asandra wasn't talking anymore. She wasn't even looking at him. Sorge and Flogg were whispering. Creed was staring at the flames. Coughing lightly, he started to apologize for not paying better attention. But as the mirling brushed a strand of hair from her eyes, in that gesture, Hadyn realized she had fallen silent on her own. She had returned to a heavy moment. For the first time since meeting her, in the smallness of that gesture, Asandra seemed like a human being. A frail little girl. Not just an angry mirling.

"Have you ever had a feeling that something was wrong?" she said, her voice fragile. She was looking at Sorge, deep in conversation with Flogg, and past him, into the dark night. "You can't prove it. You can't measure it. But you can't shake the feeling."

Hadyn took a deep, slow breath. Her question had the effect of peeling a crusted scab back to fresh, pink skin, as he had nearly done with his scalp just now. A rush of unwilled memory rose like droplets of blood that gather if the scab is pulled too soon. He thought of Mom—how the cancer had claimed her one inch at a time. Slowly at first, so much as to not be noticed. She had always been so *alive*! And then, merely sick. She and Dad said they were fighting it, that they hoped. They believed. They had caught it early, traveled across the country to the best doctors. But every night, as he drifted to sleep, the black hole in Hadyn's stomach would remain. Over a period of weeks and months, what wasn't so apparent in a single day slowly became obvious. Something was wrong. Very wrong.

And then, one day, a day like any other, Dad woke him and Ewan before school and took them downstairs. He would never forget his dad that day, pale and trembling. He said he needed to talk. Things weren't so good. Mom had been taken to the hospital during the night.

The very next day, she died. The single worst day of his life. All their lives.

Above the knot in his throat, Hadyn shaped his thought into words.

"I've had that feeling."

"Well, the people of Aion feel it *every* day. At least those of us who care to notice. Something is not right, and it haunts us. Right now, it bears a name: Nemesia. But there is darkness greater still. Great enough to consume us all. Greater than Redthorn. We feel it. Something terrible is coming."

She paused, gesturing toward the murky, hidden woods as if apologizing. "Redthorn is not truly evil. It is defiled *with* evil, a very different thing. Thorns sprout from every tree, branch, trunk, and root."

"Like a vine?"

"Like a disease. On *every* tree. Poisonous red thorns."

"You cannot walk without being pricked," the monk said, choosing that moment to rejoin the conversation. Asandra almost jumped to hear his voice. "You cannot be pricked without going mad. Jackals now call these woods their home. Worse, when the world grows dark . . ."

He shifted his eyes between the boys. His voice trailed away.

"What?" Ewan whispered.

"In every age, when the world grows dark, and the tides turn toward evil, Haurgne is seen, riding these woods again. On his wild hunt. Though he is torn by a thousand thorns, it does not matter, for he is already mad. Mad with evil and power. And Hel goes with him."

Asandra hurriedly made the sign of the circle.

"Please, my friends!" Cruedwyn exclaimed, emerging from his private reverie. "If the boys had wanted a show, they could've visited the amphitheater in Portaferry, or the Cirque, seen the Revlons dance and sing. Haurgne hasn't been seen for—what—ever? When was the last time? In the reign of Gwylfal? The time of Prophet Iff?" He turned to the boys apologetically. "Midlanders call him Herne, and say that he has antlers like a great, wild stag, cavorting with the Fey Queen on her bed. The Bittermen say he is Kurg, an evil changeling who steals children and drinks blood. For the Highland folk, he is Kr'Nunos. A man . . . no, a beast. No, a spirit! And the abbeys"—he glanced at Sorge—"they will tell you he was once the great Champion of Aion himself." He pulled a knife from his bootstrap and began sharpening it on a piece of soapstone from his satchel. "I say we've got enough problems that *can* be seen without making more up that can't."

"A fool will say anything," Asandra whispered.

"As will a fanatic," the bard replied equably.

Sorge picked up one of the spits, cut a wedge of sizzling flesh to taste. Licked his lips, pleased. He knew better than to argue theology and philosophy on an empty stomach.

"Enough talk. Nemesia is quite real. And evil enough for us all. Let's eat."

A fourth rabbit would have been nice. And more onions. Fried chicken would have been even better. Or a hamburger. *Oh!* The thought of a double Whopper with cheese made Hadyn's mouth water. He wondered how long it had been. It seemed like months.

Still, something about food around a campfire always tasted good. Cold water on a hot summer evening was even better. Unfortunately, their water was warm. Tonight, it didn't matter. Since they were all tired and sore and talked dry, the meal passed swiftly. Afterward, Sorge put out the fire, and each member of the party picked a spot to spread his blanket on the soft earth. Asandra and Sorge, each to themselves, bent low for silent evening prayers. The mirling prayed a warning hedge around them. It would not keep jackals away, but would, at the very least, startle them and wake her. After his devotion, Sorge again offered to keep the first watch. Flogg and Cruedwyn agreed to take later shifts. They worked out their plan. Pillowy clouds blew overhead, swallowing the stars whole then spitting them out again. One by one, each fell asleep.

Except Ewan, who lay awake, quietly playing his tin whistle. Which meant Hadyn lay awake, too. Actually, he didn't mind, at least not for a few minutes. The sound of Ewan's flute was comforting. And strangely stirring.

"That's nice, Ewan, really," he murmured sleepily. "You've been practicing."

Ewan paused. "Not really. You've been with me."

"Well, you've gotten better. It sounds really good."

Ewan was thoughtful. "Ever since coming, I'd say the same."

He kept playing, breathy and soft; between songs, he thought aloud: "Mom would be worried sick if she were still alive, you know? I mean, this isn't like some kid lost on aisle nine at Wal-Mart. This is another world. She'd be freaked." Sympathy flooded his voice. "Poor Dad."

Ewan had a knack for thinking and saying stuff like that. Hadyn, on the other hand, was finished with song and thought and only wanted sleep. Asandra had pressed enough of his buttons for the evening.

Hadyn sighed. "One step at a time Ewan. Before long, we'll be home."

Dreamless, they slept.

CHAPTER 26

DIVIDED

"Gone . . . he's gone."

Full of soft urgency, the phrase soaked slowly into Ewan's thoughts like rain dripping to the ground through the branches of a tree.

"Auginn's eyes! How could we have lost him?"

As red morning's light slowly crept up his face, peeling back sleep, Ewan caught little pieces of conversation volleyed back and forth. Sorge, Asandra, Flogg.

Must just be wandering . . . no, too long . . . by the river? . . . where?

Then lots of shouting. Calling Hadyn's name. Everyone, including Asandra, scurrying up and down the embankment, roaming near the black woods.

"What's going on?" Ewan mumbled, slowly stirring. Beside him, Sorge dropped to all fours, studying the soil around the campsite.

"There are many footprints here. Three. Four. Ewan—no more sleep!"

"Okay, fine."

Ewan turned, saw the blank earth where Hadyn should be, wasn't. Something finally clicked. He bolted upright.

"Where's Hadyn?"

Sorge put his hands on both Ewan's shoulders. "Don't worry. We'll find him."

"How was he *lost*?"

"No one knows. I counted, Cruedwyn counted, before we slept. Flogg was at watch. Now Hadyn's gone."

Throttling a cry of rage, Ewan dove headlong into Flogg's chest, knocking him to the ground. They tumbled. Ewan flailed his arms and fists.

"You overgrown rat! You Judas! What did you do? Sell him out? Like Gregor? Did they pay you, too?"

Sorge and Creudwyn heaved him off, kicking and thrashing.

"Ewan, stop it!" Sorge ordered. "You're acting like a fool."

"Why can't you all see it? Flogg is against us. Ask *him* where Hadyn is. He set us up!"

"Nonsense," Sorge said. "You are afraid and angry, but Flogg is no more a traitor than you. Will you keep your peace if I let you go?"

Ewan fumed. Flogg adjusted his green vest, rubbed his wrinkled snout. In morning's light, his hair and beard looked like fire. Ewan spasmed one more time, tried to lunge, then quieted. As Sorge released him, the tears came. He quickly moved off to one side.

Only one thought mattered. Hadyn had better not be dead. He repeated that again and again. *Better not, better not.* As the other four consulted together in low tones behind him, a grim foreboding settled on him, leaving a trail of bread crumbs for his thoughts to follow. Ewan struggled to ignore the trail, leave it nameless, illusory. It would not play nice. *Those five who attacked us. Four remain. They want us dead.*

He knew what that meant for Hadyn.

"Hold fast," Sorge said, "we have a plan. I know you are scared, but this tale is not yet told. We have clear tracks: three figures, no struggle. Hadyn was dragged to the river, where the tracks end. There are gouge marks in the soft earth, where they must have pulled a boat or raft ashore. I know you fear the worst, but think. If they wanted him dead, we would not be having this conversation, because you would likely be dead too."

"Why three tracks, when four survived the attack with Gregor?"

"Only three entered camp, it appears. During Flogg's watch last night, he heard noises coming from the woods. He left camp to investigate. He saw nothing. When he returned, with the fire out and the moon covered, he failed to notice Hadyn was already gone. I think one of the four made noise in the woods to distract him while the other three snuck in and carried Hadyn away." He lifted his nose, scenting the air. "Hadyn was probably drugged. The air reeks of sorcery."

Ewan peered over the Gray's shoulder at the creature standing like a tree stump, inspecting his satchel. "Treachery more like."

"You misjudge that one to your shame. You are alive *because* of Flogg, most likely."

"They would have stolen you, too, Ewan. You do understand that, don't you?" It was Asandra who spoke, busily cleaning camp and restoring the earth.

Ewan sank to the ground. "Why didn't they take us both? Why not me?"

"With five, they might have tried," said Sorge. "With only four, they couldn't risk too much noise. Or struggle. Creudwyn's sword gave us that gift."

"Cursed blade," Cruedwyn mumbled. But he held the weapon lovingly.

"How are we going to track them?" Ewan asked.

"*We* aren't . . . at least not you and I. We're heading for Stratamore."

Ewan's eyes faded to the gray color of steel. He stood. "I'm going for my brother."

"Lord Ewan, my job is clear. Get you safely to the governor. And that is what I shall do, though Helheim be emptied against me. With my last breath, if needed, I shall deliver you safely. Do you understand? I am responsible for your life."

Ewan felt rooted to the ground, unable to move.

Gently, Sorge tried to encourage. "The plan is good. Flogg and Asandra will track the raiders. They listen to the land better than I. It will speak to them and lead them to Hadyn. Creudwyn will be with them for strength of arms."

"No, I want a better plan."

"The raiders barely have the lead. We don't have time for a better plan."

On cue, swordsman, gnome, and mirling passed by, hurrying toward the river. Their gear hung from their shoulders. Though Flogg did not look at Ewan, he held his head high.

Asandra spoke as she passed by Sorge. "Solstice is in three days. I do not know what the winds say to me, but I feel a warning. Be careful, Elder."

Sorge offered his own warning. "Don't fight the jackals unless you must. It will only draw others. When you are trailed, don't meet their eyes and don't appear to run. Flogg, fire will help if you are outnumbered. You know this."

Though Flogg patted his bag, under his crusty grimace was a look of worry. Creudwyn, for his part, carried no such doom. His eyes sparkled. "Fear not, boy. The sword of Creed is cool and sharp again! We *will* find your brother."

He proudly brandished the metal of his blade, glinting in the sun, then tromped along after the others. Within moments, all three had disappeared down the slope of the land toward the river's edge.

The search for Hadyn had begun.

CHAPTER 27

CROSSING ARGO

E wan, already antsy, grew more irritable by the minute. They needed to *go*. If he could just get in motion, it might feel like he was part of the search for Hadyn. He needed to feel a part.

As Sorge packed their few belongings, he laid out the plan. They would cross the Argo, then head east, he said. Over the river, they would have open fields that bordered the woods. After a short distance, they would be on the shores of the river Hart. From there, they could secure passage on a ship—very likely one heading to Stratamore.

"Sailors give wandering monks free passage," he explained. "It is considered good luck."

Even with so little gear, packing still took nearly half an hour. Then morning prayers. Then a quick scramble down to the river. By then, Ewan could only recognize the barest hint of the three figures receding in the distance, picking their way south over muck and rock. He longed to be there, not here.

"Blood River," Sorge said, wrinkling his nose. The river was wide and deep and foul, stinking of dead fish and bugs. Shriveled, sickly grasses clung to the rocky edge. In the early sun, the waters shone with a crimson hue.

Ewan gagged. "I can't swim that. It looks . . . ill."

"As you would become if you tried. No one swims the Argo. But there is a bridge. Just inside the forest—an old rope bridge. We must be quick."

The shoreline trail soon entered the forest. Just as Asandra had said, the trees began exploding with thorns, like thousands of giant porcupines fanning their quills. Ewan focused straight ahead, tromping over pebbles and thin, stray roots, and the cracked husks of freshwater mussels. The bank was mostly wide enough for speed, but it required intense concentration and footwork to avoid low, stray braches covered with thorns. What Ewan had not comprehended from Asandra's story was how violent and unnatural the woods would seem. The trees of Redthorn were not merely tall, they were rebellious and angry, reeking of loamy, molded earth, and oozing sap like sticky gray pus. Huge roots curled along the top of the soil. The earth crawled with deformed things, bugs and worms. Blind, elongated rodents. Even the leaves were somber, in tones of olive and black. The whole forest was *wrong*, an abomination.

"Keep your eyes level, but speed up," Sorge urged. "Don't look. We're being watched."

Sorge pressed against him from behind, urging him on. Ewan noticed the red eyes, gleaming in the underbrush. He heard soft, hungry snarls.

"Don't meet their eyes. Don't appear to run. The bridge is just ahead."

High in the distance rose a blood-curdling howl. A dozen

more echoed—a chilling cacophony of bloodlust. A cold stream of fear slithered down Ewan's back. Slashes of black and gray began darting more quickly between the trees, barely hidden in shadow. They had bristling fur, wet teeth. Another howl rent the air, much closer. He nearly bolted.

"Steady . . . almost there."

Light sounds of snapping twigs mirrored the path they followed. They were definitely being tracked. Or maybe herded.

Wordless, Sorge pointed forward. The rope bridge was in view. While his description had been technically accurate, what Sorge had failed to mention was that by *old*, he meant ancient and falling apart; just like by *forest*, he meant deadly obstacle course. The ropes looked ratty, ancient. Adam-and-Eve ancient, though, as Ewan sorely reminded himself, this was hardly their world. The footpath along the water's edge led right to the base of the tree to which the bridge was fastened.

"Climb," Sorge said raggedly.

Ewan hesitated. The bridge looked even worse up close than it had at a distance. On the near side, several ropes were attached to a massive oak. Far across, the bridge was lashed to another sprawling tree and sagged deeply in the middle, high above the river, swaying in unseen winds. Wooden slats that had once formed the floor of the crosswalk had long ago rotted away. Only the main framework of ropes seemed secure, with a few tangled crossbracings.

No way.

Ewan glanced from the tree over his shoulder. A half dozen pairs of eyes were coldly fixed on him, no more than forty feet away. Seeing them, he lost a measure of will and could only stare back. They were larger, more primitive, than any wolf he had ever seen, either in his nightmares or on the Discovery Channel.

"Don't think. Just climb. Jackals are cunning. They will wait until more come. When they gather great enough numbers, they will attack."

Suprisingly, Ewan had a thought outside himself. "How in the world will Cruedwyn and Asandra make it all the way down the river chased by those things?"

"The same way we shall make it across this bridge. With courage. Now let's go."

A crude, winding staircase, carved into the trunk of the tree, wrapped around it three times before reaching the bridge above. The steps were gnarled and split, barely wide enough for feet. Sorge began whacking at the thorns that clogged the path. Slowly, he advanced, one step at a time.

The jackals began inching toward them.

"Ewan! Climb or become their next meal. But be careful! If you are pricked, stand still. I will come to you."

With sweat rolling into his eyes, Ewan began to climb. He didn't dare wipe, just blinked away the sting. He could barely breathe. The steps were narrow. Sorge hadn't gotten every thorn. It seemed forever before he reached the small platform at the top.

"I can't do this," he quavered. "We have to wait. Drive them away with fire. Build a raft. Anything but this."

"Too late," Sorge said.

Gray everywhere. Gray streamers in the sky, lacing the sun. Raspy growls beneath, gathered in a knot of gray, among rough, gray-skinned trees. Ahead of him, a monk in gray placing sandaled feet on a very old, weathered rope. Sorge leaned out to test its weight and strength. The full braid was about half as thick as a man's clenched fist. It creaked, but held.

There were two ropes for hand grips (one notably more decayed than the other). And two for their feet, both of which seemed solid. To Ewan, it didn't matter. The rest of the bridge was open to water and air below. It might as well have been a hundred miles to the other side; might as well be a high-wire act over the Grand Canyon.

Sorge drew inward for a moment of silent prayer, then shuffled carefully forward. His black, bald head caught the reflection of sun-dappled leaves. The ropes wobbled, but his feet gripped. Halfway across, he turned.

"Now, Ewan. Come."

Ewan physically *couldn't* move, except to twitch his head. "No way. I can't."

The water passing below sounded velvety and warm. Or was it a cold grave opening beneath him?

"Your world does not lie on that side of the river, Ewan. Your father, your brothers, your home—all await you on this side."

Ewan shook his head more emphatically. *No.*

Sorge edged his way back. When he got close enough, he extended his staff.

"Reach for it, little brother. I can bear your weight."

No.

"Just stretch out your hand."

Slowly, Ewan extended his hand. The staff was too far.

"Come closer."

"No, you come closer. I'm here for you."

Ewan inched forward, looked down; shouldn't have looked down. He thought he might throw up. Glinting light and water and stalking, gray fur lay below. Ready with snapping teeth, deadly jaws. Ready for blood.

Blood River.

He closed his eyes.

"Easy, easy. Keep your head up. Eyes open. Head *up*! Now

grab the rope with your left hand; take my staff with your right. That's it. Good."

The feel of the wood on his fingers felt like hope. He nudged along the bottom cord with his foot, put weight on it . . . slipped.

He cried, "Sorge!" pitching forward, fumbling for the staff.

"Hold!" Sorge shouted back, bracing his feet, as Ewan plunged between the ropes.

And Ewan held.

Desperation fueled his one-handed grip, until it occurred to him to reach for the staff with both hands. In such moments, all kinds of thoughts flash through a person's mind. Dangling above the water, Ewan thought of his dad, sitting at his computer, unable to type, pacing, praying, on the phone with the police. Not having any idea that at this moment, his son hung from a rope bridge above a poisonous river, lost in another world. All because he had crawled through that stupid rock!

The anger focused him. Calmly, he said, "I'm not a great swimmer, Sorge."

"Get ready. One, two—"

He felt a heave upward, closed his eyes.

"Put your feet out," Sorge said. "Now . . . feel the ropes. That's it, catch your wind. Slowly. Now grab here. Ewan, you need to open your eyes."

His whole body felt rubbery, like boiled meat. He wrapped his arms around the ropes, catching himself like a fly in a spider's web. When he finally peeked, the view had changed. Sorge now stood behind him, *between* him and the starting tree.

"You did that on purpose," he said indignantly.

"A happy coincidence, I assure you."

"Sorge, I hate heights. You can't make me do this."

"Just take a step, Ewan. Just one. Your foot won't slip again, I promise."

"*No.*"

Sorge's patience had run out.

"Then we have nothing but time. So answer me a riddle."

"I don't want a stupid riddle! I want to be a million miles away!"

"You aren't a million miles away. You are *here.* And I am done coddling a spoiled young man who won't make up his mind." Sorge collected himself. His expression was stern. "It's a simple riddle, really. With a simple answer. If a person pretends to sleep, can he be awakened? That's it, that's the riddle." He repeated it again, for clarity.

Ewan refused to budge, much less play any stupid riddle games. He wanted solid ground. He wanted to feel safe for once, at home in Missouri. He wanted Hadyn back.

"You must make a choice, little brother. You say you care deeply for your brother. And I believe you. But this moment is far simpler and weightier: What do *you* want? What do you *really* want?"

Ewan narrowed his eyes. Sorge met them.

"If a man pretends to sleep, he *cannot* be wakened," he said. "That is the answer. Simple, eh? A sleeping man can be wakened, for he is truly asleep. But a man who only pretends at sleep — what can you do? Ewan, we all pretend to sleep in some way or another. Likewise, we all must choose the moment of our waking. Face a thing, or do not face a thing, whatever it is. Wake or sleep. Or just sit there and talk. But *I'll* believe you want to go home — that you really want to see Hadyn — when I see you standing on the ground on the other side of this river."

Strapped to the bridge, Ewan felt the sting. He felt ashamed.

"Well, Lord Ewan? Do you want to find your brother or not? Do you want to go home or not?"

Ewan bit his lip until it bled. Tears stung his eyes.

Then, lifting one foot, he stepped.

Forward.

CHAPTER 28

DEATH ON THE RIVER

Hadyn, in a fog of pain, slowly came to realize two things: First, he had been kidnapped by zombies, and second, he was likely going to die on a foul-smelling river in whatever world lay between earth and Planet Oz. He felt like he had taken the Matrixian red pill, but instead of waking free, was now imprisoned even deeper in the nightmare.

On a raft.

It was a crude raft, barely seaworthy by the feel of the rough splinters pricking his skin and the sloshy feel of water underneath him. Almost certainly the Argo, he guessed. It had the same unmistakeable smell.

At first, still groggy from the drink they forced down his throat—a nasty, smoky liquid—he had slept. Upon waking, slack-mouthed and numb, he lay still, attentive to the sounds around him. As the concoction finally wore off enough for him to collect his wits, he realized it wasn't dark—he was blindfolded. And he wasn't paralyzed—his hands were simply bound behind his back.

A delicate lacework of light falling through the trees moved across his face. He felt the web of warmth and brightness. In the stillness of water, wind, and leaves, he sensed the nearness of others on the raft. Intuitively, he knew what had happened.

Stay calm. Breathe.

He thought of Ewan first, followed by a rash of wild fancies. Jump and swim for shore? Wouldn't do any good, not with his hands tied. Nor would it matter to shout, or they would have gagged him. And, since he was alive, they must not want him dead. Yet.

The others were probably searching for him even now. Maybe they were close?

Ewan. Are you all right?

He cleared his throat, feeling timid. These were brutes. Would he be struck for breaking the silence?

"H . . . hello?" He craned his neck like a blind man. The raft bobbed. Water splashed his cheek. "Can someone talk to me? Will someone tell me what is going on?"

Whispers. Silence. Whispers. He felt the weight of eyes staring at him. Then a shadow blotted out the gossamer sun. Something hard, metallic, cuffed him across the forehead. No time for pain. Only swooning darkness.

Yes, he would be struck.

He awoke later—how long?—in a crumpled pile on the same raft, hearing the same watery sounds. His elbow, bent under his body, tingled as the blood returned. Everything was as before, except for deeper shadows and cooler air, smelling of evening. That and a splitting headache. He was getting tired of being pecked, chased, knifed, and whacked. Blood stuck to his cheek, in his hair. He stomach-crunched himself into an upright position. A blinding light shot through his head. He nearly wretched.

That one's gonna leave a mark.

"My eyes hurt," he said softly. "My head hurts. I can't run. Will someone please . . . will you please take off this blindfold?"

More whispering. His captors seemed conflicted by his request. He recognized the first speaker's numb, ashen tone as the voice from the Stone House.

". . . no, Grayday. She would be angry."

"Nemesia said 'healthy and well.' Does that gash on his forehead look healthy? Hider remembers what she said. Don't you Hider? Maybe it needs tending."

Hider answered with a grunt. A sort-of argument followed, grousing and mostly incoherent. In the end, hands clumsily pulled the blindfold from his eyes to hang in a loop around his neck. Hadyn stared into the face of a young man, perhaps seventeen, with deep, storm-colored eyes and a face of pale, sculpted ivory, or at least it seemed like it might be, under all the grime. The boy had no instinct for space, staying within inches of Hadyn's face. Curiously, though he had just argued with the girl, he carried no trace of a grudge in his eyes. He was entirely unbothered by yielding, by anything.

Perched on his haunches, he fixed his eyes on Hadyn. Behind him, sitting cross-legged, was a girl and another boy. They also stared.

Grayday. Hider, he guessed.

The girl looked as if she might be pretty underneath the dirt and unkept hair. She was thin, waifish, ruined, like a puppy who is never fed. Maybe sixteen. Maybe thirteen. Hard to say. There was little shape to her. Her expression was a watery mixture of wide-eyed curiosity and wide-eyed dread, as if she were constantly holding her breath and constantly wondering why. Hider was overweight, with sweaty cheeks and a double-chin. His shoulder and side were wounded, his cloak torn and streaked with dried blood. Leaning to one side, favoring the wound, he winced on occasion, but little more. Based on the gashes Hadyn saw, he should have been wailing. His eyes conveyed minimal recognition of pain.

And then there was another, a young lady roughly Hadyn's age. She was clothed in layers of scarlet and white, embroidered at the neck, clasped with silver. She wore fine sandals. Her hair was long and brown. Hadyn only caught a glimpse of her, knew she was afraid. She lay crumpled like a pile of rags, bound and blindfolded.

Hadyn gathered all this in a few brief moments: the vessel of rough cut logs, lashed with vines, barely afloat; the bare movement of thick brown water grown fetid with moss and slime and small, decaying animals—frogs and rats and such—lining the rocky shore; the ghostly, contorted trees all around, carpeted with red thorns. There was little sky to see above the clutching branches. Little warmth to feel from the hidden, setting sun. The trees looked like some force had exploded from within, spined and angry, vomiting blood.

A rush of adrenaline demanded he flee, cry out, leap. Madness leaned toward him with leafy arms. He felt like joining the other prisoner, the silent girl, crumpled beyond hope. The nearness of the three who watched him, who had stalked and now captured him, caused the air to shrink around him, stole his lucidity. Almost.

Hadyn licked his lips. "There were five of you."

The leader shrugged. "Your swordsman felled Hurter at the river. The other was too wounded and weak. Poverty, my sister. We left her to the beasts of the forest."

Hadyn struggled to keep a flat expression. He did not want to appear weak.

"Do you have names?" he said quickly, to cover himself. "Real names?"

Grayday offered a wan smile, as if at a memory.

"Come on," Hadyn said carefully. "Everyone has a name. You know . . . what your parents named you when you were bor—"

"Names mean nothing. Names are illusions," said the leader. "I am called Shameface. But in truth, I am nameless."

"All right," Hadyn said slowly. "But I don't really feel right calling you that, if that's okay."

"I am nameless also," Grayday joined in. Her eyes were a cradle of wounds, her lips a plastic grin. "My parents named me something else, once. Then they sold me in the village to a fisherman who had lost his wife. He wanted a cook, a maid. He had . . . needs. My parents couldn't feed me, didn't care to try. They already had five mouths besides theirs and mine. I was one too many, they said. A mistake. Said I should go be somebody else's mistake, not theirs."

Solemn, matter-of-fact, she did not lower her eyes or look away. Hadyn did. But Grayday was not finished. "Hider will not tell you, but he was the son of a wealthy merchant. His father called him pig. Said he was slow, stupid. Fat. Worthless. Shameface was the son of a blacksmith in Bitterland. Trained to make pickaxes and hammers for the miners. He was a poor apprentice, made soft hammers that broke on the rock. He brought shame on his father. His father cast shame upon him, as did all the village. The Bittermen take pride in their metal."

"Our old names were lies," Shameface explained in monotone. "Nemesia has given us new names. Truer names. We borrow them only to speak to one another. The new names tell a story, stripped of lying words. And we are glad."

"Birth names lie. Names of pain do not," Hider mumbled.

Grayday brushed a hair from her face. "You see, life is pain. So . . ."

She waited for Hadyn to catch on. When he didn't reply, she finished for him.

". . . only the nameless escape."

Water lapped at the raft, squirting through the gaps between logs. It was a miracle they stayed afloat. Hadyn felt a battle beginning. He felt a funnel spinning inside, sucking conscious thought toward a dark edge. Grayday's tale had left him open-mouthed, speechless.

"You have had pain," Grayday said, cocking her head to one side. It was a statement, more than a question. "Everyone has."

Hadyn managed a thought in the swirling tide. Grayday's eyes climbed into his own, bored through his skull, demanding response. Three words slipped out, knifelike.

"My mother died."

"And the name she gave you?"

"Hadyn."

Shameface picked at the words as if they were pieces of food stuck in his teeth. "Hadyn is a name of memory. Memory linked to hope. To hold on to your name is to always remember the falseness of that hope. You, that boy, the one named Hadyn—*you* are the one who has felt the sorrow of a mother dying. Hope and life and promise. Lies, all of it, for they died with her. Another boy with a different name has not felt these things, because he has not borne your name. But you have, and so you are bound, name and being, to a lie. For hope and memory are also bound to that name."

Hadyn reeled. Hider spoke softly, "Those hopes will never come true."

Grayday still wore her eerie smile. Almost singsong, she said, "The nameless are free."

As if on cue, Shameface pointed to the other prisoner. "This girl. She is rich and unwise. She thinks she is loved. She has no future. But she *believes* she does. What good is such a worthless one, clinging to lies? Clinging to old words and names. We have offered her truth. We offered to let her soul become lost, as ours. She refused."

Shameface scooted near to the girl, who shivered at the awareness of his unfelt hand. The boy looked at Hadyn, then rolled the girl, hands bound, off the raft, into the water.

His face was blank as stone. He didn't even turn to watch her writhe and kick for help.

"No!" Hadyn cried. He tried to leap to his feet, to wrench his hands free. But like the girl in the water, he was bound. As he clumsily gained his legs, Hider slammed a knee into his stomach, doubling him over. He was clubbed again on the back of the head. Collapsing to the raft, darkness closed upon him swiftly. The last sounds he heard were that of the girl, thrashing in the water.

Thrashing. Screaming. Then burbling silence.

And Grayday, almost sounding pleased, said, "Now she is nameless. Now she is free."

CHAPTER 29

THE DEVOURER

"They will enter the bay soon," Nemesia informed the shadowed man before her. He was a towering figure, horned and helmeted with iron, caped in purple the color of spilled wine. He wore shimmering chain mail. A huge sword was slung at his back. In the low light, all else was hidden. If someone from the mainland were to see him, they would salute and call him Baron—Baron von Gulag. (They might wonder, for rumor was that the baron had died.) The name was like a suit of armor, a change of clothes, the latest fashion, for convenience among the world of men. The being inside was far more ancient than his appearance. His power stretched back to the beginning, from whence he earned his true name.

Devourer.

Devourer of life, of peace. The deceiver of old. He was there at the Pillar of Reckoning; there, convincing Yhü Hoder, full of bitterness and shame, to pull the string and release the arrow. He watched as Hoder's poisoned dart struck true, killing the great Aion. The Devourer had laughed; laughed and known terror, when Aion came to life again. He had been there, yes, but was not allowed to remain, banished by the reborn Aion. So came the Horned Lord to the Wild South, long ages past. Kr'Nunos, Lord of the Wild Hunt, Keeper of Hel.

Nemesia knew his true identity and addressed him with something near reverence. "I have sent a swift vessel to retrieve them and bring them here. It won't be long now, Great One."

"Them, you say?" the warlord rumbled. His deep voice rippled as thunder rolling over hills, shifting in and out of phase. It sizzled with dark energy. "Both brothers?"

"No. Only one. The other remains under the monk's protection."

The Devourer slowly clenched his gloved left fist. The sound of the black leather stretching was a warning.

"I am not pleased, witch."

Nemesia held her head high. The emerald in the circlet of silver on her brow gleamed like stars dancing in the sky, falling to earth. Her dark eyes flickered. She stood alone with the huge figure in a room of twilight and rock deep inside the Isle of Apaté. From above, javelins of light rained down through a series of slits in the central chamber of the Tower of Ravens. The air smelled of sandalwood and cloves, of ancient, dusty scrolls and leather-bound books, scattered about, marked with ominous, unreadable characters. The room was suffocating with malice.

"I have foreseen," she said quickly, softly, "that the oldest is the key to finalizing my . . . our plans. He has caused my leaders to question, which has not happened in many moons. When he falls, their spirits shall fail. Never to rise again."

"You underestimate the younger. He, too, has power. I have

felt it. My Watcher sensed it, before he was overcome by the mirling. Your mirling."

Nemesia flicked her eyes nervously, ignoring the last.

"Perhaps. But the boy is unaware."

"He stands on a threshold, passing from boy to man."

Nemesia dared to challenge. She raised her voice slightly. "I have also watched, Great One. I have spilled blood that I might look into his soul. I have seen fear."

Baron von Gulag laughed. It was an uproarious, mocking sound. It shook the tower. "Such a mighty S'Qoth witch, yet such a great fool! Never, never doubt the raw power of a young human heart, especially one trained upon destiny. Wherever they wait, fate finds them and, one day, wakes them. It is the way of Aion."

"No, Great One. Surely . . . he is caged. He thinks his brother is more special than he."

"Silence, woman! He carries a name, a name that has not been stripped from him, as with your others. A name, like oil to fire! Provoke such flames in the boy and they will rage in the man. You are surely a woman, or you would know this."

Nemesia's face flushed. She was made brave in her shame. "Are you so strong already?" she cooed. "Is your shape true? Or will you bellow at the moon tonight, dripping dew from your antlers, forgetting who you are? Are you seated in the north, ready for battle? Are the ships yet built, the Goths yet ready? The Cleavers awakened? The jackals amassed? The Watchers released? You have spent centuries roaming. You have claimed the shape of Baron von Gulag. Clever! But are you ready to face the mustered will of this land?"

The Devourer smiled dangerously. "My time is near."

"Well my time is now," Nemesia hissed. "I prepare the way before you. I weaken the will of both land and people. I prepare the shadows that sap the soul. Ten thousand Watchers will soon pour through the door I shall open for them. Why? Because I have the strength now. And I have brought the oldest Outlander here by my power! Not yours, Baron von Gulag! You forget the ally I am. You forget the power I offer. I am stealing a generation—an entire generation—all for you. Even now, my fleet of ships is bringing thousands to my shores." She approached the heavy drapes of the massive northern window, flinging them open with a thought and a twitch of her hand. Outside, sweeping down the expanse of misty, dark grass, down a long, shallow hill flowing toward the sea, she pointed. There, streaming up the hill toward the tower, line upon line of hundreds of Lost plodded along, shoulders hunched, eyes adrift, faces void of passion or thought or meaning. Like shifting fog, clinging and curling up the grass and rocks, the Nameless came, beckoned to the numbing lure of forgetfulness. And beyond, in the midst of the sea, more ships coming.

"I have amassed an army of the living dead, walking bombs, waiting to explode. They are my own, empty shells waiting to be filled with whatever I tell them to believe. They have no conscience. No power of thought. They are entirely mine. Has such a thing ever been done? Has it, O, Great One?"

As she spoke, the air around Nemesia became gray and blurry. She seemed to grow in both stature and terror. The Devourer, cloaked as a man, watched from the shadows, arms folded, unmoved. When he stepped into the beams of light, his dark eyes narrowed threateningly. He had a scarred face that was fierce and seductively handsome. Almost imperceptibly, he stretched two fingers toward her. The air in the room became a marinade of power.

Nemesia convulsed. Her body shook. Her exalted stature

shrunk as if melting. Within moments she was on her knees, limp, bowed over, gasping for air.

From someplace deep under his armor, deep within his barrel chest, he spoke, his voice pushing outward against the stones of the tower until they strained against their mortar. In truth, he never spoke above a whisper. "You are useful to me, witch. Never forget that. It is all you have."

He lowered his hand. She thirstily gulped for air.

"I have been planning for a thousand years," the Devourer said, "and a thousand more before that. And a thousand more before that. Unfathomable plans. Unstoppable plans. The power is mine. The plans are mine. The kingdom is mine, and all it contains."

Nemesia rubbed her throat. Her face was white. "Yes . . . Great One."

"This is what you will do," he said. "Find out how the Outlanders have come to be here . . . come to my world. Who called them? Archibald the fool? The coward? Why did they answer the call? Discover this. Then either convert them or destroy them. Do this, and perhaps I will allow you to continue to serve me."

He spun round, plum cloth rippling behind him. Then stopped, glancing once more out the window. He did not turn, did not need to see Nemesia glowering, spittle gathered at the corners of her ruby lips. Her smooth skin was flushed with rage.

"One more thing," he said. "Your army is nearly gathered, and it pleases me. It is greater than I thought you capable of. So at Solstice tomorrow, release the darkness. It is time."

227

CHAPTER 30

STAFF OF SHADES

The rest of the day, Nemesia fumed and fought and cursed the Baron. She focused all her strength to spite his last instruction: *Release the darkness.* She found no peace.

But powerful or no, she was, in the end, a witch. Which meant her soul was broken, a city without walls, constantly emptying itself, able to hold nothing in reserve. Hers was a brutal burden, a playland of iron and thorns. Ever, she was in torment. Ever, she was spent.

Sorcery was a grand illusion, lawlessness masquerading as power. Acolytes of the dark arts usually discovered too late the lie: They do not truly *gain* power. They surrender it. Slowly, in hidden ways, they are reduced to mere slaves, servants of darker, more clever spirits, who exert their cunning and will, leaving shells behind, unwitting channels, transmission points, that evil might gain a foothold in the world of men.

So it was that the will of the Devourer now pressed hard on

Nemesia's soul. As the day wore on, she tried in vain to compose a moment of unconflicted silence. But vengeance and blood beckoned, and she could not resist. Thinking she mocked the warlord, in rage and defiance, she slaughtered a cage full of mice, drank their blood until it ran down her neck and belly. She cut herself and called upon gods of fire and darkness. She screamed until foam formed on her lips. She pulled her hair out in chunks. Nothing she did was absent of emotion. Having long ago surrendered the sovereignty of reason to blood and fervor and vile compulsions, she had grown strong in the dark arts, for this was the secret of witchcraft.

Also, long ago, light and joy had passed from her world. She *thirsted*.

As the tormented day turned to a sleepless, tormented night, and then dawn turned to noon, she was, at last, compelled to obey. She had no choice. She was a city without walls.

So she took the Staff of Shades and climbed the steps of her high tower to the crow's nest atop, fluttering with wings. The flagstone floor was warm in the sun. A dozen birds ringed the tower ridge. Their beaded eyes watched her, ruthless and focused.

The weakened blood of Auginn. Watching. She loved the irony.

The Staff of Shades was a prized possession. Long thought lost, it had cost her dearly to find and reclaim it from the abbey, before they cast her out. For what? For pursuing deeper things, deeper truths? Truths beyond mystery, beyond the covering of light. It was, in fact, the beginning of her great plan. The staff was a relic of a different kind of menace, the age of old Hhyss One-Eye and the traitorous Raquel, wife of the great Duke Tiernon. It was Raquel's ancient ring, and a long-buried manuscript of her sorcery, that began twisting Nemesia's mind in her private studies at the Black Abbey twenty years ago.

The staff was carved of willow wood, trimmed in silver, marked with evil runes that seemed to shift shape with the light. It was a weapon of great power. Though it was heavy in her hands, once she took it up, she could not be free of it. It spoke to her in the voice of the baron.

Release me.

The stone atop the tower was carved with odd geometries: concentric circles, star shapes, other markings. Around the edges of the platform, Nemesia kept a garden of snapdragons and flycatchers, and in the center was a socket. Here, she mounted the staff. Today was High Solstice, the peak of summer's light. The perfect day to challenge the sun's supremacy. Light offered color, hope, newness. But darkness was an oily beast, a thief of virtue. The vices of man were committed mostly in darkness: murder, theft, the secret, unrestrained sins of the flesh. So, too, the Nameless were held in the spell of her power most easily when night fell or a storm came and the sky turned foul. Darkness invited evil. Thus the brilliance. To plunge the entire realm into shadow, colorless as winter, empty as a starless sky, would serve a threefold purpose: First, to sap the will of already weakened men; second, to summon what few Watchers were scattered across the land and, in succoring them, gain strength for the release of many more; third and most important, Nemesia foresaw that it would at last complete her grand design. The Nameless would be plunged beyond lethargy into the final throes of irreversible despair.

Release the darkness.

At long last, their faltering souls would yield name and nature—no more resistance. As the hues of a living world fell into gloom, gladly would they surrender the emotional burden of hope (and with hope, responsibility) for the numbing comfort of insignificance. To gaze at the sky and see shadows cover all would seem a fitting conclusion to the pain of their life. Meaninglessness would offer them a way out. No need to struggle anymore, to believe it could be better, much less that the task might fall to them to make it better. In a colored world, they might have been known or loved or cared. In a gray world, they could just give up. Give in. Expect nothing. Feel nothing, except rage. And blame. Blame others and give rage to all. Pour out rage, like water from the fountains of the deep.

A world without hope is not worth keeping. Best to just destroy it and end the pain.

So might the kingdom pass into oblivion.

Though she hated the blind obedience forced upon her by Kr'Nunos, High Solstice had been her plan all along. Indeed, it was the perfect day, the perfect symbol for her many Lost, for all the world to know that she, Nemesia the S'Qoth, had brought them to despair. The very thought unleashed insatiable hunger within.

As the sun crept to its zenith, she raised her arms, began chanting, calling for the winds of the east to mingle with the winds of the south, to rise in fury, to become unnatural. She spoke the name of each rune on the staff, along with its matching word in the old languages of Hel and suffering. She called for Watchers to gather to her, unseen, to add their will and lust and energy to her purpose. It might have been hours or days she stood in that moment, transcending time, but slowly, she sensed the gathering of invisible malevolence around her. The presence of many minds began rattling in her own, growing with intensity, gnawing at her awareness. The air grew thick with gnashing and claws, swirled with the windless flapping of many dark wings. A crescendo of voices threatened to tear Nemesia's thoughts from her conscious control, to shred her personality. She began to tremble and shake violently. As the Watchers slipped through, taking possession of her body, her eyes rolled into the back of her head. She screamed. The sound became a stream of strange words. It sounded like an iron bug scraping its wings, like tearing metal, over and over.

When the last word left her lips, she collapsed. The voices stopped. The air around the staff seemed to draw inward, bending light and time. It compressed a moment, held, then in a rush of air, dilated outward. Darkness spewed from the crown of the staff like a sick man's vomit. Incomprehensible quantities of thick, oily smoke—unlike any fire ever created—spat skyward. The substance was drawn from unseen realms, from the soul of murder, from the world of Watchers and the deep reaches of Undrwol. Passing through the rune-carved wood the way blood leaks from a wound, it stained the sky. It did not block the sun, it ate the sun. It was Unlight.

Then came the winds. Stirring at first from the south, then the east, crosswinds sucked the shadows high into the sky, began blowing them north and west across the island. Heading for the Wyld Sea and the mainland. Over the immediate vicinity of the Tower of Ravens, the sun was already being blotted out.

Nemesia lay unconscious on the ground for many hours as the Staff of Shades worked its ill design. When at last she awoke, a great shadow covered half the Isle.

It had only just begun.

"Now," she whispered, rising. The darkness fanned into the air like ink spilled in clear water. In her inner ear, she still heard the shrieking of many Watchers, urging the darkness on, feeding it with their malice, feeding *on* it. Watchers tore at her thoughts, consuming her mind. They would devour her entirely if they could. The staff was the beginning of their long-awaited doorway back into the world of men. They could sense it. They had been imprisoned for so long. They, too, were rabid with thirst. She knew this, knew the danger.

She also knew they could not devour. Not yet. They were trapped still behind the thin veil of spirit. Bound to the coldest depths of Helheim if they did not pass through the other side soon. Only temporarily, and only if summoned by power and the will of another, could they breach the Law and enter the world of men. And even then, as spirit only. How they longed for flesh! To have it, to eat it. At present, they could only torment. Nemesia heard their laughter, like a knife in her mind. She squeezed her eyes against the pain.

"Now," she whispered again, tensely. Her pale skin had turned blue, and there was no sun to warm it. Fed by Hel, the staff would not stop spewing poison until the farthest reaches of Bitterland were cast into shadow. For days and weeks and months—as long as needed.

She raised her head, heavy and haughty.

"*Now* the world will know. Now the abbey will know, and Cassock, who cast me out. Now the Nameless will know. Now even the great Horned Lord of old will know. I am *Nemesia*. I bring all the world to ruin."

CHAPTER 31

TALES OF OLD

Ewan stood placidly beside Sorge aboard a broad-bellied frigate named *Python's Eye*, loaded with casks of Befjorg mead and crates of prized whitefish, fresh from the cold waters of the north, packed in salt. The vessel slid, wind-borne, down the river Hart, a mercifully clean and mild waterway compared to the wretched Argo. The liquid sun sank low as sweeping columns of clouds boiled upward in the western sky. Mild breezes from the south had been with them all day on their trek across the stretch of grassland separating the two rivers. With each step away from the woods, Ewan's heart had lightened. But it wasn't until they had hailed a boat and boarded that he felt he could truly relax. Still, he wasn't entirely free. To the west, fanged with red, like jackals grinning after a kill, Redthorn grasped leaf and tooth toward them. But its reach fell short. Soon, they passed safely by.

"You know, I think I was even more terrified of the thorns than the jackals. We barely made it."

"Two great evils, and the wisest of the wise do not understand why. It has simply always been so."

"Actually," Ewan said softly, "I was trying to say thank you. In case you didn't notice."

"If you wish to say something, say it. A man should not pretend with words."

Ewan groaned as water foamed beneath the keel. "Are you *always* this way?"

"Yes. No. You're welcome."

They both fell silent. Ewan's thoughts, drifting from Hadyn to his father, felt like bruises. They were tender, but he pressed against them anyway, needing to feel it. Before long, his dad would have no choice but to assume they were kidnapped or dead. Two more lives to grieve. It seemed awful to think about.

Sorge, apparently sensing his need for distraction, said, "Ask me anything, Lord Ewan—three questions, if you will. But then you must rest."

Ewan ran his forefinger along the deck railing, feeling the waxy grain of the wood. "I just want to go home, Sorge." He sighed. "Tell me about the Watchers, I guess."

He was hardly interested, but Sorge's melancholy song caught his ear.

> *Auginn fierce and Runinn wise*
> *Talon, feather, night of cries,*
> *Great black wings, taking flight*
> *No more, no more, to soar the skies*
> *Brother-blood, Olfadr's friends,*
> *No more, no more, be seen again.*

"So begins the tale of faraway Isgurd and its ruler Olfadr, great and ageless. And of the two giant ravens, the brothers Auginn and Runinn, Olfadr's most beloved pets, whose names meant 'War' and 'Glory.'"

As the frigate *Python's Eye* cut south through better waters, Sorge explained, "When the Devourer was exiled from our land, Olfadr confined him to the Wild South and set a guard upon the borders that he might not return. Auginn, the larger of the two brothers, the most loyal and warlike and given to anger, was chosen to guard. He and his many thousand descendants were given many eyes for this task, though Auginn did not need them. He knew the Devourer well, for he had often travelled on hunts with Olfadr's son, Aion. This was in the time before the days of evil, when Aion and Kr'Nunos (whose true name is now forgotten) had been the best of friends. Then came the betrayal at the Pillar, and the exile, when Auginn was released to his vigil. To *watch*. To protect Karac Tor against Kr'Nunos.

"Meanwhile, Kr'Nunos had turned his vigor and craft toward shapeshifting. Eventually, he became so skilled that he lost his original shape and could not get it back. Yet with Auginn and his children ever watchful at the borders, the land remained safe."

Sorge sighed, feeling the wind on his face, like memory. "Kr'Nunos was tireless in his attempts to return. He hated the Watchers and their vigilant patrol against him. Learning of the wild magic of water, he devised a plan. He would hide himself in the belly of the great sea monster, Lavtalion. Promised with rulership of the seas, Lavtalion agreed. Thus, Kr'Nunos passed under the Watchers' eyes, deep under water. Driven by the pain of the Devourer consuming him from within, Lavtalion went as far north as the Hödurspikes, searching for the coldest water possible to ease his pain. He found the underground river Gjoll, the hidden passage to Undrwol, in the deep roots of Helheim, where all the world's waters eventually flow. There, Kr'Nunos betrayed Lavtalion and gutted the beast. From the inside out."

Ewan shriveled his face. "Gross."

"He emerged from Hel, disguised as a prince of men. Unlike the southern Watchers, the northern Watchers had never seen the Devourer, nor did they know his shape. On the high peak of Mount Agasag, he coaxed and seduced them. At his urging, the northern Watchers tricked all their brethren into attending a great council, including Auginn himself. They did not know it was a trap. Kr'Nunos slew Auginn in the presence of his many sons. Thus passed the great lord of birds.

"The sons of Auginn found themselves trapped in a web of sorcery and bloodguilt. They could neither fly nor fight, for the power of the murder had dedicated the mountain for evil, and Kr'Nunos reigned there. He violently disembodied all ten thousand of them, ripping their spirits from their flesh. So it is they remain evil spirits to this day."

Sorge shook his head, as if hearing the cries still. "It is said their cries were heard for weeks thereafter, all the way to Graywall."

Salty breezes caught in Ewan's hair. A sailor timidly approached the two of them, grinning doltishly. The man was ridiculously skinny, even more ridiculously tall.

"Don't mean to interrupt or nothing, but may I fetch ya' anything, Elder? Water or wine or apples?"

"We are quite fine, thanks. Grateful for passage to Stratamore. We require nothing."

"I'd like an apple," Ewan said. His stomach was growling.

"An apple, then! For the Elder's charge. Coming right up!" The man shuffled away quickly and hurried back, eagerly shining the red fruit on his dirty shirt. He handed it to Ewan. Ewan bit into the pale flesh hungrily, wiping the juice from his lips.

"Delicious. Thank you."

The praise emboldened the man. He turned to Sorge confidentially. "The captain's seeing a storm on the morrow's winds. Changin' south to east, which aren't normal. Never a good wind come from the Jawbone, so they say." He coughed, not bothering to cover his mouth. His breath stank of rotten gums. "Pray yer blessing on the ship, Elder — if'n we find favor with ye. And I'll be sure to pitch a coin at the chantry in Stratamore when we land." He ducked low, shuffled off, putting his hands on the first mop he could find and swabbing hard. His shipmates, busily at work themselves, lashing lines and hoisting cargo, drew together near him to whisper and, perchance, console their fears with news of a sacred blessing.

Sorge, scanning the near horizon, said, "The Bay of Champions is usually mild this time of year, but a summer squall is to be feared." He whiffed the air, glancing at the swirls of color in the clouds gathering to the east, then at the crewmen stealing furtive glances his way. Ewan thought he looked perturbed. "They are slaves, full of fear. But something has shifted. A storm *is* coming. It is High Solstice."

Ewan, whose imagination was still trapped on the peak of Mount Agasag, said, "But how can the Watchers escape Hel? Like that one Asandra caught? If they're trapped there, how do they get free?"

Sorge put his back to the railing, propping both elbows behind him. "Worship. Flesh. Since they were seduced by promises of human praise, they gain power from devotion. Holy places cause them pain. Darkness gives them sanctuary. Drawn along unseen channels to dark places, men *feel* them and wrongly perceive their presence as divine. Sacred groves and shrines are built, as we saw in the Shimlings. It is a dark circle. If enough devotion is given, the veil of their curse lifts and a door opens between worlds, allowing passage from Undrwol in spirit. But if blood is added to the worship, the evil is multiplied. The Watchers consume the flesh of the sacrifice. Whatever flesh they consume is the flesh they gain—never again lovely bodies, but maggoted corpses of claw and wing. Once embodied again, they kill without mercy. Nights turn red with slaughter. And generation after generation, the people never learn."

Ewan shuddered. A memory crested like a wave in his thoughts, of a Watcher, covered with eyes and hatred, raging. Watching *him*.

The story was finished. Night had fallen, time for stars and moon, masked in the east by a heavy drape of clouds, just as the sailor had said. Sorge spread his fingers on Ewan's head. "Now I will guess your next question: If Auginn's line are now Watchers, what are the Call Birds that brought you here? Eh? But you are a smart boy. You already know the answer. You tell me."

Ewan thought for a moment. "I'm guessing that other one, Runinn."

"Indeed. Runinn and his four sons became the legendary Call Birds. Together they launched many great souls." He frowned, puzzled. "All five were slain calling the greatest age of Champions Karac Tor has ever known, yet . . . *four* birds came to your world?"

Ewan nodded.

"Hmm. I can only guess what is at play here, based on old legends. Archibald alone will know the answer. I must say, with this one, he has greatly surprised me."

He folded his arms. "Time for sleep. Last question."

"Okay, where'd you get that armband? The one you try to hide."

Sorge looked away, toward the moon, still visible on the dark rim of the eastern clouds.

"I had a friend once. His name was Corus, the second son of a second son of a second son, stretching back many generations—a special thing for the Lotsley clan. He was an extraordinary man, the last, great Champion of our world. He gave it to me."

His face closed tight, a lock without a key. He strode over to the captain.

"Swing round the horn due west before morning," he said. "You'll miss the storm, I sense. I have friends we need to pick up on our way to the city."

Night came. Sleep came. Before drifting off, Ewan played a few simple songs on his flute. Lying on his back, staring at the stars, hearing his own music, it felt like maybe if he closed his eyes, he could wish himself back home. Then came sleep, and many dreams. In one, he heard again the melody that had opened the runestone. Only this time the tune was sung by a bright, haunting female voice—too high to be human. In the dream, he was blindfolded, groping for the voice, spellbound by the quiet power of the song. A song of doors opening, closing. Suddenly, the woman appeared before him. She had silver skin. He asked her name. *Nine*, she answered. In another dream, he was given a treasure chest. When he reached inside, his hands found a long, thin object. It was his tin whistle. When he pulled it out, he realized it was really a sword.

The visions came fast and hard, fading just as swiftly, replaced with a deep, dreamless slumber. Later, Ewan would struggle to recall them at all, though they seemed so vivid at the time. He woke briefly, sweating, then lay back down. A breeze blew.

Crickets chirped. The steady, rolling waters of the Hart carried him and Sorge under a starless sky toward Champion Bay.

CHAPTER 32

THE BOOK OF NAMES

Nestled in the lush valley at the base of the Great Rim, the White Abbey was a towering monument to the brilliance of Yhü Hoder. Not so much the abbey, per se, as the enormous edifice of white marble at its heart. The structure was a huge, perfect cube, one hundred paces square, polished white, blinding as the noon sun. It had no adornments, no spectacular, gilded columns or ornate craftsmanship, yet its simplicity and sheer size commanded awe from everyone who beheld it, with mortarless seams that were finer than human hairs and nearly invisible to the naked eye. It was the Hall of Ages, built single-handedly by Yhü to house the tens of thousands of vellum sheets which comprised the venerated Book of Names.

"And here, planted in front of the Hall nine hundred years ago, is the great tree, the Ash of Uisnwch. Brought by Soriah, may he be blessed in Isgurd forever." Alethes waved his hand absently ahead of their path to a great and beautiful tree, but his voice was flat, his eyes sunken. Having fasted for days, his features were more severe than normal (which was saying something) and his white hair smelled of smoke from the ashes placed upon his head as a daily symbol of his shame and repentance.

Melanor knew to be appropriately sober in the presence of the White Abbey's stern leader. After all, it was the most famous abbey of all, a place of legend—from its location along the Kinsman River (whose headwaters at Avl-on-Bourne were formed of Aion's sacred snow), to Uisnwch, to the great Hall and the long traditions of the Book of Names. Everything about the abbey commanded both reverence and reflection. For his part, Melanor had to squelch a kind of giddy awe. Having come of age in Tinuviel, he was well versed in the legends of the great Soriah and old Aventhorn Keep, from which the city of Tinuviel sprang. But, being initiated into the Order of the Grays at a young age, he had never travelled much. This was his first visit to another abbey, first time to lay eyes upon one of the five Great Trees and the dwarfing splendor of the Hall of Ages. He was nearly overcome.

It had been a hard four days' journey. He had arrived exhausted. His horse was lathered and thirsty. The mood of the abbey did little to restore him. It felt like a tomb, a commune of solemnity. Much more than normal, he felt sure. The only color in sight was that of garb and rank—green, yellow, tan—scribes, interpreters, and master wordsmen. Only one wore pure white, and he walked a pace or two ahead, speaking in monotone. Everywhere around Melanor, learned men and scholars bowed in alleys and lanes and courtyards, in private rooms, alone, together, whimpering, anguished, afraid. Contrite.

Indeed, such a thing had never happened.

"Such a thing!" Alethes moaned, as if reading his thoughts. His voice cracked with emotion. "Has *never* happened. Yet I wear the white. I am the high priest. I am responsible." His face hardened. "May Aion forgive me. I have horribly failed him."

Melanor wished to comfort, but could find no words. Wisely, he kept silent.

They passed under the cool shade of Uisnwch, sprawling and green, in a great circle of grass lined with white stones and yellow lilies. The tree was the only decoration marking the entry to the Hall of Ages, whose south-facing door was positioned due north of the tree. There was some symbolism to this, but Melanor could not recall it.

The door to the Hall was enormous, a solid slab the height of three men and at least four hands thick. A massive iron band formed a locking mechanism, yet when Alethes gave the door the slightest push, it swung easily open, eerily silent.

"You shall have much to report to Father Eldoran," Alethes said. He still held the letter in his hand, which Melanor had faithfully delivered. "I must confess, I am quite curious at the tidings of these youths who have come to our world. You say you saw them yourself."

"Indeed, High Priest. I saw both. They came separately and seemed quite disoriented. They wore strange clothes."

"S'Qoth perhaps? Or children of the south?"

"No. Of that I am certain. It was unlike anything we have ever seen, but not barbarian. They used strange words and phrases."

"Are you sure they were not playing an elaborate game with you?"

"I can only tell you that Father Eldoran is convinced. Even now, they journey to Stratamore. They asked nothing of us and offered no aid. Although they were impertinent at times, they struck me as quite sincere. They only wanted to return to their father and their homeland."

"And where is that, I wonder?" Alethes mused thoughtfully. "Eldoran mentioned Tal Yssen in his letter. And Artorius, the fabled king. Tell me, does he have reason to believe these boys come from the same world? I must confess, that would seem a good omen, indeed. But we cannot afford to traffic in unknown realms, Brother Melanor. The Book of Law does not allow us to experiment with these things. It could be very dangerous."

They passed together down an arched hallway full of pictures chiseled into square frames of stone. The pictures were simple, looping up and over the arch, then back again — row upon row, layer upon layer. Hundreds, perhaps thousands of carvings.

"This is the Mosaic," explained Alethes. "A history of the world, from the First Wind to the Final Fire and the War of Swords. After centuries of study, we don't comprehend even a quarter of it. Yet as you know, all of this, what you see here, the building itself and every scroll inside, was written or built or carved by one man." The high priest held his hands behind his back. He was tall and lean, with a prominent hook nose. His voice was stern with the strictures of faith. "You stand in a living prophecy made of rock, Brother Melanor. One which has never failed to guide and confirm the Way of Aion to man."

As a White to a Gray, his comment implied more. It was both diplomacy and mild spiritual rebuke. Melanor hardly noticed, and frankly, didn't care. He was too busy marvelling at the Mosaic. Some carvings he recognized, or at least could surmise. But there were far too many to see at once. "It seems impossible one man could do all this."

"And yet it is. And was. And will be. And so we believe."

Without warning, they passed beyond the Mosaic, and the

Hall of Ages was flung wide before them. The expanse within was staggeringly unexpected. The high, impenetrable ceiling was lost in shadows, save for the circles cut into the marble, each domed with one of three shades of crystal: glass, topaz, and amethyst. Through these, light drenched the floor like effulgent waterfalls. The gold and purple effect was so startling amongst the white, so ethereal, that at first Melanor did not notice the true wonder of the Hall. Lining the high walls to half their span, and forming row upon row upon row within the cavernous middle, were wooden shelves, bored with holes. And tucked into each one of these holes, a scroll.

Scrolls beyond number. Scrolls beyond imagination.

"Every soul who has ever lived, or will live, in Karac Tor," Alethes breathed. "Every scroll you see is a page in the Book of Names."

To gaze into the room, drenched in soft color, was like looking into the heart of a night sky full of stars. A kiss of light from above caught on the lip of each coiled sheaf as it barely protruded past its shelf. Millions of twinkles. The ordering of history. Blue. Yellow. White. Each light a life. Alethes allowed Melanor space to linger for several moments before aiming toward the far corner of the hall.

"These rows are decades, centuries, millennia. Advancing through time."

And so they, too, advanced past row after row lined with tall ladders on wheels, and green-robed scribes milling about, carefully tending to the parchments, the oil on the wood, the shine on the floors. He had expected the air to smell musty and old. It did not. Even at a brisk pace, it took a while to get wherever Alethes was going. Melanor felt himself getting sticky with time — the strange nearness of forgotten epochs and sprawling history. Having dared to enter such holy space, he had become a mere gnat before a great fire, transfixed in wonder, worthy only of being consumed. Even the sound of his feet on the floor seemed noisily rude to his ears.

"Here," Alethes said at last. "This is where *we* are in time. Way over there is where time began. And here," he moved back two steps, "is where we were two weeks ago, at the beginning of the Days of Awe. All of these . . . are blank." He swept his hand forward. "And not just these, but the last twenty years. It was not so last year, at the Days of Awe. Or the year before. Or ever."

Melanor studied. His eyes moved forward across time, could not help but notice that only a few rows of scrolls were left before the wall terminated at the near corner. Bare marble lay between the shelves and that corner—the only spot he had seen in the entire Hall not entirely covered with scrolls. Instead, it was overlaid with a flat sheet of pure gold.

"What's that?" he said.

"Who can know until it comes?" Alethes said enigmatically. "The end of the world? Of time? A new and glorious age? Or does the gold represent an age of fire? Karac Tor rising or falling? We don't know. But if it is the War of Swords, as many of our wisest scholars suspect, then you can see with your own eyes, we are near to the Ninth Coming. Aion, soon, shall return for the final time."

Melanor swallowed. "Where might the Outlanders be, if they were recorded here?"

"Eldoran mentioned that—a puzzling thought. Obviously, having just read your letter, I have not had much time to consider the likelihood. The fact is, we would have no way of knowing how to align their birth seasons with our way of keeping time. It is *possible* they are in our records from thirteen and fifteen years ago, but that would require much more research from our scribes than you will have time for during your stay."

"What if we were to use the date of their arrival into this world? A few days ago."

"Perhaps you haven't heard," Alethes said rather testily. "The pages of the Book are *blank*."

Immediately, Melanor recognized his mistake. Of course. He felt foolish. The boys' arrival would fall into that period of time.

Standing in a pool of amethyst light, the high priest nearly glowed. His cheekbones, made sharp and black, gave his face the look of a skull. His voice droned. It echoed in the Hall. "As I see it there are three possibilities. First and most likely, the hidden letters are the result of some sort of witchery coming from the Isle of Apaté. May that sorceress be cursed to Hel! If this is so, we should truly be afraid, for then her power is far greater than we ever thought. Nothing has ever breached these walls—neither man nor magic. Second, as stewards of the Book of Names, the White Abbey has in some way failed to maintain the standard of the Book of Law, and fallen short of the worthiness required to behold this gift any longer. If so, perhaps through our fasting vigil and repentance we might once again be found worthy. Third, some other mystery is at work, which we have never encountered, because we have never reached this point in time. This is, of course, entirely possible. But it does not ring true in my mind."

He waited, letting the silence bear down upon his guest. Melanor, instead of feeling doomed, felt a surge of inspiration. He pointed to the sheet of gold laid on white marble. "Or fourth, the end of time *is* coming. A dark age of mounting chaos. And the Book, rather than steering the way and predicting our future, holds the names of this generation in safety. It preserves them in hiddenness, until they are strong enough to throw off their shackles and take their place in the battle at the end of the age."

Alethes slowly narrowed his eyes into hard, iron points. His was the soul of a holy warrior, persuaded of the unique virtues of his order. Melanor's tone smacked of divine inspiration. It did not enjoy his approval. He stepped forward, out of the wash of light.

"Do you enter this hallowed space trailing strange ways behind you, speaking *Orn* and *Lira*? In my presence, no less? If the Blacks and Grays wish to pursue the dangers of the Nine, it is their business. We have prophecy in rock, we need no more. Only the way of the Law. Tell Eldoran what I said to you. All of it."

Feeling scolded like a puppy, Melanor shrunk away. He had never experienced any of the Gifts of Nine before. He had not presumed to do so now.

"I'm sorry, my lord. Forgive me."

"There is nothing more for you to see here."

They both turned to leave. Yet while Brother Melanor the Gray might have thought himself done with bursts of holy inspiration, the inspiration of *Lira* was not yet done with him. As they passed through the Mosaic again, another epiphany seized him.

"My lord, will you show me where in time we are in the Mosaic?"

Alethes, irritated by now, was uninterested in further conversation. He pointed.

"Somewhere in this range, in these carvings. So we think."

Melanor studied them carefully for several moments. Each picture was a simple scene or symbol. Sun on rock. A burning forest. Many fierce boats on water. A dragon with a sword. Alethes tapped his sandaled foot impatiently, but Melanor ignored him. After some time, when he was near to giving up, one caught his eye. Yes, there. There! He tried not to register surprise, did not move closer and stare, nor reach out his hand. Yet for a moment, the Gray monk felt as if, within the Hall of Ages, a new line might have just been added to the scroll of his own life. A line of simple discovery. The hairs on the back of his neck stood tingling to attention.

The carving was simple: Four boys. Four birds. And a curve of stone in a field.

Carved at the creation of the world by Yhü Hoder. In a realm called Karac Tor.

He smiled, saying nothing, and exited. Low-hanging clouds had begun knotting together like fists in the sky, casting gray upon the valley. More rain. All of Vineland had been inundated for weeks. Villages had flooded. The abbey, positioned on higher ground, felt no less bleak. All the world felt bleak.

Yet Melanor held his head high. He had seen with his own eyes, a carving.

Inexplicably, there was hope.

CHAPTER 33

THE NAMELESS

He had seen the girl rolled into the water, had shouted in horror. He vaguely remembered the blow to his head, had the bloody scab to prove it, along with a trail of dried blood down his cheek. At last, he slept, waking once more to the darkness of the blindfold. It was maddening. Worse still was the memory of the girl's body sinking slowly beneath the surface, her voiceless thrashing. The watery silence. He remembered wishing for release, to vomit; couldn't. Instead, he cried softly. He didn't care what the other three thought. The sickness in his stomach grew worse. He had never before witnessed something so brutal, so cold blooded.

He was going to die; he knew it.

Not too long after, as he passed in and out of consciousness, he felt the current of the river briefly speed up, become more choppy. The flimsy raft threatened to capsize. In the near distance, he heard other, urgent voices. Many voices. Then the raft bumped into something, bobbing in the water on large waves. The air smelled briny and open. Over the sounds of gulls, Grayday and Shameface discussed matters with other voices positioned higher above. It seemed obvious they had been approached by a larger vessel. From the tone of conversation, it was equally obvious that this was one of Nemesia's vessels.

Hadyn was hauled to his feet. A thick rope was tied around his waist. Blindfolded, bound, he whispered, "What are you doing to me?"

"Teaching you despair."

He was hoisted onto the larger ship. Shoved here, there, down a ladder, tripping over ropes and rigging. He heard the rusty hinges of a door creak open. He was roughly shoved . . . down. No ladder. No steps. Free-fall. He landed with a crunch on his shoulder and side. Air exploded from his lungs. He groaned. He thought of his mom, thought of slipping into darkness. Thought of the beauty of light and the green of trees.

I'm never going to college. Never driving or getting married.

Pain greater than his need for air seized him.

In the belly of a ship, Hadyn could do nothing but cry.

When he woke, Hadyn decided it was time to sort things out. He knew he was trapped in the belly of a boat. He knew that others were watching. He heard their whispers, curious and surprised.

"Hello?" he said. His tears were dry. "Am I alone?"

More whispering. He struggled against the ropes on his hands, but they were too tight. The effort burned his skin. He tried pressing his cheek flat against the wood to snag his blindfold. It did little but scrape the wound on his forehead, freshly split from the fall. Blood leaked down his temple, his neck.

"Is anyone else here with me? I hear you talking about me."

"We can hear you," a young woman answered blandly. In the warm darkness, Hadyn could not judge whether she was annoyed or merely weary. Or just another one of *them*.

Added another: "Seventy-two . . . now seventy-three."

"Is that how many of us there are?" Hadyn asked. "Someone tell me your name. I'm Hadyn. Where are we going?"

"The Isle of Apaté. To Nemesia, who calls us."

Hadyn scoffed. "Do I look like Nemesia called for me and I willingly came? I am bound and blindfolded. Are you?"

A long silence followed. Presently, gentle hands began unknotting his blindfold. The fabric fell to the floor. Except for a few thin bands of dusty light leaking down through loose slats and high portholes on either side, the hold of the ship was quite dark. The tattered, downcast faces of many nameless took form — the brush of light on eyes and cheekbones, huddled bodies. Most were curled up on the floor, not bothering to move or peek at him. A few stood. No one else was bound.

"What are you doing here, so special?" demanded one young man whose head was shaved. "You aren't fooling anyone. We know you aren't one of us."

Another Hadyn could not see added, "We go to a place for losers and lost. Are you one of us?"

Bodies closed in threateningly. From within the crowd, a girl intervened, the one who had first spoken.

"Let him be. Look at him. He looks as lost as any of us."

Pushing against the others, she stepped forward into a meager swath of light. She had a normal girl shape, a little full, not at all heavy, blonde hair, with timid doe eyes and a sweet half-smile. She still had spirit.

"Back!" she demanded. "Let him breathe."

Feet scuffled. Voices grumbled. Most returned to uncaring slumber. To them, Hadyn was simply one more body in an already crowded space.

"To be true, you *don't* look as lost as the rest of us," she whispered, kneeling beside him. She began daubing at his wound with a wet rag. "I am Kyra, from Portaferry."

"Is that your real name?"

"As real as any name can be. It is the name of my birth."

It was a glimmer of hope. Hadyn seized it. "My mother dreamed my name when she was pregnant with me. My dad wanted to call me Ransom. I don't know why. But one night, Mom dreamed Hadyn. They both knew it was right. It was like a gift. She always said I was a gift." He looked away. "That's what my name means."

"I don't know what Kyra means. I just know I don't like it. I never have."

"Why? It's very pretty."

"*That* is why. I am not nearly so pretty as my name."

Hadyn was taken aback, quickly realized he needed to be careful. He did not want to risk offending whatever new friend or ally he had just gained. Kyra had smooth skin and bright eyes flecked with mischief and not yet lost to Nemesia. Like the others, she was dirty and worn, but most anyone seeing her would have thought her attractive. Not beautiful but cute. And feminine, with a girlish, fluttering voice.

"I don't much like being a girl," she said, as if reading his thoughts. "Always guessing what other people think about me. I grew up watching the Revlon Cirque in Portaferry. Now those are women! So beautiful and graceful, with those huge feathers in their long, twirling hair."

"I'm sorry. I don't know what that is."

"The Cirque? Are you even from here? You talk funny."

"To be honest, I don't know how to tell you where I'm from."

"Well, *everyone* here loves the Revlon Cirque." Kyra smirked. "They are the most marvelous carnivale in all the world. Men desire them. Women envy them. Paintings of them hang in the streets. They are rich and famous." She lowered her eyes. "I do not have their shape, their face, or their fame. I never will. When I told a friend once how I wished I could be a Revlon, she laughed at me."

Hadyn spoke gently. "Not much of a friend, I'd say."

Kyra was unmoved. She pulled out a small round mirror from the folds of her gown. It fit in the palm of her hand. She gazed into it sadly. "That is only because you do not see what I see every day in the looking glass."

"What do you see?" Hadyn asked. His eyes fell on the rag she had used, clotted with his own blood. He began to feel lightheaded.

"Nemesia says there should be no boys or girls. Not male or female. We should all simply be."

"Be what?"

"Human. Free."

The hold began to spin. Kyra's voice had begun to sound as if she were underwater. Hadyn shook his head to clear it. He couldn't tell whether he was woozy from blood loss or if that freaky mind thing was happening again. He struggled to speak.

"That's the . . . dumbest thing . . . I've ever heard. Humans come in two flavors: boy and girl. If you don't start there, nothing else will make sense."

Kyra put her mirror away, pressed the rag against his wound, a little harshly. Hadyn winced. "Are you so sure?" she said. "Hatefully sure? Unbendingly sure? Arrogantly sure? Are you like all the other boys who can only think like boys? You think your strength gives you the right to hurt others. A man thing, right? Well, that is why a woman's thing is to control men. So they won't be hurt." She sighed, softened. "It doesn't matter, really. Girls hardly matter at all."

Hadyn was incredulous. "What?"

"Pretty girls matter, of course. They matter a lot."

"Who *told* you these things? Nemesia? She's a liar. Any girl—"

"Ah, you haven't been listening." Kyra smiled without joy. "Another poor trait of men. I don't want to be just *any* girl." Kyra laid her hand hesitantly on his chest. She searched for him in the dark, for common ground. "Is it so hard to imagine? I just want one thing . . . to be a Revlon."

Hadyn swallowed. "I wanted to stay in Independence. I wanted my mom to live."

"And did she? For all your wishing, did it matter?"

Hadyn swallowed hard. "Things change. Life goes on. We have to be strong."

"Yes, well . . . I guess we all want to be something we are not. That's why we are all lost. That's why we go to Nemesia. To forget what we will never be. I know I don't have to go. I *want* to go. I want to drown on her shores."

Hadyn remembered another drowning girl. Grayday's haunting, almost envious, declaration. *Now she is nameless. Now she is free.*

"If you go, you mustn't forget your name," he whispered, pleading. Somehow, that single thought still made sense to him. "What about the Book? The one everyone is written in. Doesn't

258

that mean something to you? Doesn't that matter?"

"The Book of Names?" Kyra giggled. "Scribblings from thousands of years ago? What does that have to do with me?"

"Maybe everything. Right?"

"Or maybe nothing at all."

Hadyn moaned. The sickening murk was growing worse, coagulating in his thoughts. His tongue felt thick. "I wish you could see."

Kyra faded back into the shadows.

"I see things you don't want to see. Perhaps you are the one who is bound."

No sooner had she gone, no sooner had the darkness loomed, than Hadyn forgot what was so important about their conversation in the first place. All around him, bodies swayed gently to the rocking motion of the boat. He felt queasy in both his stomach and his head. Like a newspaper imprint on silly putty, he felt the shape of his thoughts slowly stretching beyond recognition. Words — those simple containers of thought and meaning — grew mushy right at his point of actually thinking them. Feeling became an indistinguishable gallimaufry. The more he tried to concentrate, to follow a single line of thought through to clarity or resolution, the more his brain hurt.

Focus. Breathe. Think.

But focus hurt. He needed an outlet.

Perhaps . . . you are the one . . . bound.

He could feel his binding — the ropes, the knot around his wrists. Desperate for focus, he directed his thoughts to them. He remembered standing on Gregor's ship, when the sails first lurched, when he grabbed for the rope — something had spoken to him. Another peculiar word. Now, he honed in on the tone and feel, the warp and weft, of the rope at his wrists. He recognized the same, strange sense of something unfolding within. The sound of a name, whispering itself, unwrapping in his mind like a soft piece of candy, teasing him with secrets. It was so hard to focus, hard to hear.

He struggled to form the word. The word of rope. Of knotted rope. He was a namer. An opener. Somehow, this was his gift. He tried to sound it out, as he had in the Stone House. He practiced, trying to pronounce it. It was a foreign word. They probably all were.

Straining under his whispered command, the knot suddenly loosened. He felt the slack. He stopped short. For appearance's sake, he needed to leave the rope intact.

Focus. Breathe. Think.

Even as he struggled, he felt himself slipping deeper and deeper into stupor. It pressed upon him like a weight.

Focus . . .

So hard. In forgetfulness he found a semblance of peace. When he mentally relaxed, didn't fight it, relief flooded in. Each time it became harder and harder to gather the resources to think again. The sensation was unsettling. The farther they traveled, the greater the feeling that he was being transformed. Like the putty, too elastic to recognize, too squished together to distinguish. An obvious contradiction: stretched and squished.

He slumped over, closed his eyes, bit his lip. Used the pain to help him concentrate. He became porous. Language drained away. *Contradiction. Contradiction. Contradiction!* What did that word even mean? *Contra . . . diction. Dictionary. No, constitution-ary. Con . . . train . . . fiction. What was it again?*

"Are Shameface and Grayday your leaders?" he called out suddenly, sounding drunk. "Why do you follow them?"

No one answered. No one cared.

As he struggled against the ropes, his thoughts drifted to Shameface on the river. A seventeen-year-old boy. Shameface had argued with Grayday. Then, uncaring, he had simply yielded the point. No more challenge. No flare of temper. It had seemed so puzzling to Hadyn at the time how Shameface could acquiesce so easily. Now, in his slurry mess of thoughts, he finally understood why. It wasn't innate agreeableness or maturity or some sort of inner peace Shameface possessed. Quite the opposite, Shameface was simply well acquainted with defeat—with losing everything, every pleasantry, every argument, every challenge. He no longer pretended to expect otherwise.

In this, all the Lost had one thing in common. They had never felt important. To anyone.

No one cared about Hadyn either. No one was here to rescue him from becoming one of them. He was unimportant. Like Kyra. Like Shameface. He had been forced to move against his wishes. Forced to watch as his world fell apart. Forced to clear that cursed spot of land on a farm he hated. He wouldn't even be here at all if it hadn't been for how uncaring and selfish his father had been. And his brother! Getting up in the middle of the night. Chasing dreams. How foolish. How selfish. How typical. No one ever thought of what Hadyn wanted or needed.

The thought of his brother—what was his name?—made Hadyn realize he had no brother. Soon wouldn't, at least. He had no hope. He had no future. He was trapped in a surreal world, a dream. Nothing made sense. The fog in his mind—a dark, angry beast—demanded he yield, be silent. Find peace. Surrender.

Your name is Hadyn Barlow. Your name is Hadyn Barlow. . . .

It seemed impossible.

CHAPTER 34

TO STRATAMORE

I f spoken at all by sailors, the word *Argo* was usually reserved for greasy, unshaven men after a bad roll of the bones or in dimly lit taverns around tables covered with candle wax and spilled beer. They were highly colorful and never polite.

In short, the Argo was to be avoided at all cost, even in speech. So when the sailors let up a shout that they were "Argo bound!" it made Sorge laugh. But in truth, the crew was mightily cheered. Next to the crosswinds of a summer squall pinned against the Jawbone, or the mountainous waves and fierce gales famous for battering ships headed north to Yrgavien, nothing could make a crusty old seaman spit and holler worse than the mention of the cursed, red river.

Yet Sorge had spoken truly, and the *Python's Eye* hadn't felt a single drop of rain. When the captain followed his advice, heading due west upon reaching the bay, rather than cutting a more southerly course to Stratamore to attempt a quick landfall on the southern shore—as a bold captain might have preferred—the rising storm split around them, leaving them in safe waters. To aft, strings of lightning lit the tall, black thunderheads, booming with thunder, but the waves ahead remained ever steady and smooth, with a good west wind to boot. So when Sorge informed the captain that his friends were at the mouth of the Argo, no one even blinked. You don't want to risk offending the gods, or their servant, when they've brought good fortune to your ship.

As they rounded the last jut of land to the river's mouth, Ewan could hardly sit still. He nearly made his hands bleed, digging his fingers into his palms. Would Hadyn be there, smiling, waving? He opened one eye, held his breath. On shore stood three figures. Not four. Flogg, Cruedwyn, and Asandra were hunched over their fading campfire. Ewan's heart sank.

Drifting as near as they could, the *Python's Eye* dropped anchor, and the captain sent a dinghy of six men to row ashore and collect the friends of his honored guest.

Ewan was crestfallen. "They didn't get him. Why didn't they get him?"

"Take courage, Lord Ewan. Our plan was to search to this point and then rejoin. I see the chantry riddle at work. 'In division, completion . . .'" He scanned the shoreline again, shading his eyes with his hand. "It looks like they failed. But the oracle still holds, and they no doubt tracked him a good way. We'll soon know more."

"Or maybe not! What if there is no completion? What if he's dead?"

"Faith is risk. That is the only answer I know."

"Yet you believe we'll find him. What if you're wrong?"

"What if we're right? Either way, providence is at work."

Ewan repeated the word aloud. Out of the corner of his eye,

he saw a flash of silver.

"What's that?" he said.

Sorge deeply inhaled the southern wind. Thinking Ewan spoke of providence, the monk turned his attention to the eastern sky. "It means the Ever King still sits in Isgurd. And so there is hope."

But Ewan wasn't even listening anymore. He had seen the shimmering of air, the flit of motion. A dance of liquid hair. To port side, near the rear, flitting away. Aft, the sailors would say. He wandered past men heaving on ropes, toward the back of the ship.

Elysabel was there, in a corner empty except for crates of cargo. As the morning sun rose, she was nearly transparent. Her wings, like a dragonfly's, blurred the air around her. She stared at him impassively.

"Are you following me?" he murmured. She was numinous and beautiful. He wanted to touch her wings, wanted to fly away with her.

"The queen. She bid me watch over you. But you are *never* supposed to see me." She raised her chin slightly. "I do not like it that you see me."

Her eyes were hard, her tone firm. But not entirely. Ewan thought that maybe, just maybe, she was not telling the whole truth. If she did not want to be seen, she could just fly away.

Please, please don't fly away.

He heard Sorge making noise behind him, calling for him. The monk's voice was urgent. Ewan didn't care. He saw Fey.

"Will you stay with me?"

"I will not."

"Can I touch your wings?"

Elysabel fluttered back. Ewan cried out as if stricken.

"I'm sorry! I'm sorry!"

The pixie was not afraid. But she watched him curiously. "You are full of sadness. Why?"

Ewan shook his head. "It doesn't matter. There's nothing you can do."

"I can tell you a secret," Elysabel said. "Your brother lives. That is why you are sad, yes? Even now he sails to the witch's isle, beneath the great cloud."

It took time for the words to sink in. Ewan said, "Cloud?"

She pointed. He followed the line of her delicate finger. Morning continued to brighten, but far to the south a knot of darkness was growing. It didn't look like a cloud.

When he turned back, she was gone. Dazed, he heard Sorge again, calling his name.

"Ewan!"

A sailor bumped him, knocking him free of his reverie. "The monk be callin' ya, lad."

Ewan wandered, finding Sorge. He, too, was staring at the southern horizon. Anxious lines creased his face.

"Where have you been?" he demanded angrily.

Ewan spoke as if still waking. "I saw her again. The Fey. She said Hadyn is alive. He is being taken to Apaté."

"That *is* Apaté," Sorge replied tersely. A half moment later, his head whipped toward the younger Barlow. Ewan didn't move, didn't blink. Slowly, Sorge turned back to the sea. In the distance, darkness rose like a pillar into a brooding, foul sky. Beneath it lay a smallish, nondescript mass of land, floating free, shrouded in mist. He raised his voice impatiently. "Swords and blood, captain! Why aren't my friends aboard yet? Make haste, man! And then, full sail to Stratamore!"

The crew scurried. The captain fumbled an apologetic reply.

The monk had brought them luck. Best not to anger the monk. At the moment, Sorge did not seem to mind taking advantage of their superstition. Ewan heard him whisper, "Why, Nemesia? What are you doing? What evil have you begun?"

CHAPTER 35

HIGH COUNCIL

They were all gathered: that crusty old warhorse, Earl Har Hallas of Brimshane; Sáranyása—whose veil of gossamer blue accentuated more of her porcelain beauty than it hid— daughter of the Duke of Seabraith, surprising all by standing in her father's stead; pale Thorlson, called Hammerföe, Captain of the Guard of the Lady Odessa in faraway Bitterland; cunning Diamedici, from the fallen house of Faielyn, visiting in secret; and Lor'vrkeln, son of the Highland Jute, ever impatient, with blind Mac'Kalok at his side. These, the regents of government, both pretenders and those of noble birth, sat at a long, massive stone table alongside the embroidered, robed figures of the governor's many advisors and ministers. A White, a Gray, and a Black were also present, emissaries of the Holy Abbeys.

This was the High Council of Karac Tor, a throwback to the days when kings ruled and the table was surrounded by noisy barons, earls, and dukes of every province of the land. Now the table was half empty, seating barely twenty, though built for forty. At the far end, Archibald slumped in a chair carved as one piece from the massive trunk of an ancient, felled oak. His scepter lay on the table, untouched. His swollen cheeks were sallow. Beside him, Jonas watched over the proceedings with a calculating eye.

"—and still my crops are dying!" Har Hallas of the Midlands was roaring from the far end, pounding the table. The implacable stone surface (wisely commissioned by a king long ago) disallowed the drama of a wooden table, as Har was used to in his own hall in Brimshane. In Stratamore, the impact of an angry fist was nothing but a dull thump. Still, Har bellowed well enough to make his point. Everything about him was big: voice, face, arms, hair. "I've had no rain since three springs ago. And not much before. It's summer! My corn should be gold and ripening. Instead, my farmers bring baskets of shriveled black husks to my table. Not to mention thieves and jackals raiding the villages around Redthorn. And Fey Folk! Aargh! Prowling and stealing like I haven't seen in fifty years, witching the cows, frightening the townspeople. You may think it small, but they require all my will to confine to Elkwood."

"We have no crops or Fey Folk," Thorlson of Bitterland said in his heavy, gravelly voice. He was albino: shockingly white skin, hair like morning frost, a blush of color in his eyes. The effect on people was usually profound. "But our herds are sickly. Our spring foals have barely gained weight, and many are lame in the leg. This is the ninth season of puny foals. Dozens of gorse were stillborn. Our best sires no longer stud, and the mares give no milk."

Lor'vrkeln rose. "'Water is life'—so the Highlander has ever said since being led to this realm by the will of Aion through our forefather Gil. We scratch our existence out of rock and wilderness and desert. For decades now, we have warned that our deep wells are turning to sand, yet our petitions to this court for aid have gone repeatedly unanswered. Now even young children suffer with thirst as our wells run dry. We cannot grow food. Our prey die before we can hunt, before our hawks can kill." He sat down, defeated, making no attempt to mask his fear and contempt. "A people cannot live without water."

"What about the Vinelanders?" someone asked. "They are being flooded. Can they not help, or share their water?"

"The Vinelanders have no compassion for my people," Lor'vrkeln sneered. He refused to acknowledge Diamedici's presence in the room. The young prince responded only with his own brand of cool detachment. "Anyone who thinks they will offer succor or aid should drink less wine."

"Speaking of children," Har cut in, droll. "Has anyone noticed? We're running out."

A low murmur circled the stone table. A few pounded their fists in approval. He roused them further, saying, "Even if my farmers did have corn, they would have no sons of age to harvest it!"

The representative of the White Abbey stood. He wore the tan color of a master wordsman and spoke with practiced solemnity. "It is time we acknowledge the truth. Our children have turned to rebellion and witchcraft. Sons and daughters are ensnared in the spell of the sorceress across the water." His eyes roamed slowly over the assembled guests. "Everyone at this table knows this. We have all heard the excuses, the superstitious nagging of hags and old women: Ghosts wander the land! Wraiths have stolen their souls!" His voice grew icy. "I tell you, the answer is far more simple: Our youth have forgotten family and duty and obligation. They must be brought back hard to the Way."

"Brother, the *only* way you know is hard," replied the Gray across the table. A few snickered. While the Gray's tone was light, his expression was not.

"Truth *is* hard, brother," countered the White. "It pierces. Not everyone likes to hear the truth. That doesn't make it any less true. This is the Way of the Whites."

"I thought Aion was the way of all?" the Gray answered deftly, quickly adding, "Yet I yield the point, and quite concur the seriousness of the issue. It should be obvious and terrifying to all of us that the unprecedented recent events of the Book of Names have come as a judgment on all the land. They tell the story of our sins, passed down to each generation." He bowed his head politely. "I know the Whites have doubled their devotions in fasting and prayer. Yet . . . something is still missing."

"It is because Aion is *not* the way of all," whispered Sáranyása. Through her veil, she seemed to be staring at Diamedici. "Across Greenland, the Old Groves are being restored. The pagan ways are practiced again. The people dance to dark rhythms when the moon is full. They cut themselves and call down fire. My half-brother has even tracked the shape of Haurgne north past Befjorg and across into Bitterland."

"Our mountains stir," agreed white Thorlson. As he spoke, others shifted uncomfortably. It was difficult to meet the wandering gaze of his strange pink eyes. "Though they have been quiet a thousand years, they shake again. We have seen shapes of the Stag Lord in our dreams."

"As have the Blacks," added the emissary of that abbey, a tall woman with a humorless face. "Our Seers dream of nothing else. Nemesia is a face we see, and know all too well. We see also young men with hollow eye sockets, like skulls, becoming snared in a great spider's web and devoured. We see young women tear off their clothes, stand naked in the sun, full of bruises, and shake their fist at the sky. We see mysterious images of the Hall of Ages cast down in ruins. But ever of late a great shadow, shaped like a stag, lingers in the background of every picture of our dreams."

As she spoke, shadows and dread lay upon the great hall. Murmuring voices rose to fill the void. Jonas watched in careful silence while Archibald, slumped in his chair, scowled.

"Kr'Nunos, Lord of Flies, is to be feared," said Mac'Kalok. He had a scarf tied over his sightless eyes and faced forward, back straight. His scarred hands were laid flat on the table before him. "But that is not our struggle. Not yet. Not today."

"You speak wisdom, great Champion," Diamedici said kindly. Or was it sarcasm? Turning his attention to the master wordsman, he stroked his neatly trimmed beard. The room hushed to hear him. "Master Veritazian, perhaps you do speak the truth. Yet if I may be so bold, the whole truth may require a larger telling. Perhaps our youth have not forgotten their families so much as their families have forgotten *them*."

"Hear, hear!" boomed Har, loud and full of bitterness. "I lost three sons. Three—in five years! But not to some witch. Disease and hardship took them. Now I have no more heirs. You all know this. You know I would have given my soul for any one of them. I raised my boys with a firm hand, and full of love. What has happened to the fathers of this day?" His eyes circled the room slowly. He jabbed his finger at the table. "If we wish to speak a hard truth, let us begin here. If the Devourer returns, then we shall be forced in that day to face the dread of our forefathers. But . . . but! *If our children are taken from us, we are already doomed.* Nothing will be left to devour! If dames and sires value their own flesh and blood and soul so lightly, is it any wonder the children of this land eventually drift away and leave our fair shores?"

"Perhaps it is for this the herds and crops grow weak?" the Black suggested thoughtfully. "Perhaps the whole land is cursed?"

"Gentleman! Ladies!" Jonas stood at last, waving his hands. He seemed careful with the length of his sleeves. He smiled broadly. "Esteemed guests of Lord Archibald, all. Youth have always pushed against their elders, until such time as they become elders themselves. Then they complain about the next generation, just as our parents worried and complained about us. This is the way of the world. It has ever been thus and always shall. Let us deal with crops and gorse herds and necessary things. Water wells and life. Let us not grow frightened with trivial fears."

"You are a snake, Jonas," Thorlson said simply, loudly. "My lady made clear I shall not deal with you, only the good Governor Archibald, whom I wish would be free of your voice."

Jonas's lips thinned. "If you wish to have dealings with this court, then your lady will recognize that I support Archibald in the many heavy burdens he bears. I offer wise counsel. He decides on all things. And in this, he has decided that you shall speak to me."

"And what of the cloud?" asked Diamedici. "What of the darkness in the sky over the Tower of Ravens? What are we to do about that?"

Jonas clicked his tongue. "Does a Vinelander ask these things? Lord Diamedici, firstly, let me sadly remind you that you are an exile present in this court only by the good favor of our Lord Archibald, cousin to your uncle, whom you have greatly grieved. Second, Aion's mercy, young prince! Vineland is a muddy, flooding mess! Have you not seen countless dark clouds and storms? Where, pray tell, do those storm winds begin? To the east, in Isgurd, yes? Then, passing over the Isle of Apaté, to the mainland. Are dark clouds so rare? Truly, tell me?"

"This one is different."

"Different? What does that mean? Are there different kinds of dark clouds?"

"Clouds in the sky. And clouds that shoot from towers."

"Bah! A trick of the light. The governor needs your council, not your poor eyesight."

Flushing red, the prince fell silent. No one but Sáranyása caught his secret glance. Lor'vrkeln, ignoring the Minister of Justice, stood to his feet. "Lord Governor, I call upon you to lead us. The land will not bear compromise any longer while you languish in your den of comfort."

One of the court's gray-haired advisors hobbled to his feet, shaking his finger indignantly. "Mind your place, Bird Man. I will not tolerate such a tone in this court."

Lor'vrkeln did not retreat, motioning toward Diamedici. "You willingly harbor a scoundrel. Yet you take offense at *my* tone?"

Har rose. "If the son of the Jute will not be heard, then what of true and noble blood? Will you hear me, Lyson? Or what of the son of the Duke of Greenland? Why is he not present to speak?"

"Illegitimate son," Jonas countered warily. "You know the delicate diplomacy of this issue, Lord Hallas."

Lor'vrkeln shook with anger. "At least he is a fighter! Do we have so many of these that we can throw them away if their blood is mixed? Through no fault of their own?"

"I agree with you, son of the Jute," Har said. "But for once, Jonas is right. This is not the time or place for that dispute."

"When will it be the right time? Many issues are brought before this court time and time again. They all fall on deaf ears. We talk till we have no more breath. I am ready to be done with talking. I say we act. And were he *allowed* to be here, Win Shyne would say the same. Meanwhile, his father only builds more boats to tax the shipping lanes. Others with a clearer eye call it what it is: piracy."

The air grew still. Lor'vrkeln glanced to Har for support. Har lowered his eyes.

The Highlander clenched his jaw. "None of you may have the courage to say it now. But in the privacy of your own halls, you already have."

"You are as unwise as you are stupid," Sáranyása said tensely. "Little Bird Man, with your clipped wings. With your silly little hawks. How is it that the Jute sends a brute like you as diplomat to a court of your betters?"

"I fall over my tongue at your beauty," Lor'vrkeln said, bowing. "Perhaps you should stay home next time, if the speech of men offends you."

"Challenge my father all you want. The Duke of Greenland has kept the warships of Karac Tor at ready with a *reasonable* tax. For the safety of *all* the land, even your accursed wilderness. And for what? Is he thanked?"

"He doesn't have to be. He is paid."

"My father is twice the man you shall ever be."

"Twice the coward, more like, sending a woman to tend to the difficult work of governing. But that is probably unfair! In truth, does he even know you are gone? Did you come of his schemes or your own, for love? Little girl, you and the exile are fooling no one."

Sáranyása's eyes turned ice blue. "You are fool enough for us all, Bird Man."

"I agree! Guilty! Or at least I would be if I kept silent one day more, turning a blind eye like the governor, while your father rapes the seas for profit."

Sáranyása jerked to her feet. Suddenly, everyone was

standing, shouting. Swords slipped free, pointing from half a dozen men toward half a dozen throats. Har bellowed, Lor'vrkeln raged, Diamedici drew his knife, Thorlson stood coiled like a spring, ready to pounce.

Archibald gripped the armrests of his great oaken seat, stared at each face around the table. Simmering, unmoving, he ground his teeth together. Jonas shifted nervously, whispering to the governor.

"Lord Governor, what have you to say to these things?" Thorlson cried out amidst the clamor. Archibald shoved Jonas away. Guards rushed to the table, silently lowered their spears. The shouting stilled. No one moved or sat or relented. Again, Thorlson said, "Lord Governor. Look at us. The land, your people. We have need of you."

Shifting his weight, knees creaking, Archibald hauled himself to his feet. He took his scepter and flung it across the length of the table.

"You do not need me. You need a king!" he shouted, red-faced, before collapsing back into his chair. "And *I need a Champion*. One with eyes that work. One with a sword that cuts! Not another fool to join those already present round my table. Where is the Champion who will fight for me to vanquish my foes?"

The doors to the great hall swung open. All heads turned. Silhouetted in the doorway stood a monk robed in gray, a swordsman, a mirling, a young boy, and a gnome. With Sorge flanking him, Ewan stepped forward into the columned hall.

"I've come to see the good Lord Governor Archibald," Ewan declared, his voice shaking, trying his best to speak as Sorge had instructed him. He held up the silver tube and scroll. His invitation. "He Called for me. I have come at his request."

CHAPTER 36

A IS FOR AION

Later, the four of them sat in private chambers: Ewan, Sorge, Jonas, Archibald. After a brief explanation and a moment of surprise, the High Council had been dismissed, still hot and bickering, to meet again come morning after everyone's temper had cooled. Jonas had seemed quite flustered, but welcomed the visitors with a tight smile. He ordered a chamberlain, and soon a platter of freshly cut fruit was placed before them.

Archibald seemed thankful for the break. With his forefinger he traced the jewel crusted rim of his goblet of wine, sounding irritated and weary to the bone. "They want me to raise an army. They want to send spies north into the caverns under the Hödurspikes to see why the mountains shake. They want me to command Pol Shyne to launch his ships against the Tower of Ravens. They want me to give more money to the abbeys. They want me to take less advice from the abbeys. They want me to make their corn grow tall, their gorse strong, their water clean and abundant." He sighed. "I am but a man, and all the world is failing. They ask me to save it . . . as long as I save their part first."

Ewan fidgeted, feeling too much urgency to worry about breaking protocol. Or keeping it. Though the outer court had been lavish and huge, and would have been intimidating to a thirteen-year-old American kid, the plainness of the present chamber temporarily allowed him to forget his fear. He did, at least, remember Sorge's main instruction.

"*My lord,*" he said carefully. "You must have something planned. Why else would you send the Call Birds?" He spread his invitation on the table before the governor. The thick vellum glimmered with golden ink. Jonas tried to appear uninterested but leaned closer. He was a creepy old man, with rich robes and a little cap on his balding head. He had a strange birthmark on the back of his wrist. Or was it a tattoo?

Jonas read aloud. His voice sounded weak. "You have been chosen for a life of great purpose. Adventure awaits you in the Hidden Lands. *A.*"

Sorge preemptively took the blame. "Lord Governor, I apologize for our delay. Forgive me if we have taken longer than expected. We were resisted."

He explained the events leading up to their arrival, beginning with the four Call Birds, the stone arch, the abbey, Hadyn's coming, the five who hunted them, and everything leading up to the capture at Redthorn. Both Archibald and Jonas listened without comment, sipping at their drinks. Sorge further explained, as he himself had only recently learned, how Flogg, Asandra, and Cruedwyn had tracked Hadyn's raft downriver, but being greatly slowed by the difficulties of the path and numerous encounters with jackals, were prevented from ever coming near enough to attempt a rescue. They had tried to signal him through the trees, had heard his voice, seen him clubbed on the head and pass out. When they finally reached the bay, they saw him transported to one of Nemesia's vessels, bound for Apaté. That was it.

"Four invitations at the start, you say?" Jonas clucked his tongue. He fixed his filmy gaze on Ewan. "An unlucky number, to be sure. Pray tell, where are the other two boys? Did you lose them, also?"

Sorge answered Archibald, not Jonas. "The youngest two, though called, did not come. This is one of many riddles I do not understand. How can a Called one not answer? Yet in truth, forgive me, but even the two that have come do not truly wish to answer your Call, Lord Governor. Could it be for this reason that the younger ones were not allowed to cross over? I only know that the Grays have sworn to help these boys. Once the older brother is retrieved, it is their wish to return to their home and father. And so, after a long and perilous journey, we humbly request your aid and seek your counsel."

Archibald stared blankly at the burnished rim of his cup. Flame and light played in the jewels. "I'm sorry, what?"

"Call Birds, my lord. We did not even know they flew anymore. This is far beyond our knowledge. You have surprised us all. But the Grays wish to aid you in whatever manner you require. So how will you send the boys home?"

"Why are you asking me?" Archibald snorted. "Yours is the province of the divine and supernatural."

"Or, at the very least, of cheese," Jonas buzzed, dragging out the last word. He and Archibald both chuckled.

Sorge smiled politely. "Perhaps. But *you* Called them."

The governor was clearly annoyed. "Elder Sorge, I have warm regards for Father Eldoran and your fine work together. But I haven't the foggiest notion of what you are talking about."

"The letter is marked with your own hand, my lord. There, see? The letter *A*. For Archibald. Has it been so long since you sent them?"

Jonas hissed lightly at the monk's tone. On cue, the governor leaned forward, quivering with rage. His jowls flopped. "I am not the doddering old fool you and half the kingdom suppose, Gray. Do you think I don't know what I have or have not written? As if all the other demands placed upon me were not enough, now this! I've got to somehow get this boy to another world? Is that what you are telling me? Elder, I have neither seen a Call Bird nor directed one, ever, in my life. Nor have I ever seen this letter you show me now. By Aion's sword, that is not even my hand—"

A strange, distant expression passed over his face, like a cloud passing over a green field. As it did Sorge's. The air grew vivid, even perilous. Ewan didn't know why, but his pulse quickened. Jonas' eyes were wide and white. Archibald stared at the scroll.

"Could it be?" Sorge whispered, finally daring to speak.

"No," Jonas said dismissively. But his lips turned pale and trembled.

"*A* . . . Aion? Could this be the seal of the High Prince himself?"

Governor and monk slowly turned to Ewan. Archibald seemed mostly baffled, but Sorge's eyes were lit with new admiration and more than a little surprise. Ewan, dressed in every manner like a boy of Karac Tor, felt their scrutiny. All he wanted to do was shrivel away. Yet even he could not deny the numinous turn of events.

Clearing his throat, he said, "So this is, like, . . . a big deal."

Sorge spoke, drawing words as from a deep well. "To be sure, little brother. To be sure."

Jonas hurriedly whispered in the governor's ear. As they spoke, Archibald measured his young guest in feet and inches with his eyes. He put up a hand. Jonas retreated. Heavy-lidded and superior, the old man nodded once more, decisively.

"He is too small, too young."

"What?"

"You can't seriously expect us to accept this," Archibald said.

"I assure you the letter is real," Sorge challenged.

"You can assure us of nothing except that this young boy brought a letter, which you *believe* to be real."

"What about my brother?" Ewan said. "What about rescuing him?"

"Oh, don't play on so," Jonas said, smirking. "This has been a grand charade, really, but you go too far. You both should join the carnivale, I think."

Archibald twirled the rings on his fingers. "Your brother is no concern of mine. I have much more important matters of state to attend to. You may have fooled the Grays, but you will not have me chasing my own tail with your fancy schemes. I do not have time for such things. Tell me, did Lady Odessa put you up to this? I dare say you have a bit of a Bitterman's accent, eh?" He turned to Jonas, who nodded in agreement. "Now she's one that would be this clever, don't you think?"

"Oh, absolutely, Lord Governor. Definitely the lady could scheme such chicanery, to goad you into attacking the island. It's appalling, really."

Ewan saw Sorge's fist, held in his lap, clenched. "We were attacked. His brother was kidnapped. Is that part of the charade?"

"I do not deny the threat of the witch," Archibald grumbled. For a brief moment, he sounded apologetic. "She may be a threat.

She may be nothing. But *if* a threat, she is one too great to face. In either case, there is nothing I can do about it right now. Perhaps you can take comfort in this. She has attacked nothing thus far. Until now it has all been tricks and theater." He turned away. "I've made up my mind. I will not risk inciting her to rage simply because some young people are drawn to her in curiosity, drawn by this and that. It is the way of things."

"Lord Governor," Sorge pled. "You know the connection of leader to land, the sacred bond—"

"I do not need your lectures, monk. Good day to you both."

He rose, spun around. His robes flowed behind him. At the door, he paused. "Even if your story were true, even if I wanted to help—I have no knowledge of portals and no knowledge of how to return you. I'm sorry."

Rejoining the other three, they wandered out of the city, climbing the low hills to the west. Sorge needed space to think, Ewan to vent.

Cruedwyn was unusually thoughtful. "So Archibald laid no claim on the letter. And you still hold to your story, Ewan?"

"Of course. What's that supposed to mean?"

"Well, to be honest, I thought perhaps there was some other motive at work here. I've never met a world-traveler before. Good day to you."

Sorge, deep in thought, voiced them aloud. "Jonas had a mark. Did you see it, Ewan? On the underside of his wrist. I've never noticed it before. The antlers of a stag."

"I saw it. Was it a tattoo?"

Sorge seemed to chew on his own words to get the taste of

them as the five companions followed a footpath that wound up rock and scrub brush, eventually finding a small pinnacle of green surrounded by trees. There was something strange and familiar about the place. Ewan decided it reminded him of the woods outside the Gray Abbey when he first arrived.

Cruedwyn, serious but cheerful again, said, "No need to wring our hands, friends. We go to Apaté! A Creed never turns his back on a challenge, never breaks a vow. A Creed never . . ."

From his side came a low, insistent throbbing. He paused, opened his mouth—the sound grew louder—clamped his mouth shut.

"I am willing to help," he said tersely.

The humming stopped. Feeling safe, he jerked the haft.

"I'm about this close to tossing you in the ocean, do you hear me?"

No hum.

"That's right, you *know* it's the truth."

"Perhaps you should send it flowers instead?" Asandra teased. Ewan laughed. Cruedwyn gave them both a fake, honeyed smile.

"Even a blade of your skill is not enough for this challenge, Creed," Sorge said gravely. "First, we have to get there, and we can't just walk. There's not a captain at the docks that will take us." In answer to Ewan's silent question, he shook his head. "Yes, I asked. Our captain made a warding sign at me like I had just cursed his ship. If we combined *all* our funds and Creed sold his sword, we would still not have half the fare for any captain to ferry us. Not a chance."

Flogg, meanwhile, had begun pacing, muttering, hands clasped behind his back. His words were mostly incomprehensible.

"Black—Croaker," he seemed to be saying. "Only way."

Sorge also heard him. "Don't, my friend. You would be ban-ished from your kin. I will not allow it. We'll think of something else. Not the Raven Trail."

Flogg stomped a foot. "Will monk be telling Flogg what Gnomekin thinks and does?"

"What's the Raven Trail?" Ewan asked.

"A rollwol. One of the secret gnome tunnels that run under Karac Tor. The Way of the Black Croaker, gnomes would say. We say Raven Trail. Supposedly, the Raven Trail goes under Champion Bay, connecting the mainland to Apaté. But there's no guarantee we could even find it. It could be a huge waste of time."

Flogg offered a rascally grin. "Seekings and peekings. Find Croaker Way, walk to witch."

Ewan was tired of puzzles and figuring things out. He just wanted to be done. He wanted a good video game, a soft couch, some hot chocolate by the fire. As his gaze drifted to the south, he saw a stream of blue along the base of a green valley. Far away, which was where he wanted to be. Even from his vantage point on the hill, the river looked swollen from rain. The river ran parallel to the sheer face of a high cliff, stretching west as far as the eye could see. An enormous cliff. Ewan had never seen anything so huge. Grand Canyon huge. Below it, the river streamed roughly east, toward three towers. Three white towers, rising over the ridge, in the City of Kings. A black bird flew high in the sky.

Suddenly and vividly, the scene surged within him, like a waking memory of dream. Watching the bird soar overhead, he felt a rush of recognition. He *knew*.

". . . they are prized secrets," Sorge was saying. "It would be unprecedented for Flogg to break faith with his kin in this way."

Flogg grumbled, "Kin forget Uplanders, be forsaking Aion.

Forgot not and forsooken."

"What kind of bird is that in the distance?" Ewan whispered to Creudwyn, pointing.

The bard squinted into the sun. "I dunno. Looks like some sort of raven. They fly over to the mainland from Apaté all the time and feed in this valley. The island is covered with them."

That was enough. Ewan found his faith, took the leap. Providence or no.

"We take the Raven Trail," he declared with finality. The strength of his voice surprised him and everyone else. "I've dreamed this. In my world. *Before* coming here, when I dreamt the song, I saw those towers, that river, that bird, high in the sky. Cruedwyn says the ravens come from Apaté. We take their trail."

He turned to Flogg. His words trailed away, almost before he spoke them.

"I'm not sure what to say, but if you will do this for me, for my brother . . ."

Flogg grew still — not sad, not angry — just still. Like a stone planted deep in the earth. His gnarled, leathery face was proudly unbeautiful.

"Not for manling, Flogg does. For Aion, alone, who Called."

He stumped away.

CHAPTER 37

RAVEN TRAIL

They stood on the rocky shoals of the coast just south of Stratamore. The sun, bleached and globulous in the sky, grew ever darker under the strange shadows of Apaté. The capital city had prospered around one of the most pleasant coves in the kingdom. As it wrapped north and east toward Faielyn, the beaches turned to fine white powder, with water colored like the stones Highlanders gave their wives as gifts. Blue and green, like a peacock's feathers.

This was not one of those shores.

Flogg had brought them here, to a beach comprised mostly of flat sheets of rock and rough mixtures of sand and broken seashells caked with salts from the sea. The roots of a handful of particularly tenacious old trees leaned out over the water, where the back wall of earth and rock had eroded, now scooping dramatically, leaving a patchwork of nooks and crannies, like a rolling fence for the shore. Long ago, some had suggested building the King's City on top of the bald earth here—a more defensible position against seaborne raids. But old King Radygaar, who first chose the site, preferred other locations for blood and campaigns of war. Stratamore was meant for peace and commerce, fine art and illustrious diplomacy. The quiet cove to the north was far more suitable.

"Findings and bindings!"

Flogg was frustrated. They had been searching up and down the most obvious and likely stretch of land for nearly three hours. "Many wonderings for Flogg. Black Croaker less traveled. Ten tens of years."

He wiped sweat from his bulging brow, panting.

"Tell manling riddle," he said to Sorge.

Sorge winked at Ewan. "You might have noticed, we have many riddles."

"No!" Ewan said, feigning surprise.

"How do you comprehend life without riddles? Anyway, gnome children sing this song. Translated, it goes:

Trail of Birds, heed the words,
High tide no. Low tide go."

He poked the ground with his staff. "It's here somewhere."

"I've *never* heard that riddle," said Creed. "In any case, we've looked and looked. If Flogg speaks true, the shoreline has no doubt been reshaped a dozen times or more in the last hundred years. It's time to rethink, my friend. Every windcraft needs an oar."

"And just what do you suggest? This *is* our backup plan."

"I dunno. Creeds are excellent swimmers."

The monk ignored him. "Even if the shoreline has changed,

it is doubtful the caves have. The entrance must be somewhere near."

Asandra was in water up to her knees, furiously splashing about. "The riddle must mean the entrance is hidden when the tide is high, right? We are now at low tide. We've searched up and down this shore. Flogg, are you sure the Raven Trail begins here?"

Flogg bent down, put his fingers to the ground as if sucking the earth into his arms, his brain. His face paled. "Flogg kneeling, feeling, rulvôl deep below rock. Water like blood through veins. But cannot find door. Gnome magic."

"Use some of that magic then, dwarf!" Cruedwyn exclaimed. He laughed. Everything was a joke to Cruedwyn.

"It's not that kind of magic!" Asandra said nearby, pulling wet, clinging hair from her face. Though she worked near Sorge, she never spoke to him, never looked at him. Ewan couldn't help but wonder why was she even here. "Flogg refers to the way they build, which keeps things hidden. Gnomes are highly secretive. It is a prized skill to build something so well that even one of their own cannot find it."

They kept searching. Ewan grew more impatient with each passing moment. Gazing across the narrow channel of water between the mainland and Apaté — some ten miles perhaps? — he could see the island rising gray and stained from the sea. Steep shores and sharp rocks faced Stratamore. Greener fields and shallower hills curved north around the island. On the edge of that transition, between cliffs and fields, stood a tall black tower. Just a speck from here, but Sorge had pointed it out: The Tower of Ravens. A ribbon of black vapor funneled up from the tower, like ash and soot billowing from a volcano. Unlike smoke, though, it grew, rather than dissipating in the wind.

Ewan swallowed. If Hadyn was alive, he was *there*. So near, yet unreachable. To think his brother was being held prisoner, possibly in pain, in danger. So near. It made him sick.

The plan was perhaps too simple: find the Raven Trail, get across and onto the island, then Ewan would pretend to be one of the Lost and hopefully locate Hadyn. After that . . . well, they would just have to wing it. If they ever got there. Ewan's eyes wandered back to the island. This time he noted the ships docked in the small harbor on the northern side, saw what looked like thin trails of people climbing the hill toward the tower.

The Nameless.

And Hadyn, possibly, with them.

"C'mon, guys. We can do this!" he burst out. He started a cadence, like a drill sergeant on a twenty-mile run. "High . . . tide . . . no . . . low . . . tide . . . go! This is your world. Let's figure it out!"

Waves crashed on the rocks, whispered on the sand. Wind tumbled amongst brittle stalks of grass. These were the only sounds. Then Sorge started laughing.

"It's there, in the song!" he exclaimed. "The magic. Listen, Ewan just revealed it."

"I did?"

"Same words, different emphasis: 'High tide—no low tide—Go!'" He paused, thinking. "By the Nines, could it really be that simple? Is it a translation error, Flogg?"

Flogg scowled at the ground, irritated not to know. Ewan was pleased to have figured it out, although he still wasn't sure exactly *what* he had figured out. Cruedwyn was doubtful.

"Is that the best we've got? I mean, it's exactly the opposite of how it sounds at first, right?"

"I guess we'll find out when the tide comes in. Maybe the

water drains into one of these holes or caverns." Sorge's eyes lit up. "That's got to be it."

Cruedwyn, done with critical thinking, slapped his palms together and rubbed.

"By my sword," he exclaimed, "I'll grow gills if I have to! We Creeds tire of too much talk. Tonight, we swim!"

CHAPTER 38

MORE SECRETS

Nemesia's dark hair was a starless night, a raven on her shoulder. Eyes gleaming, she strolled leisurely around her prized captive.

"My honored guest," she cooed. "I've *so* looked forward to this."

Hadyn slumped in a rickety wooden chair, shirt torn, still ragged from the long hike up the slopes of Apaté and the many winding stairs to Nemesia's tower. His cheek and forearms were bruised. Though bound, he was no longer blindfolded; one eye was nearly swollen shut.

"What do you want with me?" he asked. The words scraped in his dry throat like sand. His eyes rolled here and there. Six torches burned in brackets on the walls. The circular chamber leaped with shadows. Outside, all was darkness.

"I want everything you have to give," Nemesia said sweetly, trailing one finger across his face, "which is to say, nothing. You have nothing. You *are* nothing."

"Release me then," Hadyn said. Pain and exhaustion made him reckless. "If I'm of no use, release me."

"Oh, my dear," purred the witch. "It's not what you can give me; it's what I can give you that matters. You will be part of my grand ceremony. As I said, my honored guest."

Hadyn's head felt like lead. He flopped back, laughing hoarsely.

Nemesia swept her hand toward the far wall, on which hung a huge map of all Karac Tor. She grinned, wild and beautiful.

"Behold, the banishment of hope and the darkening of all the land. The collapse of Aion's pitiful kingdom. A fitting retribution for the false promises of a faraway king, don't you think? On the morrow, we shall journey to the Sacred Grove—you and I and all my bombs—and there I shall begin returning the land to the ways of the Old Gods. The stone I throw from Apaté shall ripple out to the farthest corners of the kingdom. And my army of children shall lead them."

With his head slumped to his chest, it was hard to tell if Hadyn had heard or not. In the witch's tower, clarity was constant warfare. But something was funny. He didn't know what, but *something* was funny. He snorted. Nemesia smiled with him, at him, uncertain. Hadyn roared hysterically.

"Sacred grove—is that what you called it?" He laughed until tears rolled down his cheeks. "Sacred like my butt, maybe! Your butt!"—that really set him laughing—"I mean, I may just be a teen and all. But I'm not an idiot. You can't just rename evil, call it good, and have that mean anything." He stared at her cross-eyed, struggling to focus. "I dub thee Scary Bird Lady. Snake Charmer. Katie Couric. They're all just words. Just because you use a word doesn't make it true. You're Nemesia, the witch. The deceiver. You've stolen these kids' minds and promised them a lie. Old Gods is just another way of saying false gods."

Nemesia showed her teeth, a terrible smile frozen to her face. Seductively, her gown flowing in the light breeze, she strolled behind Hadyn, placing her hands on his head, holding it forward. Her fingernails scraped against his skin.

"You want truth? Here's the truth: You will *never* return. You know that, right? That map is the only world you've got now."

Hadyn slurred his words. "You're bluffing."

"Am I? A person only bluffs if she has something to gain."

"Or lose."

He felt daring. Probably going to die anyway, right?

"I've learned a bit since coming here. I know the Book of Names is older than you, older than all your magic. I know Aion is more powerful than *anyone*."

"You know nothing! You probably cannot even spell *Aion*. A few stories told by a failed monk — a failed warrior, a traitor — and you think you know all about my world? Tell me, Hadyn Barlow. Did Sorge tell you his story. *Our* story?"

Hadyn hesitated.

"No, of course not. It might cause you to lose faith, to know the failings of the one trusted to get you home. But since you are *so* interested in truth, allow me. It's a simple tale. Twenty years ago, I believed like you. You see, I come from another place too. Another country, far to the west. I am of mixed blood, the illegitimate daughter of a S'Qoth cult priestess and a wandering Bitterman warrior, a father I've never known. At thirteen, my gift was revealed — a foreign gift in the eyes of my mother's people, terrifying even to me at the time. When she saw my mirling power, my mother beat me, calling me heretic. I fled Quil in search of my father's land, but never made it there, eventually stumbling half-dead across the threshold of the Black Abbey. There, I was trained, nurtured. I was powerful. They found a use for me.

"Sorge travelled all the land in those days, with Corus, the great Champion. Servant and Master. They were both skilled with bow and sword, and deep friends. They took the oath of Bloodkin together, and each bore the Mark of Twine on his arm for the other. When Sorge and I met by chance, our hearts briefly entwined. But Corus also loved me. Sorge was young and temperamental. When he found out, he was wild with jealousy. He feared that Corus, with all his fame, would win my heart. And it was true. In spite of Sorge's many charms and skills, Corus became my lover. Seeing us together one night, Sorge went mad and attacked Corus. They had a mighty duel of blades. In the end, Corus could have killed him, but he withheld. Sorge fled, humiliated. In revenge, he struck a rash bargain with the Fey queen to betray his friend. Pretending repentance and submission, he led Corus into an ambush — one mere mortals could not thwart. Corus, my love, passed into shadow and bondage, and was gone. No one knows where. He is captive still."

Nemesia stared out the window with vacant, hard eyes.

"Do you know what I did, Hadyn Barlow? I cried out to Olfadr; I cried out to Aion. Do you hear me, Outlander? I cried out! Like you might, even now. I called upon my mirling skills to undo Sorge's plans, to find my love. When this did not work, I dared Aion to stop me as I turned to darker arts, older ways. I embraced the paths of my mother's people. I dared Aion to stop me, and feared him, until one day I realized I no longer cared . . . and no longer feared. By then it was *I* who was feared. So the Black Abbey cast me out. I came here, and with every step I cursed Olfadr's name."

She grew quiet. Crooked shadows crawled like vines across

the flagstone floor, the mortared walls. Dark, breathless firelight caught in her eyes.

"Now," she said, and the resolve in her voice made courage drain from Hadyn like blood from a wound. The sorceress's voice had become a silken, husky whisper. "Now, I have drawn you and thousands more like you. All to me. To the darkening which *Aion* has brought upon this land by his neglect, his lies. When you understand this, you will see I do not truly cause the darkness. My darkness merely clarifies the fact of his absence. Let him hide in faraway Isgurd forever. Let him rot in all our minds as myth and legend. The fact is, if ever Aion lived, he abandoned us long ago. Good riddance! I bring liberation. Let the world fall from him, that it might stand on its own."

The more Nemesia spoke, the more her words smudged together in his head. Hadyn tried to form an answer. "He . . . will come again." He heard his own voice as if from the bottom of a hole. For some reason, he believed.

"The famous Ninth Coming, is that it? Oh my dear, if you truly believe that, you are more lost than all my precious little bombs put together."

"My brother."

"You think he will come? Foolish boy, he's probably dead. Don't worry, you will join him soon enough if you like." She laughed. "See, Outlander? It's like I tell all my bombs. Nothing matters."

She strolled away, a flurry of wind and drama, her words echoing over and over.

Nothing matters, nothing matters.

A raven croaked. Hadyn heard his own ragged breath reflect off the stone walls.

What did it matter? Evil was so strong. He was so weak.

Nothing . . . matters. The repetition grew stronger, beating down on his mind, further wearing his defenses. Sitting alone, trapped in her tower, for the first time, Hadyn couldn't remember why he ever believed otherwise.

CHAPTER 39

UNDER THE BAY

The outline of the moon, lost in a haze of low, black vapor, was quite full. High tide had filled the beach with froth and foam. Loud, noisy waves crashed against the rock wall. The five sojourners slopped through water up to their knees, fighting the undertow, searching in the dark for what could not be seen. They were systematically sweeping north, wet and tired and frustrated.

"Listen!" Sorge shouted suddenly. "Do you hear that? It sounds like a roaring."

"I hear it!" Asandra agreed. "Right where Ewan is about to—"

In a blink, Ewan's silhouetted form disappeared into the salty water. Immediately, Sorge dove toward him—toward whatever. Flogg was sucked down next.

The short ride tumbled and twisted down a tube of rock mercifully smoothed by the long ago gnomish builder of the Raven Trail, whoever he was. They spilled in sequence, all five, from the slick channel into thirty feet of open air, plummeting into a deep reservoir fed every night by the tide.

Darkness engulfed them. Ewan could hear the steady roar of the falling water, but saw nothing, not even the shimmer of movement when he waved his hands. It was blacker than any blackness he had ever known. Treading water, he heard Cruedwyn's voice, spluttering.

"A sow giving birth . . . quite a sight, you know? Grunt, squirt, snort, *splash*! At the moment," he paused for effect, "I think I know how they feel. The piglets, I mean, not the sow."

"Flogg," Sorge said, spitting. "Can you see?"

"Aye," the gnome answered. "But flint no good."

"Asandra?"

"Yes."

"Good. Ewan?"

"Here."

Someone was testing the water, swimming tentatively. It was Flogg.

"This way. Come shoreling."

Bumped and bruised but no worse for wear, all five pulled themselves sopping wet onto an embankment of solid rock.

Creudwyn declared, "I just *love* wet chain mail! Is anyone else wet but me?"

Loose rocks scuttled about, followed by Sorge's low voice. Soon, a soft blue glow appeared, blossoming from a round stone in the monk's palm. He whispered to it, coaxing soft light. In total darkness, the effect was fairly dramatic.

"Some stones are better than others," he apologized. "A greater skill could draw out more. But this helps." He looked around. "The water must somehow drain during the day, and fill again at night."

Ewan stared at the rock, pulsing with pale color. It brightened the cave, but not his mood. Though he had tried to pretend otherwise, ever since the Stone House, he had been battling jealousy, and Sorge's rock didn't help. "Sorge . . . Hadyn has a power, right? I don't really know what it is or how he got it. You can do cool stuff with rocks. Asandra catches Watchers. . . ." He let his words trail away, hoping Sorge would catch his unspoken question. When you compete against your brother for everything, you don't like to have to spell it out.

Sorge studied his face in the dimness. "Are you concerned with power, Ewan?"

Ewan felt embarrassed.

Sorge said, "How did you come to this world? Who dreamed the way?"

Ewan reached for the inner folds of his loose-fitting shirt, relieved to feel the Irish whistle's thin metal shaft intact.

"It's not the same. You know it."

"Do I? Is your *flute* magical?"

"Look, Hadyn can't open locks on my world, not with words at least. And I'm wondering why not me?"

"Ah. Well, you should know, I asked the opposite question when you first came. Why you, I thought? When Father Eldoran said you were marked with power, I wasn't sure I believed. Nemesia fears you, and I am glad for that. But Ewan, if power is all you want, it is pointless. The substance of your heart, the choices you make, the one you serve—these are far more powerful than all the world's magic."

"Maybe, but on my world, magic is bad. Here . . . I want it. I don't want to be the only one without."

He glanced around self-consciously. Cruedwyn was busy with a cave crab dangling from his britches, hopping about and cursing.

Flogg and Asandra were still wringing water out of their clothes.

"I do not know your world," Sorge said, bending low, placing the blue stone between their faces. "But *magic* is a word, like *pleasure* or *fun*. Or *pain* or *knowledge*. There can be pleasure in evil, in selfishness, in lust, but surely not all pleasure is evil? And discipline, though painful, can be healing for the soul. Yet knowing this as I age, I still do not enjoy pain. The source from which a thing comes, and the end to which it is put, make it good or bad. Magic is a force larger than the world itself, and it is like that too."

Ewan shrunk, feeling small. "Never mind. That's not what I'm talking about."

"I know what you are talking about. Not just common stuff—grace and kindness and the power of decency—although they are quite magical when they touch you. You ask about strange realms of shadow and light, Fey Folk and Watchers, the nether regions." Sorge smiled. "Even the mysterious possibility of twinkling worlds in the far flung night sky high above our heads."

Ewan lifted his face toward the cavern ceiling. "You really think that's where I came from?"

Sorge followed his gaze. "You mean, up, up, up? Or perhaps from some other place entirely? Like where we are now, below Karac Tor, yet still *within* Karac Tor. Worlds within worlds. It's all part of the magic, Ewan. You are interested in power. I ask you, how did you come to the bottom of a tree outside the Gray Abbey?"

"I don't know. That's part of my question."

"I don't either!" Sorge said with relish. "That's part of my answer. Magic is everywhere, but it must be perceived. Aion speaks—in the Nine, the Book of Law, the Hall of Ages. Pick another word if magic doesn't suit you. But now we're talking merely about the best way to describe something, not whether the thing is right or wrong."

"To live is to see," said Asandra, who, apparently, had been listening all along. "To see is magic. So say the Highlanders."

Ewan shook his head, feeling defeated. All pretty words, but they missed his heart. "I just want to know what *my* magic is," he whispered.

"Stop magicals! Trudgings and budgings."

Sorge breathed onto his stone again, putting more strength into the light. The illumination expanded, revealing an enormous cave with a vaulted ceiling beyond the glow's reach. The walls curved upward, rough and glittering. Cones of rock jutted upward and downward, giving the cavern the look of a giant mouth lined top and bottom with ragged teeth. Intermittently, tidal water fell from above, disturbing the dark pool behind them. The only visible tunnel headed . . .

"East, I think," Sorge guessed, pointing. "Easy enough."

"Definitely east," Creudwyn added. "Creeds are practically born pointing north. Never been lost. Follow me!"

He stumbled forward, tripped on a low shelf of rock. His sword whined, wobbled.

"Probably best if I guard the rear." He hopped to his feet, brushing himself off. "You lead, Sorge. I insist."

They gathered their belongings, set off. The Raven Trail was a mess of twists and turns, but fortunately, remained a single shaft for many miles. They wound up and down narrow stairs of slippery rock, climbed steep walls, where they had to boost one up and then reach down for the next. More than once they hugged a wall of rock to their back and inched along while huge, open pits of darkness yawned before them. Ewan just stared straight ahead, thankful now for his practice on the rope bridge in Redthorn. He never would have made it otherwise.

They pressed on, as Flogg said, trudging and budging. They passed veins of yellow crystal and blue gemstones that glittered like light on water. They entered cavern after cavern of sweeping scale, with stone formations soaring beyond the reach of Sorge's light, only to pass next into narrow, claustrophobic tunnels where they had to crawl single file, on all fours, or scrape along on their bellies and elbows. Everywhere, the air was cool, mossy, damp. Once, a blast of heat hit them, but no one could tell from where.

Asandra asked, "How many miles under the bay to the island?"

Ewan hadn't even considered the fact that somewhere, far above his head, a boat might be gliding past. The thought made his throat constrict. Walls of rock closed in around him.

"Five miles. Maybe ten. I'm not sure. Flogg, how do we get out of the Raven Trail? Is the exit a trick, like the entrance?"

Flogg had no answer. They stopped twice to rest, munching on dried apricots and pork (which was slimy from the dunk in the water), then huddled together for warmth in their damp clothes. Then, more trudging. They walked until their legs ached, until they were sick of blue light and dark caves and glittering rock. When they reached a fork in the tunnel, faced with three possible branches, Flogg knelt and placed his fingers on the rough stone. His eyes became vacant and his ears no longer mattered—only the connection of flesh to stone, the voice of the deep earth, the hearing of touch.

"Trees, grass." He pointed to the center shaft. "Cry of blackwings."

No one spoke as they moved deeper into the center tunnel. Fear was turning to desperation, boring inside, subsuming their thoughts. Perhaps they *had* been hasty?

Sorge held the cool, radiant stone aloft. The path became tighter, steeper. They moved slower, breathing hard, dragging their feet. All save Flogg, who seemed downright cheerful. For the others, there simply wasn't enough light. The weight of the earth pressed upon them like a tomb. The air felt close, suffocating. They kept crawling along, every step more tedious than the last. Ewan felt near to collapse. The surface of the land, the promise of grass and light and stars just above, felt so utterly far away it caused jolts of anxiety to consider if he might ever get out. He trailed a finger along the wall to his right, wanting to feel connected to something, earth and stone, more than swallowing darkness. He felt the surface of the rock gradually become more porous, sulfurous—less the rock of common caves and mines, and more like the remnants of ancient molten flows.

"The stone is changing," he said.

"Apaté was fire mountain," Flogg replied. "Burnings and churnings. Ages gone."

"We need rest," Asandra declared. Not belligerent, just fatigued. About the time Hadyn had been kidnapped, she had seemed to soften. "We have not slept. We've traveled all night. We have no idea where we are or how far we've come. Clearer heads will serve our purpose better."

"Speak for yourself," Creudwyn boasted half-heartedly. "A Creed never tires."

But his hair was disheveled, and his eyelids sagged. When his sword wobbled in protest, he slapped tiredly at his thigh. "Oh grow up! It was just a joke."

Ewan, too, was exhausted. Sorge relented.

"I see a large chamber ahead. We'll eat there and rest for a few hours. No more."

CHAPTER 40

WOOD DREAMING

They found a river in the next chamber, flowing opposite the direction they were moving. It ended in a swirling pool, presumably disappearing into the water table deep underground. Sorge scooped his hand in the flow and lifted it to his lips.

"Fresh," he said, surprised. But then his face wrinkled. "Fresh, but strange."

They all drank, and all felt the same. The taste was nearly clean, but felt unwell in their stomachs. They found several planks of old, rotten driftwood in the chamber, along with pulleys and moldering rope dangling from somewhere up high, and the ruins of what looked like carts and crates, and a platform of some sort, decades old, with rusted gears and a metal tube that reached down into the water. Like an old pump.

"Rulvôl diggings. Gnome camp," said Flogg.

He and Cruedwyn set about gathering any scraps of wood that looked like they might still have fire in them. The gnome pulled a bulging pouch from his satchel. He sprinkled a little black powder on the wood.

"Back," he warned. Then lit it.

With a whoosh and pop, the wood caught fire. They fed it and leaned close, grateful for dry heat. They ate and slept and warmed their bones. Ewan had not realized how chattering cold he had been for so long.

When they broke camp several hours later, they followed the river. The deeper they went, the more Sorge's stone dimmed. More than once, Ewan stumbled, even though his feet had not slipped. After resting, though more alert, he found it harder and harder to concentrate. The others staggered as well.

They passed chamber after chamber connected by long, snaking tunnels. None of the passages were sculpted or refined—no arched doorways or carved columns of stone. There was evidence of workmanship in pulleys and carts, but even these were fairly primitive.

Then things changed. Ewan began noticing faint marks, black birds painted on the rock. Ravens. For so long, their path had drilled deeper into the earth. Now they seemed to be moving *up*, steeply at times. The only constant was the water, flowing down channels of rock on either side of their path. They crossed single file over natural, curved bridges of rock, while underneath the current bubbled swiftly by; again, at a dead end, they had to leap across. Ever it flowed beside them. Like salmon swimming upstream, they climbed higher and higher, creatures of darkness, wishing for light.

"I can't think straight anymore," Ewan said hopelessly. "It's like my brain's in a vice. Everything is closing in."

"The confusion of Nemesia seeps into the earth itself here," Sorge replied. "You are not tired so much as bedeviled."

They were almost climbing vertically now, up long, steep flights of cut-stone stairs—more evidence of basic craftsmanship. Small hope, but it meant someone had created the path and therefore eventually it must lead somewhere. Such was the logic, Sorge reassured. But the strange thickening of air continued. Ewan felt near to fainting. He just wanted to sleep.

So tired...

At the top of what seemed like an endless ladder of crumbling steps, splashed by water from above, Asandra's foot slipped. She cried out. Cruedwyn barely caught her wrist. Flogg barely caught Cruedwyn. They pulled one another onto the next ledge.

"Well slap my long end and call me goose," Creed breathed. "We're buggered."

And so they were. They had come upon what none were expecting: a broad, flat pool of water in a large, circular chamber. At the top of nowhere. Dead end. The narrow ledge was the only patch of rock not submerged. It overlooked the vast, still water.

"No way out. No other paths."

Sorge said, "Something doesn't feel right. Asandra, do you feel it?"

"The water is foul. Or the air. Or the trees. I'm not sure."

"Black witch," Flogg grunted. "Close. Poisons all."

Sorge hiked up his robe and stepped into the water, tracing the perimeter with his light. The lake stretched a couple hundred feet from front to back. Water poured over the sides in a shower of noisy rain.

"There must be a spring in the middle," he called back to the others. "Or a collection point for runoff water from the surface. Either way, this is the beginning of our river."

"Any tunnels? Any more passages?" Ewan asked.

Sorge shook his head. The water seemed an even depth, about

knee high. Water and roots. That was it. Gnarled, twisting fingers of wood hung down from the low ceiling, perhaps twenty feet above, smelling like moss. They groped toward the water, but only a few reached into the limpid pool. Ewan knew they must be close to the surface. He wanted to scream.

So close! The thickly matted roots seemed to hang from nothing, though obviously they were bedded to a thick layer of stone. Tangled masses broke through in their quest for water, forming a pattern of two circles, one inside another. The outer circle of roots was nearly the size of the entire area of the pool. In the center, another enormous clump snaked downward, drinking lustily. Ewan could almost hear them gulping. The tree above must be enormous.

"Of water, wood dreaming . . ." Asandra said thoughtfully.

Sorge started. "What did you say?"

The mirling raised her eyes. "I can't remember where I heard that."

"You heard it from me," Sorge said. "The riddle.

In division, completion;
In darkness, door shone;
Of water, wood dreaming;
To sunlight, from stone."

He turned a mad circle, tensing his body.

"We were divided when they stole Hadyn. Now we want to be complete again. Do you see? The promise is that in the darkness we will find a door. What does wood dream of? If you were a tree, Cruedwyn, a mighty oak, what would you dream of?"

"A pretty little maple, I'll tell you that much. Or maybe a willow, they're so graceful and—"

"Water!" The monk reached down, splashing in the pool, pointing to the hanging roots. "We will find our way to sunlight, out of the stone, through the dreaming woods." He barked a command. "Flogg!"

Already, the gnome was splashing his way toward the center tree, grasping the low roots, scuttling up with ease. Moments later, he called down:

"Flogg cannot join tree."

"He means connect with it, like he does the earth," Sorge whispered to Ewan. "This has to be it. Keep looking!" he cried.

"Maybe you should turn off your light," Ewan observed. "The riddle says, 'in darkness.'"

"Of course!"

Sorge blew out the rock like a candle. Slowly, everyone's eyes adjusted to the total darkness. Very nearly total.

"There!" Asandra whispered.

On the far wall, a thin beam of light poured down from the ceiling. Hanging beside it, like an invitation, was a long, coiled tree root.

"Or maybe a birch," Cruedwyn continued, as if he had never stopped. "They have that nice, white bark. So lovely."

Sorge grabbed the swordsman by the sleeve, hauling him toward the light. It was time to rejoin the land of the sun.

CHAPTER 41

SACRED GROVE

Really, it had been so simple, so obvious, they might have never found it. One of the largest roots had been carved of stone, weathered and shaped to perfectly mimic the gangly mass of other roots around it. On the back side, the rock was knotted into primitive, climbable steps, winding up into a hollowing of the trunk, through which faint traces of light could be seen.

They emerged carefully, one leg, one arm at a time, from the rotund belly of the great tree. Remarkably, it still lived. Cruedwyn went first, in case there was resistance. Then Sorge, Flogg, Asandra. Lastly, Ewan.

Hunched low to the ground, all five took time to squeeze clumps of grass in their fists, reveling in the feel, the smells of earth and open air. Though the sun was hidden from view, it was still *light* and felt sweet to the soul. Sorge guessed it to be late morning, nearing noon.

"See," he said, pointing. They scooted close enough to peer

over a rim of rock. From here they could see their position, on a flat-topped bulge of land, part of a series of low hills overlooking a broad sweep of valley. Not too far away, and very nearly level to their height, across a shallow ravine where a series of smaller creeks gathered water for the river in the valley below, the Tower of Ravens was sculpted from the black stone of the hillside. The structure was dominated by a tall central tower, mostly windowless, with few additional fortifications around the base. Not a true fortress, but the steep hillside offered a natural defensive position, and the walls of the tower looked imposingly solid. To the west, they saw the three white towers of glittering Stratamore and tall-masted ships gliding tranquilly in and out the King's Port. Spanning their field of view, the blue waters of the bay crawled wave upon wave toward land. Ribbons of golden beach traced the face of the island's shores.

It was a lovely sight, even draped in shadow, but it was the procession below that immediately grabbed everyone's attention. Streaming down the hillside from Nemesia's tower, a huge swath of people teemed across the shallow ravine, slowly marching up the hill toward . . . them. To the very circle of trees where they lay. The crowd was still hundreds of yards away, but the distance would close fast. A thousand, maybe two, glum youths trod along in silence, their faces smudged by the distance. Their clothing was drab and common, their line impossibly long and slow and noiseless, except for the low stampede of feet.

"I think that's Hadyn," Ewan said, his voice catching. "In the front. I'm not sure."

A hard, lovely woman with black hair led them. Nemesia, holding the Staff of Shades aloft. She wore a seductive gown, shimmering in dark hues, with a high collar, a tiara of silver, and a billowing cape. Viscous streamers of unlight trailed from the tip of her staff, chewing at the air as if eating it.

"Unexpected," Cruedwyn murmured, watching the crowd.

"They don't see us, do they? Is that why they're coming?"

"No, no." Sorge scanned the high promontory of grass. Their location was a natural outlook; yet unnatural, also. The trees were arranged with perfect symmetry, forming an outer circle of beech at the perimeter, many feet apart, with an inner circle of some sort of cedar. At the very center was a massive, ancient willow. Its great, feathered branches hung low.

"Um, Sorge. Are you seeing what I'm seeing?" Ewan said carefully.

Sorge did see. Every tree and every trunk was laced with intricate carvings. The strange symbols made you cross your eyes, or feel wobbly and ill, to look upon. Branches were hung with an assortment of chimes and bells, glass beads, amulets, daggers, and talismans made of brass. Ewan had not noticed the multifaceted sounds, so sudden and welcome was their arrival to light and land. But he heard them now. The whole grove tinkled in the gentlest of breezes, a cacophony of eerie noises.

"Now tell me, I dare you, tell me that's not a pretty tree," said Cruedwyn admiringly. "Just like I said. So graceful, folding over—"

"Creed!"

"Right. We'll need to spread ourselves. I'm thinking Flogg can lay some powder for distraction. Ewan is best positioned higher up the hill, out of harm's way." He pointed. "Behind that outcropping of rock should be perfect. The mirling should be with him. She is of no use in this battle."

"You are wrong, swordsman," Asandra said cooly. "Nemesia will try to summon Watchers. I hear them already. Even so, that outcropping is as good as anywhere. I will stay with Ewan. You will see the strength of the Blacks is not forgotten."

"Everyone's a hero," Cruedwyn said dismissively. He turned his attention to Sorge's rosewood staff. "You remember how to use a sword, don't you?"

Sorge tightened his grip. "My staff will do."

"What about one of those?" Ewan asked, pointing. Among the outer trees, strangely, were stacks of bows. And full quivers. Propped against the trunks of the inner circle were dozens of freshly carved wands. All bore similar mystic runes.

The implications were clear. Nemesia was building an arsenal. Sorge crawled a few paces and touched one of the wands, jerking his hand back as if burned. He spat on his fingers and wiped them on the grass. Something deeply unsettling was at work.

Ewan whispered, "Will somebody please tell me what's going on?"

"This is a Sacred Grove—a mockery of the term. It is a place of old magic."

Sorge struck the earth with his fist. "I knew I felt something in the water below. It all makes sense now. These roots carry blasphemy into the earth. The water we drank was defiled."

"*I* should have known, even more," Asandra said ruefully. "We are in a place of great evil. My skin is crawling."

"Mine, too," Ewan whispered.

"All very spooky, I'm sure," Cruedwyn said. "As for me . . ." He quietly pulled out his sword. The blade was long and sharp. He glanced down into the ravine. "Never taken on a thousand before. What was my previous high? Thirteen?" Sweat trickled down his cheeks. He smiled fiercely. "Today's my lucky day."

Sorge tapped him on the shoulder. "Enough boasting. What comes next?"

"Flogg makes some noise and smoke, while you and I hit the

front line and scatter their ranks. They aren't fighters. Blarmy, it looks like they're doing good to all be facing the same direction."

Sorge said, "I don't want to kill if we can avoid it. These are just children. Spellbound, not evil."

Cruedwyn nodded, as if in total agreement. "Right, right. No killing. One, two thousand, against five." He assessed his team. "Really against just two. Are you seeing the same thing I'm seeing?"

"I mean it. None. If possible."

Cruedwyn huffed. "Shall I just beat them across the shoulders with the flat of my blade? Or wave and make threatening hand gestures? Hurl clever insults? I know, I'll charm them with the mirling's tender personality!"

He winked. Asandra rolled her eyes.

"Perhaps if the bard would just wave his sword and talk," she said, "the heat might scare them all away."

Ewan snickered. Cruedwyn said, "Lovely girl, Sorge. Could we bring two of her on our next trip?"

"Stop it, both of you. I said none *if possible*. Do what you must, Creed. We have your sword and my staff. It will have to be enough."

Ewan gently intervened. "Sorge, look at how many of them there are. Your staff is *not* enough. Take one of the bows."

"I agree with the boy," said Cruedwyn.

"And I," said Flogg.

Sorge ignored them both. To Ewan, he said, "I don't expect you to understand."

Ewan pressed the point.

"I heard Eldoran, Sorge. He gave you permission. You are a master bowman."

"*Was* a master bowman."

"What about all the big talk? The Champion stuff?"

"No."

"Why? Why come all this way if—"

"No more!" Sorge said dangerously. "You have no idea the price I've paid. Once I was skilled and strong. And even more proud. Proud and stupid and brittle. I betrayed my own Bloodkin. I lost my way."

Flogg had left the conversation, was furiously at work with bags of black powder.

"All lose way," the gnome interjected. "Fallings and crawlings."

Sorge faced his friend, as if betrayed. His voice dropped to an anguished whisper. "For what, my friend? For fame? Swordplay? The last Champion of Karac Tor is lost, and my pride alone is to blame."

Cruedwyn groaned. "Allow me to pause and invite us all back to the *real* world, where a *whole lot of weird people* are coming this way, and, forgive me, I don't think it's to invite us to tea. We have a narrow moment, a decent element of surprise. If we'll just buck up and . . ."

The bard kept prattling on. Sorge let him fade into the distance. He and Ewan met eyes. "I'm sorry, Ewan. I will fight for your brother, but on my own terms. Strength and skill have cost me too dearly in the past."

Ewan shook his head. "*To you falls the privilege of righting the wrongs.* Isn't that what you told us, not so very long ago?"

For the first time since the two had met, it was Sorge who looked away.

Creudwyn was still at it. ". . . so we hit the front line. If Sorge is right, we will have profoundly confused them by then with our daring originality and wit. We grab Hadyn. Pray the gods, by then we will have had some explosions from the short one. After that, we aim for the secret tree, drop into the water, and . . ."

"And?"

"Fly. Like the bats of Hel."

Sorge didn't answer. He and Ewan were locked in a stern, complicated silence.

"They're getting closer," Asandra warned, peering down the ravine. "Our height will not hide us much longer. Minutes at most."

Cruedwyn ran his finger along the razored edge of his sword, caressing the cool steel almost lovingly. He looked to Sorge, waiting. They all did.

Sorge ran a slow hand across his bald head. "A good plan. A good plan. And yet . . ." He glanced at Ewan once more. "To tell you the truth, I've never been very good at making cheese."

"Then it is on!" Cruedwyn said, eyes shining.

"Yes, *but*. This has become more than a rescue, I think. Aion's own sacred purpose in the land is at stake. If we fight—if *I* fight—it must not be merely to snatch Hadyn and flee, but to bring deliverance. We must somehow thwart Nemesia on a larger scale."

His tone had changed. His face had changed. Everyone leaned in close. A slight breeze blew. Overhead, sun and sky were unrecognizable, void of both comfort and guidance.

The mettle in Sorge's voice was guidance enough. Even for Asandra.

"We must buy as much time as possible. Master Flogg . . . how much black powder *do* you have?"

For the first time Ewan could ever recall, the gnome grinned.

CHAPTER 42

WITCHING HOUR

S ilence. A gathering of energy.

Ravens darted and swooped above, offering faraway, throaty cries. A slight breeze swirled seaward, pleating the grass and heather. Land and water washed together at the shore. The illusion of calm left Ewan anxious that the cannonade of his heart would ruin everything. He crouched with Asandra behind the rocks and scrub and tall, knotted grass lining a shelf of rock higher up the hill. He didn't know what else to do but pray. Same for Asandra. They had all barely hidden in time.

The tip of the staff crested first, curling thick undulations of oil and vapor into the air, like emptiness or midnight. The corruption of it repulsed, then inexorably drew Ewan. He could not stop watching. Nemesia appeared next, bearing the staff, marching the last few steps up the ravine into the grove. Ewan was struck by how stunning she was, how much she embodied the fascination of darkness. Hadyn stood beside her, heading a throng of Nameless.

Ewan choked with emotion to see his brother up close. Hadyn looked drab, colorless, hollow, like all the rest. He stooped as he walked, shuffling his feet. His focus was blank, on nothing. He was badly bruised, and his face and eye were swollen.

Nemesia stood outside the grove but did not enter. She turned to address the shiftless crowd behind her.

"My precious bombs," she purred. "There is a time of power called the Witching Hour—a time when darkness spreads forth. *This* is our witching hour."

The Nameless murmured softly. Hadyn said nothing. There was no hope in his eyes. Ewan had never seen his brother like this before. He found himself turning away, willing his brain to reject the imprint of the memory, but he could not. As he watched, he saw Hadyn straining the muscles in his face, as if battling for five seconds of concentrated thought. Like a balloon deflating, the defeated expression returned. Strain again, defeat again, many times.

He had been kidnapped, beaten. He was trapped, alone. For all he knew, Ewan might be dead. His face told a story of numbness and resignation. What was there to live for?

He feels completely abandoned, Ewan thought.

It was all too much. He wanted to shout some word of hope. *Hang on!* Subconsciously, he tried to inch even a little closer. He could not stay here, could not let Hadyn feel forgotten even one second more.

"Not yet," Asandra whispered, calming him. "Hold tight. Be wise."

"It's no good," Ewan moaned. The reality of the situation was beginning to sink in. "He's as good as dead. And us with him. There's too many."

"They are empty shells. Watch and wait."

Nemesia still held the Staff of Shades aloft as she addressed the crowd of youth. "We must build a new world. A world done with pretending. In a world where light and grace and love have no meaning, we must first have the courage to admit it. In their place, we must embrace what we do know: darkness, sorrow, despair. These are the only things that are true, for they are the only things that are honest. Everything despair promises, it gives."

"*Nothing matters. Hope promises but fails,*" they answered as one.

"Come, my children. Today, the future of Karac Tor will be boldly decided. By you." She swept her arms toward the grove. "Take your places, my captains. The Witching Hour is here."

Twenty or so young men and women began filing into the grove, forming a circle around the base of the central willow. Hadyn stayed near Nemesia. The remaining mass pressed farther up and around the eastern perimeter to observe, but did not enter. Many hundreds trailed down the hill, unable to come closer.

Ewan strained to see Sorge, Flogg, Creed. Couldn't. It was such a hasty plan. Ludicrous, really. What were any of them thinking? Why bother?

Doesn't matter.

His own words bounced off the inside of his skull. He jerked as if struck.

You are not tired so much as bedeviled.

Ewan blindly felt the ground for a sharp stone, squeezing it in the palm of his hand until the pain made him gasp.

It matters.

As the leaders of the Nameless took their places, so did Nemesia. Her stride was slow and imperious. She moved past the outer circle of beech trees into the inner ring of cedars. Her gown, cut to be sensual, caught the breeze, weaving its own black spell. Hadyn shuffled slavishly beside her, baby steps, as if compelled. The sorceress approached the willow. Her back was to the east, to Isgurd. A symbolic gesture. Some inner fire caught in the thin, silver circlet in her hair, dazzling. There was no sound of crickets. No bird songs. The silence was unearthly.

Nemesia mounted the Staff of Shades into a square socket set in a paving of stones before the base of the willow. Like a snake licking the air with its tongue, the staff flicked and spit venom into the sky. Nemesia began to chant. Her tone grew louder, more cruel. Those she called her captains began to mirror her chant. As their noise swelled, outside the grove, hundreds more began droning a single note, more on the level of vibration than music. The hairs on Ewan's arms and neck rose. The sound was hypnotic, drawing him in, but Asandra tensed.

"Mismyri! They call for Watchers."

Ewan couldn't see what she saw, but he felt the stirring in the air, the movement of unseen wings. The leaves of the trees began to rustle.

"How many?"

She didn't answer. Which was answer enough.

The unlight of the Staff of Shades began to coagulate like an angry, living thing. Streams no longer slithered skyward. Instead the energy became tar-like, sticking to itself. The promontory of land on which they stood, high and green, as well as the grove and wider isle, all paled of color. A rift opened in the air, widened. Light passed from memory. Darkness writhed like a pit of cobras. Nemesia's eyes were open, but white, rolled back in her head, as ecstasy overtook her. Her fingers flexed, became splayed, bony claws, shaping and molding the dark vapors like clay, gathering the power for release. But there was no release.

THE BOOK OF NAMES

The air pressurized. The ground began to shake. The willow at the center trembled. Otherworldly sounds, cries of betrayal and murder, the traitors of Olfadr, leaked into the realm of hearing. The droning of the Nameless reached a fever pitch, demanding release.

But there was no release.

Ewan thought the staff might explode, if not the whole world. He covered his ears, unable to drown the awful sounds. The trees thrashed in a storm of wings. The noise escalated.

"Merciful Aion," Asandra said beside him. "There are thousands. We are undone."

Below, Nemesia made dying sound. Worms of darkness shivered from the staff toward every tree, twisting, snaking, sucked like water into a sponge, into a single rune—the same shape, carved into every tree. Tree trunks began dripping with unlight. Nemesia waved her hand. The chanting stopped. Only the low hum continued. And the rift. She smiled.

"Now," she said. Just one word.

Those in the inner circle obeyed. Ewan watched, not knowing their names. He did not know Shameface or Grayday, or the others gathered around the great, bowing branches of the willow. But as they fanned out, they took the wands and began dipping each in the inky blackness which poured from the Staff of Shades. The darkness transferred like an infection spreading from one shaft to another. Each wand began producing a small stream of unlight.

"Merciful Aion," Ewan heard himself say, as he looked upon stacks of dozens of wands, maybe hundreds. Arrows, too.

It seemed clear now. The staff was not enough for Nemesia's plans. Her army would take the unlight all over the land, farther, faster. Having stripped them of name and will, they would carry the darkness with them—wands for where feet could tread and arrows for where feet could not.

It was diabolical. They needed more time, Ewan knew. More time for Flogg, wherever he was. He had been wrong about the gnome. He knew it. Too late, he knew it. He hoped to be able to tell him, later. If they made it. A sense of finality was creeping upon the ritual. The window of opportunity—however paltry it seemed—was closing. To save Hadyn and stop this evil.

"We can't wait much longer," he whispered.

Asandra hushed him. Fifty wands were now infected with the same disease coming from the Staff of Shades. Now eighty, now two hundred. It was a fast process. Wands and arrowheads both. Each touched the dark rune in the center of each tree. Each came away with self-sustaining darkness.

Hadyn watched the whole thing, slack-jawed, hands bound.

One of the young leaders suddenly spoke aloud. "This tree has no bow. No arrows!"

The witch arched a wary brow. "Nonsense, I placed them myself."

Then there was Sorge. Ewan's heart leapt. There, Sorge.

"Forgive me, I borrowed it," the monk said, stepping out from behind a tree on the far northern edge. His feet were dangerously close to the cliff edge, where the knuckle of the grove dropped suddenly away to the valley below. In his arms he held a bow, stretched full, an arrow notched to the string. Aimed straight at Nemesia's heart. Ewan and Asandra faced him from the opposite side of the grove.

Nemesia inclined her head to the sound of his voice.

"So, the little mouse has decided to come out of hiding after all?" she teased, betraying no hint of surprise, her lips playing with a smile. "I'm sure I'm flattered. But really, shouldn't you be among the other little Gray mice? Pretending to be one of them, as you have for so long now? Eating your cheese. Saying your prayers. Do you want to pray together, is that it, Sorge? Surely you haven't come to fight."

A strange tingling brushed Ewan's skin, like awareness. Like someone watching.

"She's searching," Asandra said. "Feeling outward. Get down."

Ewan froze. Beside him, the mirling began to pray. The tingling on his skin became slippery, wouldn't stick. She was shielding him. Nemesia made a full survey of the grove, turning back to the man robed in charcoal with a circle-scar on his forehead. "You came alone?"

"Never alone, you know that. I come in the name of Aion. With his authority."

Nemesia curled her mouth to speak. But Sorge wasn't finished.

"And with my daughter." He paused. "*Our* daughter, Nemesia."

Asandra gasped. Ewan glanced at her. *Daughter?*

"Release the boy," Sorge commanded. "We will let you live. It's not too late for mercy."

The sorceress clicked her long nails together, laughing. The sound was mocking and seductive. "So far . . . just to hear me say no? Did you think bringing the little mirling with you would play on my heart? Of course, I should have known you would figure it out eventually. You've had twenty years to put the clues together."

Asandra's chest heaved. She had not once exhibited fear during the whole journey. Now she squeezed Ewan's arm so tightly it hurt. Her eyes welled with tears.

"He knew," she whispered. "I've hated him all my life. But he knew."

"Where is she?" Nemesia said coolly. "I sense her."

"Hidden. Safe. As she has been all her life, though she did not know it. She looks like you. She has your spirit, your gift. Your anger. But there is one difference. She is loyal to Aion."

"You dare to lecture me on loyalty?" Nemesia hissed. "Would you be so righteous before Corus, your friend? Would you tell *him* of your great code of loyalty? Do you bear his gift of friendship on your arm still?" She chewed each word like poisoned fruit. "Come now, Elder Sorge. Are you sure you're ready for this? Can a coward suddenly be brave?"

"I have made my peace with Aion," Sorge said. The feathers and single, thin shaft of the arrow were pressed against his cheek. "Long ago, and with much prayer. I am sorry for many things. About Corus. About you." He bent the bow tighter in warning. "Do not make me sorry for more."

The throbbing of magic in the grove did not subside. Hundreds of eyes were fixed on the monk, the witch. Still, the staff gushed its darkness. The trees sucked it in. But Nemesia's captains had paused. They no longer dipped the wands. Their faces were unsure. Ewan glimpsed Flogg, a small, hardly visible streak of green, blending with the grass, moving outside the field of view, from tree to tree on the outer rim. He was dropping pouches along the base of each tree.

Sorge is buying time. He's stalling.

The others did not see. Nemesia did not see. A mirling labored to shield them all with prayer.

"You will not release Watchers today, old friend," the monk said solemnly.

"Oh, but I will, *old friend*. And so much more. Darkwings are only the beginning. Soon, they shall have blood. *Blood bound, blood released*, isn't that how it goes, Sorge the Gray? From

Nemesia the Black?" She touched Hadyn on the shoulder, smiling wickedly. "I shall give the mismyri his blood and call them forth, while Aion slumbers on the green hills of Isgurd, far away. Quite beautiful, don't you think?"

Hadyn lifted his face to Sorge, desperate and blank. Even at a distance, Ewan could see the lack of recognition.

"But I am not entirely unfair. I shall let him choose." She took Hadyn's face in her hands. "Join me, fool. If you willingly do so, I shall spare your life. Another shall take your place, and their blood shall open the door, rather than your own. Regardless, know this: *The monk cannot save you.* Nor the four with him, scattered around this grove. He does not know my power. He does not know he has brought them all to ruin, including my wretched daughter. A thousand Watchers have been summoned. They are waiting. They press hard against my mind, but without blood, they cannot cross over. Magic and darkness have drawn them, but I cannot keep them here. They will return to Helheim unless there is a sacrifice." She shuddered in a spasm of pain. "I offer you this. Join me, and all my precious bombs shall be made complete in despair, to see you fall. Or resist and die. But do not expect compassion. I will not give it, even to my own."

Sorge tried to break the hold on Hadyn's mind. "Hadyn! Don't give up! For Aion, for all that you love . . . *fight* her."

It was hardly a plan. Hadyn gave no indication he heard his own name, much less anything else. Not Nemesia. Not Sorge.

Yet on some level, he understood. It was primitive; sheer will to live. Drooping, he pushed one foot forward, away from Nemesia. A silent cry for freedom.

Something tinkled at his feet. Until that moment, Ewan had not noticed the chain. Nemesia kicked with her foot. The iron between her ankle and Hadyn's snapped tight, bringing the boy to his knees. He stayed close for a reason. He had no choice.

Sorge, done with negotiations, released his arrow, too fast to follow with the eye, toward the woman he once loved. One moment it was in his hands, pulled tight against the bow. The next it was plunging toward Nemesia. No time, no space in between.

And yet the witch had time to laugh. To reach for the staff, to raise it. Time for the darkness to blossom and consume the arrow, turning it to ashes, blown away on the wind. Three more arrows, loosed by a master bowman, one-time friend of a one-time Champion. Faster than Ewan could find or focus on: notched, released. Turning to dust. All.

Nemesia pointed the staff at Sorge.

"Fool," she said.

Unlight leaped toward the monk, and only him. No more the trees, the wands. Darkness struck him like a physical blow. He jerked; Ewan almost cried out. Sorge leaned into the darkness, straining. Black fingers clawed into his mouth, slithered into his nose. The boundary of his flesh had been breached.

"Ewan!" Asandra said. "I have no magic for this."

"And you think I do?"

"You have come with power. Find it."

The younger Barlow felt desperate. Dreamlike, he heard his own voice. *No riddles. They said my magic . . . is meant to be heard.* He remembered three dreams on the boat. He remembered nine notes. He saw Sorge, saw Hadyn. On impulse, he stood. The time had come. He feared but no longer feared. The fear was too large a thing to truly be felt. It was, and he was, and yet this moment required something more. Hadyn *needed* him.

Below, Hadyn raised his eyes. Saw him. Ewan wanted to weep at the shocking bareness of recognition, like a tree stripped clean by a tornado, or a field of charred grass after a fire. Deep within

Ewan, a point of brightness flared. Yes, they were ridiculously outnumbered. There was no chance. But that's not what mattered anymore. Hadyn mattered. All his life, he had looked up to his brother, pranked him, argued with and screamed at him, laughed and fought with him. Now he would fight *for him.* Come what may. He wiggled his foot nervously, summoning courage. He pulled his baseball cap from his pocket and placed it snugly on his head. It felt good, felt right, on his head again. If he was going to fight, it could only be as himself.

He had wondered, laying low behind the rock, what this moment would require. Now he knew. He did the only thing that made any sense to him.

Any sense at all.

CHAPTER 43

SONG OF AION

In the roaring chaos of his mind, Hadyn saw a strange figure rise, standing on a ledge of rock above him. The boy was close to his own age. He wore a cap with letters on it. He held a sword in his hands. He looked familiar. With tremulous fingers, the boy lifted the sword to his mouth, filled his lungs, pursed his lips. The sword made a song.

It was song of memory, of beginnings and endings. A piercingly bright sound, clear as morning. It instantly cut through the murk of darkness, like a candle set in a window to bring travelers home. A murmur went up among the Lost. The boy began, but could not finish. Nemesia, chattering words from her mouth like a nest of rattlesnakes, knocked him backward with a thought. The weapon he played upon clattered to the ground.

Hadyn's eyes, fixed on him, finally saw. He knew. Ewan, his little brother, struggling to rise again, groping for the thin metal whistle. A gift from their mother, from Ireland.

The music had not been anything Hadyn recognized, but, dreamlike, it carried him. A long time ago, to another life. With a father he loved. Even the sorrow of that life now seemed sweet to remember. To remember anything seemed sweet. A mother, who had held him, who had known him. She was gone from his life, but not from his soul.

He saw her in his mind's eye, laughing, her blonde hair catching the light of a new day like silk and pearls. There had never been any woman like Anna Barlow. The memory came with pain. He could not stop it, could not pick and choose. It was all or nothing, good and bad. He grit his teeth to feel her again, slipping away, beyond the touch of his fingers. Fighting to live. Then gone. Hadyn might as well have been alone on that hill, as tears streamed down his face. His whole world, in that moment, was held together by the brother in his eyes, and the blonde-haired woman in his memory. In a flash, behind the pain, came sweetness. He remembered dancing with her, after school, acting like fools. He remembered her making up silly songs, just for him, then singing them at bedtime. Even when he was older, Hadyn would sing along, even when he should have felt silly. Pain stabbed him like a knife. He was *so glad* he sang with her! The pain was a searing heat. A healing heat. He remembered her teaching him how to listen to the quiet voice of God, to find him in the darkness, right before bed. He trembled.

Too much. The darkness is too much. Mom!

She could laugh and the rain would stop just to listen to the sound. Not true, of course, but that's how it had *felt*, growing up with her.

She made living fun and bright. She told stories, and the retelling was always better than the actual event. He remembered the story of her dreaming his name, giving it to him like a gift.

She gave it to him now, in his memory. A final gift. A command to live again.

Hadyn!

His brother was shouting the same word. Standing on the high outcropping, shaking his fist in the air, shouting his name.

"You are Hadyn Barlow! Son of Reggie and Anna Barlow! You are *my* brother. I am *your* brother. I am Ewan Barlow! We are lost, but we are not Lost, because we know who we are!"

Nemesia's face became a dark rage. She ordered her captains, "Get him!"

Ewan still stood, still shouted. He waved his whistle like a banner on the field of battle. "Do you hear me, Hadyn! Do you remember who you are? You have to *want* it."

The pain. The loss. The memories that burned like hot metal, that could make a day a hated thing. The move to a new place, the loss of friends. Dreadful days. Better days, yet unlived. Somehow worth living. All of it wrapped up in human flesh, shaped of a life, given a name.

His name.

He wanted it.

Some things come hard and take a long time. Others turn course in a moment. Another day, maybe, would tell the difference. For now, he only knew that he *wanted*, he chose—and in the choosing, the haze lifted, like a harbor fog pushed by the wind. His eyes cleared. For the first time in many months, Hadyn knew himself and was glad for the knowing. He felt his bound hands, his tender, swollen cheek. Felt a tidal wave of anger rise from his core.

Nemesia flailed one arm wildly toward Ewan, demanding action from the Nameless. The staff bucked wildly in her hands. She dared not lift it from the monk, who shuddered in a bubble of darkness, eyes bulging. His skin had turned from a deep, natural color to a pale, sickly brown. He was dying. Hadyn absorbed all this in an instant. Saw a man—what was his name? . . . Creed?—sprinting from somewhere, sword drawn—why was he laughing?—crashing against the tide of lost youth who pressed toward Ewan, waving their wands and sharp-toothed arrows. He saw Creed move like a man consumed, his blade an extension of his being, like a brush for a painter, an artist, flashing with silver and fire and death.

Hadyn knew his task. He spoke a word, the word he had learned on the ship. In his quiet thoughts, of ropes and knots. Binding unbound, the knot grew slack. It could not do otherwise. Its name had been spoken by one who knew the power of names.

Nemesia's captains surged toward Ewan, while the mass on the hill watched, stunned, incapable of thought. No different from any other day.

Except for one difference. Their eyes were on Ewan. *Not* Nemesia.

Hadyn tried to wriggle his foot lose from the iron band. The metal bit into his ankle.

"I can't get free!" he shouted above the din. "Somebody help! Creed!"

And then, the music again. The same haunting, familiar melody, played to fullness now, unbroken. Nine notes, played once through, then twice. Ewan had reclaimed his flute, his footing. From the ground where he lay, Hadyn was awed. Seeing some twenty people climbing toward him, carrying rocks and wands and magic, blind with rage, Ewan did not flee. Thankfully, the steep, crumbly hill slowed his pursuers. But they were getting close. Three times Ewan played. One of the Lost threw a large stone.

"Ewan!" Hadyn choked. "Watch out!"

Ewan ducked, immediately putting the flute to his mouth again. Somehow, he had become even more deeply rooted to that place on the rock. A part of the land itself. A conduit of light.

Nine notes, again. Only nine. A melody beyond compare. Five times, six, the melody played. Doorways to other worlds.

"The Song of Aion?" Nemesia sneered. "Is it magic now? Who taught him that song?"

In his mind, Hadyn answered her fiercely. *Aion did.*

Ewan repeated the melody again, for the eighth time. A pulse. The witch felt it first.

Then, nine.

"No!" she screamed.

Power quivered in the ground, down the rock to Hadyn's body, to his feet. Something sharp and metallic pinged loudly, multiple times, like firecrackers in succession. Every link in the chain which bound him snapped, the shackle tore. He fell backward, scooted away.

"The Song of Aion!" he shouted. He was free.

Nemesia turned her staff upon Ewan. Its power never reached him. Waves of energy rippled from the place where he stood, rising like the crest of a wave, colliding in the center of the grove. A battle ensued between the song of light and the staff of dark. Ewan continued to play. The darkness wavered. Freed, Sorge gasped at the breach, finding air. When Ewan paused for breath, the darkness waxed strong again.

Hadyn heard the monk grunt, motioning with his hands. A circle. More.

"Keep playing!" he shouted up the hill.

A girl passed by Nemesia. It was Grayday, headed toward Ewan, to stop him. The sorceress grabbed Grayday by a handful of her hair and threw her to the ground. A fount of strange words bubbled from the witch's mouth, foaming. For a moment, she released the staff. It fell to the earth, sizzling and sputtering. A second reprieve. Growling, the witch seized a blade of black onyx from the folds of her gown and lunged for Grayday's throat.

Hadyn didn't think. He lunged too. This time toward the witch, not away. He caught Nemesia broadside, knocking her to the ground.

"Grayday," he groaned, his face on the ground near the girl's. Grayday's eyes were white. "Don't die. Not for her. Wake up. Run."

Nemesia kicked at Hadyn. Her foot landed in his gut. She slashed at him. He rolled away. Coiled from the force of her swing, she uncoiled even faster. Her return slash caught Hadyn off guard, biting deeply into his arm. He fell back, squeezing the wound to staunch the blood.

Meanwhile, a half-dozen young men — those who had escaped Cruedwyn's sword — were nearly upon Ewan. Though their footholds were weak, they were close enough it hardly mattered. Ewan's song began to falter. He was not trained to play for so long, and his lungs burned. He stopped, took a large stone in hand, and lobbed it toward the nearest two. He felt faint, but his aim was good. They tumbled into one another, down the hillside. Instantly, Creed was upon those two. They did not rise again.

"I will climb!" Creed called. "You play! Keep your song!"

Ewan stumbled, lightheaded. But he played. At the bottom, Grayday cowered underneath Hadyn, sobbing. Nemesia screamed in rage, pointing to a different girl amongst the stupified throng on the edge of the grove. "You! Come!"

The girl did not flinch. Wide-eyed, vacant stare — same as the rest — she came.

"No!" Hadyn wailed.

"I am Shy Eyes," the girl said.

"Doesn't matter," said the witch.

Like the strike of a scorpion's tail, Nemesia drew a quick, sharp line with her knife. The girl's throat ribboned with red. She fell to the ground, bubbling. Nemesia chanted strange words. Shy Eyes's body shook. Nemesia lifted her face to the sky. It was now or never. The darkness had prepared the way. They were gathered.

"Watchers! Traitors to Aion! Mismyri, come! I shed blood for thee. The door is open."

Through the ruptured rift of air created by the staff, Watchers poured forth. In the span of a moment, a thousand had split through. Immediately, they began tearing at the flesh of the dead girl. In their disembodied state, they could only consume dead flesh. Living spirits were beyond their reach, save for terror and dread. But when their grisly feast was done, they swerved at the gathered host anyway. Their shrieks were the sound of tearing metal, a rabid sow giving birth. A basilisk sound, cold and bone-chilling. It was madness in the brain. Some Nameless watched, awed, their eyes rolling back in their heads. Other hundreds scattered in terror. Hadyn felt himself slipping again into despair, to hear that sound, to see the earth beneath where Shy Eyes had fallen smeared with nothing but red.

Still Ewan played. Like a Champion of old, he stood his ground as dark wings raked around him. Hadyn clung to the lifeline of his brother's flute. Aion's song. A thousand Watchers had entered, and nearly a thousand had already fled, lusty with freedom, bent on vengeance and worship elsewhere. But with words of power, Nemesia seized the will of the last three, ordering them to strike at Ewan. At first they fought, squealing. Their long, toothy beaks and many eyes — their black, foul feathers — stank of mold and decay. But then, shuddering with delight, they understood. More blood. They reared in the air and swooped. If the Lost could kill him, they could drink their fill. So drive him to madness first.

"No!" Hadyn whimpered. Out of the corner of his eye, he saw Sorge struggling to his feet, pale as death. Dark tendrils still clung to his body like seaweed. He saw the monk steady himself. Barely able to stand, he gathered energy for prayer, from prayer. One by one, the last tendrils fell away. He was too weak to do more. Hadyn flicked his eyes, seeing a dash of movement among the bases of the far beech trees. He saw Cruedwyn roll and flow like a river among stones, as he fought the last three of those he could reach, bringing each to the ground in turn.

And then, in the anguished slowness of a single moment, he saw three Watchers, wretched and vile, streak toward his brother with death and lust in their eyes. Their claws were outstretched, like razors, ready for blood.

Rising from behind the rocks with her hands lifted high, the daughter of Nemesia met them with eyes closed. A pillow of pale light, almost invisible, caught the breeze like a sail to form a canopy above her. Above Ewan. The Watchers reared back.

"Mismyri yl maal eStyblerian! Aione portismaal sanos!"

Watchers, you cannot come near. Aion forbids it.

The Watchers beat their wings furiously, rolling their many eyes to and fro. They snapped hungrily, chomping their beaks, bone on bone. Asandra had no mirror of blessed water, had no ring of men trained in the Wall of Binding. She was a strong mirling, but it was still just one against three. Her barrier would not hold long.

Growling, doglike, Nemesia took the staff from where it lay on the ground.

"Mismyri, om!"

The Watchers heard, flying to the staff like moths to a flame. They drank its viscous fumes, gathering strength.

"Kill them," she said in a fell voice. "Drink their blood. Gain flesh."

"Look around you, Nemesia!" Sorge rasped from a distance. "Your plans are undone. You will not win this generation. Give up."

Hadyn, nearby, continued to shelter Grayday. The arm of his shirt was torn and soaked red. He tried to edge nearer to the witch. His one goal, one purpose in this battle had become clear: Get the staff.

Nemesia spun to face him. "You could have been among my best and most wretched."

She jabbed at him. Hadyn ducked, choking on the vapors that trailed the staff. In a limber twirl, she spun to face Ewan, releasing a burst of darkness. Asandra's covering wavered. The Watchers pounded against it.

Then back to Hadyn, she swung. She was strong, fast; fueled with sorcery. An idea formed in Hadyn's brain. Half-formed, really. He didn't know if he could pull it off without much more practice. This was all so new. Nudging his thoughts toward the chain where it lay shattered by Aion's Song, he stretched his awareness, feeling for the secrets and substance of iron. He saw it in the half-light, cold, dark, and gray, untouched by the sun, moldable with heat and light. Hard as night. He asked it questions. It did not answer. It was iron. Unfeeling.

Too hard. Not enough time or skill yet. Something else.

She swung again. He rolled, nearer to Sorge this time, who still heaved for air and had no strength. Unlight was like drinking poison from a cup.

"Just . . . hold on, Sorge."

The monk grunted. Watchers, empowered by the Staff, pounded at Asandra's canopy. Her hands were outstretched, but she was bent low under the weight of their wings. Their cries were torment to the mind of a mirling. They were three, she one. She began to crumble.

Creed had scrambled up the hill by now, shouting insults and pulling on the heels of the ones above him, who had also made the climb. The highest of these had his fingers on the ledge of rock at Ewan's feet.

"Shameface!" Nemesia screamed to the boy. "Kill him."

Ewan tried to step on his fingers, but Shameface grabbed Ewan's foot. Twisting, he dropped Ewan to his knees. Ewan cried out in pain. Cried out a command.

"Flogg!"

There was no response, only more struggle. Ewan and the boy, older by several years and stronger, tangled arms and rolled together down the slope, tearing at each other's face and throat. Rocks gouged and scraped their skin. The Watchers, seeing their prey emerge from under the cursed Black's protection, screeched and swooped.

Hadyn started to run. Suddenly, he could not move at all.

As if waking from a long sleep, the earth shuddered. Under Hadyn's feet, the ground rose to meet him in a massive explosion that rocked the grove, followed by a quick series of lesser explosions. *Flogg!* Earth and grass shot into the air, which immediately thickened with smoke. Tree trunks along the outer rim splintered, sending chunks of wood flying. One of the Lost howled as a large, sharp piece struck his leg, shattering the bone. Cruedwyn, who had slipped down the hill near to one of the trees, was thrown twenty feet. Trees began falling toward the center and outward down the steep cliff face. Roots groaned, snapped.

Nemesia fought for balance. The Watchers hesitated.

For a split second, the force of the explosion left everyone rattled, including the witch. The only sound was the gruff voice of a gnome, fuming somewhere amid the smoke. Only a moment. That's all any of them had.

It was enough.

"Smashings and flashings!" Flogg said angrily. "Want crashings!"

The next thing Hadyn saw was Flogg's leather satchel, the whole thing, arcing through the crowded air. When it landed, the explosion was deafening, followed by a loud cracking sound. A line formed in the stressed earth, creeping left and right and forward, spidering out, following thin places in the rock down to the dome underneath their feet where the pool of water lay unseen. Hadyn saw nothing but the staff. He no longer saw Ewan fighting for his life, nor Sorge staggering forward. Naming iron had been too hard. Too unknown. But there was something else he knew. He bent down, carefully, took it in his hands. It made no sense to try this. It was too soon, he was too untrained. Still, he *knew*. In his heart. The fibres, the weft, the shape of the knot, the strength of the thing. He knew the binding, for it had bound him. And so he tried.

Nemesia was distracted by Flogg, by Sorge stumbling toward her. He would have no better chance. Ridiculous thoughts scurried through his head, like how it would have helped if he had ever been a cowboy, ever been in a rodeo. At the moment, he wouldn't mind getting that chance someday. He balled one end of the rope in his fist. Threw the other end toward the staff.

It sailed, missed.

City boy, they called him at school. Newland was sounding better all the time.

"Nemesia, have done!" Sorge said.

She paused. She stared at the monk with a strange look on her face. Mere seconds. Visible fissures laced through the earth, tearing apart the grass. Rock against rock, grating. Loud reports here and there as the stone skeleton of the grove fractured. Hadyn threw the rope again.

This time, yes.

In midair, he said a word, the word of knotted rope. The appellation was as foreign to his ears as a clanging lock in the Stone House, yet as true as his own name. He spoke, and as the rope looped around the staff, it found itself, wove together. He jerked with all his might. The staff sprang loose from Nemesia's grip. He caught it. He didn't know why he ran then. Didn't even think about it. He just ran.

"I will bring all of Hel to your door!" Nemesia screamed, wheeling round.

"Get back!" Hadyn shouted, scooping Sorge by his arm, hobbling away. "Everyone, back!"

Nemesia's eyes flashed. She opened her mouth, had barely begun her final incantation when the earth split. The belly of the grove, severely weakened, finally collapsed. Willow tree and all, earth and rock, folded upon themselves, dragging Nemesia down. She clawed at the ground briefly. Sorge tore free of Hadyn, stumbling back toward her, grasping for her hands. He could not get close enough. The ground was too fragile. Nemesia looked up at him with one last terrified look.

"Find Corus, Sorge. Find him. Tell him Nemesia stayed true."

She plummeted below.

CHAPTER 44

COMPLETION

A s the dust settled, streams of pebbles rattled and clattered into the pit where the grove had once been. For a long time, nobody moved or spoke. Overhead, the heights of the sky remained clogged with darkness, but around the island the lower shadows began to dissipate a little. Some few, stray sunbeams made their way through.

The Watchers had fled, ready for power and spoil purchased elsewhere at lesser cost. They had no desire to remain so near to a mirling, risking recapture, if they did not have to. With Nemesia gone, they did *not* have to. Sorge lay near the edge of the cavity, clenching and unclenching his fist, shaking. Asandra lay beside him, weeping.

"You knew?" she said at last. Hidden in her words was something fragile, a question of worth. Of years and tears and anger. Sorge was unwilling to look at her, but he nodded.

"I was a different man, then."

"Why didn't you come to me? I suffered so much, piecing stories together. I came to hate you."

"I carried you in my thoughts every day, Asandra. I have failed at so many things in my life. But you were never one of them. Even so, I hoped you would grow, free of my sins. I hoped you would never have to know. It was a risk, but I thought you might have a better chance, a fresher start, without me. Without the burden of knowing who your mother was."

"I was born to a woman, not a mother," Asandra said bitterly. "At least I could have had a father."

Sorge stared at his hands, the ground. He had no words.

Ewan hobbled to his brother. Hadyn grabbed a fistful of Ewan's clothes, pulled him into an embrace. His hands shook, as if the moment might pass and all be a dream.

"It was so dark," he whispered. "I thought I was forgotten."

He started to pull away. Ewan held tight, unwilling to let go.

"Never," said the younger brother, his voice muffled, his face pressed against Hadyn's chest. When he finally pulled away, saw Hadyn's battered face, he wrinkled his nose. "You look awful."

Hadyn smiled weakly. They both did. A relief valve had opened.

All six took turns gazing down upon Nemesia. Her body was broken, her legs and arms bent at odd angles, splayed across the body of a cedar tree in the water below. Sorge extended a hand, palm out.

"May Aion have mercy. On us all."

He took Asandra's hand. She allowed it. Realizing many eyes still watched them, the monk addressed the stragglers who had not fled, who waited for direction. Their confusion was almost painful to witness. They truly were *Lost*.

"Nemesia was a cruel master to all of you," he said, raising his voice. He had regained a measure of strength but shook as if he was cold. "She stole your name. Your future. She was going to use you for great evil, whether you lived or died." He pointed to the bloody ground where Shy Eyes had lain. "If you do not believe me, ask this one."

Gradually, as he spoke, the darkness broke. As did the stupor of thought for all of them. Faces stared at the green grass, the blue water far below, each other, as if for the first time. They murmured amongst themselves. One voice grew loud. Though Hadyn could not see her, to his ears, it sounded like Kyra. The girl from the boat.

"What do we do now?"

"Go home to your families," Sorge said. "Most have not been as wrong toward you as you think. You have been bedeviled. In fact, they likely grieve, thinking you are dead. If they have wronged you, forgive them. If they do not want you, go to an abbey for sanctuary or find work in a village. Most of you are of age. Claim your name again. Make a life."

He had no strength to say more. The crowd slowly dispersed, waved away by a hobbled Creed. To where, Hadyn had no idea. How do you strip a soul and then put it back together again? He had felt that ravaging, if only for a few days. Healing would take time.

Asandra began tending to the wounded, and there were many. As it happened, Cruedwyn had not dealt a single fatal blow fending off Nemesia's captains. Such was his skill, thrusting and jabbing to nonvital areas, crippling for a time. But not killing. Many of these lay on the ground, bleeding, moaning.

"I wouldn't have guessed," Ewan said. "It looked like you were on a rampage."

Creed put his arm around Ewan's shoulders. "Ah, my boy. A skill as precise as mine is closer akin to a surgeon's blade than a brutish club. I do what I intend, strike where I aim. Never more. Never less."

Within seconds, he was tearing his sword belt loose, cursing, casting the molten blade to the ground. He pushed three fingers to his lips to keep from howling at the pain.

"Maybe sometimes . . . less."

The grove was a tangled mess of carnage: collapsed earth, exploded trees, shattered rocks. The six picked their way carefully around the areas that had survived the blast, that had not fallen inward. The trees that survived, they defaced. Sorge, though weak, displayed angry passion in cleansing the bark of its wicked markings. Asandra gathered elements of wood, stone, water, held them in her hands, raised them to the sky, offering prayers to heal the land. It would take more than she could give, but it was a start.

Since the ritual was never completed, the strange darkness was not sealed upon the wands and arrows. Slowly, it began to fade. Sorge ordered all the implements collected, thrown in a pile, and burned. He remained until he personally witnessed each consumed to the very last puff of ash—except the Staff of Shades. Its power fire could not destroy. Sorge wrapped the profane thing in his cloak.

"Such great evil," he said thoughtfully, glancing at the gray, clearing sky. For days, the Staff of Shades had burned, stolen light, sending shadows across the bay to the mainland. It would affect the people it touched. Perhaps not as far and wide as Nemesia's full intent. But darkness like this was sticky. It fascinated. It prepared souls for evil. It would require attention, care, prayer. The land was already so weak.

Steadfast spirit. Mercy of Aion.

This, too, would take time.

Hours had passed. Hadyn felt an urge to look upon Nemesia once more, for closure. Standing near the edge, he peered into the gaping hole.

"Sorge!"

Sorge came. The others came. Nemesia was gone.

"Should've killed her when we had the chance," Creed said. "Made sure."

"Fallings could not live," Flogg said. "Not human."

Sorge said nothing. He lifted his hood so that none could see.

They made their way, limping, torn, down the ravine, into the valley, to the shore below. They found empty, waiting boats—skiffs, schooners, keels, flat-bottomed barges—and selected one they thought they could manage. None of them were sailors. Some of the Lost milled about the shore. Several young men and women asked to go with them. One of them was Grayday.

"What is your real name?" Hadyn asked her. "Tell me now."

"I don't remember."

They took her on board, with a few others who seemed most ready to leave. They did not have room for very many. They did their best to mount a single sail and caught a southerly wind for Stratamore.

Elysabel had seen many things in her five hundred years. But nothing quite like this. Power and courage. Pain and betrayal. Tears and blood and hope. Maybe it had always been so. Maybe she had simply never taken the time to watch so closely. But the queen had commanded: *watch.*

So she had. For days. After seeing the older brother hauled to the island, she had stayed with the younger. She had been with him in the chamber with the one they called governor. Such fancy, important men. So much talking! She had followed them under the waters, through the caves. The younger brother was fiercely devoted. The older was strong, had held firm. She saw all this but did not understand.

It was not for her to understand, only to convey. The queen would expect a report soon. She had much to tell. But for the first time she could ever remember, it seemed strange to leave, to go from here to there. She had grown attached. She wanted the boy to see her again. To talk to him.

It was forbidden. Dangerous. Didn't change the wanting.

Away she flew, leaving them on the blue water, in their old boat. As she lifted into the sky, the younger one turned unexpectedly, as if he had heard a noise. His gaze followed the slant of light she disappeared into. Just in time, she hoped.

Still, she wondered.

CHAPTER 45

A HERO'S WELCOME

All the next day, prior to their audience with Archibald, they rested beneath the castle's three white towers. They didn't know it, but stable boys, chamberlains, scullery maids, and cooks were abuzz with tales of their deeds. Court officials whispered nervously, being highly attuned to any shift in the balance of power. *Troublemakers*, they said amongst themselves.

Asandra slept all night and half the next day, rose, ate some bread, and slept again. Sorge recovered more quickly, though the darkness, or Nemesia's loss, had clearly taken something from him. He was quieter, his gaze less intense. He spent much time alone. Flogg wandered in the small woods within the palace grounds, looking for mushrooms, grumbling over the loss of his satchel, though of course he would soon fashion another one. Cruedwyn, whose back was miraculously unbroken by the force

353

of the blast, suffered with a smile while two flouncy, pretty-faced maidens nursed his bruised bones and muscles.

Hadyn and Ewan were mostly a mess. They felt elation, relief, dejection, triumph. Upon waking, they sat in their room, eating grapes and honeybread and dried meat, contemplating the last three weeks. So much had happened. So much gained and lost.

"It wasn't how I expected," Ewan said, mostly to himself. "The adventure."

Hadyn nodded, his eyes swimming with memory, pain. "Nope."

"Didn't know it would be like this."

Hadyn said nothing.

Light slanted into their room. Motes of dust danced in the beams. A sudden feeling of awkwardness, of the nearness of the other, forced their gazes apart, unsure what to say or how to say it. How do you shape pain and magic into words? How was it possible to feel altogether foreign about a place, yet drenched with *aliveness* right where you sat? In one breath, homesick yet glad? Torn from comfort, yet strangely at peace. The only thing worse than the thought of staying one more day . . . was the thought of suddenly getting their wish and going home. They both felt it. Neither dared speak it.

"What do we do now?" Ewan said, intentionally vague.

Hadyn nibbled at a grape, held up empty hands, equally elusive. "Honest to God, I don't know."

He thought a moment, studying the floor, the crumbling mortar of the ancient walls, as if they might hold hidden clues. "I get this weird feeling Dad might have known about a world like this. Or at least suspected. He and Mom had been researching for years. Then they bought the old farm."

"For the runestone."

"Because an ACP might be there, in Newland."

Ewan was grateful for the distraction from his own inner world. He pondered.

"What's that even mean? Ancient Civilization Portal?"

"Heck, I don't know. Dad's always been knee deep in British stuff, though. Celts and all. Wales. Ireland. It's weird, I can't explain it. But it kind of feels like that here. Like an alternate universe. Know what I mean?"

"Camelot," Ewan said, smiling. He was fighting tears.

"Something like that."

Ewan's voice began to crack. "We were supposed to go with Dad on his next trip. What if we're stuck here forever?"

The older boy wrapped his arm awkwardly around the younger's neck. "I miss home, too. You know that's a big deal for me to say." He paused. "And yet . . ."

"I know. You hate Newland."

"No . . . no. A part of me feels at home *here*, too."

Like a dark secret loosed, Hadyn knew it was true. Even Ewan felt strangely released to hear it spoken. Both fell silent again. For Hadyn, Newland was foreign and friendless, while Karac Tor had only brought great pain into his life. Yet for all the pain, his time in the Hidden Lands was a revelation. Home had become more than a place, more than a spot on the map. Home was an idea, a strange convolution of emotion, identity, and experience. He took note of Ewan's gray green eyes, the shining rim of hope he saw there. Hope, the color of tears. The belief that one day, somehow, they *would* make it back.

For his part, Ewan knew he was not done in this world. What good would it do to escape to home and then only wish to be back here again? Here, where it was dreadful, dangerous. Here, where he saw Fey and his music released power. Here there were friends:

Sorge, Cruedwyn. Even Flogg. In a matter of seconds, both boys bounced from one extreme to the other—urgency to leave, desperation, anxiety; to never leave, hope, adventure.

Both groped toward the center again, toward one another. The space between their words became an apology of sorts, for questions without answers and feelings beyond explanation. In the muddle, a blessing emerged: At least they had each other. In the silence, both seemed to agree that Karac Tor *had* called to them. And, as Sorge had long ago pointed out, they had answered.

That part of the ache was certain. Returning home was not.

Hadyn put aside his own questions and turned his strength to comfort his brother. In that moment, he grew, became more of a man. This time, on Ewan's shoulder, his fingers did not shake.

"No matter what, we'll make it home. We'll see Dad again. Soon."

By mid-afternoon all six of them were rested, collected, washed, fed, and ready. Archibald, having met privately with Sorge, now received the ragtag troupe in his courtroom, surrounded by advisors. Except Jonas. The Minister of Justice was notably absent.

"So you've stirred up a real hornet's nest, monk." Archibald lifted his sagging chin with contempt. "Nemesia was not a friend. Any fool could see that. But at least she was docile. Now you have made issues. For us all."

The six glanced at one another, stunned. Had he not listened to Sorge, earlier that day, debriefing in the governor's private study? The full onslaught of darkness had only narrowly been averted, yet a thousand Watchers now streaked through the air of Karac Tor, *unbound.* Their presence would be felt. Very little was required to bring the cursed beasts to flesh. And the darkness of the Staff of Shades? Such arcana was difficult to calculate, but light had been consumed, devoured by unlight. It could never be restored. What opportunities for evil might now be possible that had not been before? How could the unimaginable be anticipated? Darkness, fundamentally, was blindness.

"Nemesia was destroyed," Asandra said contemptuously. Sorge subtly motioned her with his hand. *Shh.*

Archibald scoffed. "Is she? Then show me. Show me the body!"

Asandra either did not notice Sorge's hand or did not care. "Clearly, she was moved."

"Clearly, you say? By whom? Fool of a mirling. A renegade may act as he, or she, likes, but a *ruler* must consider all factors. I said she was docile before. Do you think she will be tame if she lives?"

"It is unlikely she lives," Sorge said calmly.

"Jonas believes it. We consulted. Before he left on matters of state."

"Be that as it may, with respect, the pot you say we stirred was boiling before, and most certainly would have soon spilled over. The only difference would be a guest in your land dead and even greater evil unleashed. Far greater."

"So you say." Archibald sniffed, unmoved.

"My lord, you saw the creeping shadow. You heard the explosions. She sat at your doorstep and mocked you with her plans. It is she who stole their names from the Book. Her power could not be ignored."

Archibald uncoiled like a spring. "Yet you feel quite comfortable ignoring me? My will? You know nothing of diplomacy, Gray. Or affairs of state. Do you think me a mongrel by the trash heap, to speak to me so, telling me what to do, whom to fear? I will decide what is right!"

He stood for several moments, quivering, red with rage. Then he collected himself. Looping his thumbs in the belt of his robe, he turned his attention to the Barlow brothers.

"And here we have the young heroes, right? You should keep better counsel——"

"Kindly, sir," Hadyn interrupted. He felt no loyalty to a fool. "The only counsel we really want is how to get home."

Archibald narrowed his eyes. Impertinent boy. "Yes, well, on that, I cannot help you. I informed your brother as much before he went off making a mess of things for *me*. As if I didn't already have enough problems, and now a dead witch come back to life."

"They saved my life, you know. This group of troublemakers. You weren't there."

The governor fell heavily into his seat, made a noise, dismissed them with a wave. Most of his advisors behaved in similar fashion, though a few seemed troubled, even embarrassed. Sorge did not dawdle. He rose, bowed, and left.

Their sandaled feet padded softly on the polished marble slab, past the great doors, past the Governor's Elite, with spears and helmets plumed in blue. In the council hall, Hadyn heard Archibald call out, "Before you go, Elder! I think I should see this staff you spoke about. The shadow-maker. Perhaps it has usefulness."

His request rang out, sharp as a spear point gripped in the hands of the silent guards. Sorge left it there, unanswered. He did not break stride.

CHAPTER 46

ON THE ROAD

Once outside the castle, Sorge gave full vent to his rage. "Fool of a man!" he spat. His braided ponytail snapped on his head. "*Give* him the staff? Him? Does he really think?"

They stood now in the bustling lanes of the city outside the outer wall and ramparts. Street performers danced. Merchants hawked beads, silver, wine, rope, food. Metalsmiths clanged upon horseshoes and shovels and links of chain in a cascade of sparks. The air smelled of smoke, meat, and unwashed bodies. As they had marched away from the governor's audience hall, Archibald had called for them once more, demanding they return. Even so, no guard rose to prevent them. No escort had been detached.

Sorge leaned his face to the sky as if wringing answers from the clouds. "We should go to the White Abbey," he said slowly. "The Book of Law will tell us how to deal with the staff. It cannot be left with Archibald."

"Might the Whites know something to help *us*?" Hadyn

reminded. "You know?"

"Indeed . . . why didn't I think of that?"

"Sorge, it is time. I cannot continue on." Asandra smiled wanly. Her eyes were on her father. "I must go to Seabraith. I'm quite late."

"I must go too," Cruedwyn added, squinting into the sun. "Somewhere."

"And that would be . . . ?" Ewan let the question trail away. He had grown quite fond of the bard, but he hardly believed a word the man said.

"Oh, the Highlands, perhaps. Or maybe Aventhorn Keep. A charming place, the old city and the new. You should go sometime. Perhaps I'll get inspired to write a song."

"It wouldn't have anything to do with the fact that Pol Shyne has driven the League from there, would it?" Asandra teased.

"Has he? I had no idea!" Creed exclaimed, putting his hand on his heart as if wounded. "Elder, will you allow this from your own daughter? What does she take me for? I'll have you know I come from a long line of courageous bards. An even longer line of Creeds, who never walk away from a fight, who never — "

"Cruedwyn," Hadyn warned.

"Packed in my bag! A blessing beyond compare. Allow me my moment!"

Sorge grinned. "Come with us as far as Faielyn. Then sail to Tinuviel if you need. Truth be told, we may need your sword again."

He extended his hand, awaiting a clasp. Cruedwyn shadowed his eyes. "I see. A blessed donkey is better than a yoke of oxen. Is that what you're saying?"

"I would never speak so poorly of donkeys," Sorge said with mock gravity.

"Marvelous. A witty monk."

Ewan laughed out loud, but the bard quickly sobered. "Truth be told, I could probably use a friend even more than you could use a sword."

He took Sorge's offered grip and winked at the boys. "Somebody has to keep you boys alive. Otherwise, all you've got is Sorge. And his Mighty Stick of Peace."

Sorge thumped Creed in the stomach. Both laughed.

They bade farewell to Asandra. The parting was especially bittersweet for her father. With no easy means of closure, Sorge had avoided the moment as long as he could. Their road from this point was unknown, but a common future was no longer impossible to imagine. Not that it would be easy. They didn't know how to talk to each other about the guilt, the hurt. They simply pulled aside, exchanging whispered words, meant only for each other, where both expressed a willingness to start. The fact was (and all could see it), Asandra had noticeably lightened in the last two days—lightened by about twenty years. She was still quite prickly, but there was a new grace. She offered the sign of the circle to her five friends, a blessing of peace, lingering most in her farewell to Hadyn as if waiting for an answer, though no question had been asked. Hadyn felt the intensity of her eyes, returning it without words. He was nearly sixteen, still a boy through and through. Unsure what her gaze might mean, he was equally unwilling to let the moment simply slip away.

"Good-bye, Asandra," he said. "Maybe another time."

She smiled. "Another place."

Then turned and walked away.

The journey to the White Abbey took two weeks. Maybe three. The road, a well-used merchant's path, many centuries old, was usually hard-packed and deep with ruts, but not in the fickle weather of late. Amazingly, it still bristled with traffic; carts pulled by oxen or donkeys laden with produce, rugs, or barrels of wine, headed to market in the King's City or one of many lesser villages along the way. The road stayed a stone's throw from the broad curves of the Kinsman River, which bulged and frothed as it overspilled its banks, leaving broad swaths of fields under water, including, at times, the road. It was slow, messy going.

The waterway traced its supply to the legendary headwaters of Mount Bourne, where Yhü first drank the forbidden melted snow of Aion's sacred mountain, and the familiar doom was laid upon him: to record the entire future of his enormous, extended lineage. Every soul to spring from his loins, housed in the Hall of Ages. The Book of Names thus became both punishment and redemption, for it promised his progeny, though cursed, would regain their glory in his name. It promised, one day, victory.

The full tale was much longer, but stories like this flowed from Sorge like water from a new well. He seemed eager to share them and only occasionally tired of the relentless questions that followed. The boys learned more about Karac Tor than they could ever remember, probably more even than they knew about their own world. For Hadyn, the tales had the ring of something true, almost familiar. Every now and then Flogg would interject a comment. Creed mainly listened, occasionally cracking jokes. Usually, he seemed content with silence, which offered the added blessing of his never having to peel off his sword. Perhaps he was learning.

It rained frequently. They traveled soaked as often as dry, tramping and stamping, as Flogg might say, through deep ruts of mud. Quite wearisome. Even Cruedwyn's normally high spirits were hard pressed. Their campfires would not burn. Their skin seemed permanently pruned and chilled. But at least there were no jackals, no Watchers. No Nemesia, no Lost. And maybe, just maybe, the rain was washing them clean.

About the midway point, the road forked. One leg headed north to Faielyn. The other proceeded on to the abbey. For days, rain or no rain, the path had presented them with staggering, dramatic beauty. Vineland was a long valley of lush grass and sweeping blue skies. It was the first undiminished stretch of fertile fields and clean, rushing water they had yet encountered. So much of the Midlands—at least what they had seen over the hills toward Threefork—had been bleak and dry and brownish gray. Forsaken. Like Redthorn, cursed to its roots. And then Apaté, trapped in shadows. Not a pretty first impression. But here, when the sun burst through and the rain dried, colors shimmered with vibrancy, causing even the memory of Nemesia's dark island to fade. Carefully cultivated vineyards of fat, sweet grapes filled the air with fragrant aromas. Red stucco homes dotted the hillsides. Young children played and danced and sang; in the mud, of all things. But they looked happy.

Such was the valley. A soothing gift to the soul. The Rim (so Sorge called it) was another matter entirely, for it both intimidated and inspired. As a natural phenomena, it was beyond fathoming—a looming, imposing, impossible wall of solid rock, rising to the south across the Kinsman and paralleling the river's path. It was simply enormous. The unbroken cliff line soared skyward with no warning, no preliminary foothills. Rather, it was as if the earth had merely broken into two chunks along that line, with one portion dropping low and forming the green swath of Vineland to the north and the other, sudden and terrifying, protruding from the earth a thousand feet straight up to the Highlands. The sheer climb — or drop, depending on where you stood — was solid granite, and it stretched nearly a hundred miles from Stratamore all the way to the White Abbey. To look at it was to shrivel into smallness.

At some point along the way, Ewan realized these were the very cliffs, the same river, he had seen from the hill north of Stratamore, the day they decided to take the Raven Trail. It was the extended landscape of his first dream.

"Up and over, there . . . the Highlands," Sorge explained. "Fierce warriors. Shapeshifters, once. Aion welcomed them to Karac Tor long ago, but banned them from shapeshifting, for that was the way of Kr'Nunos. They are called Bird People. If you see a hawk or kestrel circling above the ridge, a Highlander's likely there, unseen. When there is war, since they can no longer change shape, they will swoop down from the Rim on great false wings they wear on their arms. It is a fearsome sight, to see the sky darkened with Highland warriors. For this reason, there is little love between them and the people of this valley. They are called Bird Men but not kindly."

They kept a leisurely pace, continuing to regain strength, eating often, gathering fresh, wild herbs and vegetables and wild game. With Flogg's help, they ate like royalty. Ewan, many days past, had apologized to the gnome for his rudeness and suspicion. The two were actually beginning to be friends. Around the fire, more stories flowed. More and more. The rich history of the land began to seep deeply into the Barlows. Without their realizing it, Karac Tor was beginning to define their frame of reference for life.

After roughly a week, just past the fork in the road to Faielyn, Ewan noticed a series of structures on the ridge, identical in shape and size, like giant, flat stone slabs. Perched on the edge of the

Rim, they overlooked Vineland and Redthorn like guards at attention. They were enormous to be visible at such a great distance.

"The Sentinels," Sorge said, before Ewan could ask. "A mystery to all. No one knows who built them or what purpose they serve. They are ancient beyond all memory, all story or legend or song. They have marks that no one can read."

Ewan glanced at Hadyn, mouthed a question. *ACPs?* Hadyn shrugged.

"Nine," the older Barlow mused, almost to himself. Louder, he said, "I count nine Sentinels, Sorge. There's the Nine Gifts. Nine notes in Aion's Song . . ."

Sorge took up the rhythm. "Nine Powers, Nine Worlds, Nine Elements, Nine Sacred Names, Nine Secrets, Nine Sentinels, Nine Sleepers, Nine Stars, Nine Sorrows, Nine Songs. Yes, clever boy. Nine is very important. It is a most sacred number — *the* most. It is the number of Aion, who has come eight times before and will come again. The Ninth Coming. The War of Swords. Which reminds me!" Sorge grabbed Ewan, tousled his hair. "How *did* you know the Song of Aion? And beautifully played, I might add."

"That was the song at the portal. It's what opened the door."

Sorge froze. "What did you say?"

"The nine notes. It—"

"Opened the door. Yes, that's what I thought."

He turned to Flogg, spoke, as if quoting.

"Doors shall open, doors shall close . . ."

"Oh, even I know *that* one," Cruedwyn exclaimed. "It's been set to at least a dozen different tunes over the years. The old land barons love to hear it. 'Cause it's spooky, I suppose."

Groping, Sorge closed his eyes. It took him a moment to catch the rhythm.

"In final days come final woes;
Doors shall open, doors shall close.
Forgotten curse blight the land,
Four names, one blood—fall or stand."

Ewan felt a chill rush up his spine.

"Another *Orn*?"

Sorge began to pace, prodding the ground with his staff. High above, a kestrel cried, alone in the wind.

"It's nothing, or so I've often thought. An ancient riddle. A prophecy, some believe. Maybe nonsense." He turned to Flogg. "Forgotten curse. How would you say that?"

The gnome thought a moment.

"Curse of forgetting."

"Merciful Aion," Sorge whispered, his face grown pale. "Nemesia. The Lost. The Book of Names."

After that, he would not speak for many days.

CHAPTER 47

REVENGE

His body, covered in thick fur, glistened with the milky dew of early morning. He had lain in the woods all night. He had ridden hard for two weeks, then three, then four. Ridden his great steed named Vyle, a midnight stallion with red eyes. Jackals had run with him through Redthorn. Watchers, fresh from their release at Apaté, swarmed overhead and called to him from the Midland sky. They hated him, for he had made them what they were. But they were forever enslaved to his will.

The Devourer relished the thought of his plans. In a crevasse of rock and dirt, in the woods near the Gray Abbey, lay the broken body of Melanor, Brother of the Grays. His neck snapped. Kr'Nunos laughed. It pleased him to know the shape of the man before him, already cold on the earth, would wield the knife. It was a good and wicked plan.

Kr'Nunos, the Devourer, was a shapeshifter. Not always so. But long ago, having learned the power of false forms, he had gladly traded his essence for the ability to become another appearance, whatever he might need or want. Whatever, whenever *he* wanted, not some faraway princeling in Isgurd. Even so long ago, he had loved running with the wild beasts. Loved their power, their wild mating, their killing and thunder. It was drunken rebellion for his soul. And so it happened, in the ancient, darkly spun past, that he lost himself, became the beast.

He was in his natural form now—the only form that was natural anymore—with muscled man's legs, a pelt of fine hair on his naked chest, a beastly, handsome face and heavy crown of giant antlers. He was not masked as the baron. That form was needed from time to time, as were others. The shape of the baron, the fear it brought, served him well. It would prove even more valuable in the days to come, he knew. But it was so hard to hold another shape for long. He could only do it with great effort, for short periods. Yet every day, he improved, got stronger. His patience was paying off. He had hidden for a long time. Walking among men, as men. Killing them in secret, taking their place as needed so no one would know. He could do that. *Become* . . . as long as their bodies were freed from their souls, he could take their shape. All over the kingdom, he was known by many names, many faces. Current names, no longer only the legends and myths of old. He relished the old names, the fear of them, most of all. But his new tactic was much more cunning. It was no longer only fear and power, but strategy and timing. And plans many layers deep, plans that would ultimately lead to total dominion. Wrapped in the skin and flesh of common men, he had sown his seeds. In many places, they had already taken root.

A low sound of pleasure bubbled and frothed on his lips. He nursed it as he nursed his anger. For eons, he had drunk deep from the well of hate. At long last, his time had come again. His army of Goths was growing, deep under the mountains of the north. An entire generation of humanity was stranded in nothingness, incapable of resistance. The Watchers were released. Jackals multiplied. Yes, he was very near.

Rising now from the earth, he bayed at the waning moon, overcome, as a beast would be, by forces deep within the light in the sky, the sway of the night. He expelled hard air from his wet nostrils in great, gushing breaths, saw them feather out and fade in the moonbeams. His hair was matted with maggots and sticks and creeping bugs. And the still-wet blood of Brother Melanor, who had come out to the forest, late at night, to pray.

The smell of the monk's blood drove the Devourer mad. He thirsted for more. For revenge. The old man would become a problem soon. He was in the way already. He had intervened too much. Outside, in the woods, Kr'Nunos had left his horse where it was tethered, and begun walking. This would not take long. His enormous shape shadowed the already darkened ground. The branched horns of his antlers waved slightly to and fro as he strode. He shook. Cried out. A pained, beastly sound. Sounds of squishing and cracking came from his skin, his teeth, his bones.

By the time he reached the abbey in the dark, his form had changed.

In the shape of Brother Melanor, he passed through the halls. A few other brothers had also risen by now, so early. But most slept. Those who were awake were sealed in their rooms, kneeling for prayer. None knew his plan. None could have known.

Melanor reached his destination swiftly. The door was unlocked. Eldoran never locked his door. None of them did. This was a place of peace. They prayed, tilled the earth, tended orphanages, made cheese.

Melanor reached into his gray robe, pulled out a knife. He

entered. The Father of the Grays snored rhythmically. His gray beard and hair were mussed. Only the faintest traces of light passed through the small window, enough to see the pale white circle burned onto the skin of his forehead so long ago — some fifty years, when he first took his vows.

The Devourer waited in the room for a long time. He wanted more light. Wanted Eldoran to see the shape of Melanor. To despair of the efforts of his life, before he died.

When it was light enough, just enough, the lips of Melanor moved.

"Father, awaken."

Eldoran stirred, saw his friend. He sat up in bed, still groggy. His lips were dry and a trail of spittle had collected in his beard.

"What's wrong friend?"

"I came to tell you," Melanor said, "that the day of Aion has passed. The time of the Horned Lord has come!"

A swift stab of the knife. Again and again. Eldoran did not even have time to gasp. Crimson fluid spewed from his belly and chest, trickled from his mouth. He dropped to the ground, gurgling, clutching the hand of his brother, the one who had taken his life. Only the hand he held was a different hand. There was a mark that Melanor never had. That the Devourer could never hide. Some things cannot be hidden.

On the underside of the wrist. The antlered shape of a great stag.

CHAPTER 48

THE RAVNA'S RIDDLE

At the White Abbey, dusty from the road and weary, the travelers were greeted with a mixture of warmth and reserve. Honored guests, and potential trouble. In particular, Hadyn and Ewan were viewed with outright suspicion. Yet the sign of the circle was offered to each of them, and they were allowed to enter in peace. An older man with a shock of white hair, dressed in tan, guided them around a series of paved stone walkways to a large building made of mud brick, whitewashed with lime. Inside, down a narrow hall, they passed room after room with more men in tan robes bent over tall desks, poring over meticulous copies of the Book of Law.

"Master wordsmen," Cruedwyn whispered, with high, intentional drama. "Learned men."

At the end of the hall, the narrow corridor swelled to a large vaulted space, ringed with still more men, these dressed in yellow. More desks, too. The faces of the men were taut, anxious. Each had a quill, a pot of ink, and several sheaves of paper. Letter by letter, they transcribed sacred writ. The room was heavy with silence and shuffling paper, scratching quills. A stern, regal man wandered slowly behind each, looking over their shoulders. He alone was dressed in white. When he saw his visitors, he immediately appraised the brothers coldly. Raising a steady, hushing hand, he escorted them outside.

"High Priest," Sorge began deferentially, once they were outside again.

"No need for pleasantries, Elder. Word travels fast. We have heard of your dealings with Nemesia. Though you may be surprised, I agree with Governor Archibald. Your actions were rash and ill considered. You should have consulted us first."

"The boy's life was in danger, your grace. We were *all* in danger."

Alethes said nothing, letting the silence tell his doubt. Sorge procured the folded mass of twine and fabric slung over his shoulder, opened it, held up the Staff of Shades for Alethes to see. The high priest reflexively formed a circle with his hands, warding off evil.

"Aion's mercy. Put it away," he snapped. "This is holy ground."

"All the more reason to entrust it to the Whites. Let the Book of Law destroy it."

Even so, Alethes would not touch the staff, so Sorge was forced to carry it further. They resumed walking again, ambling along a garden path past various smaller abodes. Green-clad scribes tended herbs and squash and lentil patches here, diligent in manual labor until their spiritual rigors, come afternoon. They

THE BOOK of NAMES

did not look happy. Though the White Abbey had finally set aside its fasting and mourning, it was far from at peace with itself.

As they strolled, Alethes did not move his head, but his eyes strayed constantly toward the boys. "So. You are the royal visitors from another world?" He made no attempt to hide his disbelief.

"I guess that's right," Hadyn answered.

"No, no, no. No guessing," Alethes reprimanded, as if schooling them. "We must be sure. We must test. We must *validate*."

They approached another building. Two monks at the door nodded to the high priest. Sorge paused outside.

"With all due respect, your grace. *I* am sure of it. As is Father Eldoran."

"The Whites"—Alethes sniffed—"will make their own assessment."

"And just how will you make certain?"

"A test. The simplest test of all."

He pushed against the door. When it swung open, a cry rang out. A cry of surprise. Recognition.

"Hadyn! Ewan!"

A flurry of motion. A warm, familiar body pounced on both. Hadyn was stunned.

"Gabe?"

Gabe grinned fiercely, all noise and words and excited gesticulations.

"I can talk to birds!" he exclaimed. "Can you believe it? I come here—wherever we are, Kractor or whatever—and I can talk to birds. They know my voice! What in the world does that mean?"

Hadyn and Ewan stared, dumbstruck. Sorge, likewise. Alethes, carefully observing their interactions, stroked his chin. He had apparently heard this much already. Gabe, like a gushing river, kept chattering away. Until he saw Flogg. He jumped. Flogg crinkled his snout in retort. Gabe jumped again. Creed burst out laughing at both of them.

"Hold it, hold it!" Hadyn shouted, baffled, throwing his hands in the air. "Wait, what . . . how?"

Beaming, the youngest twin unrolled a scroll. Gilded in gold. Signed at bottom with a large, scrollwork *A*.

Then started chattering again. It went like this . . .

He and Garret had found the scrolls under Hadyn's bed, right? The morning Hadyn and Ewan went missing. *(Sorry, we know. It's your room, not ours.)* Thought about telling Dad, didn't want to worry him. Figured Hadyn and Ewan had gone to the briar patch early. Risky. Knew they weren't supposed to go. Grabbed a backpack. Flashlights. Other stuff. Took the scrolls. Why? Don't know. Crawled to the back, through the tunnel. Lights glowed. Then through the rock thingy. Bam! (Gabe made a smack with his hands.)

"What was the name of that place again?" he asked.

"Ga'Haim," said Alethes, unamused, but relaxing. The test, it seemed, had largely been passed. "Ga'Haim, capital of the Highlands."

"Anyway, right. Ga'Haim. Landed in a wilderness there. Near the city. Hot! Surrounded by ravens. Heard them talking. Can you believe it? Birds, talking! Then a Bird Man showed up. Oops, a Wingman. A Highlander. Took me to the city, to their leader. The Jute?"

Alethes, once again: "K'vrkeln the Jute. Clanlord of the Highlanders."

"And boy, is he one serious dude!" Gabe said. "He didn't know what to do with me, so he sent one of his Wingmen to bring me here. I flew! Off the Rim. About peed my pants, but here I am.

Can you believe it?"

"No," Hadyn said, smiling. "Yes. How long have you been here?"

"I dunno. Weeks."

Sorge shook his head. "Bless you, Ravna! And your glorious riddle!" He burst out laughing, shouting. "To live in such a day!"

Everyone turned toward the monk in gray. Sorge drew out his words. "Hadyn Barlow, Ewan Barlow, Garret Barlow, Gabe Barlow. 'Four names, one blood.'" He glanced at Alethes. "Doors shall open, doors shall close."

Flogg nodded slowly. "Final days. Final woes."

Alethes stepped back as if he had been pushed. Color drained from his face. He reached for the wall to steady himself.

"Can it be?" he murmured.

Sorge flashed a broad white smile. "Your grace, look at them! How can it not be?"

"Yes, yes, I see. Obviously, something . . ." He wiped his eyes, wide awake. His voice was dry, like a bag full of stones. "I see it now, or begin to. But if it is true, then it can mean only one thing."

"The War of Swords," Sorge acknowledged. "It is coming. We approach the unknown, the sheet of gold. The end of time."

Alethes nodded slowly. "Easy, Gray. We must not pretend to know what is not *specifically* decreed. I, for one, will not go down that road. And yet it is clear to me now I have been traveling in circles, stubborn and blind. Aion have mercy, I am twice a fool. Unwilling to admit both the turning of the age and the full scope of evil. The blank pages. I should have known."

"Excuse me," Ewan interrupted. "Where's Garret?"

Hadyn spun around, feeling the hair on the back of his neck begin to rise. *Where* was *Garret?* They all looked at Gabe.

Gabe shrugged. "For the millionth time, I don't know. He's with some guy. Someplace else. I tried to tell the Jute."

Hadyn tried to keep a calm tone. "Tell me exactly what happened, Gabe."

"You won't be able to figure it out either. Besides, the guy said he'd be fine."

"What guy? Gabe, what guy?"

Gabe put his hand on his hip, as if put upon, or caught giving away a secret. "Okay, here's the deal. When we both went through that arch thingy, it got all dark and weird and stayed that way for a couple of minutes. I couldn't see anything, couldn't see Garret. But I heard him talking. Like someone else was in there with us. When it got all bright again, I was laying there on the rocks outside—"

"Ga'Haim."

"Right. And Garret was gone."

"The other voice," Hadyn pressed him. "What did it say?"

"It said Garret needed to go with him."

"Him? Who's him? Did he say his name?"

Gabe scrunched his face. His mop of blond hair hung over his eyes.

"I think it was Taliesin."

Sorge inhaled sharply. Alethes sat, heavily, on a nearby chair. Even Hadyn seemed to pale at the sound of the name.

"Gabe, say it again. What was his name?"

Gabe rolled his eyes. "Taliesin. Taliesin. He said he would take Garret to another place, and that it was for the good of all. Garret asked about Dad, then they left. I don't know any more than that, I promise."

Sorge leaned forward, rubbing his fingers in slow circles. "Gabe, I am a friend of your brothers. We've been through many adventures. Let me say the name I hear you saying. Please listen closely."

Gabe nodded, waited.

Sorge fixed his eyes on the boy, then carefully pronounced the name.

"Tal Yssen."

"That's it," Gabe smiled. "You got it."

All the air sucked out of the room. Ewan didn't have a clue what was going on, yet even Cruedwyn seemed dumbstruck. Hadyn had heard that name. He'd read it many times. From old earth legends. A name of legend on Karac Tor, too.

Alethes held his head in his hands, moaning. Sorge was caught up in wonder. "The greatest mirling of the Black Abbey . . . *alive?*"

Hadyn tried to stop his fingers, his voice, from shaking. He repeated the word. *Mirling.* A door connected to a series of more doors, revelation upon revelation, all suddenly opened at once. In his imagination, epiphany roared.

"Tal Yssen was a *mirling?*" he said softly, swallowing hard. His heart pounded.

"The most famous of all. It was said he talked to Fey." Sorge caught up to his own stream of thought. His eyes widened. "And built doorways to other worlds."

Hadyn stood in a daze. He could hardly believe his next words. "Sorge, you need to know. This man, Taliesin, is part of our history, too. Sort of. From a long time ago. Most don't even know about him anymore, at least not by that name. Nothing more than legend, now. But he is better known by another name. Now I know why. To us, he's *Merlin.*"

"What?" Ewan gasped.

Alethes shook his head, pounded his fist. His white hair was nappy and frayed. "It's all too much. You must be silent now! These events are beyond all reckoning. I must think! I must consult the Books. I have missed so many things."

His voice sounded full of doom. He looked from one brother to the next. His vision was unfocused. Lastly, to Sorge.

"What do you seek now, your grace? In the Books."

"An answer. To an obvious question: Do we win?"

His words formed pressure in the air. Hadyn had felt it before. Not so long ago, but forever it seemed. Not the same, but similar enough. A day of magic.

Today was not gray and cold, as it had been that day, but the same clean smell of ozone tingled in the air, from lightning and rain all across Vineland. *Then*, the oldest Barlow hadn't the eyes to see. He hadn't known anything about anything, really. Except starting over, missing Mom. He had been a stranger in a strange land, had spent all his time and emotion hating life.

Things were different now.

He glanced at Ewan. His brother's face held a devotion that matched his own, and that was good. Hadyn felt clarity, the fierce pleasure of a question that did not need words to be answered. How could he deny the amazing turn of events? Adventure beyond imagination. Gabe, too, was eager. Always ready to charge ahead. He would have to find his own answers along the way. Sorge, on the other hand, and Alethes and Flogg, had all grown strangely quiet. They seemed troubled beyond words, all searching for the same answer to Alethes's question.

Cruedwyn alone licked his lips, smelling battle.

"Whatever you say next," he offered, eyes firm on Hadyn. "You have a Creed with you."

Hadyn had no idea what he was about to say. Not a clue. For some reason, he trusted himself to say it anyway. To find the words, if he would just open his mouth.

So he did.

"A Call came, from your world to ours. We answered it." He found the eyes of each man in the room, young and old. "I don't know if we will win, but I have an answer for all of us. With our four names, with our one blood, I give you that answer . . . *we fight.*"

CHAPTER 1

TALIESIN

Darkness like a blindfold. Warm air, close to his skin. Garret felt panic rising. For some reason, it stayed in his belly. He heard his own voice, as if from a great distance:

"Who are *you*? And where am I?"

So much had happened. Such a short period of time. Only moments ago, they had scampered to the back of the tunnel with scrolls in hand. Winter cold, this morning. Cool light, falling from the sun, rising from the gray earth. Strange marks, glowing. Arch of rock. He hadn't known what to do. Neither had Gabe.

Curiously, Garret went first. Not the usual way of things. Why had he changed it up? But there he was, under the arch. Through the arch. Behind him, Gabe followed. That's when the darkness came, when light was swallowed. He had heard Gabe, laughing like it was an amusement park ride or something. Even felt him nearby, in the brush of arms and legs. There was a swirl of air, a sensation of movement, of falling. Something like wetness splashed over him, like plunging into water head first. Yet he remained dry. In the confusion that followed, they were separated.

"Gabe!" he cried out.

Faint and far away, he heard his brother call back to him. Then another voice, chuckling. A near, touchable voice. Not mocking, not vindictive. Amused. An old man's voice.

"Who are you?" Garret asked nervously.

The voice that answered from the warm darkness was clear:

"Before my release, I was many shapes:
I was a slender, enchanted sword;
Raindrops in the air, a star's white beam;
A word in letters, a book in origin;
I was a lamp of light for a year, and half again;
A bridge that stretched an estuary for sixty and six;
I was a path, a kestrel, I was a coracle in blue water."

The voice was pleasant, crackling with humor. "Many words have been written about me. For me. Words like these, wondering how I survive through time, how I move between worlds." A pause. "It makes for nice poetry, at least."

"Where am I?" Garret demanded. He was blind in the darkness.

"In between is the best I can tell you. We're on a journey, you and I. You'll see your brothers again soon enough. All of them. Don't worry, lad. I've been waiting for this for a long time"

Garret's tone became quite serious. "How do you know about Hadyn and Ewan?"

The old man's voice became even lighter. "Ah, how many times have I been asked that question? Eh? *How do you know?*

How did you do that? How, how, how! I know the same way I know about your letter—signed by the High Prince himself, no less. I just *know*."

"So you know about the scroll, too?"

The old man chuckled. "Many things, lad. I know many things. I have lived a very long time."

"Tell me your name then. I can't see you."

In the darkness, he felt a firm, gentle hand on his arm.

"Tal Yssen," answered the old man. "My name is Tal Yssen."

The rushing sensation came again. Darkness, changing colors, remained dark. Gabe's voice faded into distance, then nothingness. The next awareness Garret had was of sudden, pale blue skies and the smell of goats. His feet stood on firm ground—no more floating or plunging. He took a step, through something. Turned. Energy vibrated around him. At his back was another arch, similar to the one in the briar patch, but much larger, made of fitted, mortared stone. They stood alone, he and the man named Tal Yssen, on a solitary hill of green, surrounded by flatlands. Other than hedgerows of wild hazel and sparse outcroppings of hawthorn and elm, the hill was the only major feature, like someone had dropped it there by mistake. It rose, tall and sudden, shorn of trees, utterly alone, with vast sweeps of green on every side. A worn footpath wound down the hill, past a stand of trees, toward a clutch of wattle and daub buildings. One of them, larger than the rest, was circle shaped, with a cross-shaped beam rising from the center of the thatched roof. It looked to Garret like an old church. Near to these simple structures, but far for his eyes, hunching over like giant mushrooms, small brown figures worked in rows, tilling the earth.

"What is this place?" he said softly. Tal Yssen, he now realized, was perhaps sixty years old. He had a short-cropped, silver-white beard and a hawk's beak for a nose. He wore long leather breeches, a blue tunic, and a dark blue cloak, fastened at his neck with a silver brooch. His eyes were the color of new-tilled earth, and just as warm.

"You have not merely come to a place, but also a time," said Tal Yssen. "You stand in Ynys-Witrin, in the year of our Lord 539. This is your world, my boy. A long time ago."

"Ynis whatdja say?"

"Do not trouble over words. In your day and age, it will be known by other names."

"Okay, and the *five thirty-nine* part? Five thirty-nine? Really?"

Garret put his watch to his face. The timepiece was shaped like the logo of the Kansas City Chiefs. A gift from Dad last year, for Christmas. Their first Christmas without Mom. Growing up in Independence, the Chiefs had always been Mom's favorite team—thus, the family's favorite. He never took it off. And it kept great time. But now, the digital display was frozen at 7:43.

Maybe when I entered the arch? he wondered.

The seconds meter, reading twenty-seven, didn't move either. Perplexed, Garret tapped his finger on the glass top. This made *no* sense.

"That device will do you no good here," Tal Yssen informed him equably.

Garret whirled, as if hoping to find a hidden camera, some reality game show host, smiling. Up until now he had felt strangely calm. But that was fading.

"Please tell me what's happening," he said, not rudely. "Did we come through that thing? Is it like that Stargate thing on Sci-Fi?"

"We stand on the Great Tor, the hill at the heart of all of Breton." Tal Yssen swept his hands below and to the west. "Not long ago, this region was a seaport for Caesar's troops. Later it became an impassable marsh, and the ships withdrew. Now, after heavy rains, it often becomes a vast, freshwater lake. The waters rise, making an island of the tor. The abbey, below, usually remains just above the waters' reach. And this"—the old man, who did not seem old at all, swung round to the stone arch—"this is called Myrddin Esgyll."

"Myrddin what?"

"A doorway, like the one on your father's land. Centuries hence, another structure will be built atop the tor. But the builders, fearing the magic of this rock—both to lose it and to keep it—will be very clever in their design. They will hide this arch in the shape of the main entrance. And so it shall endure forever."

Garret put out his hands as if to steady himself, even though there was nothing to lean on. His voice began to rise. "I don't understand. What are you talking about?"

Tal Yssen began walking down the footpath, motioning him to follow.

"It is a holy place, with a holy purpose, Garret ap Reggie Barlow. Here, the king shall return. From here, the truth shall spread to all of Breton."

"You aren't making any sense!" Garret called back with exasperation. He began walking faster to catch up. "What king? Where's my brother, my dad? Why have you brought me here?"

The calm feeling had definitely worn off.

As they strode down the hill, a flock of black and white spotted goats came trotting up, amiably chewing their cud, neck bells tinkling. A young monk in brown, with a bald pate and an easy smile, nursed them along the same footpath with his staff. His head was down. Then up. He stopped. A mama goat bleated for her kid.

"Taliesin the Merlin?" the man whispered hoarsely. Then, gaining strength, over and over again, he shouted excitedly. "Taliesin the Merlin! Taliesin the Merlin!"

His words rolled down the long waving grass to the monks busily tilling the earth below. They all looked up, paused, then burst into motion.

Garret was a bright, meticulous child, with patterns of thought much like his older brother, Hadyn. He tended to absorb information quickly — structuring, categorizing, digesting, interpreting.

"Wait a minute. Hold it! *The* Merlin?"

"That is what they call me, yes," Tal Yssen said, almost embarrassed. "In truth, it is what I *do*, not who I am. I am a mirling. But they think it is my title, and it does no good to tell them otherwise, I assure you." His expression sobered. "Stay close. It is about to get even more strange."

They drew near the base of the hill. In the circle of huts, a dozen monks halted their garden tending. They held their crude tools nervously, watching him. They were mostly young, a few older. Garret, feeling weird about the whole thing, decided to wait in the shade of a great hawthorn tree. Wait and watch. His mind spun.

An old, wrinkled monk emerged from one of the huts. The younger ones fanned apart to make room for him, bowing slightly as he passed by. His skin was weathered and cracked with age, and one eye was blind, but his vision was not so poor that he could not recognize his visitor.

"Ah, Taliesin. Welcome again, my friend. It has been too long."

He hobbled toward Tal Yssen, and the two embraced. Garret strained to hear what they said. Tal Yssen whispered something. Garret heard only the reply.

"Yes, she is here, don't worry," said the old monk, gesturing. "The autumn rains will bring the water to us. We have a vessel ready. She waits inside for you."

"And?"

"And what? She waits. She sits and speaks nothing. She trembles. She writes. She cries. She hardly eats."

From the very same hut, rising as if beckoned, stepped a woman of bruised, exquisite beauty. She was a contradiction in her plain woolen shift, her doe eyes — wide, innocent, weary with secrets. Seeing Tal Yssen, she immediately lowered her gaze. Strands of hair feathered in the breeze, covering her face. She did not bother to push them away.

"My queen," Tal Yssen said quietly. Garret could not tell if his tone was one of surprise, or sorrow. Perhaps judgment?

The woman kept her eyes to the ground for a long while. When she finally looked up, they glistened in the sun.

"Mock me if you must, Merlin. I am no queen, and you know it. I am a beggar. I am the shame of the kingdom."

"I do not mock," Tal Yssen said gently. "You are, and ever shall be, the wife of my lord."

Garret tried to hear compassion in his voice; did not. Yet there was a sort of kindness. The older monk did not intervene. The breeze that had blown earlier now became still. A warm smell of melons, fresh mint, and peppers filled the empty space between them. Not far away, a goat bell jangled.

"Artorius is no more," the woman said. Touching her fingers

tentatively to her lips, her voice faltered. "A queen must have a king."

"And love must pass beyond the grave, or it is hardly love. Will the queen stay true? Can she?"

The woman swallowed hard, raised her chin. A speck of pride and fire glinted in her dark eyes.

"Ever the puppet master, eh, Merlin? The wise sage, the prophet. The kingmaker. Well, the puppet is dead. You know it as well as I."

"He has passed into another world, Gwenhwyfar. That is what I know."

"I saw him fall!" she shouted. "I felt the coldness of his skin. Damn you, do not play with my heart!"

Tal Yssen's voice stretched, hardened, becoming a thin, sharp razor. "I am not the one who has played with hearts, my queen. Not I. Not Artorius. I loved the king with all my soul."

"And did I not?" Gwenhwyfar cried. "Is that what you imply? You think I *meant* to betray him? To hurt him so? You think I shall ever forget the look in his eyes? To the day I die, I tell you, old wizard, I shall not."

Tal Yssen nodded slowly. "Indeed, such grace will be rare, I think. You and the king's Champion shall grow old with your memories. Earned at such great cost."

"Thus, I go," Gwenhwyfar said quickly. "To Almsbury. To live out my days in seclusion, in service to the Lord. As penance." She clutched a handful of the loose fabric of her dress, balled it up in her hands. "Some wounds can never be healed, Merlin. Not even by you."

"For wounds of the soul, 'tis especially true. True enough of my lord's mortal wounds, had I left him in the care of mortals. But I did not."

Gwenhwyfar lashed out, "Stop it! You would have me believe he sailed to Avalon, is that it? To these very shores, when the rains came last? With your lover, the faerie? Her sisters? Is that it, Merlin?" She laughed bitterly. Such a beautiful face, dark molasses hair. So much lost in the gray mist.

In four strides, he was upon her, looming. Gwenhwyfar looked caught, like a rare bird trapped in a cage. Shame covered her face.

"Will you be *true*, my queen?" he demanded. "What will you give, in hope of love? In hope of redemption?"

Gwenhwyfar slowly regained her composure. Rising to her full height, she met Tal Yssen's fierce brown gaze; a flicker, a moment of cold connection. Something broke loose behind her eyes. The challenge passed. She turned without a word, entered the hut. Returned moments later with a small note, folded, sealed with red wax. She pressed the note into Tal Yssen's hands, took a ring from her finger, and gave it to him.

"These," she said flatly. "These are what I will give."

She entered the hut again and closed the door hard. Tal Yssen stared at the place where she had stood, the place behind the door where she went. His shoulders sagged. He started to take a step toward her, to follow her path. Half step, stopped. Looked at the letter, the ring in his open palm. He turned.

"Come, Garret ap Barlow," he said. "We are done here."

CHAPTER 2

MOUNT AGASAG

Saliva and blood spattered the wall, flung from the face of a broken man. A Champion, once. Now in chains. His head flopped as though his spine were no longer attached. The fist that had struck him, gloved in leather and mail, jerked at his bloody chin, forced it up.

"I told you to look!" thundered Baron von Gulag (for that was his present shape). His prisoner had limp hair and a long, ragged beard, laced with gray and knotted with frozen water like pearls on a necklace. His face was scarred almost beyond recognition. His eyes, haggard. The Baron rumbled with laughter at the sight of him. Pitiful creature. Fool. Mighty Corus. He struck him again, thundering, "Look, I say!"

The two were alone in a chamber of blue cold, deep under a mountain of snow and ice—Mt. Agasag. Though he practiced the Baron's shape now, there was no real need to use the dead man's voice. Not here, in his own domain. Besides, whatever the shape,

whatever the voice, it was Kr'Nunos who spoke. He bore an antlered mark on the skin of his wrist, a mark he could not forsake
even with countless shapechangings. His captive cared nothing
for pain or life. Each day was grinding torment. Long ago, Corus
had given up on living.

Yet Kr'Nunos would not let him die.

Agasag was the tallest peak in the upper reaches of the
Hödurspikes, that place of terror and legend whose cavernous
base was the doorway to Hel. Far above, connected by the rough,
sulfurous shaft of Agasag's volcanic past, was the massive chamber where thousands of years ago, the Devourer had seduced and
debauched the noble Watchers, enslaving them forever.

The Baron took perverse pleasure in his routine with Corus.
He would lift the former Champion thousands of feet through
the shaft, to the very heights, and cause him to look across the
empty miles of vast, frozen tundra, toward the Frostmarch. Look
south, to Karac Tor, lost in dream and darkness beyond the silver
peaks. He would describe his plans of coming devastation in delicious detail: the army of Goths, lurking below, unformed, waiting
in the mud and rock of Hel; the Watchers; the darkness. Day by
day, week by week, Corus was made to endure, to listen and live.
It had been years. Ever since he had been taken from the Fey.
Whenever it pleased the Horned Lord, he would bring Corus to
this place and taunt him, then cast him once more to the lower
regions, keeping him alive on gruel and brown water.

"Do you see the lands you once protected, now ravaged, now
raped?" Baron von Gulag sneered.

Corus neither answered nor moved. He was stripped nearly
naked, left to shiver where he hung from thick, iron manacles.
His breath was frost, his proud physique nothing but skin and
bones and pain, thinned with hunger and striped with lashes

from a bone whip. He didn't even try to focus his fevered eyes. His mouth drooled freely.

"I will destroy it all," said the Baron. "Down to the very last tree. Down to the very last maiden and child. Down to the last seed in the cold ground. The Hall of Ages will be no more. The Sentinels will fall. And I will make Mt. Bourne my footstool."

He spoke these and other blasphemies, again and again. He reminded Corus of his great love, Nemesia, now a witch in the Baron's service. Told him of the Staff of Shades, the darkening of the land, the stealing of names, the release of Watchers. Told him of a governor, ruling in Stratamore, who was weak and easily controlled.

He did not tell him of the interruption of his plans, nor the coming of the Outlanders. They were trivialities. Minor annoyances.

When he was done, the Baron descended into Hel, leaving Corus to freeze in the bitter wind. The deep world was impossibly vast, a network of subterranean chambers and countless pits scraped out of hard, blood-stained rock. The main level of Hel was called Angwyn. Other places had other purposes, and below all, deep in the bowels of the earth, lay Undrwol, a place outside and beyond even the Baron's power. But here in Angwyn, Kr'Nunos was building. Massive beams connected complex wooden frameworks to arched bridges, to pulleys with ropes, to buckets and carts and long extension arms. Smithfires burned everywhere. The clang of hammers on anvils, the burst of sparks, was unceasing.

And then there were the great pits, stone craters full of gears, of machinery; pits of iron ore and copper, even algathon, so rare. The raw materials progressed through smelting pits to eventually form huge stores of long iron spikes and nails made of copper. Smaller pits sparkled with jewels and gold, and great piles of dirt and rock. But most terrifying of all was the bones. Great piles of bones, like mountains, stretched as far as the eye could see. Bones of dead things.

Thousands labored in firelight and steam, with hammers, axe and rope. Their oiled bodies moved and struggled in the dark like maggots on a carcass. They were S'Qoth man-slaves, brought by the Baron from Quil. They were dressed in animal skins and feathers, had faces painted green and black, with strange markings on their arms. Big, beefy overlords stood on platforms of wood, or mingled amongst the slaves, shouting curses in the brutal language of the S'Qoth, snapping whips.

"We are nearly ready, Great One," grinned a tall overlord, missing teeth. He bowed to Baron von Gulag.

"You have earth?" the Baron said.

"From Röckval, as you commanded, my lord."

"Then give me a test, Oruuwn. Let us make a creature in my image."

The man took a short gorse horn and blew two blasts. Immediately, overlords began barking orders, whistling, gesturing. Slaves scrambled, crying out as whips nicked their skin. Wood was brought. A fire was lit. A barrel of dark, oily fluid was poured into a smaller cavity, which soon began to boil. Next, bones were hauled—bones of bull and jackal and human—along with shovels of rock. Sharpened iron spikes, a handful of copper nails, then mud, water, sawdust. All were thrown together into the bubbling cauldron. Pleased, Baron von Gulag folded his great arms on his iron-plated chest, his robe billowing in the heat. When the time was right, he stretched out his hand, spoke a command. The bubbling intensified. The liquid began to thicken, coagulate. Slaves and overlords gathered round, whispering and clenching their fists, toothy with delight.

"Arise!" the Baron rumbled.

Something took form. From the cauldron, a crumbling beast of earth and bone. It was man-shaped, but faceless, with bulging, nondescript features. A rough outline of head, torso, arms, legs. A cavity of ribs was clearly visible along its midsection, and long, iron spikes protruded from the stumps of its fingerless hands. Standing to its feet, dripping mud, it showed a gaping maw, and a mess of jagged, copper nails for teeth. A noise came from its mouth—a sound like the movement of wind through winter-crusted leaves; a gasping, nothing sound. The beast stood eight feet tall, was thick as a tree. It had no eyes.

Kr'Nunos took a clump of new soil from a separate pile. He pressed it like clay into the beast's belly, then stepped back, said a final word.

The creature seemed to shiver, become aware.

Then started killing.

No roar of rage, no warning. No emotion or cause. Only the cold grind of rock and bone, and heavy arms swiveling left and right. It was not fast, and yet it punctured half a dozen S'Qoth through chest and skull as easily as a man might snap a twig, or put a knife in a tomato. The strength of the beast was the strength of the earth—the hardness of stone, the bite of metal. One S'Qoth, leaping upon it from behind, shouted and pounded the beast's head with an iron rod. He struck wildly. The beast neither flinched nor cried out. It clamped upon the slave and, as a child might bite into an apple, ripped the man's arm from his shoulder, let it drop to the ground. The Quil man hit the cavern floor screaming, fumbling about in shock for his severed limb. The other S'Qoth fell back, unsure. They formed a loose circle beyond the beast's reach. Strangely, it no longer lashed out. Its path now unobstructed, it began moving relentlessly in one direction—toward the Baron, with arms raised, ready to strike. When it drew near, about to strike, Baron von Gulag merely stepped out of the creature's path. A test. The S'Qoth hissed in fear. Again, the beast did not veer. It lowered its arms, lumbered on. Straight path.

"Attack it from behind!" the Baron commanded.

Overlords and other S'Qoth grabbed shovels, spikes, axes. They rained down blows upon the creature's backside, then jumped back warily. Unfazed, the beast did not bother to retaliate. It faced one direction, a magnet pointing, offering a silent cry.

Eventually it reached an impasse, a wall of rock. Even then it did not change course. Methodically, it began assaulting the stone, as if to break it apart. It struck with crushing force. It would go through, not around.

The Baron smiled, pleased. He spoke a word that rattled on his lips, made the S'Qoth cover their ears. Instantly, the beast crumbled, collapsing into a loose heap of bone and rock and mud.

"Behold, what I have created!" he cried aloud to the men cowering around him. "The first of my great army of Goths." His voice dropped to a low rumble. "Let the people of Röckval tremble."

ABOUT THE AUTHOR

Dean "D. Barkley" Briggs is the author of *The God Spot* (Word Publishing) and *The Most Important Little Boy in the World* (W Publishing). He is father to four magnificent young men, born to him and his late wife. Recently remarried, Dean and his wife, Jeanie (also a former widow), now share eight magnificent children. They live in the Midwest. Visit www.hiddenlands .net for more info.

Want more fantasy reading? Check out the SWORD OF LYRIC series!

The Restorer

Sharon Hinck
ISBN-13: 978-1-60006-131-8
ISBN-10: 1-60006-131-1

Meet Susan, a housewife and soccer mom whose dreams stretch far beyond her ordinary world. While studying the book of Judges, Susan longs to be a modern-day Deborah, a prophet and leader who God used to deliver the ancient nation of Israel from destruction. Susan gets her wish for adventure when she stumbles through a portal into an alternate universe and encounters a nation locked in a fierce struggle for its survival.

The Restorer's Son

Sharon Hinck
ISBN-13: 978-1-60006-132-5
ISBN-10: 1-60006-132-X

Plunged again into the gray world of Lyric and Hazor, Susan and Mark search frantically for their teenage son, Jake, as all signs hint that a trusted ally has betrayed them and threatens their son. Assassins and political intrigue, false leads, and near misses beset their path, which will lead them into the dark prisons of Hazor before the One's purpose is revealed.

The Restorer's Journey

Sharon Hinck
ISBN-13: 978-1-60006-133-2
ISBN-10: 1-60006-133-8

With a loved one's life at stake, Jake charges through the portal into Lyric to stage a dramatic rescue, trusting that the signs that mark him as Restorer will guarantee success. But everything familiar in Lyric has vanished, swept away by deadly lies and a corrupt king. As inexorable forces conspire to turn him from his purpose, Jake finds his path leading to places beyond his courage.

To order copies, visit your local Christian bookstore, call NavPress at 1-800-366-7788, or log on to www.navpress.com.
To locate a Christian bookstore near you, call 1-800-991-7747.

BE TRANSFORMED